ABOUT THE AUTHOR

From an early age, Martin was enchanted with old movies
from Hollywood's golden era — from the dawn of the talkies
in the late 1920s to the close of the studio system in the late
1950s — and has spent many a happy hour watching the likes
of Garland, Gable, Crawford, Garbo, Grant, Miller, Kelly,
Astaire, Rogers, Turner, and Welles go through their paces.

It felt inevitable that he would someday end up writing
about them.

Originally from Melbourne, Australia, Martin moved to Los
Angeles in the mid-90s where he now works as a writer,
blogger, webmaster, and tour guide.

www.MartinTurnbull.com

This book is dedicated to

ANNA DOUVLOS

because some friendships are
deeply felt from the very start.

ISBN-13: 978-1546976035

ISBN-10: 1546976035

TINSELTOWN CONFIDENTIAL

a novel

by

Martin Turnbull

Book Seven in the Hollywood's Garden of Allah novels.

CHAPTER 1

When Kathryn Massey stepped out of the limousine in front of the Pantages Theatre, flashbulbs exploded along the sidewalk. She closed her eyes and turned her head before she realized how crummy she'd look in the papers the next day. She turned back around, but the photographers had moved on to the next car, from which Fred Astaire was unfolding his lean frame. He waved to the fans and they roared with excitement.

Fred greeted Kathryn with a kiss to the cheek.

"Nervous?" she asked.

He kept his smile wide. "Piece of cake."

"Since when is hosting the Academy Awards a piece of cake?"

"Since the day I realized they were never going to give me one. You won't see me sweating through *my* tux."

Kathryn's date, Leo Presnell, emerged from the limo behind her. She introduced him to Fred, and together with Fred's wife, Phyllis, they bustled past a tight core of press photographers and into the theater's foyer.

It was Kathryn who felt nervous. Her friend Bette Davis was the odds-on favorite for *All About Eve* tonight, but she had stiff competition from Gloria Swanson and *Sunset Boulevard*. Kathryn feared that Bette and her costar Anne Baxter might split their votes and hand the Oscar to Gloria.

Bette had telephoned Kathryn that morning, wailing, "What if they don't call my name? What if it goes to Gloria instead? How many more Margo Channings am I likely to get a crack at?"

Kathryn had no good answers, but she proposed a fortifying pre-show whiskey at the Frolic Room next door to the Pantages. But then Leo was late picking her up at the Garden of Allah, and they became ensnarled in the traffic clogging Hollywood and Vine. They arrived with only forty-five minutes to showtime. Surely Bette was already running the gamut of press, fans, and well-wishers.

"Do you see her?"

"No," Leo said, "but I need to use the john. If you find her, blame everything on me."

"I fully intend to."

Leo's afternoon meeting with NBC hadn't unfolded the way he expected. He worked for Sunbeam Mixmaster, who cosponsored Kathryn's radio show with Betty Crocker. It was supposed to be a casual get-together with the network brass, which Kathryn assumed meant a three-martini lunch at Perino's. Instead, they'd lowered the boom that *Window on Hollywood* had cratered to number twenty-two in the ratings—not great news for a show that had once nudged the top five.

Leo melted away, pointing to the knot of people besieging Ava Gardner and Frank Sinatra. Rumors were swirling that Ava had moved in with Frank. Not that Hollywood cared much about a glamour couple living in sin, but the vast expanse between Los Angeles and New York did. Kathryn knew if she could pull a wedding date out of them, it would keep the NBC hounds at bay for a while.

As she elbowed her way toward them, she spotted Bette posing on the mezzanine steps, backlit by a spotlight suspended from the second-floor balcony. "Bette! BETTE!" But the din bouncing off the Art Deco angles swallowed her voice.

Marilyn Monroe angled the right shoulder of a gauzy concoction Gwendolyn Brick had made for her, and sliced through the tightening crowd toward Bette. She arrived at the bottom step just as Bette kissed George Sanders goodbye.

Marilyn waved, tilted onto her toes, and called to Bette, who doused her with a critical once-over, then turned her back, leaving Marilyn in her shadow.

A pocket of space opened up in front of Kathryn. She went to raise her hand again, but someone yanked it down—Arlene Curtis, a neighbor at the Garden of Allah.

"Thank God I found you—I just got accosted by Walter Winchell!"

"Is he drunk?" *Walter Winchell drunk and handsy at the Oscars? Now THAT is a great story.*

Arlene pulled a face. "No, but he was full of questions about Mayer."

Louis B. Mayer was to be honored tonight for "distinguished service to the motion picture industry." It wasn't as exciting as the award in Bette's crosshairs, but a gleaming Oscar perched on a mantelpiece was nothing to sneer at.

Arlene drew in closer. "I'm not supposed to say anything, but my boss has been reviewing Mayer's contract." Arlene was chief legal secretary for MGM's principal attorney.

"Reviewing it for what?"

"Loopholes. They want to cancel it three years early."

"That's outrageous! He's L.B.! He *is* Hollywood! Are they forgetting that *King Solomon's Mines* made nearly ten million?"

"Not too long ago, we would've dominated the top ten. I get the feeling Mr. Schenck feels it's time for a change."

"Are you sure?"

"Who do you think's been typing the memos to New York?" Arlene knotted her fingers. "A year or so ago, I ran into Mr. Mayer at the commissary. I could tell he recognized me from—you know."

Arlene was working in a brothel above the Sunset Strip when Kathryn's friend met her at an MGM management party.

"We swapped an I-know-who-you-are look. Would you believe he actually came up to me and said it was nice to see me doing so well for myself? He never said a word to anyone about my past. What they're doing is real rotten. Mr. Mayer deserves better."

"Do you think Winchell's caught wind of this?"

"With Walter Winchell, it's safest to err on the side of probably."

The lights dimmed for a moment, and a deep voice announced that the ceremony for the twenty-third Academy Awards would commence in ten minutes.

Kathryn thanked Arlene and made her way to her seat in the twelfth row next to Leo, five rows behind Bette and several behind Marilyn.

The news about Mayer consumed her thoughts as *All About Eve* won six Oscars, Judy Holliday won for *Born Yesterday*, Dean Martin and Jerry Lewis sang "Bibbidi-Bobbidi-Boo" from the new Disney cartoon, and Edith Head picked up two Best Costume Designs for *All About Eve* and *Samson and Delilah*.

By the time Darryl Zanuck was accepting his Thalberg Award, Kathryn was wondering how best to tip off Mayer. Did he even need to be tipped off? If there was a groundswell brewing, surely his stoolies had already told him.

When Charles Brackett presented Mayer with his honorary Oscar, Kathryn was struck by the self-effacing way Mayer approached the podium. All finagling flew out of her head when Mayer gave his unexpectedly brief speech.

"This is truly a thrilling experience," he said, looking at nobody in particular. "I've been very fortunate in being honored in many ways, but this stands out above all because it's from the men and women in the industry I love and have worked so hard in. And it fills me with humility and a great sense of responsibility to the future years to come."

By the time he shook hands with Brackett and made his way out of the spotlight, Kathryn felt like a rat. *He's been good to you,* she castigated herself. *He's given you scoops over Louella and Hedda and Sheilah, made you the envy of the dance floor, and found work for Marcus when he was blacklisted. No,* she decided, *at the very least, I need to make sure he knows what's going on.*

After the ceremony, as the theater rustled with silk, organza, chiffon, and congratulations—sincere or otherwise—Kathryn found Bette and her indomitable mother, Ruthie. They both wore faces bleaker than a Massachusetts ice storm. Bette met Kathryn with a jaundiced eye.

"Don't worry," Bette said, "I possess no sharp objects. Everyone's jugular will survive the night intact."

"Are you terribly disappointed?" Kathryn asked.

"I'm ropeable! This was my last shot. It's all grandmothers and character parts from here on out."

"You don't know that."

"Just you watch. I'll be the go-to dame for the Crazy Spinster Neighbor and Grandma with Dementia roles." Bette's disdainful gaze landed on Marilyn as she chatted with Bill Holden and Joe Mankiewicz. "She's what they want now. Pretty, blonde, and dumb as dirt. Just look at who they gave Best Actress to this evening."

"Neither Judy Holliday nor Marilyn Monroe is dumb as dirt," Kathryn interjected. "If that's the way you're going to be, I'll leave you to stew in your own juices."

"Please don't," Bette conceded. "You're right. Let's go find a drink before anybody else wants to bury me in their heartfelt sympathies."

"I just want to give Mayer my best wishes. I'll meet you out front. Leo's there somewhere with a limo big enough for the LA Rams."

Kathryn picked her way backstage, where Edith Head buttonholed her. "I'd forgotten how heavy these little golden guys are!"

Kathryn doubted that. Edith's first Oscar, just last year for *The Heiress*, stood on a prominent shelf in her office. Still, two Oscars in one night was a significant achievement.

As she embraced Edith, Kathryn spotted Mayer slipping out the stage door. She made her excuses and followed him into the service lane behind the theater, mildly surprised to find it vacant except for Mayer staring at his award.

As she drew closer, she caught his contemptuous look.

Mayer lifted his Oscar so that it caught the light of a street lamp at the end of the alley. "I just heard someone calling this my Kiss of Death Award."

"That's awfully mean-spirited."

"In other words, the Thanks for Everything But Your Best Work Is Behind You So Please Get Lost Award."

"If you don't want it, I'm sure Bette Davis would love to—"

"I meant what I said tonight."

"I could tell."

Mayer lowered the trophy. "That comment left a bitter taste in my mouth, but I'm not going to let it spoil a memorable night, so thank you for seeking me out. I appreciate that."

Kathryn fought the urge to fidget with her clutch purse as Mayer raised a wary eyebrow. "I came to offer you my congratulations, but also to see if you know what's going on with your contract."

"How do you mean?"

He's not as well connected as I assumed. Maybe that's the problem. "You need to know that Nick Schenck and your head of legal have been combing it for something that will allow them to cancel it early."

Mayer tried to keep his face immobile. "I don't believe you." His voice had turned acerbic.

"My source is pretty good."

"Tell me who told you."

"I can't, but she is on your side."

"You're playing with my career, my legacy, on the word of some *girl*?"

Kathryn started to wish she'd kept her trap shut. "It appears Winchell's caught a whiff of it, although I'm not sure how much he knows. The point is, someone's looking to sink your career—"

"No, Miss Massey. The point is tonight was to be a career highlight."

Don't shoot the messenger, Bucko. "When did I get demoted from Kathryn to Miss Massey?"

"When you decided to shove rumors of my demise in my face."

"I came out here to warn you. If I'd known I was going to get accused of—"

"Of what? Fishing for one of your precious scoops? I've always considered you a cut above Louella and Hedda. But now I have to wonder if I've been wrong about you this entire time."

Kathryn dropped her gaze to his Oscar. He gripped it between two fingers, dangling it by its head like a stale cigar.

They were suddenly drenched in the headlights of Mayer's roaring limo. She stepped back as it pulled up. Mayer got in and slammed the door, leaving Kathryn to choke on the exhaust and wish she were more like Louella and Hedda. They wouldn't hesitate for a second to announce this betrayal to the world.

CHAPTER 2

Gwendolyn Brick sat behind the counter of her store on the
Sunset Strip and stared at her telephone. She'd refreshed her
front-window mannequins, finished the final touches on a
dress she'd made for James Stewart's wife, and banished
every dust mote in sight.

Kathryn always phoned her the morning after the
Academy Awards to fill her in on who won what, who wore
what, and who flirted with whom. But it was coming up to
one o'clock in the afternoon, and still no call. Had it been a
calamity? Had Kathryn gotten blitzed and fought with Leo
again? Gwendolyn hoped it wasn't at some post-ceremony
party in front of half of Hollywood.

Gwendolyn had had her doubts when Kathryn became
romantically involved with her radio program's sponsor, but
in the past year Leo had been nothing but a gentleman.

She decided to give it until one o'clock before she called.

The second hand on Gwendolyn's watch was ticking
toward twelve when the bell above her front door tinkled
and in walked one of her most loyal customers, Marilyn
Monroe, accompanied by a stylishly dressed man in his
early thirties.

Gwendolyn rushed forward to greet her. "So? How did
it go? Were you nervous?"

"Are you kidding?" Marilyn brushed a lock of blond hair
out of her eyes. "I was nervous as all get-out. Fred Astaire
gave me a kiss for good luck, but that just made me worse. I
kept thinking, Fred Astaire just kissed me. Me! How did I
get to be so lucky?"

"Oh, I don't know. Looks? Charm? Broad appeal, perhaps? And did you see Bette?"

Marilyn pursed her lips. "I tried to play nice, honest I did. How your pal Kathryn can be friendly with her, I just don't know."

"So you weren't too upset for Bette when she lost?"

Marilyn permitted herself a sly smirk. "When they announced Judy's name, Bette looked like Medea who'd just overdosed on Dexamyl."

"And what about the dress?"

Marilyn's handsome companion gave a quiet yip. "Our girl here looked thoroughly enchanting in your dress." He had a friendly face and thick, dark hair, and an unassuming way about him. Gwendolyn wondered if this was the latest beau. Marilyn hooked him by the arm. "This is Billy. Billy, this is Gwendolyn."

He smiled an impish grin. "Marilyn tells me you're the Gwendolyn of the infamous Ruby Courtland cards."

Gwendolyn maintained her professional smile but inwardly sighed.

"Yes!" Marilyn exclaimed. "The dress was utter perfection, but now I need something new. Something real memorable."

"Everything you wear is memorable."

"But I don't want it to be all flashy and 'Look at me trying hard to catch your attention.' I need . . ." Marilyn's eyes drifted as she struggled to articulate what she had in mind.

Billy had wandered away to inspect a display along the eastern wall. Gwendolyn watched him finger an emerald green suit with a peplum skirt that she'd just put out this morning.

"How about you tell me where you plan on wearing it," Gwendolyn suggested.

"Well!" she said breathlessly, "Billy told me that there are whispers doing the rounds at the studio that Zanuck's considering upping my six-month contract to a full seven years!"

"Jackpot!" Gwendolyn grabbed her hands. "Finally, you're getting your due."

"Not yet I haven't. But I want to make a good impression on the first day of *Love Nest*. We start on the twenty-first of next month, and Zanuck will be there for the first read-through, so I want him to see me and think, She's got it together."

"So we want flattering but sensible, memorable but understated."

"But not too understated."

"Noteworthy but not desperate."

"That's it exactly!"

"This is perfect!" Billy held up a conventional shirtdress of gray worsted with a matching sewn-in belt, three-quarter sleeves, and a contrasting collar. It wasn't what Gwendolyn normally stocked, but she got them for cheap from a bankrupted wholesaler and planned on adding sparkle to them later.

"No!" Gwendolyn exclaimed. "That won't do at all!"

Marilyn giggled. "He doesn't mean for me."

Billy brought the dress to the counter. "Sorry for the subterfuge, but if I didn't find anything I liked, I figured I could sneak away undetected."

"Subterfuge?"

"Billy usually goes by his last name: Travilla."

Gwendolyn couldn't help the double take she shot toward Billy.

Edith Head had mentioned this costume designer to Gwendolyn a number of times, usually in glowing terms, and Edith wasn't the type to hand out praise like boxes of See's candies.

"You're at Warners, right?" Gwendolyn asked.

"Was," Marilyn said. "He's at Fox now. And if Zanuck gives me that seven-year contract, Billy here will be designing my costumes. He's an absolute whiz."

"I don't know about that," he conceded. "I appear to have bitten off more than I can chew. I've been so busy doing Betty Grable for *Meet Me After the Show*, and Gene Tierney for *On The Riviera* that I've fallen behind. Patricia Neal is about to start some science fiction picture called *The Day the Earth Stood Still*. She only wears two outfits on screen — thank God — but I clean forgot!"

"Surely Fox's wardrobe department —"

"You'd think so, but nope. Then Marilyn mentioned she was coming here and said you might come to my rescue." He faced the store. "You've got some nice stuff here. Real impressive. Lives up to its reputation."

Gwendolyn said she was glad he thought so, but she cringed to know that of all the smart and pretty creations she had on display, she was selling Billy Travilla the dullest outfit in her store.

"Are these all your designs?" he asked.

"Fifty-fifty." She pointed to the eveningwear, hoping he might see something better than the gray shirtwaist. "Most of those are mine."

"Have you designed for the screen? These are very screen-ready."

"I'm friendly with Edith Head, so perhaps I've been influenced by her style."

"Her lines are clean, whereas yours are soft, more feminine. I like it very much." He returned to the counter. "If you could wrap this up, I ought to be getting back to the studio."

It wasn't until after the two of them left that Gwendolyn realized Kathryn still hadn't called. She picked up the phone and dialed the *Hollywood Reporter*. The switchboard operator was putting her through when Billy Travilla walked back in. She slammed the phone down.

"I've just had a thought," he said. "I know the wardrobe guy on *Dragnet*. He's in over his head, so I was wondering if he could call on you?"

"*Dragnet*?" Gwendolyn frowned. "That's all cops in suits. What help could I be?"

"It's the women's roles. He hasn't got a clue and is getting no help. It might be anything from the sort of shirtdress I just bought to more elegant eveningwear. Can I give him your number?"

"If you think I could help, sure."

She was redialing Kathryn's number when she wondered what she'd just said yes to.

CHAPTER 3

The sign at 720 Wilshire Boulevard featured a circus clown lugging a bass drum with a hole punched into one side. The neon blinked on and off: *The Broken Drum – you can't beat it!*

Of all places, Kathryn wondered why Mayer wanted to meet her at a burger joint eight blocks from Santa Monica Beach, and on a Tuesday afternoon, no less.

The location wasn't the only puzzle piece. Mayer's invitation arrived in the hands of an old guy with grizzled white hair and pale eyes, rheumy with fatigue. He shuffled up to her desk last week, handed her a sealed envelope, and waited there for her reply.

The last time Kathryn saw Mayer, he accused her of fishing for scoops. It wasn't the accusation that stung as much as his venomous tone.

She let her resentment fester as she wrote a thinly veiled blind item that she nearly sent to print, but at the last minute swapped with the announcement that Frank Sinatra and Ava Gardner planned to marry in November. For the next few weeks, she flayed herself for being weak.

When the wheezing go-between appeared in front of her like the Ghost of Oscars Past, curiosity replaced her umbrage.

She pushed open the Broken Drum's weathered door and walked inside. It was a typical beach-town diner: booths on the right, a counter along the left, and a checkerboard of tables in between.

A waitress with dyed-black hair told her, "Anywhere you like, hon. I'll be with you in two shakes."

A lone figure in a homburg sat in the booth at the far end. He beckoned her to join him.

Mayer wore a sleek navy blue suit that probably cost more than the waitress made in a year. His shirt was regulation white and his necktie was charcoal, but he hadn't tied it well. Its cockeyed angle looked foreign on someone who always took great pains to dress immaculately.

She slid into the booth. "Come here often?"

He picked up his menu. "When the grandkids were young, yes. They loved the double cheeseburgers."

The waitress took their orders — chili for him, tuna salad for her. Kathryn waited until they were alone again before she spoke.

"I assume this is a conversation you don't want anyone to overhear."

He unfolded a meager paper napkin that was bound to disintegrate within minutes and placed it on his lap. "I owe you an apology. My behavior after the Oscars, it was unconscionable."

"It wasn't easy for me to tell you," she said, "but I imagine it must have been harder for you to hear. Especially with that Distinguished Service Oscar weighing you down. I hoped my source was wrong."

He looked like he'd been shoved through a meat grinder. "She wasn't."

"How long have you helmed MGM?"

"Twenty-seven years."

"And this is how they treat you?"

"It appears so."

"Not that they'll get away with it."

The waitress arrived with their lunch. The plates were chipped and the cutlery battered, but the food smelled as good as anything at the Bullocks Wilshire Tea Room.

"Thank you for saying that. I've found myself questioning the loyalty of everyone around me."

Kathryn thought about the scores of actors, directors, writers, and union leaders Mayer had screwed over in the name of greater company profits.

He shoved his aluminum spoon deep into the chili. "My attorney says that loophole is pretty solid, so I don't know if I can head them off at the pass. But it won't be for lack of trying, I can promise you."

Kathryn was glad he still had some fight in him. His hair — what was left of it — was all silver now. Surely he'd reached the age when most men coasted gently into retirement. "Good for you."

"If you hadn't tipped me off, this coup — and that's what this is, you know, a goddamned *coup* — it might have slipped past without me being any the wiser. So I want to thank you, and return the favor."

Kathryn had told Gwennie weeks ago that if Mayer apologized, she wanted Gene Kelly and Leslie Caron, MGM's new French discovery, to be guests on her show. The two were about to start filming the ballet sequence for *An American in Paris*, and Kathryn sensed that it would be the studio's hit of the year.

Kathryn sat up, ready to make her request, when Mayer said, "How about I come onto your show?"

A chunk of tuna salad sent her into a coughing fit that she barely managed to quell by swallowing half her iced tea, but it gave her a chance to collect her thoughts.

"I was going to shoot for Gene Kelly, but if *you* want to come onto my show, that would be spectacular!"

"I was thinking perhaps a retrospective of MGM's history, highlighting the films I've helped pilot to the screen."

Kathryn shook her head. "Rather than look back on past glories, maybe you could talk about the exciting projects your studio has lined up, like this *American in Paris* picture. And *Quo Vadis* — you could talk about that, too." His eyes darkened. "Or we could go with a retrospective — "

"No, no. Looking ahead. That's a wonderful idea. There's another matter I wish to talk to you about. It involves *Quo Vadis*, in a way."

A rowdy bunch of teenagers burst into the diner, taking up most of the counter. They fired their orders at the waitress, who told them all to pipe down and quit making so much noise.

"Do you know where Marcus Adler is?" Mayer asked.

When the Hollywood blacklist blocked every one of Marcus' career paths, he'd been forced to pursue work in Europe. He'd been gone five months, and Kathryn missed him like mad.

"I got a letter from him last week. *Quo Vadis* has finished shooting, but he's still in Rome."

"You need to convince him to come back."

"Personally, I'd love nothing better, but the last time I looked, the blacklist was still in effect."

Mayer lowered his voice, not that anybody was nearby. "A couple of weeks ago, I met with Winchell. I let him talk about himself for a while before I started dropping vague hints about this rumor of my possible coup."

"I'm sure he knew what you were up to."

"Probably. At any rate, I think he didn't know as much as he let on to your source—who I assume was Arlene from our legal department?"

Kathryn was impressed. Schenck and his cronies were sure going to have a fight on their hands. "You think Winchell was just fishing?"

"I do, but then he started talking about Senator McCarthy."

Kathryn pushed away the remnants of her tuna salad. "I thought J. Parnell Thomas was bad, but that guy's a rabid dog with a rotted bone."

"According to Winchell, McCarthy's decided that Red hunting has gotten everyone about as far as they will go, so he's brewing a new campaign. He believes the homos working inside the government are a huge security risk."

"How does he figure that?"

"Because they're open for blackmail."

"So what's his plan?"

"To treat homos the way HUAC treated Commies."

___

20

Kathryn wondered what any of this had to do with bringing Marcus home.

"Winchell and McCarthy are cut from the same cloth," Mayer said. "Neither of them cares who their sacrificial lamb is. Winchell brought up your marriage to Adler. He must have said the words 'lavender marriage' and 'lavender scare' five or six times."

Whether or not Hollywood was truly awash with Commies was debatable, but Hollywood was undeniably nipple deep in queers.

Kathryn said, "You know as well as I do that lavender marriages are as common as false eyelashes here. So why should I convince Marcus to come back to Hollywood if the likes of Walter Winchell and Joe McCarthy are planning on—"

"I got the impression that Winchell plans to use your marriage to Marcus as an example by which all marriages in Hollywood should be judged. He talked about how Marcus has gone on the lam—"

"He's hardly on the lam!" Kathryn protested. "If anything, he was painted into a corner and pushed out the window."

"Do you think that's how Winchell's going to put it?"

Kathryn suddenly felt like she'd been cornered, too. "What do you have in mind?"

"I can help get Marcus off the blacklist."

"You can?"

"But only as far as the graylist."

"Wait! What? There's a *graylist*?"

Mayer shifted uneasily in his seat. "There is."

"Who's on it?"

"People who have been accused of being Commies, or at least fellow travelers, but without much proof."

"It must be a hell of a long list."

"These people haven't been blackballed outright, but just branded 'Hire with caution.' I can get him on it, but he'll have to get himself off it under his own steam. And he can't do that from Italy."

Kathryn let out a long breath. Like any good columnist, she maintained a network of contacts and tipsters that spiderwebbed across Los Angeles. She figured that if she had never heard of this graylist, it must be more classified than the Manhattan Project.

Mayer said, "I don't know if I'll be able to scuttle these plans to get rid of me. However, if Schenck is successful, *Quo Vadis* might be the final movie I approve. Therefore, it's important to me that it's a huge hit. I want to send you to Rome."

"Send me? All the way to . . . *Italy*?"

"I want you to write a big article heralding a new era in filmmaking. Hollywood is partnering with postwar Europe. European talent and sensibilities plus the Hollywood money that's stuck over there. It's a whole new world of moviemaking and MGM is at the forefront, and *Quo Vadis* is the vanguard. I even have the title: 'Hollywood on the Tiber.' How does that sound?"

Kathryn could only nod. *I'm going to Italy! To see Marcus! I'll get him back home if I have to gag him with spaghetti and throw him into a steamer trunk.*

CHAPTER 4

Marcus Adler had never seen Cinecittà's reconstructed Roman Forum entirely deserted. For months, he'd meandered through hordes of extras griping about scratchy togas and helmets that dug into their scalps. But today, he had the back lot to himself.

With production on *Quo Vadis* completed, the cast and crew had packed up their costumes, makeup kits, scripts, and cameras, and boarded their Pan Am Stratocruisers, leaving him alone for the first time since November.

The four Corinthian columns outside the emperor's palace stood fifty feet high. Marcus didn't know what the palace itself would look like — the special effects team in Hollywood would insert it later — but he imagined it would dwarf everything. On each side rose thirty-foot statues on plinths of heavy timber painted like gold and jade. Even close up, the crew had done a first-rate job.

In the center lay the forecourt where priestesses in white and purple had danced in praise of Roman gods. Marcus wasn't convinced that any of it was authentic to Nero's Rome, but he had no doubt that the crane shots that took hours to orchestrate would look spectacular on screen.

It had been cloudy all morning, but as Marcus leaned against a copper urn, the sun broke through and shone directly onto Minerva, the goddess of wisdom and war; her golden head glowed as though Jupiter himself had adorned her. Marcus peered through his camera's viewfinder and waited for the sun to shift just a fraction and light up her stern face.

"FRIENDS! ROMANS! COUNTRYMEN! LEND ME YOUR QUEERS!"

He knew the voice as well as he knew his own. But it was supposed to be six thousand miles away reporting on the grosses for *Royal Wedding* and which star shoved what body part into wet cement out front of Grauman's.

He lowered his camera. "I hear it but I don't believe it."

"Some lazy Roman soldier left his spear thingy behind. If you don't turn around this instant, I'm going to skewer you with it."

Marcus drank in the sight of Kathryn standing ten feet away, wearing a smile as wide as the Appian Way. A glisten of tears filled her smoky brown eyes.

"Come here, you big lug!" She dropped the spear and threw herself into his arms.

Her hair smelled of roses and vanilla. He'd forgotten how soft it was, like eiderdown.

They hugged each other until their muscles gave out.

"What are you doing here?" he gasped. "And why didn't you tell me you were coming? I could have met you at the airport."

Kathryn pulled a white handkerchief from her sleeve and dabbed at her eyes. "Before I left LA, I sent a telegram to the production office."

"They closed it down a week and a half ago."

"I figured as much, so I went to your pensione, where I met your landlady."

"Ah! The redoubtable Signora Scatena."

"She's a force of nature."

"That's what it takes to survive Mussolini, the Blackshirts, and the allied invasion."

"I tried to ask her where you were, but she kept wanting to feed me."

"You should've let her. She takes zucchini flowers, fills them with mozzarella cheese and anchovies, dips them in batter, and throws them into the deep fry. You'll think you've gone to heaven."

"So then she starts hollering 'Cinecittà! Cinecittà!' I flagged down a taxi and yelled 'Cinecittà! Cinecittà!' and here we are."

"Gosh, but it's good to see you. I thought I'd be okay after the cast and crew left, but my plaster pals here" — Marcus waved his hand toward the enormous golden gods— "aren't the conversationalists I hoped they'd be."

She wrapped an arm around his waist and lay her head on his shoulder. "I'm so glad to be here."

"Why *are* you here?"

"I come at the behest of L.B. Mayer. Officially, it's for a story on the new Hollywood. Coproductions with Europe, that sort of thing. He wants me to call it 'Hollywood on the Tiber.'"

"That's got a certain ring to it."

"Assuming my readers know where or what the Tiber is."

The Roman sun had started to burn through the morning haze, heating up the painted concrete. Marcus knew from experience that if they didn't find some shade, they'd start sweating like a pair of centurions. He led her up the stairs to a shady bench behind the columns where Robert Taylor and Peter Ustinov sat between takes.

She took his hands in hers. Her gloves were made of silky kid leather.

"I've come to bring you home."

His face shot up. "To LA?"

"To LA, to Hollywood, and to the Garden of Allah, where you belong."

"This is Italy," he told her gently. "No HUAC, no Red baiting, no jostling for the next prestige picture. In addition to which, the exchange rate is fantastic, so is the Chianti, and did I mention the zucchini flowers?" She didn't even smile. "Of course I miss you, and Gwennie, and Doris, and Bertie, and everyone, but honestly, the prospect of going back to that rat race . . ."

He watched her earnest face soften as she shifted gears. "How's Oliver? He must be doing better now."

Marcus dropped her hands, got to his feet, and leaned against the column. He'd become used to experiencing the Forum so full and alive; it was jarring to see it empty. "I've lost him."

"WHAT? You don't mean—? Oliver is—?"

He felt her beside him, her hand on his arm. "I could have phrased that better," he admitted. "What I meant was that I've lost him to the Church."

"What church?"

He poked her in the ribs. "You're in Rome now, remember? There's only one Church."

Kathryn pulled her eyebrows together. "Oh, honey, I've been awake for nine thousand hours. You need to spell things out for me."

Marcus knew he'd have to explain what had happened to Kathryn and Gwendolyn sooner or later, but he hadn't figured on doing it in person. He sat her back down on the bench.

"Moving over here gave us a whole fresh start. It drew us together again, and removed him from those dope pushers and their temptations. Stitching together the *Quo Vadis* script turned out to be an all-consuming beast, but once that was done, Mervyn asked me to be the on-set photographer. This has been a monumental undertaking and he wanted it chronicled. Turns out I've got quite a feel for it. Between the script and the photography, I was very preoccupied."

"Where did that leave Oliver?"

"He needed to keep busy, so he decided to learn Italian. I was around it all the time so I managed to pick it up, almost by osmosis. But he wanted to learn it properly, so he enrolled in a language school run by the Jesuits to teach Italian and Latin to Catholics who are coming to the Vatican."

"If you're going to learn Latin, learn it from the Jesuits."

"That's what I thought. I was busy with my work on set, so I was happy he found something that absorbed him so much, especially after everything he'd been through. As production went on, I started taking on extra duties that Mervyn's assistant director couldn't tackle. I got so busy that I just didn't notice what was going on with him." Marcus let out a muted groan. "He had a religious awakening. Leastways, that's how he described it in the letter he wrote telling me that he'd enrolled to become a novice."

"A novice what?"

"That's the word for people who want to join the Jesuit order."

"HE'S A PRIEST?!"

Kathryn's voice echoed off the concrete, startling a pair of doves nesting atop a gigantic column. They squawked as they shot into the sky.

"Not yet. Technically, I think he's a postulant. Or is that just for nuns? You wouldn't believe how complex Church hierarchy is. At any rate, he'll soon be taking the Jesuit vows of poverty and obedience to Christ and the Pope. In there somewhere is also a vow of chastity, so that lets me out."

"Jesus!"

"Literally."

"Did you try and talk him out of it?"

"He didn't give me the chance. I came home from work one night real late, so I snuck around in the dark, trying not to wake him, until I realized he wasn't even there. He'd left a letter on the table saying how he'd had a powerful epiphany and that he was joining the Church."

"He ran off to join a monastery and told you about it *in a note*?"

"He'd been trying to find a time to tell me, but I left for the studio before dawn and rarely got home before ten."

"You're not blaming yourself, are you?"

"Looking back, there were signs that I could have picked up on. He said the path he'd chosen was free of indecision and brought him a depth of serenity he hadn't felt for a long time — if ever. Besides, getting the news over a glass of Chianti or in a *Dear John* letter, does it really matter in the long run?"

"*I* think it does."

"Not when you're competing with God."

That shut her up.

They sat in silence, listening to the wind whip around the statues dotting the piazza. She squeezed his hand. "I hate that you had to go through that alone."

Marcus had kept Oliver's letter for a week, rereading it several times a day, until it became too painful and he set his cigarette lighter to it in the bathtub. "I've had better weeks."

"So he's reverted to form."

"How do you mean?"

"Isn't his father some sort of preacher? And his granddad, too?"

Marcus stared vacantly at the pagan gods and marveled at how he could have forgotten that Oliver came from a long line of Bible thumpers. Since the *Quo Vadis* company departed Rome, he'd come to regard the statues as his companions and confidants, but now he saw them for what they were: plaster and wood parading as marble and gold.

"I've been moping around here like such a sad sack, but you're right," he told Kathryn. "It's in his blood."

"So there's nothing to keep you here?" Kathryn asked.

"There's plenty to keep me here."

"Like?"

Marcus counted off his reasons, one finger at a time. "Spaghetti alla carbonara, fettuccine alfredo, saltimbocca alla Romana, bruschetta, limoncello, and I'm telling you, Signora Scatena's zucchini flowers!"

"I'm serious." She whacked him on the arm. "I had a meeting with Mayer. He told me to bring you back."

"But what did he say, exactly?"

"That you were one of his few writers capable of seeing a script through from start to finish. Most screenwriters are specialists, good with structure, or dialogue, or endings, but you can do it all. He said, 'A chap like that is precious to the industry. We can't afford to lose him. Especially now.'"

Praise from Caesar is praise indeed. "What did he mean, 'especially now'?"

Kathryn got to her feet, pulling Marcus up with her. Hooking her arm through his, she told him to take her on a tour of the Roman Forum. She felt woozy, and someone had told her if she could stay awake until sundown, she'd recover faster.

He led her down the palace steps and around temples and through piazzas as she related Nick Schenck's conspiracy to bring Mayer down, and how Senator McCarthy was hatching a Lavender Scare to lasso all the homos who hadn't already been branded Commies.

Kathryn was finishing up her speech when they strolled into a gargantuan colosseum. Or at least half of one – the half needed for shooting. Even a partial colosseum with thirty rows of seats for thousands of extras was an impressive sight.

"Do you know what we filmed here?" Marcus asked.

"Chariot race?"

"It's *Quo Vadis*, not *Ben-Hur*. This is where Nero throws the Christians to the lions."

"Did they use real lions during filming?"

"Lots, and boy were they hungry."

"Sounds horrible."

"Not as horrible as being thrown to McCarthy, Winchell, Hoover, and Breen."

"I know," Kathryn conceded, "it's just that –"

Marcus dug the edge of his wingtip into the floor of the stadium where a fist-sized stain of fake blood tinged the dirt. "It was bad enough being branded Red, but lavender too? No thanks."

"But you see –"

"So I come back to LA . . . and do what? I'm still blacklisted, so I hardly see the point of —"

"Will you let me speak?"

Marcus made a gesture: *The colosseum is yours.*

"Mayer can get you off the blacklist."

"How? Wave a wand?"

"There's a catch."

"It wouldn't be Hollywood without one."

As Kathryn explained what the graylist was, it began to dawn on Marcus that maybe the landscape back home really had changed.

"So how do I get off this so-called graylist?" he asked.

"We have to figure that out ourselves. But you can't do it from all the way over here." She stuck out that determined little chin he'd missed so much. "Gwennie's last words to me were 'If you come home alone, I'll kill you both.' And you know how she is with scissors."

He glided a hand around her shoulders. "I need to think about this."

"I know." She paused. "Meanwhile, how's about you show me Rome?"

"Sure. But first we need to stop at *la pensione della Scatena.*"

"What for?"

"Did I not mention the zucchini flowers?"

CHAPTER 5

It was coming up on closing time on Friday night — nine o'clock — when the telephone rang at Chez Gwendolyn. It wasn't unusual for someone to call so late. Gwendolyn figured it must be Kathryn or Marcus with last-minute dinner plans. Al Levy's Tavern, Bit of Sweden, the Cock'n Bull, Little Hungary, Bublichki's — they'd been to nearly all their old haunts since Kathryn fetched Marcus back from Italy.

The only places they avoided were the Italian joints. "Once you've had Mama Scatena's," Marcus declared, "it's hard to go back."

Gwendolyn picked up the phone and heard a high-pitched, breathy giggle that could only belong to one person.

"Marilyn?"

The giggle became a squeal. "He did it! That son of a bitch actually put his money where his mouth is."

Gwendolyn clenched the receiver. "Zanuck?"

"Full contract. Seven years. Annual pay increases. It's everything I've ever hoped for. I can scarcely believe it!"

"Tell me you've signed the contract and it's a done deal."

From what Gwendolyn had seen over the years, contracts were works in progress that changed according to box office receipts, gossip-column innuendo, and the physical charms of the focus-pulling chorine third from the end.

"At four o'clock this afternoon. Photographers from the *Times*, the *Examiner*, and *Life* were there. The guy from *Life* even said he might be able to swing me a cover. Can you imagine? Me? On the cover of *Life*?"

Gwendolyn thought of the snowy gown sprinkled with diamantes that she'd just finished. "I don't find that so hard to imagine." Even if—or when—Marilyn got that cover, she'd probably wear a Travilla original. But if not, what a coup that would be.

"Listen, the reason why I'm calling," Marilyn said, "is that a bunch of us are going out to celebrate and I want you to join us."

"Just tell me when and where."

"Ten o'clock at the Crescendo. But don't be late—Louis Armstrong is playing at eleven, so it'll be packed."

The Crescendo was a pocket-sized nightclub next to Mocambo, which would give her time to cherry-pick a sensational dress before dashing home to the Garden to freshen up.

"I'll meet you at the bar."

She was pulling out a knee-length chiffon cocktail number in deep apricot—not quite right for a late-night club, but the low neckline more than made up for it—when the phone rang again.

"Sorry, Marcus," she said into the receiver, "but you're too late."

A worried voice she didn't recognize made a grunting sound. "I was told you're open till nine. It's only ten to."

Gwendolyn laid the apricot number across her counter. "Sorry, I was expecting—never mind. How can I help you?"

"This is Raymond Bourke." The guy said his name as though Gwendolyn should recognize it.

"Have we met, Mr. Bourke?"

"Billy Travilla said I could call on you if need be. I do wardrobe for *Dragnet*, and I'm in trouble."

"Of course! How may I help?"

"We're about to start shooting a new episode and the murdered secretary got re-cast twenty minutes ago. Republic's wardrobe is mostly moth-eaten cowgirls and Wild West hookers. Can I send this girl over?"

"You mean right now?"

"Call is at seven A.M. She's a secretary so it don't gotta be nothing fancy. I'm working with a real tight budget here, Miss Brick. I can afford twenty bucks and not a penny more. You got anything to fit the bill?"

Gwendolyn pulled her apricot dress off the counter and told the guy yes, she had several things that should work.

"Great, because she's on her way. Her name's Hannah. Mail me the receipt."

Six minutes later, a plump, middle-aged woman with a henna rinse and a grim frown burst through the door. She slapped her generously curved sides. "Never in all my days have I witnessed such a collection of amateurs as that *Dragnet* bunch. Have you been over there? Don't bother, not if you prefer your sanity intact. Jumpin' Jehosaphat on a pogo stick, it's like the Keystone Kops." She held up a meaty index finger. "They didn't have anything bigger than a size twelve. Now, of course, I'm the first to admit that I'm no size six, but I ask you!"

Gwendolyn rattled through a quick mental stock. "What size would you say you are?"

"Sixteen on a good day. Otherwise, eighteen."

That usually meant twenty, which narrowed the options considerably. Gwendolyn's usual clientele were ex-model types who subsisted largely on pep pills to get through arduous days of shopping and art galleries.

Hannah opened her purse and pulled out a ragged twenty. "That Bourke schlemiel said as long as this covers the bill, tax included, I can pick whatever I want."

Gwendolyn glanced at the clock. "Is this your first job?"

"I've been a radio actress for years, but of course appearance is less of an issue. This is my first television role, so I'm hoping it'll open the door to new kinds of work." Hannah picked out a dress that was at least two sizes too small for her. "How much is this?"

"Twenty-four ninety-five."

"Pity."

In the end, she picked a brown suit with dark blue lapels that was a little snug across the back, but a fortified corset would fix that.

Two minutes after ten, Gwendolyn saw the woman through the door.

Fortunately the apricot number wasn't tricky to get into — side zippers were dress designers' gift to the single woman. Gwendolyn pulled a brush through her hair and touched up her makeup, then hurried to the nightclub.

Like most of the joints that dotted LA's social scene, the Crescendo featured a pretty hat check girl inside the front door and a maître d' podium where a tuxedoed gent stood with a ready smile. The walls of the Crescendo's squarish interior were swathed in deep purple drapes. A pall of cigarette smoke already shrouded the improvisational jazz trio in the corner.

Marilyn's eight-top table had one empty seat. "There you are!" She was radiant in shimmering blue.

"I had a last-minute customer."

Marilyn rattled off a bunch of names as she introduced the table. Gwendolyn caught only the last two on the end. "That's Ben Nye, my makeup maestro on *Love Nest*. What this man can't do with foundation and blush just isn't worth knowing. And next to him is Jack Paar. He's an actor, but don't hold that against him." She pointed at the empty seat next to Jack. "That's yours, honey. And of course you know Billy."

An unattached hand waved away a dense cloud of cigar smoke, revealing Billy Travilla. "Nice to see you again." His eyes ran down Gwendolyn's dress; approval hoisted an eyebrow. "If that color looks as good on you in the daytime as it does under this dim lighting, you should wear it more often."

She thanked him and slid onto the seat.

Marilyn heaved a magnum out of a chrome ice bucket and announced, "We have champagne!"

"No, sweetie," Ben told her, "I think you'll find that one's empty."

Marilyn flipped it and pouted when only a few drips trickled out. "We've finished two already?"

"We're a thirsty bunch." Billy faced Gwendolyn. "It's been quite a day, as you can imagine."

The maître d' arrived with a fresh bottle, lined up eight flutes, and filled them in a well-practiced swoop twelve inches above the table.

Gwendolyn grabbed her glass and took a deep swig.

"Quite a day for you, too?" Billy asked.

"I have you to thank. Or blame. I'm not sure which."

The jazz trio launched into a meandering interpretation of "Heebie Jeebies," an early hit for Louis Armstrong from back in his Hot Five days that Gwendolyn knew because Tallulah Bankhead insisted on playing it at every Garden party she crashed.

"I got an SOS from your *Dragnet* pal," Gwendolyn told him.

"Raymond still has that job?"

"He called me ten minutes before closing, all worked up into a lather because he had to costume an actress for an episode tomorrow and they had nothing for her."

"You were able to help him out?"

"And for less than twenty bucks."

He leaned back and rubbed a finger along his jawline thoughtfully.

"What?" she asked.

"You just impressed the right person."

"I hardly think he's the right man for that job."

"God, no. He shouldn't be there at all, but he's the producer's brother-in-law. Michael Meshekoff is quite the big cheese over at Republic because of that show. My guess is you just made your mark on a nice chunk of Gouda."

A smooth voice came over the speakers. "Ladies and gentlemen, the Crescendo is proud to welcome the incomparable Mr. Louis Armstrong."

The house lights dimmed and footlights rimming the stage glowed as the most skilled trumpeter in America stepped forward. Marilyn released a howl and her costar, Jack, let out a two-fingered whistle.

From the corner of her eye, Gwendolyn could see Billy Travilla sizing her up. It wasn't sexual—she knew when a come-on was looming—but she wasn't sure what he had on his mind. All she knew was that Armstrong was nearly halfway through "C'est Si Bon" before Travilla took his eyes off her.

CHAPTER 6

Marcus read the sign at Villa Nova. "Here?"

"We're sick of everything else," Kathryn told him.

"And I miss the osso buco," Gwendolyn added.

"And the crepe suzettes," Doris put in.

"Crepe suzettes are French," Marcus said. "Signora Scatena wouldn't serve — "

Kathryn prodded him in his shoulder, right at the soft part where she knew it would hurt. "But most of all, we're sick of hearing about Signora Scatena. You don't give up wine just because you can no longer drink Chateau Lafitte."

Marcus was aware that he'd become a bit of a snob about Italian food, and that he viewed his time in Europe through golden lenses that made California feel like a pallid imitation. Everything back there was infused with centuries of tradition: food, wine, architecture, churches. LA felt as flimsy as the MGM back lot now.

It had only recently dawned on him that he was bound to return to the States eventually, and the longer he stayed over there, the harder it would have been to readjust. Although he'd been back for nearly four weeks now, he was still easing himself into a pace he'd once taken for granted. In the time he was away, even his barber had gone out of business.

Was nothing forever in this town?

Marcus relented and held the door open for his friends.

It was Friday night, but well after nine thirty, so Gwendolyn could close the store; the evening rush had passed and the room was busy but not packed. They were seated near the rear and opened their oversized menus.

As the others debated the merits of the piccione and the baccala, or maybe the bistecca rusticana, Marcus began to see that, sweet though it was, his time wandering Cinecittà's Roman Forum photographing farmers' sons in scratchy togas wasn't real life. Nobody picks up and moves to Europe any more than they pick up and move into a storybook. It was time to get his life back on track.

He'd have to determine what this graylist was so he could figure out how to get off it. He kept asking around, but so far had nothing.

Kathryn closed her menu. "I need fortification after that preview this afternoon. Just the title alone should have given me a clue: *The Thing from Another World*. Ugh!"

This was another development during Marcus' absence: the semi-underground genre of science fiction had wormed its way onto the screen. "I wouldn't have thought that was your kind of movie," he said.

"It's not, but word around town is that Howard Hawks directed it."

Marcus couldn't imagine that someone who guided *His Girl Friday*, *To Have and Have Not*, and *Bringing Up Baby* to the screen would bother with a story about a plant-based alien found frozen in the Arctic.

A waiter swept past with four plates of chicken cacciatore loaded with garlic, and Marcus remembered the little place down at the end of Via Giuseppe Salvioli whose chicken cacciatora surpassed even the culinary wizardry of Signora Scatena. It was where he went pretty much every night after he found Oliver's letter. Two days before he left Rome, he dropped a note at the seminary telling Oliver of his plans, but heard nothing back. He wished now he'd left his address with the signora, just in case.

"I'm glad you chose this place," he announced. "That chicken cacciatora smelled good; I think I'll order it."

Kathryn followed the progress of a couple heading toward the back corner. "Don't look now, but L.B. and Lorena Mayer just appeared."

"Is that so strange?"

"Since those rumors started, I never see him anywhere." She drummed her fingernails on the tabletop. "I wonder what this means."

"That he's hungry?" Doris suggested.

"He's more of a Romanoff's kind of guy. And look at the way they've buried themselves behind their menus, acting like a couple of Garbos."

The waiter arrived. Marcus watched the Mayers as they placed their orders. As soon as the waiter departed, he told the girls to whistle when his chicken cacciatora arrived.

He was only halfway around the thicket of tables when Mayer caught sight of him. He looked like a mallard on opening day. His second wife, a pleasant woman in her mid-forties, lay a placating hand on her husband's forearm.

"Hello, L.B.," Marcus said as he approached their table. "I just wanted to give you my appreciation for what you did."

Mayer nodded silently, keeping his eyes on the glass ashtray in front of him.

"You're Marcus Adler, aren't you?" Lorena asked. "Why don't you join us?"

Mayer's flash of anger at his wife was hard to miss.

"No, no," Marcus said. "I only wanted to make a quick stop to say thank you."

"Nonsense," Lorena said. "Please join us. If only for a moment."

Marcus sat down slowly.

"You're just back from Italy, aren't you?"

Marcus had never seen Lorena up close before, and he was surprised to find her a younger, prettier, more appealing version of Louella Parsons. She was also nobody's fool if she knew who Marcus was and where he'd been.

"I am," Marcus said.

She sipped her rosé. "I've heard Rome is still recovering from the war."

"There's lots of building and restoration going on, which gives it a real vitality. You can almost taste the liveliness in the air. And they're mad about movies. Cinecittà must be seen to be believed. My whole time there was quite an experience, and I have your husband to thank for it."

The three of them sat in awkward silence until Marcus couldn't stand it any longer.

"So this graylist. Nobody's got any advice for me. About how to get off it, I mean."

"It's only the top brass who know about it," Mayer replied.

"I've got a few ideas for movies and thought perhaps I could pitch them around town."

Mayer shook his head as though he couldn't bear to hear another word. "You'll have to find some other way." He drained his whiskey and motioned the waiter for a refill. "I got you onto the graylist, but you're still blacklisted as a writer. You need to acquire a new skill."

"Is a job at MGM out of the question? Perhaps I could learn a new trade, such as lighting, or —"

Lorena stiffened.

Mayer picked up a book of Villa Nova matches and started turning it over and over. "You want my advice, Adler? Here it is: *Trust nobody*. They're all bastards and will pick you over like vultures first chance they get. HUAC and their supporters have crushed the Commies, so they need a new boogieman. They know it, and this McCarthy bastard knows it, too. Do not underestimate him."

"I hear he's intent on creating a Lavender Scare. Seeing as how HUAC has practically decimated the creative side of the industry, perhaps you and your counterparts —"

"I don't have any counterparts," Mayer snapped. "Or at least won't, soon enough."

"I'm not sure I follow."

Mayer set his mouth to a surly frown. "I'm being forced to resign."

"But MGM without you is unimaginable. Surely they —"

"They've got him right where they want him," Lorena said. "Louis is right, Mr. Adler. Trust nobody."

"They're trying to control how the news gets out. Well, screw that, and screw them." Mayer lit a Havana and pointed it toward Kathryn. "Tell her I'll be in touch. Real soon. Meanwhile, good luck to you, Adler. From here on in, you're on your own."

CHAPTER 7

Kathryn burst through the front doors of the Zephyr Room, pulling off her gloves like she was plucking a chicken, each finger marking a fresh irritation.

That little shit!

No, he's a big shit!

What a nerve!

After sixteen years!

And HE questions MY loyalty?

With its all-white décor and intricately sculpted ornamentation around the curved bar, the Zephyr Room was a picture of understated elegance. But Kathryn could have been at some grimy dive down the seedy end of Sunset for all she cared.

She found Leo at a corner table.

"I ordered you a manhattan," he said, "although maybe I ought to have made it a double."

"Wait till you hear *this*!" She sank into her chair as the bartender delivered a pair of manhattans. "Give us five minutes," she told the guy, "then bring over another round."

Leo clinked his glass against Kathryn's. "What's happened?"

A pianist started tinkling a Rosemary Clooney tune in the opposite corner. It was the first quiet moment she'd had all afternoon. "I'm sure you had a busy day, too. Dealing with bosses and their unmitigating egos, and how they question your loyalty after sixteen years."

"As a matter of fact, I had a pretty good day."

Leo was a decent guy, good-looking, great taste, successful, and hot stuff in the sack. He didn't deserve to sit through a long-winded rant, but if she didn't get this off her chest, it would smolder.

"Get this: Wilkerson's wife is pregnant. At sixty-one, he's going to have a kid. You know what he told me? The day the kid pops out, he's going to give up gambling. Said he had an epiphany." She raised her empty cocktail glass and jiggled it to catch the bartender's attention. "I'll believe that when I see it."

"Seeing is believing."

"So he calls me in. Tells me about the baby. Goo-goo, ga-ga, baby-baby-baby, blah-blah, fine. Then he says, 'I've got a bone to pick with you.' 'About what?' I ask him. Suddenly, he's all beady little raccoon eyes. 'About the big announcement on your show last Friday,' he says."

The morning after that evening at the Villa Nova, Kathryn got a five-star telegram at the Garden of Allah requesting her presence at the Mayers' home in the canyons behind the Hotel Bel-Air. She drove through the deserted Sunday streets and pulled into the driveway on St. Cloud Road with clammy palms.

Lorena served coffee and sweet rolls in their sunny living room, where a radio played wispy minuets and nimble waltzes. Kathryn was tempted to blow the whistle on the blatant stagecraft, but she could see how tough it was for this man who'd plowed every waking moment into keeping his dominion at the forefront of American culture. If he wanted to pretend that he was perfectly at ease with being dethroned, she could play along—especially if it meant she would walk out with the biggest scoop of her career.

Which she did.

By some sort of miracle, the news remained locked up until days later when she stood in front of the NBC mike and tried to steady the papers shaking in her hand. Her announcement sent shockwaves through the industry, prompting a landslide of phone calls, notes, and telegrams.

She was still riding high when Wilkerson's secretary announced that she'd been summoned.

All job-well-done expectations flew from her mind when Wilkerson planted his palms on the mahogany desk, his face pale with fury. "EXPLAIN YOURSELF!"

"I thought you'd be pleased." She sat down in one of the chairs facing his desk, hoping he'd do the same. He didn't. "I've been hearing from people all over the country. We scooped Louella, Hedda, Winchell, and *Variety*."

Wilkerson thumped the desk. "You didn't even tell me! That story belonged on a two-inch banner headline in the *Hollywood Reporter*."

"But you got your headline."

"A day later!"

"It wasn't even twelve hours between my show and us going to print."

"The point is you didn't confide in me. Remember that time you learned Vivien Leigh got Scarlett? Who was the first person you came running to?"

That was hardly the same situation. At the time, Kathryn was miserable working at *Life* magazine and used the news as leverage to return to the *Reporter*. But Wilkerson was in no mood for logic.

"Mayer gave me his exclusive on the condition that I break the news on my radio show."

Wilkerson opened his mouth, then closed it again. He returned to his chair, but perched on the edge. "My beef with you," he clipped every word with a calibrated snap, "is that you didn't trust me with the story of the decade."

"You're absolutely right," she conceded. "I didn't trust you with it because I didn't trust *anyone* with it. Not my friends. Not my producer. Not even my boss. I couldn't take that sort of risk."

"WHERE'S YOUR LOYALTY?" The question exploded out of him like a Chinese firecracker. "I thought I could at least count on you. This galls me, Kathryn. It absolutely galls me."

"And it galls me that you're even questioning my loyalty."

"After the way you have turned your back on the *Reporter*, I do!"

Kathryn shot to her feet. "The whole point of the radio show was to raise the profile of the *Reporter* to a national level. The whole country is talking about us!"

"You need to start thinking about what's more important to you: your column or your radio show. Now get out of my office. I've got a paper to run."

Kathryn signaled the Zephyr Room bartender for a third round. "Thank you for listening," she said, stroking the hair on the back of Leo's knuckles.

He smiled, but said nothing. To prove that she had gotten it all off her chest, she said nothing as well.

"Did I ever tell you I have two younger brothers?" he asked.

"Twins, right?"

"They came along fourteen years after I was born, which means I have experience dealing with little boys. Wilkerson is stamping his foot because he didn't get the shiny prize first."

Kathryn pictured her six-foot boss in a sailor suit with short trousers and a hat with a white ribbon. "You're plenty smart, Mr. Presnell."

"How about I take him out for a round of golf at the LA Country Club for some man-to-man time?"

She leaned over and kissed his lips.

"I've got some news that will cheer you up," he said.

"I'm all ears."

"I met with NBC today, and boy, were they ever busting out the smiles. They said your bombshell virtually guarantees this Friday's show will leap back into the top ten, possibly even top five, which puts you within striking distance of Winchell."

The tension headache that had been pounding Kathryn's temples started to recede.

"So," Leo continued, "I have pitched to my boss an idea I've been incubating." He shifted in his seat, a little apprehensively, it struck Kathryn—unusual for a guy who rarely showed his nerves. "Remember that cake demonstration—where you had those housewives eating out of your hand? Well, me and my counterpart at Betty Crocker want to sponsor a nationwide tour replicating that demo."

Kathryn had been nervous as hell that day at the May Company and managed to pull it off only by the sheerest of flukes.

He watched her face. "Hear me out. Ten cities in fifteen days. Two of them Fridays, so you'll be broadcasting from Denver and Pittsburgh, and we'll fly in some big movie star. The tour will culminate in a special program, which NBC will promote the living daylights out of, and it'll take place at Rockefeller Center."

"In New York?!" It could have been the three manhattans she'd downed in rash succession, but Kathryn felt her heart skip a beat.

Leo lay his right hand over her left. "I'm already in talks with Duke Ellington and Benny Goodman as guests."

"*Both* of them?"

"I haven't come to the best part yet."

Kathryn wondered if a fourth manhattan was too much.

"NBC is putting together a stunt they're calling Golden Aerial Day. They want to broadcast your show on both radio *and* television, in New York *and* Los Angeles simultaneously. It'll be a first. Kathryn Massey of the *Hollywood Reporter* baking a Betty Crocker cake using a Sunbeam Mixmaster on NBC radio and television. Everybody wins. Which is how I will pitch it to Baby Boy Wilkerson when I take him out for golf."

Kathryn's "Holy mackerel!" came out so softly that she doubted Leo even heard it. Suddenly, the place felt cramped and hot. "I need fresh air."

* * *

As they strolled along Wilshire toward the Town House Hotel, visions of Central Park, Bergdorf Goodman, Radio City Music Hall, and the Rainbow Room jostled in Kathryn's imagination.

She grabbed Leo's arm and squeezed it. "Can we stay at the Plaza?"

"I don't see why not."

"And Rumpelmayer's!" She loved how that name rolled off the tongue. "Do you know where it is?"

He laughed gently. "The St. Moritz Hotel."

"I don't even care if the ice cream is second-rate."

"I can assure you it's not."

They walked in contented silence until Kathryn said, "Is it strange I've never seen New York? I've always been so busy here with some crisis or celebration, a hit that's hit or a flop that's flopped."

"You got away from it long enough to go to Rome."

"I had extra incentive to bring Marcus back. Plus, before I left, I was up to midnight every night writing as many columns as I could. But it won't be like that this time. I could do my column on the road. When we get to New York—"

A realization dropped on Kathryn from what felt like a great height.

"Do you know where Sing Sing is?" she asked as lightly as she could.

"Near Tarrytown. Maybe forty miles." He pulled his arm from her grip. "Oh no," he warned, waving a finger at her. "No, no, no. Don't even think of it."

"But he's my father. This might be my only chance to meet him."

Leo bunched his hands into fists and shoved them into his pockets. "I don't want you spending one second contemplating anything like that."

She stepped ahead and blocked his path. "I don't know that it's up to you."

He looked like he wanted to punch a hole in the brick wall beside them.

"You have no idea how long and how hard I've been working to stitch this deal together. It's the most ambitious project I've ever done, and I did it for you."

Under different circumstances, she'd have told him not to kid himself about that. "It just means slipping up to Tarrytown. An hour to get there, an hour with him, and an hour back. Nobody'll know."

"By the time you get to New York, you'll be even more famous across the country than you already are. What if you get recognized?" Spittle was starting to collect in the corners of his mouth. "I'm surprised your illegitimacy has stayed secret. But on top of that, you want to risk the revelation that your father is in prison? Let's not forget he was convicted of selling secrets to goddamned Nazis."

"My mom thinks he's innocent."

He inched forward. "Do you want him to be the next Julius Rosenberg?"

"How did the Rosenbergs come into this?"

"They're housed on death row at Sing Sing." He started with the finger waving again. "I forbid it. There's too much at stake and I will *not* let you sabotage it just because you want to visit your long-lost daddy."

He went to add more, but Kathryn's handbag to the side of his shoulder stopped him cold.

* * *

It was well past eleven by the time Kathryn returned home. A few lights were on in villas scattered throughout the Garden, but Marcus' was dark. She was still contemplating the sort of reception she'd get if she woke him up when the light in his kitchen went on. She knocked on his door.

He opened it, his hair tousled, without his glasses, and wearing only his pajama bottoms. "What's going on?"

"Are you awake enough for me to unload my troubles?"

He smiled lazily and took her by the hand. Newspapers and magazines crowded his sofa. He shoved them to the floor and patted the space beside him.

He kept his face in neutral while she spewed out the details of her horrible day. When she was done, he asked, "Did you really hit Leo with your purse?"

Kathryn grimaced. "I do kind of feel bad about that. But he was treating me like a four-year-old, telling me what I can and can't do."

"He does have a stake in all this — both personally and professionally."

"Okay, so I behaved like a bitch. I get it."

He leaned his head on a hand and slow-blinked at her. "En route to Italy last year, I wanted to stop off in New York. But I had to be on the set of *Quo Vadis* so I didn't see it."

"You want me to send a picture postcard?"

He sandwiched her hand between his and kissed her fingertips. "I'm suggesting that I meet you in New York. We could take a carriage ride in Central Park. Climb the Statue of Liberty. Catch a Broadway show — I hear *The King and I* is marvelous. Shall we dance, pom pom pom!"

"That does sound fun."

"And maybe at some point, *I* could slip away. Upstate. Pay someone a visit. On your behalf. Without anybody knowing."

Kathryn didn't feel the tears coming, but when they did, they burst out of her in heaving sobs as Marcus guided her to his chest and muffled them before someone called the cops.

CHAPTER 8

The stink of ammonia hit Gwendolyn as soon as she walked into the deserted production offices of *Dragnet*. She fanned her purse to clear the air.

"Hello? Is anybody here?" No answer. "HELLOO-OO!"

Since the night that plump actress landed on her doorstep, Raymond Bourke had come to her again and again, and *Dragnet* had proved to be a handy sideline. So when a tetchy secretary called to say that the producer wanted to see her in his office, she was more than happy to oblige. But she couldn't make it over into the Valley until after she closed the store.

"That'll be fine," the secretary replied. "Our offices will be the only ones with the lights on."

Gwendolyn called out again.

"I'll be right with you." The man's voice sounded friendly enough, but it was hard to determine its origin.

Gwendolyn wandered over to a poster hanging on the wall. It was a duplicate of the billboards that NBC had plastered across town advertising how *Dragnet* would be back with new episodes in September and reminding viewers that Sgt. Joe Friday wants the facts. Just the facts, ma'am.

"You must be Miss Brick."

Michael Meshekoff wore no tie and disheveled hair. They shook hands.

"I was just about to pour myself a drink. I have brandy, whiskey, and some pretty good scotch. I could probably even rustle up some sherry, if you'd prefer."

It had been a tiring day for Gwendolyn, too. She'd endured an unexpectedly long fitting session for the wife of the director of *David and Bathsheba*. Fox had high hopes for the picture, and the director's wife had equally high hopes for the dress she'd wear to the premiere in August.

"A sherry would be nice."

Meshekoff's office was expansive but spare. A long, deep tartan sofa along the wall made Gwendolyn question whether accepting a drink was such a good idea. But he directed her to the chairs in front of his desk as he produced glasses and poured their drinks. He sat a sherry in front of her and took the other seat.

"It's late, so I'll come to the point." Meshekoff frowned the frown of someone with an unsavory task ahead of him. "I'm stretched pretty thin, and it only just recently came to my attention that you've been helping Raymond out with women's wardrobe."

Gwendolyn sampled the sherry. It was top shelf. "If that's a problem, you could've just called me. I wouldn't have taken offense." *Drats. That* Dragnet *money's been paying half my store rent.*

"I had to fire Raymond Bourke this morning," Meshekoff said. "Some people just aren't cut out for working at this pace. Miss Brick, I'd like to offer you the job of managing the wardrobe department for my show."

"Me?" Gwendolyn forced her sherry down. "I'm hardly —"

"I live across the street from Billy Travilla and his wife, Dona. We often stop for a chat when I'm out walking my dog. We got talking the other day and —"

"He suggested me?" Gwendolyn pictured the look on Billy's face that night at the Crescendo. "I'm sorry, Mr. Meshekoff —"

"Call me Mike."

"Thank you, but I have a store to run, clients to serve."

"NBC just increased our budget."

"Still, I'm going to have to decline your offer."

Meshekoff slid his scotch onto the desk and raked his fingers through his hair. "I'm a desperate man, Miss Brick. A weekly television show is like a battle cruiser: it stops for nobody."

"*Dragnet* is cops and detectives and bad guys," Gwendolyn said. "You need a man running your wardrobe department, but one with good taste in women's apparel."

"What I need is a replacement, but quick."

"Tell me, Mike, do you remember a haberdashery called Tattler's Tuxedos?"

"Sure. My dad always got his formalwear there. And when it came time for me to get my first suit, that's where we shopped."

"What if I could get Horton Tattler for you?"

Meshekoff planted his elbows on his knees and knitted his fingers together. "I know he fell on hard times, and all, but the Tattler name still carries a note of prestige."

"May I borrow your phone?"

* * *

Gwendolyn hadn't been in the Vine Street Brown Derby in the three years since she'd opened her store, so she was pleased to see it hadn't changed significantly. She suspected the booths had been reupholstered in the same rich, warm red, and the walls freshly repainted, too. But the place still had that same welcoming air. And of course the Derby wouldn't be the Derby without the celebrity caricatures covering every inch of vertical space in neatly ordered lines.

Horton Tattler was already seated in one of the booths. When he stood to greet her, it enabled her to take in the full sight of him.

When Mike Meshekoff said that Horton had fallen on hard times, he was more right than he knew. The war had seen his once-notable fortunes dwindle, and after the restoration of peace, they hadn't turned around until Gwendolyn gave him a stake in her original fragrance.

Horton held his arms out wide, revealing his suit's fraying cuffs. As she drew closer, she could see the faded colors in his yellow silk tie. "What a surprise to get your call," he exclaimed. "And what a rare treat to see you, my darling girl."

She returned his hug, noting that he no longer wore his Tattler's eau de cologne. She smelled only Lux soap.

They slipped into the booth and accepted menus from the waiter. From the angle of his eyes, she could tell Horton was skimming the bottom of the page for the cheaper items.

"This is my treat." She waved away his protests. "I invited you, not the other way around, so none of this old-fashioned 'the man must always pay' nonsense. And besides, I've got an ulterior motive. I'm about to ask a favor, so the least I can do is pick up the check."

Mike Meshekoff was so enthusiastic at the thought of having Horton run wardrobe that Gwendolyn didn't want to let him down. After placing their drink order, she asked Horton if he watched *Dragnet*.

"I probably would if I could afford a television set."

"Here's the thing: I've been helping out the guy in charge of wardrobe. I get a call when he's stuck for a pretty outfit. Last night, I had a meeting with the producer."

"You *are* moving with a fast crowd these days."

"Not really. At any rate, he had to fire his wardrobe guy. So now he's in the hole for a replacement, and wanted me to take over. I guess he thought my store would just run itself. I told him no, but offered up a Plan B."

A group seated at a long table at the end of the restaurant broke into cheers as the maître d' presented them with a birthday cake spiked with a lit sparkler.

"You're my Plan B."

Horton blinked. "What?"

"You should have seen the look on his face when he heard your name. His father used to shop with you all the time."

"Who is this chap?"

"Meshekoff."

The waiter arrived with their drinks and asked if they were ready to order dinner, but Gwendolyn shooed him away.

"I do remember that guy," Horton said. "He only bought formal from me, but always the finest stuff. He had a kid, as I recall. A son."

"You sold him his first suit. His name's Mike."

"And he's the producer on *Dragnet*?"

"He is, and I want you to consider taking the job of running the wardrobe department."

Horton pressed his hands to his mouth, his eyes bulging and unblinking.

"You don't need to give me your answer right this very minute," Gwendolyn told him.

He groped his pockets for a handkerchief and found one in the breast pocket of his jacket. He yanked it out with a quiet yip and pressed it to his eyes. Amid the hubbub of the restaurant, Gwendolyn couldn't quite make out his strangled mutterings. Something about the embarrassment of losing something.

"Do you need a moment to collect yourself?" Gwendolyn asked. "Perhaps you might want to—?"

He expelled himself from the booth with a jerky nod, and scuttled, head down, toward the men's room.

Gwendolyn picked up the menu and pretended to study it. After a few minutes, Horton hadn't returned, but she did spot a familiar face.

Herman Dewberry had been her boss at Bullocks. In fact, he was responsible for her becoming the go-to dressmaker for a clandestine community of crossdressers she'd never known existed. When Gwendolyn decided to open her own store, Herman was one of the first people she told.

She waved; he motioned for her to join him.

His dinner companion had a vaguely Victorian air about him, rather like a genteel walrus. He did not stand when Gwendolyn approached their table, as Herman did, but he kissed her hand and asked her to join them.

"A moment or two, perhaps."

Herman jacked a thumb toward the bathroom door. "Would you like me to go check on him?"

"He just got a bit of a shock. A good one." The door remained stationary. "I hope. Let's give him a few minutes."

Herman said, "Please allow me to introduce my boss, Maxwell Schofield. Max, this is Gwendolyn Brick. She used to work for us in the fragrance department, and was quite the saleswoman too, I might add."

Schofield stroked the gold tiepin in his cravat. He leaned toward the center of the table and took in a deep sniff. "You're wearing Sunset Boulevard, are you not?"

"I am. I —"

"My daughter is mad for it. So are half her friends. I know when she's had a gang of them over to the house. The place smacks of it."

Gwendolyn couldn't tell if he was complaining or simply making an observation.

"Max," Herman said, "do you remember I brought up Miss Brick in our recent management conference?"

Schofield's silvery brows started twitching as his milky blue eyes took in a new appreciation of this girl at his table. "Chez Gwendolyn? On the Sunset Strip?"

"That's me."

"So this Sunset Boulevard perfume everybody is so mad for, it's yours?" Schofield thumped the table. "That puts an entirely new complexion on the matter."

"It does?"

"Miss Brick!" Schofield said, "I have a proposition for you." A fat Dutch Masters cigar had been sitting neglected in the ashtray. He picked it up and took a deep pull.

There was still no sign of Horton.

"We would like — very much, I might add — to stock your perfume."

"*My* Sunset Boulevard? In *your* stores?" The offer left Gwendolyn a little breathless.

Pull yourself together, she told herself. *This is a business deal. Don't stammer like an ingénue in a Jerome Kern musical.*

"I've done very well with my perfume, but its major selling point has been its exclusivity at my store, and my store alone."

"It's a draw card," Schofield said. "It's what pulls your customers in. While they're there, you show them a pair of opera gloves, maybe a scarf, which happens to be draped over the most expensive outfit in your collection. Miss Brick, retail is my life; I understand the process thoroughly. That's why we're prepared to offer you a handsome deal."

She peeked at Herman. He shot back, "A *very* handsome deal."

"I'll need some time to think about this," she said. "Perhaps if you could put something in writing?"

"I'm sure we could get a formal proposal in the mail to Miss Brick by this time next week."

Horton started picking his way through the restaurant; the color had returned to his cheeks. She thanked both men, shaking their hands like a businesswoman should, and arrived at their booth at the same time as Horton.

"I'm so very sorry about that. Such a display from a gentleman of my advanced years."

"This is the Brown Derby," Gwendolyn reminded him. "You think they haven't seen worse?"

"Perhaps you're right."

"So, the *Dragnet* job?"

"Tell him I can start tomorrow if need be."

"Wonderful!" Gwendolyn clapped her hands. "It's quite possible Mike will take you up on that."

Horton jutted his head toward Herman's table. "That wasn't Maxwell Schofield I saw you with, was it?"

"You know him?"

"Back in my Tattler's Tuxedos days, we frequently did business together."

"Is he a good guy? Can I trust him?"

"Absolutely. He comes from the 'His word is his bond' school of business. Why?"

Gwendolyn related the offer Schofield had just made.

"You're going to take it, aren't you?" Horton asked.

"I should at least see the offer first. When it comes in, maybe I could show it to you?"

"Of course, but if it comes from Schofield, you can be sure it's a square deal." After a heavy pause, his voice took on a choking quality. "My dear, thank you for this opportunity with *Dragnet*. I won't let you down."

The bunch at the end of the room with the sparkling birthday cake let off three raucous hip-hip-hoorays. Gwendolyn raised her glass. "Between my Bullocks and your *Dragnet*, it almost feels like they're cheering us on."

CHAPTER 9

The set of Humphrey Bogart's new picture looked to Marcus like it had been cobbled together from discarded plans for Rick's Café Américain: plain walls, ceiling fans, scattered tables. He'd never given much thought to what 1920s Syria resembled, but he guessed it wasn't 1940s Morocco. Still, the geometric tiles were a nice touch, and so was the decorative arch behind the bar.

Marcus pulled at the collar of his French soldier's uniform. The leather strap secured across his chest pressed the brass buttons into his ribs and he wished he hadn't declined the offer of talcum powder. But Doris' last words to him that morning were,

"The Screen Extras Guild can get pretty jumpy if they know a nonmember is on set, so keep a low profile. Just nod and say 'Yes, sir.' The union rep is a vindictive little creep who goes out of his way to throw grief at me, so don't give him a chance, *capisce*?"

Marcus hadn't found a scrap of work in three months. As much as he liked being back in LA, his mind kept wandering back to his favorite Roman bistros, thick with the aroma of garlic, tomatoes, roasted eggplant, and fried onions. And the coffee — strong, black espresso from elaborate contraptions Jules Verne might have dreamed up. Stovetop espresso pots were okay in a pinch, but the watery swill they served in American diners was like comparing a Keystone Kops short to a Technicolor musical out of MGM's Freed Unit.

When Marcus' duties shifted from screenwriter to on-set photographer for *Quo Vadis*, Mervyn LeRoy intentionally neglected to tell the location accountant to adjust his pay accordingly. Consequently, Marcus returned home with a healthy wad of cash, but American dollars went a lot further in Europe than they did in LA.

A week ago, Marcus checked his bank balance and was horrified to learn that he barely had enough to cover next month's rent for his cheap room in the Garden of Allah's main house. Kathryn had offered to let him crash on her sofa, but pride and independence choked off anything but "No thanks."

He needed to find work — and fast.

His sister, Doris, came to the rescue. She worked at Columbia juggling soundstages and personnel logistics between the studio's feature film production and its television shows.

He was thankful for the work, even when she told him it was on the set of *Sirocco*. Bogie had lived at the Garden a couple of times, and Marcus saw him as a colleague. But now Bogie was one of the world's biggest movie stars, and Marcus was a guy in the background suffocating in a French soldier's uniform for less per day than Bogie probably spent on tobacco.

As extras started to file onto the set, the assistant director cupped his hands to his mouth. "Take a seat at any table. When the cameras start rolling, keep in mind that you joined the French army to be a soldier, but you're stuck in Damascus where it's hot and boring and the locals resent the crap out of you. You've come to the Moulin Rouge for relaxation, booze, and the chance you might pick up a broad who'll let you feel her up for a Syrian pound or two."

A redheaded guy with more freckles than sense stuck his hand up. "How much is a Syrian pound worth?"

"What difference does that make?"

"Should I be peeling off one bill or two?"

The guy behind the arched bar wore a red fez and a white smock buttoned at the shoulder.

"Hey, Charlie! Do you think anyone in the Levant is going to see this picture? Just shut the hell up, sit the hell down, and do what the man says."

He lifted the fez from his head, revealing a dark purple birthmark the shape of the Carthay Circle Theatre tower. Marcus headed toward a four-top table on the far side of the set. Doris' lecture had included a strong warning to avoid the guy with the birthmark. "That's Pierce. He's the Guild rep. A real union guy. A-1 stickler for the rules. If he finds out that there's a nonmember working on one of his sets, there'll be hell to pay. Mostly by me."

Marcus passed a raised platform where four musicians in smocks and fezzes were seated. He took a seat with his back to the bartender; a pair of soldiers in uniform soon joined him. One of them, barely twenty, moved with the gangly angles of a baby giraffe. Behind him was Freckles, who the union rep had just yelled at. They were soon joined by a fourth, a Gilbert Roland type—if Roland was twenty years older and had spent his life picking fruit by day and chugging liquor by night.

"Morning, gents." Roland cracked an affable smile and suddenly looked like the most authentic French soldier on the set. "I see Mr. Pierce is with us today."

"Is that good?" the giraffe asked.

Freckles grunted.

"He doesn't stand for any bullshit from management," the lookalike replied. "He knows how long they can work us without a break, and if they go a single minute overtime, he'll blow the whistle. Literally. He's got one under that costume and he won't hesitate to use it."

"But Bogie's a decent guy, right?"

"I ain't saying he's not. But this is his production company, so he's got one eye on the script and one eye on the budget. Most producers push their luck, but never when Pierce has his beady little peepers on them. I do hope you remembered to bring your union card."

Marcus stopped tugging at his stiff collar. "Why?"

"I was on a Maria Montez picture last year; you should've seen what he did to a poor slave girl when she couldn't produce her card."

"What if I don't have it on me?" Marcus asked.

"Why wouldn't you? It's a union requirement."

"Because I changed my clothes at the last minute and left my wallet in my other pants."

Freckles winced. "In that case, if Pierce starts coming around doing a card check, that's the time you crawl under the table."

Marcus nodded as blithely as he could and said nothing more.

The director and cameraman took a black-haired belly dancer through her seductive gyrations around the set and past the table where Bogie in an incongruous bow tie sat next to an appropriately greasy cohort sucking a cigar.

Marcus didn't think Bogie would care about finding him in such reduced circumstances, but Marcus wasn't sure he was up to enduring that sort of conversation. He kept his eyes pinned on a carved wooden screen at the rear of the set as his tablemates talked about how extras were treated at the various studios and which directors were heartless bastards to the faceless bodies that filled their backgrounds.

Two hours later, the crew was still setting up lighting and camera angles for the belly dance, and the conversation around Marcus' table had drifted into a word game called "I'm Going on a Picnic." The Gilbert Roland lookalike got bored with that and changed it to "I'm Going to an Orgy." He won the first two rounds and was about to suggest a third when he grimaced.

"I could tell Pierce was in a pissy mood."

Marcus didn't dare turn around.

During the word games, a steady stream of crew had disappeared behind the wooden screen and reappeared with tools or props. Marcus was halfway to the exit when a surly assistant blocked his path. "You can't leave the set. We're about to start shooting."

"But I need to use—"

"We'll be starting soon."

"What is this, elementary school? I need a hall pass to go to the little boys' room?"

"Please return to your table."

Pierce was now halfway across the set, checking the four musicians' union cards. "The men's room is right around the corner. I'll be two minutes, tops."

The assistant jabbed a pudgy finger past Marcus' shoulder. "Back to your table. *Now*."

Marcus didn't want to get Doris into trouble, but he really needed the dough, too. He took the long way back, looping around a plaster column. When he was out of the assistant's sight, he faked a loud sneeze. Bogie, who had stepped onto the set to confer with the director, caught sight of Marcus as Pierce reached Gilbert Roland, Freckles, and Baby Giraffe.

Marcus walked toward Bogie with his hand outstretched. Bogie grabbed it and shook it with gusto. "I heard you were back in town."

"Sometimes I wonder why."

The smile dropped away from Bogie's face. "You made the right choice. Long term, I mean."

"I'm glad *you* think so."

"When you start producing your own pictures, people treat you differently. They show you things that you might not have otherwise seen." Bogie waited until Pierce walked past them to the final table on the set. "Like lists, for instance."

So the graylist wasn't a term describing a political point of view, but a physical list that some secretary had typed up?

Bogie presented Marcus with a wry smile. "Is it true Mayer got you onto it?" Marcus nodded. "Makes a guy speculate what he did to get you there."

Marcus had often wondered if Mayer had pulled in a favor. Had he threatened someone? Marcus should have asked him at Villa Nova, but Mayer wasn't in the chattiest of moods that night. "Are you dropping a hint?"

Bogie shook his head. "No, no. Just wondered. Not that it matters—his days are numbered."

The burly assistant approached them. "The director is ready when you are."

Bogie thanked the guy and waited till he was out of earshot. "I'm off to the Belgian Congo with Huston and Hepburn soon. Perhaps when I get back, we can have you and Kathryn over to the house. The kid's nearly two and a half now, running all over like a demon."

It was a nice offer, but Marcus knew it was just one of those things people say. As Bogie took his position behind a table laden with food, Marcus returned to Gilbert, Freckles, and Baby Giraffe.

Freckles said, "If you know Bogie well enough to walk up and say hi, what the hell are you doing here with the rest of us schlubs?"

Marcus shrugged off the question with a noncommittal smile. Pierce was back behind the bar, the tassel dangling from his red fez bobbing up and down as he polished shot glasses with the intensity of a surgeon.

To Marcus' immediate right sat a woman in her late sixties with huge Betty Boop eyes and dyed-black hair marcelled into waves and pinned back with a diamond barrette.

As the belly dancer whirled and shimmied through take after take, Marcus tried to remember where he'd met the woman before. By the time the cast and crew were dismissed for lunch, he concluded it must have been at a Garden of Allah party. There had been so many over the years that they blurred together like watercolors left in the rain.

He crossed the Columbia lot to the casting building to see if Doris was available for lunch, but her office was empty, so he left a note and headed to the commissary. By that time, most of the cast had been through the line and fused into groups.

He bought a deviled Virginia ham and cheese sandwich and searched for a spare seat. A hand shot up over the heads and waved. It was Betty Boop, motioning him to join her.

"You don't remember me." It was more of an accusation than a question.

He slid his tray onto the table. "I do, but the circumstances escape me."

"I used to live next door to your friend Oliver."

Even with that, it took Marcus a moment to place her. "Regina, right?"

She widened her round eyes. "I'm impressed. We only met once or twice." She stuck out her hand. "And you are — I want to say Malcolm?"

"Close. Marcus." Her fingers felt knobby with arthritis. "I don't remember your hair being so dark."

"I was probably a raving redhead when we met. But it looks wishy-washy in black-and-white, so I dyed it."

"The marcels suit you."

"Pah! What a pain. Takes me two hours, and for what? To sit in the background and watch Bertha the Belly Dancer shake her talents in our face? If this wasn't the only work I could get, I'd be out of here faster than a jackrabbit with a firecracker shoved up his butt. This is your first time working background?"

"Yep."

"Boring as hell, ain't it?"

In the years holed up in his screenwriter office, Marcus hadn't spent much time on sets. There was always another script to finish, and never enough time. He'd heard this work was a whole lot of "hurry up and wait," but actually doing it was a revelation. "I should have brought a book."

She squinted at him as she stirred her coleslaw with her fork. "I always got the impression from Oliver that you were some big mucky-muck. MGM, wasn't it?"

"Emphasis on 'was.'"

Regina raised her painted-on eyebrows, erasing the crow's feet from her face. "This cockamamie business sure can be cruel."

Marcus hadn't been too sure about Oliver's crackpot neighbor when he met her a few years ago.

She'd come across as a wacko has-been who'd come to Hollywood with stars in her eyes and ended up facedown in the gutter, missing a shoe, a glove, her best hat, and the last forty bucks in her pocketbook.

"I think of this cockamamie business more as a game of Russian roulette," he said. "Sometimes you get to live another day; sometimes you're being strong-armed through the exit along with the rest of the bums."

She crackled a throaty laugh. "Oh, you're funny! Oliver never told me that. How's he doing these days?"

He bit into his ham sandwich to buy time. Was there a *Reader's Digest* version of Oliver's tortuous trek from bucolic sanatorium to Catholic seminary? By the time he swallowed, he decided there wasn't. "Fine, last I heard."

Regina gave a pout that Shirley Temple would have envied. "You two busted up? What a shame. You lonesome?" She opened her purse and pulled out a business card with her name, address, and telephone number printed on it. The name read: Regina La Plante.

"I thought your name was Horne," he said.

"La Plante's my professional name. Lookit, in a few weeks, there's going to be a retrospective at the Silent Movie Theatre. You ever been?"

It was a small neighborhood theater on Fairfax Avenue that specialized in the silent movies everybody else had forgotten. Marcus admitted that he hadn't.

"I need a date, and you're it," she told him, getting to her feet. "But we better be heading back, otherwise Persnickety Pierce will give us the evil eye, and trust me, you don't want that."

CHAPTER 10

Gwendolyn had never been one for omens. She thought of herself as a "make your own luck" type of gal. But roaring up Wilshire in her neighbor's beat-up, prewar Pontiac, she wondered if she should revise her theory.

The lights at the corner of Wilshire and Western changed to red. Gwendolyn slammed on the brakes, forcing them to squeal like a box of hamsters. She slid her hands off the steering wheel and let them drop into her lap. "It's only twenty to twelve," she told herself. "Plenty of time. And it's not like they can start without you."

When she agreed to Maxwell Schofield's proposal, she hadn't expected things to move along at such a clip. The contract arrived within four days, and by the following Friday, they'd already set a launch date. Three weeks ago, a special messenger arrived with a mockup of the huge advertisement they planned to take out in the *Herald-Examiner* declaring August 15, 1951, to be "Sunset Boulevard Day" at all five Bullocks stores, with a splashy event at Bullocks Wilshire that promised French champagne and handcrafted chocolates from Edelweiss of Beverly Hills.

But Gwendolyn's excitement took a nosedive when her car refused to start in the Garden of Allah parking lot. She was hurrying back to her apartment to call a cab when she encountered Bertie, who appeared to be getting in from the night before. Gwendolyn didn't stop to ask for particulars and was about to excuse herself when Bertie offered to loan her car—a big old jalopy that stalled three times between the Garden and Western Avenue.

Across the street, the sun broke through the clouds. It bathed the blue-green tiles of the Wiltern Theatre in a radiant glow, leaving Gwendolyn to wonder if perhaps she should have chosen something more glamorous than her aubergine and black suit. She'd wanted to look like a serious businesswoman, but now she felt like a funeral director's widow pulling up in a clunky firetrap that stank of kerosene.

A banner hung from the Bullocks Wilshire's first-floor window:

SUNSET BOULEVARD PERFUME
NOW EXCLUSIVELY AVAILABLE AT BULLOCKS STORES

I bet they wish I'd called it Wilshire Boulevard.

She swung into the parking lot and braked to a screeching halt under the Art Deco porte cochère. She smoothed her pearl necklace, pulled at her cuffs, and checked the watch. Five to twelve—right on time. No harm, no foul.

PAH! Omens, schmomens.

She pushed open the frosted glass doors. The gleaming marble walls, the heels clicking across the tiled floor, and the intermingled scents of a dozen fragrances conspired to fill her with a pang of nostalgia. Suddenly, she felt like Gloria Swanson returning to Paramount in *Sunset Boulevard.*

A banner like the one outside hung across the central hall over the same glass and mahogany counter where Gwendolyn used to sell perfume to studio wives and executives' mistresses. A twelve-inch-tall bottle of Sunset Boulevard and a coordinating eighteen-inch package made for a striking display. But no one was there.

Where was the champagne? Where were the chocolates? They wouldn't be anywhere but the perfume department, would they?

Maxwell Schofield charged toward her with all his Victorian walrusness, his arms outstretched, followed closely by Herman Dewberry.

"Oh, Miss Brick!" he panted. "Such *dreadful* timing!"

Gwendolyn's hands flew to her cheeks. "Do I have the wrong day?

"Naturally none of us could possibly have foreseen what's happened, but nevertheless—" He stopped when Herman nudged him.

"I don't think Miss Brick has heard," Herman said. "About Hearst?"

Gwendolyn shook her head.

"William Randolph Hearst died last night," Schofield explained. "All the journalists and columnists we lined up to cover the big launch, of course they're all now on the other side of town trying to talk to Marion Davies."

"Or the maid, or the undertaker, or the pool man," Herman added. "Beverly Hills must be a madhouse right now. We were hoping for a big to-do but damned Hearst had the last word, even as he cashes in his chips. I'm sorry but it's just us—and twenty bottles of Bollinger."

Gwendolyn stroked the side of the oversized Sunset Boulevard. "Timing really is everything, huh?"

The clatter of high heels reverberated against the acreage of black-and-gray marble as Marilyn Monroe tottered toward them in a halter-necked sundress that she'd bought at Chez Gwendolyn several weeks back. Trailing behind her was an attractive woman Gwendolyn didn't recognize, mid-thirties and sporting a tennis tan. Beside her was a gaunt fellow in a brown suit and a beaten fedora that badly needed steaming.

Marilyn waved a white handkerchief. "I was afraid I'd miss everything!" She peered around. "Today's the day, right? The fifteenth?"

The guy in the fedora snapped his fingers. "Ah! Hearst, right?"

"You mean nobody came just because that silly old coot died?" Marilyn asked.

Gwendolyn grabbed her hand. "You did."

"Of course! I was your very first Sunset Boulevard customer, remember?"

Gwendolyn nodded. Back then, Marilyn was just some knockout blonde who bought two bottles as soon as she smelled it.

"You should've told me," the guy said. "That'll make great copy for my article."

"Are you with the papers?"

"I'm sorry, everybody," Marilyn said. "This is Mister...?"

"Arlington. Like the cemetery. From the *Herald-Examiner*."

"But you're a Hearst paper," Gwendolyn said. "Shouldn't you be off somewhere reporting on the boss?"

Arlington shook his head. "We can't fill the entire paper with the old man. And besides, this story's got great human interest. The girl behind the perfume counter becomes the entrepreneur with her own perfume. It's like an old Joan Crawford movie, brought to life. Trust me, my editor will be thrilled."

Marilyn dabbed her forehead with the dainty handkerchief. "The publicity department at Fox assigned Mr. Arlington here for a sort of 'day in the life' piece about me."

"You being the first customer for this stuff is perfect!" Arlington exclaimed. "This article's just about writing itself."

"You said you're from the *Herald-Examiner*?" Schofield asked. "We've taken out half-page ads with your paper starting tomorrow. I don't suppose you have any sway in placing our ads alongside your article?"

"I'll be sure to mention it." Arlington unhooked the camera slung from his shoulder and suggested a photo with Gwendolyn and Marilyn standing on each side of the display bottle.

Onlookers started to gather around them. As Arlington snapped a few pictures, Gwendolyn could see that it wasn't her perfume that was drawing them in. A college-aged girl with a long ponytail stepped forward.

"Excuse me, but you're Marilyn Monroe, aren't you? I saw you in *All About Eve* and thought you were keen. May I please have your autograph?"

As photogenic as Marilyn was on the screen, Gwendolyn had always considered her more attractive in person. During her time at the Cocoanut Grove, and later at Bullocks, Gwendolyn had seen that elusive "It" factor in a number of actresses: Garbo, Lana, Rita, Vivien, Ava. And she'd seen it the night Marilyn first came into Chez Gwendolyn.

But *this* Marilyn radiated an aura that attracted curiosity from society matrons, teenagers, intellectuals, and trust-fund babies alike. None of them could resist the orbital tug of a woman who was only starting to realize the force of her own gravitational pull. There weren't as many of them as Gwendolyn had hoped might show up today, but it was better than standing around on her lonesome.

Gwendolyn leaned back and whispered to Herman. "Would now be a good time to break out the Bollinger?"

He nodded and headed toward his office.

"This is happening more and more."

It was the woman Marilyn had arrived with. She wore her hair in a bob and possessed a sweet smile.

"I don't think we've met," Gwendolyn said, extending her hand. "I'm Gwendolyn Brick."

"Marilyn talked about you the whole drive over," the woman replied, shaking her hand. "I'm Dona Drake."

"Have you known Marilyn long?"

"Since she started at Fox. I'm married to Billy Travilla."

"Oh, yes? Your husband does such wonderful work!"

Dona tilted her head toward Marilyn.

"A few months ago, he told me he's found his muse. He said it's going to be like Joan Crawford and Adrian." Marilyn let out a peal of laughter. "She's getting good at this PR game. We've spent all morning with that newspaper guy. She's been perfectly charming the whole time and hasn't thrown him one personal scrap. That girl learns fast."

"She's headed for such big things."

"That's what Billy said, too." Marilyn had been cagey about her childhood, but over the past couple of years, Gwendolyn had gleaned a few details. An unstable mother. In and out of orphanages. It all sounded pretty rough. "Billy isn't convinced that she's built to cope with that sort of fame."

"Emotionally, you mean?" Gwendolyn offered.

Dona nodded. "You need two feet planted firmly on the ground to survive it."

Fans and autograph hounds besieged Marilyn. Waiters in smart red jackets appeared with silver trays of champagne flutes and porcelain plates loaded with chocolates.

"Billy encouraged me to befriend her," Dona added. "She's mentioned you a bunch of times, so when your launch came up the same day as this *Herald-Examiner* walk-around, the stars aligned."

Gwendolyn thought of her dead car back at the Garden and how an hour ago she'd doubted the stars were aligned except perhaps in the worst possible way. "I haven't seen Billy since Marilyn got her contract and a bunch of us went out to celebrate."

"I was doing press on *Valentino* at the time. Billy told me it was quite a night. And he said to tell you that we're planning to go see Ella Fitzgerald at the Dunbar and are putting a table together. We'd love for you to come."

The Dunbar was the most famous of the jazz clubs that lined Central Avenue south of downtown LA. It had earned a reputation as the best place west of the Mississippi and south of Chicago to experience the raw passion of Negro music.

Gwendolyn had always wanted to see a show there, but had never mustered up the courage. She told Dona to count her in as the chatter surrounding them intensified a notch or two.

Schofield appeared at Gwendolyn's other side.

"Shall we?"

He guided her to the front of her old counter, where he cleared his throat. "LADIES AND GENTLEMEN." He waited for the crowd to simmer down. A bit of a tall order, Gwendolyn thought, considering he'd just plied them with champagne. "What an exciting day!" he exclaimed.

Some wisenheimer at the back called out, "Not for Hearst, it ain't!"

Schofield seized on the laugh that followed. "If your name is William Randolph Hearst, then perhaps you're right. I'll grant you that."

Even though he came across like he'd just stepped out of a Dickensian gentlemen's club, it was clear Schofield knew how to work an audience.

Gwendolyn took a deep breath to relax herself.

"However," he continued, "if your name is Bullocks, today is a wonderfully bright day indeed."

Gwendolyn wished Horton could have been there. He was as responsible for Sunset Boulevard as anyone. He found the guy who came up with the formula and designed the packaging, but *Dragnet* kept him busy six days a week now.

On Wednesdays, he sent her the script via bike messenger, and on Thursdays, she sent it back marked up with female wardrobe suggestions taken from what she had in stock. Their budget was growing, so the arrangement now benefited them both. Horton hadn't been this happy in a very long time. She smiled to herself and hoisted a champagne flute. *Horton, old chap, this one's for you.*

CHAPTER 11

Marcus opened the passenger door of his Ford and held his hand out for Regina. She gripped it as she hoisted herself inside.

"Thank you, my dear boy," she rasped. "These joints ain't what they used to be. But with L.B. Mayer gone from MGM, what is?"

He closed the door, returned to the driver's side and slipped in behind the steering wheel. "You look very chichi, I must say."

"It's nice to be noticed, I must say."

Her outfit featured black and white bugle beads tightly woven into entwined diamonds and zigzags. The sum total of what Marcus knew about women's clothing came from being around Gwendolyn, but even he knew it must have taken months to sew.

He merged onto Melrose Avenue. "It looks original; the dress, I mean."

"It is! Oh my, what an eye you have."

Regina held up her arm so that the passing streetlights picked up the sparkle in the beading. "It's a Paul Poiret, but I don't suppose you've heard of him." Marcus admitted that he hadn't. "He was Elsa Schiaparelli's mentor."

The traffic was unusually light and they were making good time. He turned onto Gower. "Perhaps I ought to have worn a tux."

"Why didn't you?"

"I thought we were just going to the movies."

The laugh that followed — a tinkling pixie giggle that sounded like it'd first been dragged across broken glass — reminded him of Madame Nazimova.

"I suppose you could call it that." Regina contemplated the Paramount soundstages silhouetted against the pink dusk to their left. "You ever worked there?"

"Nope, but I know the head of the writing department."

Marcus and Quentin Luckett met during the war when Quentin was angling to get his boyfriend an MGM contract. But they hadn't seen each other since well before the word HUAC was enough to give everybody an attack of the vapors.

They pulled up alongside the RKO globe at the corner of Gower and Melrose. Regina gazed up at it.

"How come you haven't called in a favor to see if he can get you working background? Or maybe even a dress extra. They pay more for that, especially if you wear your own tux."

Marcus hit the gas and took the corner on what felt like two wheels, and charged west toward the Silent Movie Theater. "I'm not that desperate yet."

Since Doris helped him join the Screen Extras Guild, Marcus had been working regularly at Columbia. He hoped that by physically being there, an opportunity to lift himself off the graylist might come about. After six weeks of sitting in fake nightclubs and walking down pretend New York streets, he'd started to wonder if he was just kidding himself.

"You want to explain that?" Regina sounded huffy now.

"Explain what?"

"That crack about being desperate."

"It's just that Quentin and I were once on par with each other — he at Paramount, me at MGM. He's still way up there, and I'm way down here. It's just hard to —"

"So it's a matter of pride?"

"I never quite thought about it like that, but I guess so, yes."

Asking Quentin for background work involved swallowing a pumpkin-sized wedge of humble pie, and Marcus wasn't sure he could force it down yet.

Just past the high school Marcus swung the car onto Fairfax Avenue where a pair of spotlights swept the sky. In contrast to the usual extravaganza of sculpted plaster scrolls and blazing neon, this theater was an unassuming edifice of clean lines squatting behind an unadorned marquee. A crowd rigged out in gowns and tuxes as formal as Regina's extravaganza gathered in the doorways and spilled across the sidewalk.

Regina pointed to an empty parking space out front of the theater. "We can park there."

"I'm not so sure about that," Marcus said. "Looks to me like they're saving it."

"For a smart cookie, you sure are a dum-dum. Read the marquee."

REGINA LA PLANTE
RETROSPECTIVE TONITE!

"You made enough movies to fill a retrospective?"

"That's what the sign says, doesn't it?" She was smiling now, smug as a fox.

"I had no idea you starred in silent pictures."

"It wouldn't hurt to ask a question once in a while." She gestured toward the theater. "Come on. They're waiting for me."

The vintage Paris gown now made sense. "I wish you'd said something. I'd have dressed up."

"Trust me, sweet cakes, they won't be looking at you."

Regina climbed out of Marcus' car as though her joints weren't the slightest bit screaming from arthritis. "Bless you all!"

She threw out double-handed kisses like fistfuls of confetti to her applauding fans as a middle-aged guy who looked like Monopoly's Uncle Pennybags rushed toward her. "Miss La Plante!"

He thrust out a bouquet of white roses.

Regina pulled a *For me?* face, and took in a deep sniff of their scent. She lifted her Betty Boop eyes heavenward. "Thank you! Thank you all!" Now she sounded like Lynn Fontanne in the third act of *Pygmalion*. "I couldn't be more tickled." She hooked Marcus by the elbow; he felt her weight as she leaned on him. "But why are we all standing around in the night air? Let's go in and enjoy the show!"

Marcus cupped her elbow and guided her into the foyer. As they inched forward, he observed that at forty-five, he was the youngest person there — by twenty years.

Most of the men had done their best to squeeze into dinner jackets; their front buttons were straining to hold everything in place. The women had turned out in their best silks and brocades. Marcus detected the pall of mothballs mingling with the cigarette smoke. While no one matched Regina's French original, it was a sophisticated parade that probably hadn't seen the light of day since the stock market crashed.

Mr. Monopoly reappeared in front of them. "We've reserved the best seats — fifth row, center!"

"How perfect. And how thoughtful! Thank you very much. This is all so thrilling."

Once they were settled in Row E, Marcus nudged Regina's shoulder. "Can I get a potted history?"

"Remember Essanay Studios?"

"In Chicago?"

"I grew up on Winnemac Avenue, just a block north. First background, then bit parts, then featured roles. I worked with them all: Wallace Beery, Ben Turpin, Colleen Moore. Glorious like you wouldn't believe. But then they moved to California, so I did, too. Thomas Ince saw me in a picture with Francis X. Bushman —"

"No kidding? I met Bushman at the opening night party at the Garden of Allah. He was my first —"

"Do you want to hear this or not?"

"Beg your pardon. Go on."

"So Thomas — lovely man, by the by — he offered me a contract paying me five times what I'd been earning. He threw every role at me: nurses, hookers, secretaries, vamps, housewives. My favorite was *Priscilla Propeller*. I played a lady archeologist who becomes an aviatrix."

"Sounds logical."

"It wasn't in the least, but it was a huge hit, so who cares? You'll see it tonight."

"I'm glad."

"I worked for Thomas maybe five or six years until he died in the mid twenties. His studio was sold to DeMille, but my contract wasn't part of the deal. I finagled a sound test for Goldwyn, but I just didn't record well. My voice was considered too high — I hadn't started smoking yet so I came off sounding like a chicken beak dragged across a 78 record."

"I'm sure you weren't *that* bad."

"I'm quoting Goldwyn himself. But that's okay, I had ten fabulous years." Regina lifted her palms to the theater's low-slung ceiling. "And now this!"

Mr. Monopoly walked in front of the screen to a round of applause. "Welcome to the Silent Movie Theater. Tonight we get to re-experience the visual delight that was — IS! — Miss Regina La Plante. I can see that she needs no introduction, so let's plunge ourselves into my favorite, 1912's *Corinne Rides the Rails*."

"I'd forgotten all about Corinne!" Regina whispered into Marcus' ear. "You'll enjoy this one."

* * *

The table at Canter's Deli was supposed to sit eight; somehow they managed to squeeze in eleven, with Marcus at one end and Regina holding court at the other.

He could scarcely hear her over the lively hubbub, so he turned to his neighbor, a tiny woman whose forearms heaved with silver bangles and bracelets and who wore her hair in a Louise Brooks pageboy.

Her name was Linda Sunshine — she swore up and down it was her real name — and she got her start standing in for Lillian Gish on the set of *Broken Blossoms*.

"Lillian liked me so much, I stood in for her all the way up to *La Bohème*. But I got into the most awful fight with King Vidor. He had me barred from the MGM lot, so I went to Paramount where I got a part in their first talkie, *Interference*. It starred Bill Powell and I had a *mah*velous scene with him. We kept cutting each other up, and oh my goodness, the director got so mad! But Bill calmed him down fast enough. I swear that man could charm the trunk off an elephant. And I know about elephants. I was in *Elephant Boy* with Sabu."

Across from Marcus sat a wizened old Brit with a choleric frown who'd made a "very tidy career playing butlers, chauffeurs, and maître d's at every major studio you could name, and a few you probably couldn't" until a nasty fall at Malibu Canyon crushed his serving hand.

Next to Linda was a big-boned gal with flaming orange hair who had acted opposite Ann Sothern in all ten Maisie movies. Linda Sunshine told Marcus in a hoarse whisper that she "goes by the name of April-Mae June even though we know she's just Wanda Berkowitz from Queens."

The table conversation drifted to what everyone was doing now. Marcus expected them to wax nostalgic for the good old days, but they sat up like jackrabbits and gushed about how busy they were.

Everyone else Marcus had encountered since returning to Hollywood complained about how television was slaughtering feature films, and how "that repugnant little box in the living room corner was gobbling up every last member of the moviegoing public."

But episodic television's insatiable appetite chewed through writers, directors, cast and crew, so this group found itself constantly in work.

April-Mae June declared, "Especially them there westerns. Why, just last month, I worked on *The Cisco Kid*, *Adventures of Kit Carson*, *Hopalong Cassidy*, and *The Lone Ranger*. All those homesteaders and wagon trains. It's a gold mine!" She tapped Marcus on his nose. "I can see you playing a honky-tonk barkeep. They need a new one on *Lone Ranger*. I could put in a good word for you."

Marcus picked at the remnants of his brisket. It felt like more than just a year and a half since he worked on *The Lone Ranger*, first as a writer, then as the de facto head of writing when the show supervisor, Anson Purvis, fell ill. And she wanted him to stand behind a bar and serve sarsaparillas to cowboys? No thank you.

Regina picked up on Marcus' reticence and swerved into a funny tale involving a libidinous bull and a circus clown on the set of *Corinne Rides the Rails*. Soon everyone was sharing stories of working every movie from *Intolerance* up.

Marcus could have listened to these peoples' recollections all night, but just before midnight, Regina flagged him with a not-too-subtle I'm-done eyebrow lift. The party broke up and Marcus escorted Regina to his car. He pulled a U-turn as Regina fished around in her beaded purse.

"You don't mind, do you?" She lit a match and a pungent aroma filled his car, taking him back to the first time they met.

"You still smoking that mary jane?" he asked.

"Please tell me you're not one of those wet blankets." She let out a long, straight plume.

"I live at the Garden of Allah, not the St. Benedict Monastery."

"Thank Christ for that!" Regina passed the reefer across to him. Even though Robert Mitchum's marijuana arrest a couple of years back had done much to diminish marijuana's reputation as a danger to society, Marcus hadn't gotten around to trying it. He rather liked the irony that his first puff came from a quirky dame old enough to have worked with Ben Turpin.

He accepted the cigarette and took in a drag. A moment or two later, a breezy lightheadedness rippled through his body. "Thanks for a wonderful night, you dark little horse, you." His words came out slightly slurred; he eased off on the gas. "You might have warned me."

Regina took the reefer back. "You just went through a red light."

Marcus checked his rearview mirror. "I did?"

"Pull over and we'll sit a spell."

He parked at the curb and switched off his engine. A vision of Oliver dressed in a flowing black cassock that turned into a swan drifted through his mind, though he wasn't sure why. "I felt woefully underdressed tonight," he said. "Not to mention my clapped-out junkmobile of a car. If I'd known, I could've arranged for a nicer vehicle—"

She drilled him with a sharp look. "What did you learn tonight?"

"To be more curious about people."

"I'm asking a serious question."

"I *am* being serious. All that time we've spent sitting around those sets, I never asked about your background. I feel like a very self-centered nitwit right now."

Regina stubbed out the nub of her marijuana cigarette. "Why did you clam up when April-Mae brought up *The Lone Ranger*?" Regina's line of questioning was killing off his pleasantly wafting sensation. "It hit a nerve, that much was obvious."

The headlights of a car barreling down Hollywood Boulevard lit Regina's face. The way she pushed her brows together and softly strummed her fingernails on the dashboard reminded him again of Alla. It encouraged him to share his history with the show, what happened with Purvis, and the fallout of being listed in *Red Channels*.

She stayed silent while he spoke, then finally said, "You're a schmuck."

Her declaration snuffed out the last vestige of marijuana left in Marcus' system. "Come again?"

"That gang at Canter's, you heard their stories. They've worked with Griffith, Cagney, Lombard, and now they're standing around drafty sets, dressed up like farmers' wives and prospectors and churchgoers, sometimes for hours on end. Did you hear any of them complain? No. And you know why? Not just because they like to pay their rent and buy new shoes once in a while. They also like to feel as though they can still contribute. Okay, so most days it's just walking back and forth across some phony-baloney British village square or podunk cattle town. But thanks to television, it's regular. Correct me if I'm wrong, but I don't exactly see you flush with cash, so maybe it's time to pull your head out of your ass."

He eyeballed her dead reefer while he tried to think of an appropriate response.

"Look." She eased off the preaching a notch. "I can see why you wouldn't want to go back to *The Lone Ranger*, but how about this: my friend Lucy Ball—"

"Lucille Ball is a friend of yours?"

"We shared a dressing room at RKO way back when. Anyway, she and her husband are putting together a new TV show. I could call in a favor and maybe get you regular work doing background. They shoot at General Services Studios over on—"

"Las Palmas Avenue. Yes, I know it."

"So what's with the face?"

"General Services Studios is where *Lone Ranger* shoots."

"Remember when I said that it's time to pull your head out of your ass?"

"I'm pulling it out as we speak."

"So if I call in my favor with Lucy, it won't be for nothing, will it?"

"Absolutely not."

She stared at him, not blinking. "So are you going to take me home, or do I have to walk?"

He started his engine, and pulled back onto Hollywood Boulevard. Without another word, she lit the remnants of her cigarette and handed it to him.

CHAPTER 12

Kathryn threaded a fresh sheet of paper into her typewriter. Her fingers poised over the keys but remained paralyzed in midair. After an entire minute of indecision, she told herself to just start typing. Sometimes it was better to let the column write itself.

> *The word out of merrie olde Londontown is that director William Wyler has found his princess. Over the protests of Paramount brass, he wants to film his next pic,* Roman Holiday, *in Hollywood on the Tiber. Here are three things I can tell you about the frontrunner: She's a gamine newbie named Audrey Hepburn; she's a ballet dancer; and she's not related to The Other Hepburn.*
>
> *And speaking of The Other Hepburn, she plans to end her MGM contract with the Cukor-helmed* Pat and Mike.

Kathryn lit another cigarette. The real news wasn't the casting of this Hepburn nobody, but that the most tarnished screenwriter of the Hollywood Ten, Dalton Trumbo, had written the movie but couldn't be credited on what had all the earmarks of a hit.

She took another drag and doodled the word "graylist" on her steno pad.

———

When she arrived on the *Quo Vadis* set, she'd immediately noticed the gray creeping into Marcus' temples. She thought he looked rather distinguished, but the next morning, when she looked at herself in the hotel vanity, she found a gray hair of her very own.

The discovery shocked her to the core.

"Gray" meant "middle-aged," which meant there now were as many productive years behind her as there were ahead. Gray hair marked the beginning of the end. Suddenly, it felt like there weren't enough hours in the day to push back against unspoken accusations of *has-been* and *past-her-prime*.

But meanwhile, she had a million tasks and only ten little fingers.

She picked up her jangling phone.

"The boss wants to see you." It was Wilkerson's secretary.

"Right now? I've got three more columns to write before I can get out the door. I'm going to see Lili St. Cyr at Ciro's tonight, after which I'll have to do a write-up—"

"Okay, so I'll explain that you can't see him because you're going to see a stripper."

She told Vera she'd be there in a couple of minutes. She banged out a few more sentences about Katharine Hepburn's imminent departure from MGM. First Mayer and now Hepburn? Sometimes it really did feel like the end of civilization.

She walked into Billy Wilkerson's office without knocking, then wished she had when she saw that her boss was not alone.

Wilkerson rose from his desk. "Ah, Kathryn, come in, come in." He was using his statesman voice, which he employed when he was trying to impress someone.

The man seated with his back to Kathryn got to his feet.

He was a clean-cut, neatly turned-out gentleman in his late thirties, with a knowing twinkle in his eye and a hey-there-sweetcheeks smile on his face.

Kathryn felt the fine hair at the nape of her neck stand up as she ran through the possible scenarios that could explain why *Variety*'s lead columnist was standing in Wilkerson's office.

"Kathryn," Wilkerson said, "this is Mike Connolly."

"So nice to finally meet you." Connolly's handshake had all the firmness of last week's dinner napkin. "I'm surprised we haven't met already."

Because I've avoided you like a dose of the clap.

Kathryn disagreed with pretty much everything Connolly wrote: politics, religion, censorship, daring casting choices, and anyone whose view diverged from his own. Both Louella and Hedda flew their broomsticks around the same right-hand end of the political spectrum, so that wasn't what bothered Kathryn. Connolly's perspective lacked flexibility and nuance. The only acceptable opinion on any given subject was his, and anyone with an alternate position should take cover.

On the plus side, he was well read and possessed an Algonquinesque wit. She would have admired his dexterity with language but for his inclination to use the royal plural.

Now that they were face-to-face, she could see he was a swisher. All those years at the Garden had sharpened Kathryn's senses. One look at Connolly and she could tell he was a vicious queen bee — or could turn into one with a few drinks inside him.

Intuition warned her to proceed carefully. Columnists from rival papers rarely stepped into hostile territory.

"Yes," Kathryn said mildly, "it is remarkable we've never bumped into each other." She shot Wilkerson a *Why is this guy here?*

"I have news!" Wilkerson beamed like a five-year-old at Christmas. "Starting next week, Mr. Connolly will be taking over the *Rambling Reporter* column."

Kathryn felt like she'd been kicked in the groin. For the past sixteen years, she'd worked six, sometimes seven days a week to ensure that the industry read her *Window on Hollywood* first, thus reducing the *Rambling Reporter* to an I'll-read-it-when-I-get-around-to-it.

"Is that right?" Kathryn reminded herself that she would be absent from the office for a few weeks, so now might not be a great time to make a bad first impression. "In that case, welcome to the *Reporter*—rambling and otherwise."

Connolly thanked her and reached for the white straw panama on Wilkerson's desk. "I must skedaddle," he said. "I have an interview lined up with Billy Graham. Did you see his Christian Western, *Mr. Texas*, at the Bowl last week?"

Kathryn couldn't think of anything more tedious. She shook her head.

"I thought it a pretty good first movie. If the God-fearing Mr. Graham plans on getting into the film biz, it would behoove the *Hollywood Reporter* to get in tight with him. 'Bye now!"

Kathryn waited until he was outside earshot. "A warning might have been nice."

Wilkerson was already holding his hands up. "Don't go reading anything into this. He's no Ruby Courtland. He'll do the gossipy, trivial celebrity stuff, which will free you up to tackle what you do best: highbrow, industry-wide issues."

"Fine." She had more columns to write and it was already after three o'clock. "I'm just saying that—"

"You want I should consult you on all staff appointments, or just when assigning columns?"

She ignored his no-win question. "Aren't you going to wish me good luck? I'm off on my national tour tomorrow. Baking cakes from here to Fifth Avenue."

He came out from behind his desk and planted a paternal kiss on her cheek. "I was planning to make a speech at lunchtime, but . . ."

"But Mike Connolly. Yeah, I know."

"Break a leg. Do they say that in radio?"

"Just hope I don't embarrass myself in front of America's housewives."

"Do us proud, Massey. We'll keep your seat warm while you're gone."

That's what I'm afraid of.

* * *

Earlier in the year, Kathryn's antenna had quivered when Ciro's announced that they would soon be presenting Lili St. Cyr. While Gypsy Rose Lee cast witty asides as she discarded items of clothing that revealed very little, Lili had curves and legs and cleavage, and wasn't shy in letting her fans know that they would see as much of her as the law permitted.

Over the past year or so, Kathryn had seen a gradual dwindling of nightclub attendance.

Until recently, people had thought nothing of going home to change, put on fresh makeup, and drive clear across town to the Biltmore Bowl or Mocambo or King's Tropical Inn. But now there was a box in the living room that could serve up entertainment with the flick of a knob. Wasn't it easier to forgo all that effort and watch *Toast of the Town* or *Arthur Godfrey's Talent Scouts* instead?

Just as movie house audiences were shrinking, nightclubs needed to book headliners if they were going to draw people off their sofas. And that meant matching the ever-increasing fees that Las Vegas casinos paid.

Kathryn dragged Marcus along when Ciro's debuted "the stripper on the Strip." Even though Kathryn thought the act bravely toed the line between provocative and indecent, she wasn't sure it was right for audiences raised on Xavier Cougat, Marlene Dietrich, and Joe E. Lewis. But St. Cyr packed houses and garnered inches of press.

After she wowed Las Vegas, Ciro's announced a return engagement for a much-trumpeted 1,250 smackers per week. Kathryn hadn't felt any great need to see the show again until the stacked cigarette girl at Ciro's called her to suggest she might want to book a table—on Thursday night, specifically. When Kathryn asked why, Phyllis said, "Yesterday, the bartender told me not to call in sick tomorrow. When I asked why, he tried to make out like he was just fooling around, but I got me a strong intuition that you should be here."

It was the last thing Kathryn felt like doing, but if she could leave town with a strong story, she could ride it for a few days.

The club was jam-packed. Bogie was there—without Bacall; Lana Turner was too, with the boyfriend-du-jour, Lex Barker, the screen's latest Tarzan. Chatter boomed through the main room.

Kathryn managed to finish her columns by six o'clock, but packing for her three-week trip proved more arduous than she'd bargained for. Leo had given her a clothing allowance, which she promptly spent at Chez Gwendolyn. What seemed like a godsend became a problem when she tried to fit everything into her steamer trunk. Thankfully, Bertie had one she could borrow, but pulling it out of the Garden of Allah's basement wasted time she didn't have.

Consequently, Kathryn made it to Ciro's just in time to order a manhattan as she joined Marcus, Gwendolyn, and Leo at their ringside table.

"Have I missed anything?" she asked over the din.

"Too packed for tablehopping," Marcus said. "Mostly been air-kiss blowing and I'll-call-you-soon handkerchief waving."

Kathryn found Phyllis on the other side of the room tending to Ronnie Reagan. It was too close to showtime to say hello. She swigged a mouthful of manhattan.

He'll do the trivial celebrity stuff while you stick to the highbrow issues.

As high-falutin' as that sounded, people preferred bitchy gossip about who's screwing who behind whose back to industry issues like blacklists in an industry that was losing customers to an easy alternative.

Kathryn tapped a fingernail against her glass. Connolly had never hidden his right-wing views. Was Wilkerson getting sick of her liberal politics? She pulled out her final cigarette and lit it. Connolly starting at the *Reporter* when she was on tour for weeks was one hell of a coincidence. *And besides, who said I can't write bitchy gossip? Look where I am right now — about to watch a stripper go through her paces.*

Marcus tapped her forearm and discreetly pointed toward the bar. "That brown suit has been watching us since you sat down. And by 'us' I mean 'you.'"

The guy looked like a hoodlum who spent his nights in the mob's back room counting the clams. "Someone needs to cook him a meal."

Leo's hand slid on top of hers. "Everything okay?"

The five musicians took up their instruments as the house lights faded to soft twilight. The drums started to roll, then over the loudspeakers, "The best dressed *un*dressed lady in the theater — please welcome Miss Lili St. Cyr!"

As the lights came up, the striking blonde appeared in a swirl of mink and jewels. The curtains parted to reveal a translucent bathtub. The centerpiece of Lily's act was taking a leisurely bath followed by a protracted ritual of wrapping herself in a large white towel as she selected a dress.

For a striptease, the act possessed a level of elegance not previously seen on the Sunset Strip. Although she lacked the pipes of Piaf and wasn't a powder keg like Kay Thompson, she got away with being erotic but not dirty because she refused to take herself seriously. And it was a good thing she didn't. The woman was probably in her mid-thirties now. Too early for gray hair, but it'd start showing before long.

And God knows, the years peel away faster and faster, Kathryn thought. *Good for Lili for making the most of them. She probably knows there's always going to be someone younger and prettier waiting in the wings.*

The lights lowered as Lili made her exit amid enthusiastic, albeit restrained, applause. Kathryn pulled out her notepad and made a few notes. She wasn't quite finished when she felt a tap on her shoulder. It was Phyllis, the cigarette girl.

"You might want to get backstage."

"Why?"

"A police captain by the name of Sutton just walked in. I hadda deal with him when I worked at Florentine Gardens. The gal with him's got 'lady cop' written all over her."

"Is Lili being arrested?" Kathryn was already on her feet.

Phyllis pointed to a side door the band had used. "It'll take you to the dressing rooms."

Kathryn picked her way around the crowded tables. A blitzed Mickey Rooney called her over, but she pretended not to hear. The door opened to a narrow corridor. On the left was a fire escape leading to Sunset; to the right a short hallway opened onto a large square space with several doorways. A few people milled around, including some band members and an anxious Latin-lover type, presumably Lili's latest husband. Kathryn knocked on the door signposted with a star.

"Enter!"

Lili was dressed in a floor-length white silk robe, seated at her makeup mirror. She dabbed at the sweat on her forehead. "You're Kathryn Massey, aren't you? I noticed you in the audience tonight. Come on in. I'm so happy you came back to see me."

Kathryn took a tentative step into the spacious dressing room that was crammed with sparkling costumes and props. "My information could be wrong, but apparently, members of the police are in the house right now."

"Cops?" Lili stood up and tightened the sash around her waist. "I've shown more flesh in burlesque houses far less classy than this."

"Still, you might—"

A loud knock on the door cut Kathryn off. A stern woman in a utilitarian suit strode into the dressing room and headed for the sequined G-string hanging from the armrest of Lili's sofa. A thickset guy followed her.

"Miss St. Cyr," he announced, "I'm Captain Sutton, and I am placing you under arrest for an indecent performance and lewdly exposing your person."

He sounded so archaic that Kathryn burst out laughing. "Oh, come on," she said. "It's not like we saw anything."

"Please get dressed, Miss St. Cyr. We're taking you downtown."

Lili slowed her movements. "Okay, but I'm not wearing anything under this robe." She grabbed Kathryn and headed toward a dressing area behind an elaborate Oriental screen lacquered black with red and white storks. "Don't fret your panties, you two," she said over her shoulder. "There's only one door out of here, and you're standing in front of it."

Behind the screen, Lili dropped her robe to reveal that she was quite naked. She grabbed her bra. "What'll I do?" she whispered.

Up close and without the benefit of baby pink spotlights, Lili looked older and more careworn.

"So this wasn't a publicity stunt?" Kathryn asked.

Lili's blue eyes widened in genuine surprise—or at least what appeared to be. She pointed to a linen skirt, which Kathryn unzipped and held open for her.

"I was tipped off about this."

"By who?"

Kathryn thought of the semi-sleazy guy Marcus had pointed out, and played a hunch. "Did you see the character at the back of the room? The skinny one in the hat."

"No." Lili lifted her arms to let Kathryn zip her in.

"Miss St. Cyr!" Captain Sutton knew a thing or two about voice projection. "If you please?"

"There isn't even a window I can crawl out of, so hold your goddamned horses." Lili put on a matching jacket and pointed to a shoebox leaning against the wall. "Personally, I think Hover's behind this." Herbert Hover was Ciro's owner, as well as its master of publicity who, Kathryn had noticed lately, had started to compete more strenuously with Mocambo farther down the Strip.

Kathryn pulled a pair of leather pumps out of the box and laid them on the carpet. She extended a hand to help Lili slip into them. "Let me see what I can find out."

Kathryn stepped out from behind the Oriental screen. Sutton made a gesture with his thumb, indicating that she should scram.

Three times as many lookie-loos now filled the spacious area outside Lili's dressing room.

Kathryn recognized three different press agents, several reporters including Florabel Muir from the *Los Angeles Mirror*, some freelance photographers, and half a dozen members of the Beverly Hills police department. The whole thing reeked of a setup. Kathryn was sure that Lili believed any publicity is good publicity, but the shock in her eyes was hard to fake. Either way, this was the sort of bitchy gossip Wilkerson now wanted to leave to Mike Connolly.

The hell with that.

As Captain Sutton and his cohort escorted Lili out of the dressing room, Kathryn spotted the skinny creep. He was leaning against the far wall, one leg cocked up against the brickwork, flipping a used matchstick around the tips of his fingers.

Sutton escorted Lili from the building amid a cacophony of reporters' questions and flashing lightbulbs. Kathryn expected the guy to follow the spectacle, but his gaze remained on the tumult, his matchstick in constant motion.

"Do you know anything about this?" Kathryn asked him.

He dropped his matchstick and blinked in slow motion. "Can't help you there."

"I noticed you before the show."

His mouth curved into a smirk. "I was warned about your powers of observation."

Behind Kathryn, the stage door to the street slammed shut, leaving them alone. "Warned? By who?"

"I'm not at liberty to say, ma'am." He tipped his hat and went to step around her, but she grabbed his elbow.

"I'll pay you double."

"Double what?"

She couldn't tell if he didn't know what she meant or was well-versed in bluffing someone's bluff. "Double whatever you're being paid to observe me." She knew she sounded paranoid and might have caved but for the greedy sneer on his face.

He lifted a shoulder as though to say, *Your money's as good as anyone's.* "Thirty an hour. Been here four hours. You gonna fork out two hundred and forty bucks for a name?"

Am I? It's not like I have that sort of cash sitting at the bottom of my purse, and this isn't the sort of thing that a lady writes a check for.

"I didn't think so." He pushed himself away from the wall.

She panicked. "I'm heading out of town tomorrow. What if I leave an envelope for you at the reception desk?"

"*Hollywood Reporter* or NBC?"

Kathryn realized too late that the banks were closed and wouldn't reopen before she left for Union Station tomorrow. If she did a whip around the table out front, she was sure she could come up with two hundred and forty, no questions asked. "The *Reporter.*"

"If there's no dough waiting for me, it'll go into the report."

Kathryn felt like she'd walked into an Ida Lupino movie. "Fair enough."

"Winchell," he said. "First name: Walter."

CHAPTER 13

The butterflies in Gwendolyn's stomach slugged each other as she and Marcus entered the Dunbar Hotel. Even though Billy Travilla had assured her that a party of six white folks in a Negro nightclub wouldn't be a problem, she wasn't convinced.

A quartet of two-story arched windows dominated the hotel's foyer where groups of people waited for friends or stopped for a smoke.

"Do you see them?" Marcus asked.

Gwendolyn tried to ignore the shooting stares. "No. Maybe we should all have come down together so that you and I could avoid sticking out like a couple of pasty thumbs."

A barrel-chested bouncer in a dark maroon suit and matching tie ran a fingernail along his silver tiepin as he watched Gwendolyn and Marcus try to blend in. Not that that was likely, considering Gwendolyn's sunflower yellow cocktail dress.

The bouncer in maroon headed toward them like a slow-motion locomotive. He was still several yards away when he tilted his head.

"You two with the Travilla party?"

Gwendolyn said they were.

"Mr. Travilla told me to keep an eye out for you. He's been delayed at the studio and asked that I escort you inside."

The main showroom was bigger than she expected, and packed with cocktail tables.

Gwendolyn felt the heat of every eyeball in the place as she and Marcus followed the guy down a central aisle. He stood aside and gestured toward a front table for six with a hand-lettered sign: *Reserved.*

"You want me to send over a waiter or wait until—"

"Now would be great, thanks," Marcus jumped in.

He offered Gwendolyn a Camel. She'd recently switched from Luckies to Pall Mall, but a Camel would do in a pinch. Being the only white people in a Central Avenue jazz club qualified as "a pinch."

A whiff of Sunset Boulevard perfume drifted past Gwendolyn, and she did what she always did whenever she encountered it in public: tried to guess who might be wearing it.

She sorted through the Sunday-best suits and fascinator hats until she landed on a woman around her age, swathed in sable.

A waiter appeared; Marcus ordered manhattans.

The woman in the sable studied Gwendolyn like an amateur birdwatcher: *I've heard of such creatures, but I've never actually seen one in the wild.*

Her escort muttered into her ear. She told him no and went to pull at his arm, but he was too quick for her. He squeezed past their neighbors and sat down on the stage's edge.

"You two sure you're in the" —he made a circular motion with his hand, indicating the rest of the room— "right place?"

"Are we not welcome?" Gwendolyn looked at the front doors hoping to see Travilla or Marilyn, but found only the maroon Sherman tank.

"I didn't say that."

"We just came to hear Ella Fitzgerald sing, that's all," Marcus said.

"Funny how you got front-row seats, and all."

"We weren't expecting that," Gwendolyn put in. "Our friends—"

"This ain't the bus," he snapped. "You white folks can't be expecting to get shown to the front any old time you want. Some of us, we been following Miss Ella's career since she sang at the Harlem Opera House. If you want to watch her from the front row, why don't you see her at your fancy Cocoanut Grove?"

"We didn't ask for a front-row table," Marcus said. "Our friends made the booking—"

"Always some other cracker, huh?"

"Is that your wife you're with?" Gwendolyn asked. The guy's eyes narrowed. She motioned for her to join them.

Hesitant at first, the woman obliged, and was soon standing next to her husband.

"My name is Gwendolyn," she told the couple, "and this is my good friend, Marcus. Perhaps you'd like to watch the show with us?"

Marcus stared at her with a slow eyebrow raise.

"Sit? With you?" the woman said. "Together? At the same table? Well, that just wouldn't be right."

"It's okay by us if it's okay by you."

The couple swapped looks. Gwendolyn took advantage of their hesitation. "Are you wearing Sunset Boulevard?"

The woman blinked several times.

"It smells wonderful on you." Sable or no sable, Bullocks Wilshire was not a progressive environment. "May I ask where you got it?"

Suspicion clouded the woman's face. She stared back at Gwendolyn until she snapped out of her reverie and plunked herself down next to her husband.

"Well!" She hunched forward conspiratorially. "My friend Bessie, she worked at the main Bullocks store, downtown. Accounts receivable, or some such. I'm not even sure what that means; all I know is that it qualifies her for the staff discount. So I got her to get me a bottle. But now I'm in a pickle because that damned Bessie, she switched to the May Company, and now I'm nearly out of my favorite perfume!"

Gwendolyn reached into her purse and pulled out a business card. She slid it across the table. "Why don't you come see me?"

The woman studied the card. When she peered up again, admiration had shoved aside the hostility. "Y'all're Miss Gwendolyn? *The* Miss Gwendolyn?" She faced Marcus as though she wasn't prepared to believe anything more out of Gwendolyn's mouth.

Marcus nodded. "The one and only."

"Well, if that don't beat the chickens from the coop."

Her eyes flared wide and her mouth dropped open again. A wave of agitation rippled through the audience. "Land sakes! Who is *that*?"

Gwendolyn breathed out in relief. *Please, please, please.*

Marilyn Monroe floated down the middle aisle in an off-the-shoulder cocktail dress of blood-red silk overlaid with black mesh, and opera gloves in black satin. She spotted Gwendolyn and waved a handkerchief of matching lace, pretending not to notice how every head in the room had turned in her direction.

The woman in sable nudged her husband. "Jeremiah, these good people's friends have arrived so it's time we headed back to our table."

"But you said—"

"Never mind what I said. Now, *git.*"

"My goodness!" Marilyn exclaimed. "Parking was such a problem." She cheek-pressed Gwendolyn, then stepped aside. "You remember Jack, don't you?"

The chap with the cute cleft in his chin appeared from behind. "Jack Paar. Nice to see you again." He wedged himself between tables and sat down next to Marcus to allow Billy and Dona Travilla easier access to the last two seats.

"I didn't expect to stand out quite so—distinctly." Billy motioned for the waiter.

"We were nearly shown the exit," Marcus said, "but thankfully Gwennie here had the presence of mind to head off a scene."

Marilyn nudged Gwendolyn. "I always suspected you'd be a cool head in a crisis."

It had been just a couple of months since the perfume launch at Bullocks, but the changes in Marilyn were plainly evident. She carried herself with greater poise. The pronounced wiggle in her walk had given way to a graceful sway. Every movement declared, *This is me. Look or ignore. Like me or don't.*

A slight frown shot across her radiant face. "What?" she asked Gwendolyn.

"Looks like someone's been getting full marks at charm school."

Marilyn lifted her blue eyes toward the smoky ceiling. "When they put you under contract, they get their money's worth. Acting lessons, singing coach, voice teacher, dance class, deportment, publicity photos, costume fittings."

"You mean you don't just stand there and emote?"

"That's the ever-loving least of it." She stared at the empty stage in contemplation. "Well, maybe not the *least*, but what it takes to get in front of a camera, it's like Niagara Falls — it never ends!"

The waiter was depositing a round of drinks onto the cramped table when the house lights dimmed and Ella Fitzgerald made her entrance amid a barrage of applause and whistles. She'd swept her hair into an updo and crowned her head with curls. The style flattered her full face, and so did the rhinestones encircling her neck. But as Gwendolyn's eyes lowered to take in the dress, her mouth dropped open.

* * *

They begged Ella for a fourth encore, but three was her limit. The Dunbar's house lights came up, leaving Gwendolyn wrung out. The woman could turn a note by putting an extra puff of air behind it and spin it like a billiard ball as she broke your heart while you weren't looking.

Gwendolyn turned to Dona. "Is she always that breathtaking?

"Always."

"How many times have you seen her?"

"Oh, tons! Ella and I are good friends. In fact, we're heading backstage now to say hello. Would you like to come?" Dona rose to her feet and pointed to a side door. "She's right through there."

The backstage area wasn't the tumult Gwendolyn expected. Two crewmembers were stowing away lights and ropes, and the drummer shared a cigarette with the pianist, but otherwise it was deserted.

A red door stood slightly ajar. Dona knocked and pushed it open. "I hope you're decent!" She stepped into the dressing room, motioning for everyone to follow her.

There was just enough space for a vanity and basin, a loveseat, and a chipped wooden changing screen. Ella stood in the middle with her arms outstretched, still in that awful dress. Broad pink and orange horizontal stripes sprinkled with green sequins? And a V-shaped neckline that wasn't even centered properly? There was nothing in Ella's outfit that did her the slightest favor.

She enveloped Dona in her arms and kissed her, continental style, before doing the same with Billy.

Dona introduced Marilyn and Jack, Marcus and Gwendolyn.

"I've been wanting to see you perform for such a long time!" Gwendolyn didn't care that she sounded like a teenager with a crush.

"I hope I was worth the wait." Ella slung her hands on her hips. "But don't think I missed that look on your face when I walked onstage."

Oh, dear. "My face?"

"Uh-huh. You looked like someone just puked up on your wedding dress."

"I don't know why you'd think . . ." She let the end of her sentence drift away.

"You don't like my gown, do you?"

Gwendolyn looked to Billy for guidance. He crossed his eyes as though to say, "It's horrible," then mouthed the words, "Be honest."

"I feel," Gwendolyn started gingerly, "that you deserve better."

"FINALLY!" Ella threw her hands up toward the dusty chandelier. "Lay it on me."

Marilyn started to giggle; so did Jack Parr. Billy Travilla could no longer contain himself. "Who on earth makes these monstrosities for you? Helen Keller?"

Ella shook her head sadly. "An old friend of the family. It was supposed to be a one-off, but she keeps making 'em. Damn if they don't get uglier and uglier."

"You have to make her stop," Billy said. "You want people to hear your voice, not your dress."

Gwendolyn stepped forward. "First of all, these horizontal stripes? No, no, no."

"They make me look like a goddamned whale!" Ella hollered.

"Only Charlotte Greenwood can get away with horizontals. And if you're going with sequins, do it on solid colors. Maroon, maybe, like what the bouncer out front is wearing, with a black lace décolletage. Like Marilyn's. But for Pete's sake, get someone who knows how to center a neckline. This is off by half an inch."

"It never did feel right."

Gwendolyn fished another card from out of her purse and placed it in Ella's hands. "I have at least seven pieces in my store that would suit you. And if you don't fancy them, I'll make you something. Any style, any color, any fabric." She ran her finger down the pink and orange stripes. "Anything but that."

CHAPTER 14

The set of *I Love Lucy* took Marcus by surprise. He was used to the gargantuan masterpieces built for feature films, where a single home could take up to two or three soundstages. The sets needed for a film often required half a dozen or more. But everything for *I Love Lucy* was designed to fit into a single soundstage at General Services Studios. They were laid out in a long line so that the live studio audience could see what was going on and, hopefully, laugh its ass off.

As it turned out, Regina couldn't get Marcus onto the show as an extra because they only did scenes that required no more than six actors. As a consolation prize, however, Regina got him a seat in the audience.

"At the very least you'll get to see how a TV show is filmed," she told him. "You'll be amazed how fast they work. And keep an eye out for Jess."

Lucille Ball and her husband, Desi Arnaz, may have been the public faces of *I Love Lucy*, but it was the lead writer, Jess Oppenheimer, who captained the ship. Regina had worked with him on *The Lifebuoy Show* when she was scraping up work on radio.

"*I Love Lucy* has been a hit right out of the gate," Regina said to Marcus, "and hit shows need ancillary writing, like ad copy, radio promos. You could do that, couldn't you?"

Marcus didn't share with her how bleak his finances were. Beans-and-rice-for-lunch-and-dinner bleak. Move-out-of-the-Garden-of-Allah-and-find-someplace-cheaper bleak. He wasn't sure that writing ad copy and promos could get him off the graylist, but he had no doubt he could do it in his sleep.

The day before filming, he sat at his bedside table and banged out a few examples. He had them in his jacket pocket just in case an opportunity presented itself.

The bleachers filled up with a hundred members of the public, all of them twittering with excitement. Production companies hadn't offered the chance to watch filming since the silent days.

Regina described Jess as "in his late thirties, but he's going bald so he looks like he's already hit forty, especially with those big, round eyeglasses. He's got a sympathetic face, but don't be fooled. He's Charlie-in-charge, and everybody jumps to the general."

A guy resembling that description walked onto the living room set to confer with the director. He held a book with the word NUMEROLOGY printed in large letters across the front.

Marcus leaned over the rail. "Say, buddy," he said to one of the cameramen, "the guy in the checked jacket, that's Mr. Oppenheimer, right?"

The cameraman nodded.

"Excuse me, sir." A security guard, almost as broad as he was tall, tapped Marcus on the shoulder. "Please remain in your seat. The crew must be free from distraction."

Marcus began to pull his ad copy from his jacket. "I was just trying to —"

"I know, I know. It's real exciting seeing this stuff up close, but everybody here has a job to do, and you don't make it any easier by interrupting 'em."

Marcus showed the guy his papers. "Mr. Oppenheimer —"

"Remember how I said everybody here's got a job? Well, mine is ejecting uncooperative audience members."

A voice came over the PA. "Cast and crew, to your places. This is a take."

When Lucille Ball walked out onto the kitchen set, her red hair blazed under the studio lights. "Ready for a terrific show?"

After the audience roared its answer, she stepped close enough for Marcus to see the sky blue of her eyes. She made a little speech about how glad she was that they could join her today and that their job was to have a good time. Marcus wasn't sure if he imagined it, but about halfway through her spiel, Ball appeared to do a double take when she spotted someone in his section.

She took her seat at the Ricardos' kitchen counter and set the numerology book in front of her, then pulled a face of comic concentration. "Ready when you are, Mr. Daniels!"

* * *

Marcus hadn't yet caught an episode of *I Love Lucy*, so he came to this filming cold. It didn't take long to figure out that Lucy was the kook who never learned her lesson, and Ricky was her straight man forever wishing he'd married some regular girl instead of this henna-rinsed wacko he'd fallen for.

Between takes, Marcus could see this wasn't just a superficial duplication of how Lucille and Desi were in real life. The pair of them — but especially Lucille — were keen to land every joke for maximum response, and were open to any suggestion to improve the script.

Regina was right: Marcus was staggered by how quickly they moved through the script. The cast and crew worked together with a singlemindedness that allowed them to burn through page after page. At MGM, it took weeks to get through half an hour of screen time, but these people got it done in hours. Then suddenly, they were finished.

As Marcus stood to leave, he felt his attempts at copywriting push against the inside of his jacket. Maybe he could break away and find Oppenheimer's office? The production offices were probably in the same buildings as the *Lone Ranger*'s. He didn't want to bump into anyone he knew there, but this might be his only chance.

By the time he figured this out, he was the last person left on the bleachers, and the security guard was coming his way.

"Just leaving now!" Marcus moved toward the stairs.

The guard blocked his path. "Come with me." He led Marcus along the front row and down a short flight of stairs to the kitchen set, and had him take a seat where Lucy had opened the episode.

Marcus took out his dummy promos and was surprised to hear a woman's voice greet him. "Hello!"

Lucille Ball was dressed in a snugly tailored, floor-length duster. She held out her hand as she approached. "You must be Marcus."

"I am." He took her hand and returned her firm shake.

She sat in the same chair she'd used in the opening scene. Close up, her eyes were almost cobalt blue, but softer, inviting. Somehow, she managed to give him the impression that she'd winked at him without actually winking. "We know someone in common."

"We're bound to, considering we were at MGM at the same time."

"I'm talking about Kathryn Massey."

Marcus knew everybody Kathryn knew, and the name Lucille Ball was not on that list.

"We only met for the first time recently when she took me to lunch at Perino's." She laughed. "We were at it for three hours. She's a smart cookie, that one."

Marcus slipped his papers back inside his jacket. Whatever the reason he was here, it wasn't to write ad copy. "Don't I know it."

"She mentioned you a couple of times. I knew you from your HUAC appearance, and when I spotted you tonight, it got me thinking." Ball strummed her lacquered nails on the counter in a rapid rat-a-tat-tat. "I have some work for you, if you're available."

"I am."

"Kathryn told me that you were Mervyn LeRoy's on-set photographer for *Quo Vadis*."

"Oh, she did, huh?"

"Was she talking out of school?"

Marcus uncrossed his legs and sat up straighter.

"Did Kathryn ask you to give me a job? I could use one, God knows, but I don't go for charity—"

Ball thumped the counter. "Glad to hear it! No, Kathryn didn't ask anything. She just mentioned you in passing, but a week later I was over at Deborah Kerr's place and she showed me your book."

"My what?"

"Coffee table book. The photos you took during the production of *Quo Vadis*."

At the end of an all-night shoot when everybody was dead on their feet, Marcus joked about turning his shots into a book so they'd have some recollection of what they'd done. Mervyn LeRoy laughed but gave no indication he would do anything like that.

"Ah, the *Quo Vadis* book."

"It got me thinking." She lifted her chin and narrowed her eyes. The softness was gone; in its place was the composed confidence of a businesswoman. "I have a hunch that this silly little show we're doing, with its wacky housewife and her long-suffering—but more importantly, *minority*—husband will be groundbreaking."

Marcus thought that was a stretch. But maybe not. It was impressive the way they filmed with three cameras at the same time.

"And if I'm right, I want it documented," Ball said. "Everything. The writing room, the rehearsals, costume fittings, filming, end-of-season parties, promotional tours. You'll get full access, right across the board. Two hundred a week while we're in production. What do you say?"

Marcus longed to say yes, but felt it wouldn't be right unless he was sure that Ball was fully aware of the facts. One of these days, he could have a conversation like this and not have to bring up the past, but that day seemed a long way off. "I have what some people think of as a sketchy background."

Ball ran a finger through a vivid red curl. "You're referring to those HUAC bastards?"

"I am, but—"

"Are you aware of *my* Commie past?"

"You? I find that very hard to believe, Miss Ball."

"What if I were to tell you that back in 1936, I became a registered voter with the Communist Party?"

"You're a — *member*?"

"I'm not a Commie, Mr. Adler, so let's do away with that deer-in-the-headlights face. I come from a close family, and had a grandfather whom I adored. He asked me to do it."

"You became a Commie to please grandpa?"

"It was 1936; we were still feeling the effects of the Depression. *Commie* wasn't a four-letter word like it is now. I knew zilch from nada, except that I loved my grandpa and would do anything to please him. It's not like I attended meetings or anything. I'm as Commie as Little Orphan Annie, but there are records somewhere, and one of them has my name on it."

"Does HUAC know any of this?" Marcus asked. "Or the FBI?"

"I think we can assume it'll come up sooner or later."

"And why are you telling me this?"

Lucille Ball laid a hand on his arm. "Because I want you to know that this blacklisting fiasco makes my blood boil. I want to help anyone who's been unfairly mistreated. And also because when the tables are turned on me, as I assume they will be, maybe I'll need you to help me through shark-infested waters." She squeezed his wrist. "So what d'you say, you little Pinko stinko, you? Are you on board?"

Marcus smiled at his new boss with the flaming red hair, the sharp blue eyes, and the secret Commie past, and thought of Mayer's advice to acquire a new skill.

"You bet your last bottle of henna I am."

Ball slapped the sides of her face in horror. "Anything but that!"

CHAPTER 15

Kathryn stood behind her mock counter in her mock kitchen and maintained a mock smile as her director, Dex, fussed with the display of cake mixes and cookbooks. He was having a devil of a time getting them to sit right.

Kathryn still found it hard to grasp that her face was about to be seen in New York and Los Angeles at the very same time.

At each of the ten stops on Kathryn's Sunbeam Mixmaster-Betty Crocker tour, the crowds were bigger than anticipated. She'd thought she'd just show up at some department store and do her shtick, then head back to the hotel to work on her next column.

But Denver and Pittsburgh had been whole different slices of lemon chiffon cake.

Susan Hayward joined her in Denver. Even though she played the lead in the biggest hit of the year – *David and Bathsheba* – Kathryn wasn't prepared for the multitudes who jammed the homewares department at Sears to see a movie star in the flesh. Nor did she expect Susan to yell, "I can't bake for nuts!" Kathryn wasn't sure how the cake-mix fight came across to the listeners at home, but the store audience ate it up.

When Randolph Scott joined her at Kaufmann's department store in Pittsburgh, the ladies damn near broke the barrier. Not that Kathryn blamed them. Scott gave "gorgeous" a whole new meaning.

Dex adjusted *Betty Crocker's Picture Cook Book* again. "How's that, Mac? Still flaring the lights?"

A voice came over the PA. "Perfect! Don't anybody touch it."

"You got everything you need?" Dex asked Kathryn. She told him no and asked if he'd seen Leo.

"In the control booth." He squinted. "You're too shiny."

Kathryn already felt self-conscious. Radio required nothing elaborate, so she wasn't prepared for the suffocating layers of dark pancake makeup and setting powder the NBC makeup guy had applied earlier.

She circled her face with an index finger. "I feel like I'm in blackface."

"Our cameras need masses of light, so be prepared to feel like a rotisserie chicken, too. If it's any comfort, Adelaide is enduring the same torture in LA."

For the past few years, actress Adelaide Hawley had been portraying Betty Crocker in print and television ads. She'd done so well that a recent poll showed most American housewives believed Betty Crocker was a real person. The woman playing her was the second most recognizable female in the country after Eleanor Roosevelt. It was Kathryn's idea to have "America's First Lady of Food" on the California end of the transcontinental cable, and the executives were hyperventilating with excitement.

The studio doors banged open and the audience stampeded in. Kathryn walked out from behind the counter. "Welcome, everybody. No need to rush. Every seat is a good one!"

A pigtailed teenager squeaked, "You look funny."

"I do, don't I?" Kathryn flung her arms out. "I feel like Al Jolson in *The Jazz Singer*!" Everybody giggled. "We're here to bake cakes and make history. I've never done anything like this, so I need to know that you're behind m—"

The "me" stuck in her throat when she spotted an unsettlingly familiar face in the very last seat of the front row.

What is Winchell doing here?

He blinked at her with supercilious indolence.

A makeup artist in a blue smock appeared by her side and muttered how perspiration would be the death of her. Kathryn turned her back on Winchell and let the woman powder her down.

Over the PA came a different voice. "Five minutes and counting. I need everybody in place, please."

The makeup woman gave Kathryn a final swipe with the powder brush and wished her luck in a *you'll-need-it* tone that Kathryn didn't appreciate.

"Lights!"

The blanket of light singed Kathryn's retinas and she let out a piercing shriek. She cringed when she heard the audience gasp. She turned away not only to hide her embarrassment, but to shield herself from the contempt on Winchell's face.

For the first time all morning, she thought of Marcus and wondered if he was having a better time than she was.

* * *

As Marcus pulled into the prison parking lot, he realized that he'd been expecting Hollywood's version of Sing Sing: tangled barbed wire stretching interminably in both directions, dozens of armed guards with loaded rifles cocked and ready, spotlights raking the driveway, and maybe Cagney or Bogie making a run for it.

The reality was rather mundane.

The gravel parking lot held only a handful of cars. A fifteen-foot wooden gate painted dark green was the sole feature of a twenty-foot wall of gray stone that blocked the view of the Hudson River.

Marcus climbed out of his rented Pontiac and walked to the gate — it was more like a barn door. When a curt voice on the intercom told him to state his business, he said that he'd come to visit an inmate, and gave Danford's name. The intercom went silent for a full thirty seconds — a long time to be standing outside a prison whose name alone brought on the heebie-jeebies.

It was a miracle he was here at all.

Once he got the *I Love Lucy* job, he thought he would have to bow out of the New York trip with Kathryn. But a fight had broken out among the key players about the show's direction and the sitcom took a hiatus. By pure dumb luck, it was the same week Kathryn was ending her tour in New York.

But now that he was standing outside the infamous prison, Marcus didn't feel all that lucky.

The gate slid open just enough for Marcus to step into a small courtyard. Bare concrete floor. Iron bars on three sides. Metal clanking against metal.

An armed guard pointed him to a sign — *VISITORS* — next to a door that slid open as Marcus approached. A guard whose sullen face matched the voice over the intercom patted him down, then directed him to a room the length of a football field.

The smell of fresh paint filled the air, but the dreary brown walls could have been painted at any time in the last twenty years. A long wooden table the width of a Chasen's booth ran down the middle of the room; along the center a ten-inch barrier separated the sides.

Three couples sat along the length of the table, inmates on one side, wives on the other. A guard told Marcus to sit anywhere he chose.

A metal door clanged open to reveal a figure wearing gray twill trousers and matching jacket, and a drab white shirt buttoned to the collar. As the prisoner approached, Marcus thought about what Kathryn had said over breakfast at the Plaza that morning.

"I only have it on my mother's say-so that this guy is my father, so I want you to look for signs of anything we might have in common. The same nose, maybe, or similar hand gestures. Apparently, we can inherit those through our genes, like hair color."

Marcus got the impression that Kathryn wouldn't be altogether disappointed if this jailbird convicted of treason wasn't related to her after all.

But as prisoner 16391–1258 drew closer, any doubt that he was Kathryn's father evaporated. Danford possessed the same determined jaw, the same intense gaze from the same dark hazel eyes, and the same dead-straight hair that no amount of home perms or professional marcelling could conquer.

Marcus stood. "Hello, Mr. Danford."

He regarded Marcus tentatively. "I saw your name on the visitor roster, but I'm afraid it doesn't ring any bells."

"It wouldn't."

The two men took their seats on opposite sides of the broad table.

"It's been a long time since anybody paid me a visit," Danford said. "We're allotted twenty minutes, so please, let's not waste time on social pleasantries."

As Danford leaned back and crossed his legs, Marcus saw a hint of the old-money society family that liked to claim it reached back to the Boston Tea Party.

"Are you some sort of lawyer, Mr. Adler? Or reporter, perhaps?"

"No, nothing like that." Marcus forced a smile. He'd seen those eyebrows furrow a thousand times — when Kathryn was getting riled up over Louella's column or an injustice Harry Cohn had perpetrated on some naïve Columbia starlet. "This is more of a social call. I'm here . . ." It was a weightier moment than Marcus had anticipated. The stifling confinement of the place closed in on him; he felt the chill of the concrete permeate to his bones.

"Spit it out, son," Danford told him.

"I'm here on behalf of Kathryn Massey."

The man had no response.

Oh, for crying out loud, Marcus thought. *I'm going to have to tell him who she is.*

* * *

Kathryn stared down the lens of the one-eyed monster and wondered if it was picking up the line of sweat at her hairline. She felt it trickle behind her left ear and seep down her neck inside the collar of her dress.

"Adelaide?" she said. "Are you still with us?"

Kathryn thought it ironic that unknown thousands of people could watch her and Adelaide Hawley bake cakes on both coasts and the only person who couldn't see it was her.

Do they even have television sets in Sing Sing? If this were a movie, Marcus would be pointing me out to Danford right now — Oh, sweet Jesus! I called her Adelaide!

Dex's final instruction was, "Do not call her Adelaide. To America, she is Betty Crocker."

Kathryn could hear only static. Had they lost the connection?

Kathryn cupped her hands around her mouth. "Paging Betty Crocker! Are you still with us?"

So far, the broadcast had gone well. The green bulb on top of the camera lit up right on cue, and Kathryn hadn't stumbled over her welcoming words. And when she'd called for Betty Crocker to join her in Los Angeles, Adelaide's voice came through crisp and clear.

After Leo had outlined how Golden Aerial Day would work, Kathryn had asked whether the historic broadcast that enabled LA and New York to tune to the same program deserved better subject matter than baking some stupid cake. Leo had pointed out that without the lemon chiffon cake, the Betty Crocker people wouldn't be interested in sponsoring the event, and Kathryn's national tour would be off.

Kathryn held her smile through several ponderous seconds of dead air and waited for Adelaide to respond.

"I'm here, Kathryn!" she exclaimed. "I accidentally hit my microphone with a spatula."

"Did it hit you back?"

The studio audience laughed. So did Adelaide after a delay. "I don't know how big your microphone is, but I wouldn't want to stumble across mine in a dark alley."

Her remark made Kathryn think of Winchell. She hadn't seen him in a year, not since the night of the *All About Eve* premiere at Grauman's. Whatever he was here for, it was for more than just a baking demonstration.

The bell on Kathryn's fake oven tinged. "Betty?" Kathryn said toward her microphone, "my timer is going off. That must mean yours is, too."

"Ringing like a church bell!"

"In that case, here we go!"

Kathryn opened the oven door and pulled out a fluffy yellow cake. The Betty Crocker people wouldn't take a chance that her cake would flop on live television, so someone had baked a principal lemon chiffon as well as a backup. A stagehand had inserted it into the back of the oven just minutes before.

Kathryn pulled it out and lifted it in front of her. "Mmmm!" she exclaimed exactly as she'd done at each of her department store shows. "You're absolutely right, Betty! Your method really does guarantee a perfect cake every time I bake, cake after cake after cake."

It was a corny line, but it paraphrased the TV ads. In truth, Kathryn really did enjoy lemon chiffon, so she wasn't lying. But it irked her that they couldn't have come up with something more substantial for her to do.

Dead air. No Adelaide. Low-humming static.

Through the open oven door, Kathryn heard Dex whisper, "We've lost her. You've got fifteen seconds to wrap up. Thank Betty, thank the viewers for watching, say your goodbyes, and keep the cake in full view."

Without a television set to show her what the viewers could see, Kathryn held the cake in place and let the cameraman frame her. She babbled her closing remarks and maintained her smile until she heard Dex announce, "And we're out!" The lights switched off, and suddenly the temperature dipped twenty degrees.

"Thank you, everybody!" Kathryn exclaimed.

She sought out Winchell's face. He wasn't there. It was rude of him to walk out during the broadcast, but she was relieved. A stagehand brought her a towel and she blotted the sweat tracks that streaked her white makeup.

The guy handed her a note. "Mr. Winchell told me to give you this after the show."

She unfolded the paper with dread and skimmed his message.

"Oh, crap."

* * *

Thomas Danford tilted his head. "Tell me that name again."

"Kathryn Massey."

"You say it like I should know who that is."

"She's a columnist with the *Hollywood Reporter*."

"Hollywood, huh? Are you from Los Angeles too, Mr. Adler?"

Marcus nodded. "Kathryn and I are very good friends."

"And why has she sent you here?"

Marcus decided a friendly smile might help ease the shock. "Because . . . she is . . . your . . . daughter."

His words hit like a series of punches. With each successive blow, Danford bowed lower and lower until his forehead hung over the tabletop. He stayed that way until he had sufficiently marshaled his wits and rose to meet Marcus in the eye.

"Will you explain how you came to be here? And please remember that our time is fleeting."

Marcus gave Danford a précis of Kathryn's encounter with a photograph on the set of *Sunset Boulevard* of her four-year-old self sitting on the knee of a man that her mother later explained was her father, who was currently locked up in Sing Sing for treason.

Danford threaded his fingers together. "So she's a columnist with — which paper?"

"The *Hollywood Reporter*, but she's syndicated across the country and has her own radio show, *Window on Hollywood*. Today she's hosting the very first two-coast simultaneous television transmission."

"I thought her name was Violet." Anguish cut through his voice like a scythe. "That's what her mother told me at the time."

Yep, Marcus thought, *that sounds very Francine. Give him a fake name and put him off the scent.*

Danford dropped his head into his hands. "Tell me more about my daughter. What is she like? What is she good at? Is she married? Happy? Healthy? Do I have grandchildren?"

Danford kept his eyes down while Marcus answered his questions in the last minutes of their allotted time. When Marcus was done, Danford's eyes were blunted with agony.

"I'm glad you came and not her."

"She wanted to. Desperately. But it was—" Marcus groped for a gentler substitute for "career suicide." Fortunately, Danford saved him the trouble.

"I couldn't bear her to see me like this. It would be the ultimate humiliation."

One of the guards behind Danford caught Marcus' eye. He tapped his wrist.

"There's a question I know Kathryn's got on her mind."

"Am I guilty of treason?" The guy was every bit as sharp as his daughter—or was it the other way around? "I've been tried by a panel of my peers and found guilty, so does it really matter?"

"It does to her."

"Mr. Adler, I could tell you that I'm innocent and that I was framed, but I live in an institution where ninety percent of the men say the same thing, so there's no reason my daughter should believe me. But tell her thank you for doubting that I could really commit such a crime."

The guard started walking toward them.

"Francine thinks you're innocent," Marcus said.

Danford raised his eyebrows in appreciative surprise. "Kathryn must forget about me. Nothing good can come from the press catching wind that we are father and daughter." A shadow fell across him as he stood. "One black sheep per family is more than enough; two is overkill." The guard clamped a hand on his shoulder and pulled him away from the table.

Marcus jumped up. "What do you mean 'two'?"

The guard lifted his flattened palm toward Marcus. "Please exit the way you came in."

"There's only Kathryn and Francine," Marcus pressed. "Who are you talking about?"

The only sound in the hall was his voice echoing off the cold concrete.

* * *

Kathryn's week was a blur of firsts, bests, and unforgettables. *Guys and Dolls* at the 46th Street Theatre, *The King and I* at the St. James, and *Paint Your Wagon* at the Schubert; shopping at Bergdorf Goodman and Tiffany's; a Central Park carriage ride; the top of the Empire State Building; lobster Newburg at Delmonico's and pastrami at Carnegie Deli.

Leo said yes to everything she asked for.

A banana split sundae at Rumpelmayer's? Yes!

A ferry to the Statue of Liberty? Yes!

The Abstract Expressionism exhibit at the Met? Yes!

It was a dream come true . . . until she got that note from Winchell:

> *Meet me at the Stork Club*
> *3 East 53rd St*
> *I'll leave your name with the maître d'*
> *10 PM tomorrow night*
> *Punctuality is a virtue*
> *W.W.*

For such a famous place, the Stork Club had an unassuming frontage. A black canvas awning stretched from the door to the curb with the name painted plainly in white.

When Kathryn gave her name to the maître d', he led her into the innermost sanctum: the Cub Room. All eyes fixated on Kathryn as a waiter in a crisp, tight tux led her through the thicket to the most famous table in the city: Number 50, from which Winchell spied, joked, interviewed, and gathered material for his gossip column.

Winchell was dressed in a dark blue suit teamed with a necktie of a gorgeous shade of blue that reminded Kathryn of the jacaranda trees that bloomed along Santa Monica Boulevard in the early summer. It would be the perfect gift for Marcus.

What a doll he'd been to drive up to Sing Sing. With his writerly eye for detail, he described the chill of the air, the clanging of the metal doors, the way her father walked, the shape of his face, and the weary edge to his voice. Danford was probably right to advise her to put distance between them, but who was this black sheep?

Winchell rose when Kathryn approached. "Right on time." He motioned toward the seat to his right.

"Punctuality is a virtue, don't you know?"

"I do, but not everybody agrees with me."

A waiter appeared and Kathryn ordered a sidecar.

"The Long Island duckling à l'orange is very good," Winchell said, "as are the broiled jumbo El Panama shrimps Provençale."

Kathryn scanned the room and spotted Orson Welles at a table near the front. If she'd seen him, she would have stopped to say hello, if only to show Winchell she was not without contacts and allies — even in New York.

"Your demonstration yesterday," Winchell said. "You handled yourself like a pro. Very impressive."

"Imagine how impressed you'd have been if you'd stayed to the end."

"I wanted to." *Why do I find that hard to swallow?* "But I had a previous engagement." *Like fun you did.* "And you know what a stickler I am for punctuality." *All I know is you've called me here where you've got home advantage.* "I saw enough to be able to talk about it in my column tomorrow." *Then why delay mentioning it for two days?*

She tapped the armrests of her chair. "Is this where Hoover sits?"

"Interesting that you should bring up Hoover."

"It's because I have a theory."

There was a pause as Winchell gave a quasi-military salute to a brownnoser in a straw boater a few tables away, then lit a Lucky Strike with well-oiled dexterity. "Theory about what?"

Marcus had been on his fourth sidecar at Tavern on the Green last night when he decided Winchell shared Hoover's grudge against Kathryn. Since the end of the Prohibition, Winchell had been filling inches in the *New York Daily Mirror* with his tête-à-têtes with Hoover, and it was safe to assume Hoover had told him about the time Kathryn went toe-to-toe with him. She'd only just gotten away with it. "A theory about you and Hoover," she said.

Winchell neither smiled nor scoffed. "What about us?"

"You're in cahoots."

"Against who?"

"Me."

"You know how paranoid that sounds, don't you?"

Her theory hadn't seemed so extreme over boeuf bourguignon, but now it sounded a tad ridiculous. She persisted anyway.

"I stood up to Hoover once; he doesn't like that. Nor does he forget it. And since my announcement about Mayer's ousting, my ratings have soared. And I think that makes you nervous."

He shot a plume of cigarette smoke from the side of his mouth. "You do, huh?"

"Furthermore, I made it onto television first and I think that burns your derrière."

That last part had only just occurred to her as she observed how every one of the well-heeled guests surrounding them nodded and cowed like he was King George.

"Is that what you think?"

"If *you* appeared on television before *I* had, I'd be jealous as hell."

That wasn't true at all, but Kathryn had been around enough egomaniacs to know how to soften them up.

"That's quite a theory you've worked up there, Miss Massey. You got anything to back it up?"

"Your man in LA."

"You'll need to be more specific than that."

As she described the skinny creep from the night of St. Cyr's arrest, Winchell listened with admirable restraint. But the twitch of his upper lip and tiny spasm in his pinkie finger gave him away.

"You really should pay him more to ensure his loyalty," Kathryn told Winchell. "He may as well have 'mercenary louse' tattooed across his forehead."

"He's not my louse." Winchell winced when he realized he'd overshot the truth. "Not mine alone, at any rate."

"Who else does he belong to?"

He gave Kathryn a level look. "Joe McCarthy. He hates you, by the way."

"McCarthy? We've never even met," she said. "Why would he hate me?"

"Because of what you've done."

"What have *I* done?"

"Joseph McCarthy is loyal, if nothing else. He never forgets a friend."

Oh, God, Kathryn thought.

Ruby Courtland's words from the night of the *All About Eve* premiere came back to her: "My dad and Senator Joe went to the same college. They're old pals, and Hoover knows it."

If there are fifteen million people in New York, how come the same names keep circling me like hornets: Hoover, Winchell, McCarthy, Courtland. "I thought you hated Ruby's father," she said.

Winchell jabbed his cigarette into the air between them. "Otis Courtland is a miserable piece of shit and I hope he spends eternity eating Hitler's puke in hell." He sank back against his seat. "But McCarthy thinks he's a stand-up guy because they went to Marquette together. Ergo—"

"Ergo, I'm at the top of his bitch list because I contributed to his daughter's downfall and subsequent ride on the midnight train to I-don't-care-where."

The waiter appeared. Kathryn ordered the Long Island duckling à l'orange, then nearly laughed out loud when her host ordered the stuffed boneless Cornish hen à la Walter Winchell with a straight face.

"So tell me, Walter, is this invitation purely a social call?"

"I figured you'd enjoy the view from Table Fifty."

The atmosphere of the Cub Room was every bit as rarified as she'd hoped. There were enough famous figures, furs, and facelifts here for a week of columns. Henry Fonda and Leland Heyward, both ex-husbands of Margaret Sullavan, had joined Orson Welles at his table near the front, and Kathryn longed to be with them, listening to a conversation that was probably meandering around every topic except the obvious one.

"I must say," she admitted, "it's lived up to its reputation. But I can't help feeling there's another reason you summoned me."

"As a matter of fact, there is. I recently made a trip up north along the Hudson River to pay someone a visit."

"I assume you didn't go for the fishing."

"Oh, I went fishing, all right."

The waiter appeared with fresh drinks, clearing the empty glasses and replacing the ashtray without making eye contact.

"What did you think of him?" Kathryn asked.

"I keep current with Boston politics, but only peripherally. The Danford case was a sensation. I heard rumors about it being a frame-up. They died off when he was convicted. But the facts of the case stayed with me. Somehow, they just didn't add up."

"You think he's innocent?"

"I'm saying that I wasn't convinced. I went to see him because if he's innocent, and if there's a way to prove it, it would make for the sort of headlines I relish."

"How did he strike you?"

Winchell sucked the juice out of the orange slice garnishing his drink. "Even in prison stripes, with a crew cut and a three-day beard, he's quite credible. But he's also resigned to his fate."

But surely someone with Danford's background was smart enough to see the advantages of having an advocate as powerful as Winchell on the outside.

"Why are you telling me all this?" Kathryn asked.

"I thought you'd like to know."

"Are you setting me up to owe you a favor?"

"If I was, would it be so bad?"

It wouldn't, but the thought was enough to make her squirm in her seat.

CHAPTER 16

Kathryn and Marcus walked around back of the Chateau Marmont to Francine Massey's rented bungalow. Kathryn's mother had been the hotel's head telephone operator for years and qualified for cheap employee housing on site.

Even though the Marmont was within walking distance of the Garden of Allah, Kathryn and Francine didn't often see each other, preferring to maintain a friendly truce at a distance. But inevitably some rabid issue would rear up and before anyone could say "You're so alike," they'd be butting heads.

Kathryn paused at Francine's front door. "This black sheep thing, it could be anyone. It could even be worse than being locked away in Sing Sing for treason."

"Let's not jump to any conclusions." Marcus took her left hand and stroked the top of it. "She may not even know."

"Maybe I'm better off not knowing. There's a lot to be said for plausible deniability."

Kathryn tried to pull away, but Marcus tightened his grip. "I believe it was Confucius who said, 'Ignorance is bliss . . . unless there's a possibility that Walter Winchell might also know and use it against you in the court of café society.'"

She couldn't help but smile. "You're a nut."

"And nuts are delicious." He released her hand. "You want me to take the lead?"

"This is about my family. But I doubt I can remain objective. Not with Lady Dahlia in there."

"So that's a yes?"

The door swung open. "How much longer are you two planning on standing there?"

Kathryn blushed, wondering if her mother heard the Lady Dahlia crack.

In the fifteen years she'd lived in her compact employee housing, Francine had scarcely changed anything, so when Kathryn walked in and found everything had changed, she was thrown off guard.

The brown leather loveseat that had always been against the left wall was now a low-slung cream sofa against the front wall. The two mismatched chairs were now a single club chair, and the seaman's chest Francine had always used for a coffee table was gone. So was the bookshelf full of dahlias, and she had painted the living room light yellow.

"Do you like it?" Francine asked.

Aside from Marcus and Gwendolyn, one of the few constants in Kathryn's life had been her mother. Although they rarely got along, hers was an unvarnished opinion she could count on, and her home was one she could walk into and know where everything was. "It feels like a whole different place."

"I redecorated."

"It looks peculiar without your dahlias," Marcus said.

"They're a lot of work," Francine said blithely, and pointed to the sofa.

The two of them took a seat. The redecoration had thrown Kathryn a curve ball. She pulled a face at Marcus. *Yes, I want you to take the lead.*

"Francine," he pressed his hands together, "when Kathryn and I were in New York, I rented a car and drove up to Sing Sing."

Francine leaned a hip against the club chair. "Please tell me you didn't."

"I did. And—"

"What on earth were you hoping to achieve?" She faced her daughter. "Did *you* know about this?"

Kathryn nodded.

"You swore to me you'd have no communication with him. You sat right here in this room and *promised* me—"

"You asked me to promise, but I didn't actually promise you anything. And even if I did, you can't hold me to it. He's my father! Don't I deserve to know him, even just a little?"

"Not when he's serving time."

"But you said yourself that you didn't think he was guilty."

"Tell that to Louella and Hedda when the truth comes out. At least you were sensible enough to send a scouting party." She dropped into the chair and asked Marcus, "Did they let you see him? In person? How was he?"

"Despite his reduced circumstances—"

"There's an understatement."

"He's still a very impressive gentleman. I can see why you fell for him."

"I'm so very grateful for your approval."

See? Kathryn thought. *This is why it's hard to be around you.* "Will you please just listen to what Marcus has to say?"

"Obviously, I have no choice—"

"So anyway," Marcus cut her off, "I saw him, told him who his daughter is, and he said it would be better for everyone concerned if there was no contact between them."

Francine ran her fingernails back and forth across the double strand of pearls slung at the base of her throat. The rapid click-click-click-click grated on Kathryn's nerves; she fought to keep silent.

"But that's not why we've come," Marcus continued.

"Well now, this just gets better and better. I hope you took notes; perhaps one day you can turn it into a movie. Oh, that's right, you're not allowed to write them anymore, are you?"

"Mother!"

"As the guard was leading him away," Marcus continued, "Thomas said to me, 'One black sheep in the family is more than enough.'"

The irritating click-click-click against the pearls halted. A windowpane rattled as a fire engine rumbled along Sunset. Francine waited until the siren's wail petered out. "And now you want to know who this black sheep is."

"His side of the family or ours?" Kathryn asked.

Francine rubbed the tips of her fingers across her forehead. "Have you ever wondered why I've never talked about my family?"

"My whole life," Kathryn replied. "But there was always a high brick wall around the past. And a wide moat. Filled with sharks. But no drawbridge."

"Well then, here's your drawbridge. I have a brother. His real name is Camden Caldecott; we called him Cam."

"What do you mean, 'his real name'?"

"He now goes by the name of Sheldon Voss." She glared at them expectantly, but the name drew a blank. "You might want to pick up an East Coast newspaper once in a while."

"So he's famous enough to make the papers?"

"For the past thirty years, he's eked out a living as an itinerant tent revival evangelist."

"I thought you were going to say 'serial killer'!" Kathryn burst out. "Or that he was the real Lindbergh baby kidnapper. A Bible thumper doesn't sound nearly so bad."

"Shows what you know."

"Go on, Francine," Marcus said softly.

"Growing up, Cam was a wonderful older brother. He looked out for me, and I adored him. But all hell broke loose when I fell pregnant. He was away at college at the time, and he came thundering home and made an ugly scene. He was outraged beyond reason. Screaming, yelling, virtually frothing at the mouth. In the middle of all that, poor Thomas arrived on the doorstep. Talk about bad timing. Cam just about killed him. Accusations of rape, threatening to call the cops. Oh, it was terrible. Thomas fled down the street, but Cam could barely be placated.

"I managed to convince him that I was okay and he should go back to college in Philadelphia. Next thing I know, I get a letter from him saying that he's had a religious conversion and was dropping out to become a preacher."

Kathryn perched on the edge of the sofa. "But why is this such a big, dark secret? If he wants to spend his life roaming the countryside pontificating—"

"BECAUSE HE'S A LIAR, AND A CHEAT, AND A THIEF, AND A CHISELER, AND AN UTTER FRAUD!"

For all her contrariness, Kathryn's mother wasn't a screamer. She always kept her emotions buttoned down while she made her point with a strong, trenchant line. But yelling fit to bust a jugular was as unheard of as redecorating.

"Why is he a liar and a cheat?" Kathryn used the measured tone she usually reserved for movie stars hopped up on bennies or going through an incendiary divorce.

Francine rubbed her forehead until her bunched-up shoulders drooped. "I've been keeping track of him over the years using a clipping service."

"So he was good at this preaching business?"

"If only that were the case, dear." The 'dear' was a good sign. Francine tended to only use it in her more relaxed moods. "Unfortunately, my brother has rarely been out of trouble for long. Theft, forgery, swindling, defrauding the recently bereaved, the infirm, the just plain ignorant."

"In other words, easy targets," Marcus said.

"Precisely. Always in the name of the Lord, and always petty stuff that won't get him a long stretch in the county lock-up. Usually he'd skip town. He's wandered all over. And if that's the way he stayed, I wouldn't be quite so worried. But then Billy Graham showed up."

A few years after the war, the Southern Baptist minister struck a deep chord with conservative, middle-class Protestants. He was now the most famous preacher in America, thanks to his *Hour of Decision* radio show.

"What does Billy Graham have to do with your brother?" Kathryn asked. *Or my uncle. Oh my God, I've got an uncle!*

For someone who'd spent her whole life thinking her only blood relative was her unpredictably crabby mother, the idea that she had an uncle pushed Kathryn into uncharted territory.

"Cam — or should I say Sheldon — has gotten it into his head that he wants to be the next Billy Graham. Only bigger. And knowing him as I do, he's figured out a way to take his petty grafts and swindles and turn them into monstrous cons."

"All in the name of the Lord," Marcus said.

"Precisely. He can be a very charismatic man when he wants to be. His Labor Day meeting in Wichita drew five thousand people." Francine wagged a warning finger at Kathryn. "Let me be crystal clear. Cam has no moral compass, and even fewer scruples. I am ashamed and appalled that we're related. That's why I've remained so tight-lipped about my past. It was bad enough that you were an illegitimate birth, but you've got a charlatan evangelist for an uncle and a father in the slammer. You can't finesse your way out of circumstances like that in your profession. Yes, I built a wall and dug a moat around you. That was because I tried to protect you from it all. But you had to go and dig, didn't you?" Francine was on her feet now. "Dig, dig, dig! So now you're like a dog with a pile of moldy, old bones. Are you happy?"

* * *

Kathryn and Marcus walked in silence until they were within sight of the big neon *GARDEN OF ALLAH VILLAS* sign facing Sunset.

"So," Marcus said, "you've got an uncle."

"Seems that way."

"But of course he's not just any regular uncle. Oh no, you had to go and get yourself Elmer Gantry."

At the corner of Havenhurst, Kathryn perched her rear end on the low brick wall and pulled Marcus down with her. "You know what worries me? Winchell and Hoover are thick as thieves."

"And now this McCarthy clown is in the picture."

"And where we have McCarthy, we have Otis Courtland. But why are we talking about them?"

"Between the four of them, that's a hell of a wide network of spies and informers. The question is, do any of them even suspect that I'm related to this Sheldon Voss guy?"

Marcus pulled out his gold cigarette lighter and started flipping it, Cagney style. It caught the light of the neon sign flashing white and gold behind him in the chilly November air. "You need to assume the worst. You're a threat to Winchell's supremacy on radio; you stood up to Hoover without blinking; and you publicly embarrassed Courtland's daughter. That's three strikes against you right there."

"What about McCarthy?"

The rush hour traffic crawled along Sunset. It had been growing heavier lately — the evening peak hour now stretched to an evening peak hour-and-a-half.

Marcus said, "McCarthy's a real jerk, and jerks are hard to predict. So you better watch your Ps and Qs — and it wouldn't hurt to watch the rest of the alphabet while you're at it."

Kathryn dropped her head into her hands and wondered if it was too late to take a job as a secretary at some dismal ball bearings factory. What a relief it would be to simply type up letters, file away invoices, and get coffee for a middle-aged boss whose greatest ambition was to reach retirement before a heart attack laid him out at an Atlantic City convention.

Nice work if you can get it.

CHAPTER 17

1951 was Chez Gwendolyn's fourth Christmas, and it struck Gwendolyn that every year, the Christmas rush arrived earlier and earlier. Was that because holiday parties started sooner? Or because her store was more famous now that *Sunset Boulevard* was available in all the Bullocks stores? Whatever the reason, by the second Friday of December, she was so busy that she started to consider engaging someone to help her through the rush.

As she changed the *OPEN* sign on her front door to *CLOSED*, she ran her mind through a meager list of candidates. She kicked off her heels and decided she was too tired to care about that right now. It was well past nine and she was starving, but she had to tally her intake for the day.

She heard three slow knocks at her back door. The only people who did that were delivery drivers.

She ignored it.

Thirty seconds ticked past.

Another three loud knocks.

She slid back into her heels and thrust aside the black curtain separating the salon from the workroom out back. She pulled open the alley door and Ella Fitzgerald stepped out of the shadows.

"Oh my!" Gwendolyn exclaimed. "What a surprise." She widened the door. "Come on in."

Ella pointed behind her to a figure cloaked in the gloom. "This here is my good pal, Isobel Jenkins."

"Remember me?" she asked. It was the woman Gwendolyn and Marcus had tangled with at the Dunbar.

"Hello again," Gwendolyn said. "Come in, come in! You don't have to wait in the alley! Why didn't you just come to the front door?"

"Oh, sugar, no. I wouldn't dream of putting you in such a position. We just thought it best to wait out back until you'd closed."

She guided the women through the workshop into the salon. "How long were you two out there?"

"Not long. Maybe twenty minutes. Now, you told me you had a whole bunch of outfits you thought would suit me."

"Hold on a minute." Gwendolyn shifted her weight from one aching foot to the other. "You stood in that stinky old alley until I was closed? Why for heaven's sake didn't you just come through the front like regular—"

Ella gently tapped Gwendolyn's wrist.

Gwendolyn felt the heat of a furious blush sear her face. "What can I do for you ladies?"

Isobel headed for a white dress with dark orange embroidery across the bust and neckline. "Ella, honey, I can see you in that."

Ella pressed a finger to her chin. "I do like that one, I must say. But it might be hard to find a lipstick to match. Do you have it in red?"

"I'm sorry—but—I have to say this. You're Ella Fitzgerald," Gwendolyn blurted out. "You've played some of the ritziest nightclubs in the country."

"Yeah," Isobel jeered, "now ask Miss Ella if she's allowed to walk in through the front door of those swelegant establishments, or does she have to slink in via the kitchen, and hope she doesn't end up with marinara stains all over her dress?"

"But that doesn't still happen, does it?" Gwendolyn asked Ella.

"See?" Isobel scolded Ella.

"I said I *hoped* she was different."

"And what did *I* say?" Isobel turned to Gwendolyn. "I said, 'Sitting through a show down Central Avenue with Travilla's wife don't make her anymore understanding than any other nice white girl out there.'"

Ella waved a dismissive hand at her friend. "Don't pay her no nevermind.

"This is 1951!" Gwendolyn exclaimed. "Circumstances change, people change, attitudes change."

Isobel stepped forward, her eyes blazing. "Lemme tell you something: back in the twenties, I was a chorus girl at the Cotton Club up in Harlem. Twenty-five dollars a week they paid me; that was a king's ransom to me and my poor black behind. But we hadda walk in via the kitchen. And worse, they didn't even give us no proper place to pee. We hadda go in the basin *in the wings.* Downright humiliating, is what it was. And if you think it's any different thirty years later, you're living in a bubble."

Those words torpedoed Gwendolyn back to her tenth birthday party. When her best friend, Joey, failed to show up, her mother rolled those watery blue eyes of hers and growled, "You're living in a bubble that someone's just achin' to prick. Little Joey won't be coming around no more and that's all there is to it."

Standing in the middle of her Sunset Strip store thirty years later, Gwendolyn could still hear the shake in her voice as she asked her mother why not.

"When you were just a little bitty snip, I didn't mind you playing dollies and hopscotch with the neighbor's maid's daughter. However, there comes a time when it's no longer appropriate. You need to start mixing with your equals."

Gwendolyn cried for two straight days, but she never saw or heard from Joey again.

Gwendolyn tried not to hate her mother for what she'd done. Even at the age of ten, she was able to grasp that Desiréé Boyington, of the Savannah Boyingtons, was a victim of a hopelessly obsolete upbringing.

Gwendolyn's grandmother, Rosamond, had brought up Desiréé as though the South's halcyon days were still in full flower, even though Rosamond herself had never experienced them. The opening shots of the Civil War rent the air over Fort Sumter as Rosamond's wet nurse weaned her among crinolines, magnolia blossoms, and mint juleps on the family's cotton plantation. And yet there was Desiréé, standing in that squalid little kitchen in Hollywood, Florida, more than fifty years after Appomattox, pretending it was still 1840.

"It's been a hundred years since the Emancipation Proclamation," Gwendolyn said. "You have the right to enter like everybody else."

Ella and Isabella looked at each other askance.

"As fine as that sentiment is," Ella said, "that just ain't how the world works."

Gwendolyn marched to the CLOSED sign and switched it back to OPEN.

"Sweetie," Ella said, "I hear a twang in your voice, so I suspect you know what we're talking about."

It hadn't taken Gwendolyn long to realize that "Southern" was a euphemism for "country-hick stupid" in LA, so she'd worked hard to lose her Southern lilt. But every now and then, a split vowel snuck out while she wasn't looking.

"I do," Gwendolyn admitted, "but I figured it didn't matter out here."

"Of course that's what you figured," Isobel said. "You're white, you're pretty, you have a store on the Sunset Strip, you have your own perfume."

Gwendolyn wanted to tell this woman that she'd spent the last of her money on developing her fragrance. Its failure would have wiped out everything she possessed.

"But this is my store, so I get to run it however I see fit."

"I suspect that's not as true as you'd like to think," Ella said.

"And I'd like to believe that we've made more progress than that."

"This isn't Arkansas."

"And it ain't *Lost Horizon*, either."

Gwendolyn uncrossed her arms. "My store, my rules," she told Ella and Isobel. "There'll be no more creeping in through the back door. Okay?"

"If you say so."

"I do. And you can tell your friends."

CHAPTER 18

As Kathryn walked along the brick path to Humphrey Bogart and Betty Bacall's home in the Hollywood Hills, she found herself listing to the right. If Leo hadn't called her at lunchtime, she'd probably have stayed in bed all afternoon.

Purple and pink petunias lined the edges of the garden path. Bacall's voice from the previous night came back to Kathryn in blurred snippets.

"I planted them myself, you know. On my hands and knees, every last goddamned one of them."

Kathryn remembered someone challenging her. "I don't believe a word of it!" Was it Kate Hepburn? Or John Huston's wife? Whoever it was managed to spill her zinfandel all over the table.

That was when Bogie said, "See? *This* is why Dave Chasen covers his linens with glass."

Kathryn's memory of what happened next faded in and out. James Agee talked to her — or rather, *at* her — about some novel he'd been working on since 1940-whenever. She no longer possessed lucid recall of the one-sided conversation. If it came to that, she no longer had lucid recall of the entire evening.

It had started out entertainingly enough.

Bogie called to say he had a print of his new movie.

When reports had started to filter back to Hollywood about the rigors of filming in the Belgian Congo, everyone thought *The African Queen* was a turkey in the making. But when it went into post-production, the bees started buzzing that Bogie, Hepburn, and Huston had made a career-defining picture.

Bogie's invitation to the secret advance viewing came with a caveat: "Say nothing to nobody," which Kathryn interpreted as, "I don't exactly have permission to run this movie."

The movie was warm, funny, thrilling, and romantic. The gang of lucky viewers that emerged from the screening room on the United Artists lot were so high on what they'd just seen that when someone suggested dinner at Chasen's, they piled into cars and tore down Beverly Boulevard.

But now it was twenty-four hours later and Kathryn's head was teetering on the edge of splitting open. A fistful of aspirin was the only thing keeping her upright.

Kathryn rang the bell—not that it was likely to be heard over the blasts of laughter and clatter of ice hitting glass. She opened the door and plowed into a heated conversation about Palm Springs between Frank Sinatra, Judy Garland, and David Niven.

When Judy spotted Kathryn, she cried out, "I give UP!" and left the two men. She pulled Kathryn into a hug. "They're arguing about investing in real estate out in the desert. I keep reminding them that it's just a pile of sand but they don't want to hear it."

Kathryn hadn't seen Judy since the party Gene Kelly threw a year ago to celebrate the success of *Summer Stock*. Judy had barely survived production and hadn't looked at all well that night. But now her liquid brown eyes shone clear and bright with a vitality that a mountain of pills couldn't extinguish.

"I thought you were still laying them in the aisles at the Palace," Kathryn said. "I tried to get tickets when I was in New York, but they couldn't be had for love nor money."

For the past couple of months, Judy had enjoyed a triumphant comeback at the Palace Theatre, prompting Kathryn to devote an entire column entitled "Don't Kick Her Yet—Judy's Far From Down."

"You should have called me," Judy scolded. "Yes, I'm still there. But I must confess, it's exhausting. I asked Sid if perhaps we could take a few days off and get out of that cold. So here I am. This is my only party. Otherwise, I'll be sleeping so soundly they'll think I'm dead."

Now that Judy's marriage to Vincente Minnelli was over, rumors of a romance between Judy and her manager, Sid Luft, were rife. "Is Sid here tonight?" Kathryn asked.

"He stayed in New York. Once the Palace run ends, we're looking at bringing the show to LA."

"You are?" Kathryn spun her head around too fast.

"Oh my dear, you're looking a little green around the gills. You weren't at Chasen's last night, were you?"

Kathryn admitted that she was.

"We need to get you some hair of the dog."

Judy led Kathryn to the curved bar in the corner of a packed living room. "And speaking of successes, congratulations on yours," Judy exclaimed, pouring them each a generous Glenfiddich on the rocks. "Number three!" They clinked glasses.

Kathryn's cross-country tour had succeeded on every level.

Her Golden Aerial Day broadcast set a new record of ratings for a midweek midday broadcast, so the suits were all smiles. The following week, *Window on Hollywood* entered the top-ten primetime radio shows nationwide, and in the first week of December, it lassoed the number three slot in the ratings, just behind *Lux Radio Theater* and *The Walter Winchell Show*.

A few days after Kathryn returned from New York, Leo dropped his bombshell.

The suits at NBC, Sunbeam Mixmaster, and Betty Crocker were extending a five-hundred-dollar bonus for every week she stayed in the top ten, and an extra five hundred for every week she beat Winchell.

But Kathryn knew that her recent bump in ratings was just that. What she needed was a whammo-blammo guest that would compel listeners to tune in. A guest like Judy Garland.

"To you!" Kathryn said, clinking Judy's glass again. "It must be great to be back on top."

Judy waved to Eddie Bracken and his wife. "Between us chickens, it's all been a bit overwhelming."

Three gulps into her Glenfiddich, Kathryn could feel her hangover dissipate. "But in a good way, right?"

"Playing the Palace is a truly wonderful experience, but honestly, I don't know how Ethel does it. She did *Annie Get Your Gun* for three years and only missed two shows. Can you believe that?"

Kathryn curved her eyebrows upward into what she hoped was a beseeching-not-begging face. "Any chance I could lure you onto my radio show?"

"I fly back Tuesday night."

So much for that.

They talked shop for a while, about Lena Horne missing out on *Show Boat*, whether or not Lili St. Cyr's arrest was a publicity stunt, how Gene Kelly's new movie about Hollywood's switch to sound was the talk of the MGM lot. Inevitably, Judy was dragged away, this time by June Allyson to settle a dispute between Dick Powell and Frank Sinatra over Lorenz Hart.

An old Johnny Mercer tune, "Autumn Leaves," floated overhead.

Kathryn tried to catch Betty's eye, but she was busy playing hostess. Over the past few years, she'd transformed the Bogart-Bacall home into a place where A-listers could show up, no makeup, no girdle, no toupee, and just be themselves.

A solitary figure standing at the bookcase caught Kathryn's eye.

She picked a circuitous path, hoping she could see what book lay open in the actor's hands, but it was impossible in the gentle lamplight. She drew close to him. "Surprising, isn't it?"

The guy wasn't even thirty yet, but he exuded the power of General Patton—if Patton was dripping with enough testosterone to make every woman in the country swoon.

"What?" he asked.

Kathryn indicated the crammed shelves with her whiskey tumbler.

"That Bogie would read Plato, Emerson, and Shakespeare."

The guy rolled his shoulders back to face her more squarely. "You can judge a person by the books on his shelf."

His dark eyes drank her in. The ice in her drink tinkled against the side of her glass; she steadied it with her other hand. "Uh-huh."

He held up Walt Whitman's *Leaves of Grass*. "One of my favorite poems is 'I Sing the Body Electric.' Do you know it?"

What Kathryn knew about poetry could fill Thumbelina's thimble. She shook her head.

He intensified his stare with a penetrating scowl. "Be not ashamed women, your privilege encloses the rest, and is the exit of the rest. You are the gates of the body, and you are the gates of the soul."

Kathryn had no idea what any of that meant, but it had the intended effect. She swallowed. Hard. "I see what you mean."

"Stirring, isn't it?"

"Just like your *Streetcar* performance."

The first time Kathryn had heard Marlon Brando's name was when he hit it big on Broadway. After that, every other conversation started with, "Have you heard about this Brando guy burning up the Ethel Barrymore Theatre?"

His photos showed a brooding actor with an impenetrable gaze, but it wasn't until Elia Kazan's movie version of *A Streetcar Named Desire* hit the screens that Kathryn saw what people were going gaga over. But now, with him standing two feet away from her, radiating star power like Clark Gable or Gary Cooper, she felt like Alice in Wonderland falling down the rabbit hole.

Brando allowed her a reticent smile. "Thank you."

"I'm sorry." Kathryn shifted her whiskey to her left hand and offered her right to him. "I should have introduced myself. I'm Kathryn Massey."

"I know who you are." He held her hand like it was a delicate bird. "I'm surprised people like you are invited to shindigs like these."

The heat from his hand traveled up her arm. "The Bogarts and I have a history." He raised an eyebrow and let go of her hand. "We've lived at the Garden of Allah at several different times over the years. That's the hotel up on Sunset. Have you been there?"

Kathryn knew full well that Brando had never been to the Garden of Allah. If he had, it would've been the talk of the place.

Brando shook his head. "Was that an invitation?"

"Are you always this flirty?"

Brando snapped the book shut and slipped it back into its place on the shelf. "Someone told me the only women I should flirt with are the four queens: Louella, Hedda, Sheilah, and you. She told me, 'Charm them, and they'll charm the world for you.'"

"And who is this 'she'?"

"Irene."

Only the woman's first name was necessary.

Irene Mayer Selznick was the daughter of Louis B. and ex-wife of David O. She fled Hollywood for New York after her marriage ended and became a Broadway producer whose first play was the sensation of the '47-'48 season. It solidified Tennessee Williams' career and launched Marlon Brando into the stratosphere.

"Irene is very level-headed," Kathryn said. "I'd take her advice, if I were you."

"You know what else she told me?"

Kathryn breathed in his scent: a heady mixture of coffee, loose tobacco, a musty cologne that reminded her of her lost love, Roy, and — oddly — amaretto, which clung to his clothes like sweat.

"What did she tell you?"

"Irene said flirting wouldn't work on you."

"What am I, made of ice?"

Brando tilted his head back and bared his movie-star smile. "It was a compliment, Miss Massey. She thinks you're too astute for that bullshit."

Between the tumbler of whiskey and the amaretto sweat, Kathryn could barely feel her face. She hoped to God she wasn't blushing. Leo was a good man, kind, attentive, watched out for her interests, enthusiastic in bed. But for all that, he didn't arouse the sort of heat radiating from this lady-killer. Then again, few men did, even in Hollywood.

"I knew I liked Irene." She threw off a laugh, shooting for Noel-Coward-esque mirth. "Mr. Brando, I have a radio show —"

"Now that we've met, I'll be sure to tune in some time."

In someone else, his insolence would have come across as uncouth, but in this beefcake with brains, it read as seductive.

"The way you recited Walt Whitman just now —"

"What of it?"

"I was hoping you might agree to come on my show and recite 'I Sing the Body Electric.' Or perhaps some Shakespeare." She'd heard Joe Mankiewicz hoped to film *Julius Caesar* and was considering Brando for Marc Antony.

Brando's smile dropped away like it'd been slapped off his face. "Do I look like a whore?"

"What? No, of course not. I just thought —"

"You thought that I'm like every other actor in this one-note town." His voice cut through Peggy Lee's "Why Don't You Do Right?" "That I'll do whatever it takes to get picked up like some two-bit streetwalker."

"Hold on a minute!" Kathryn set her empty glass down with a thump that turned heads. "I just thought—"

"A guy hits big and everybody wants a piece of him. Well, fuck you, lady." He suddenly looked as raw and jagged as Stanley Kowalski in the street with his t-shirt ripped from his torso. Brando took in the rest of the room. "And fuck ALL of you."

He shoved Kathryn into the bookcase and stormed out into the cold December night. The whole room stared at Kathryn. *What the hell just happened?* The only body in motion was Betty Bacall.

"Did he hurt you?"

Kathryn waved dismissively to everyone. "Everything's fine!" Then to Betty, "Where's your nearest powder room?"

"Use the one upstairs, first door on the left."

The door opened into the master bathroom with his and hers sinks and thick green hand towels that matched the "Autumn in New England" décor. She took stock of her reflection in the mirror and castigated herself for not thinking further ahead than the end of her tour.

She opened her handbag and pulled out her lipstick for a repair job, but she didn't have the energy for even that. She wished she'd gone to Leo's company Christmas bash at the Beverly Hills Hotel instead. The crowd there wouldn't have half the sparkle of the people downstairs, but they wouldn't be half the work, either.

As she dropped her lipstick into her pocketbook, she scanned the headlines of the *Washington Post* on the counter. Its headline read

VOSS WORKS UP LATHER FOR THE LORD.

Kathryn snatched up the newspaper. The article reported on a tent revival in Washington, DC, held by Sheldon Voss, "the fervent evangelist dripping with liturgical sweat." J. Edgar Hoover and Senator Joseph McCarthy had been in attendance, thus validating Voss' campaign of moral righteousness.

The article speculated that Hoover and McCarthy had received advance word of Voss' announcement that next summer, he would be spreading his message in a transcontinental caravan called the "Sea to Shining Sea March." Twelve stops were planned: Washington, D.C., Pittsburgh, Columbus, Cincinnati, St. Louis, Memphis, Dallas, Oklahoma City, Denver, Albuquerque, Phoenix, and Los Angeles. Only, he didn't call it Los Angeles, but the "Sodom and Gomorrah of these great United States," and "a cesspit of sin and debauchery, filled with Communists and deviants whose souls I can hear crying out for redemption."

Kathryn flung open the bathroom door and strode into the hallway, almost colliding with Frank Sinatra.

"Whoa, Nellie!" he laughed as she ran into his arms. "Is there a cattle stampede I oughta know about?"

Flustered, all she could do was mumble an apology and tell him how nice it was to see him.

"You didn't let that bozo get to you, I hope?"

"No, no," she told him, "I was just feeling . . ." . . . *an impending sense of doom called Uncle Sheldon.*

"Judy and I were chatting just now, and she told me that you're in need."

"Of what?"

"A guest. For your radio show."

Sinatra's blue eyes glistened with anxiety. The guy was in an awful slump. The public hadn't approved of the way he broke up his marriage to tie the knot with Ava Gardner, and he'd started his first run in Vegas at Desert Inn where, according to one report, he was "playing to half-filled houses of wildcatters and ranchers."

She smiled. "How does two songs and a comedy routine sound?"

"For you, baby, I'll stand on my head and juggle flaming swords while belching 'The Star-Spangled Banner.'"

Oh my God, she realized, *Sinatra's more desperate than I am.*

CHAPTER 19

When Hattie McDaniel walked into Chez Gwendolyn during the first week of 1952, Gwendolyn panicked, then mounted her blandest smile and welcomed Hattie and the friend who trailed behind her. "Let me guess," Gwendolyn said. "Ella sent you?"

Hattie's full, round face broke into a smile as she trooped forward. "She told us you have so much loveliness on offer that we might not be able to choose." Uncertainty flickered across her eyes.

Gwendolyn ignored it.

"Welcome! What sort of apparel are you looking for? Everyday street-wear? Formal? Performance?"

"I've been asked to take over the role of Beulah in *The Beulah Show* now that they've moved production to Hollywood. Ethel Waters' loss is my gain! I'm going to be doing a whole lot of press, so I need some pretty new duds." Hattie called to her friend. "Dorothy? Come join us, darlin'."

Hattie's friend was a slim, light-skinned girl, very pretty with a shy smile.

"This is my friend, Dorothy Dandridge," Hattie said, "or as I like to call her, Melmendi, Queen of the Ashuba." She let out the high-pitched giggle she made famous as the O'Haras' Mammy.

Dorothy told Hattie to hush her big mouth.

"Dorothy here is an actress, too," Hattie explained. "And a mighty fine one, as she demonstrated earlier this year in *Tarzan's Peril*."

"You're never going to let me live it down, are you?"

"Not if I can help it."

"We can't all have *Gone with the Wind* on our resume."

Hattie giggled again. "No, child, we sure cain't. Dorothy sings like a dream and is working up an act to pitch around town in between films. So she's going to need some stage outfits, like you did for Ella."

When Gwendolyn moved out from behind the counter, Hattie took in a full measure of her. "Have we met?"

Gwendolyn shook her head and pulled out a poinsettia-red suit in shot silk. "I don't have it in your size, but I could whip one up by the end of the week."

"You sew, too?" Dorothy held a floaty floor-length gown of white chiffon. It was several sizes too big for her, but it would pick up the spotlight at Ciro's beautifully.

"Anything you want," Gwendolyn told her. "Maybe a strapless version of what you've got in your hand." She faced Hattie again and held up the suit. "Something like this?"

Hattie still wore a puzzled frown. She tsked several times. "I know your face."

The silver bell above the front door tinkled, saving Gwendolyn from having to confess.

The three honey blondes who burst through the door cackling like extras on *The Snake Pit* were regulars Kathryn had dubbed the Tinseltown Triplets. Gwendolyn suspected they lived on cigarettes and black coffee, but they had excellent taste and bottomless allowances from their studio-exec husbands, who were probably schtupping starlets and secretaries right this very minute.

"Hello, ladies," she called out. "I'll be with you in a moment."

They stopped just inside the door, their smiles fading as they took in the sight of Hattie and Dorothy.

The triplet with the biggest bosom grimaced as though she were about to pass gas. "May we have a private word?"

Hattie shoved the shot silk suit into Gwendolyn's hand. "We'll be taking our leave now."

It didn't take Einstein to figure out what the "private word" was going to be. It was one thing to tell Ella Fitzgerald she was welcome when it was nine thirty at night, with nobody around. It was a whole other thing to take a stand in the full light of day from clients who dropped hundreds of dollars whenever their shopping itch demanded scratching.

"It's all right, child." Resignation bled from Hattie's face. "I've been staring at those sort of faces my entire life. And I'm the one with the Academy award at home. Ironic, huh?"

Dorothy joined them. "That white chiffon is awful dreamy," she said, "but we didn't come to cause you trouble."

"Try it on," Gwendolyn told her, ignoring the triplets. "It's too large for you, but it'll give us an idea of how to fix it."

One of the triplets cleared her throat like the narrator in a French farce.

"And Hattie, there's a light woolen suit near where you found the first one, more of a paprika red. The workroom's got tons of space to try everything. I'll be back to check on you."

She approached the three bottle blondes. "Ladies?" she said sweetly.

The one with the big boobs lowered her voice to a genteel but firm whisper. "Surely you can see how inappropriate it is for you to be attending this sort of clientele."

Gwendolyn had hoped she might be able to negotiate a middle ground. She took a half-step back and whispered, "You think they don't have enough money?"

"That's not what we mean," Triplet Number Two said, "and I'm pretty sure you know it."

Gwendolyn shook her head slowly and smiled, sweet as cotton candy. "I really don't."

"We're only looking out for your best interests."

"Trust us, Gwendolyn, you wouldn't want word to get out about this."

"About what?"

"Don't force us to say it out loud."

"I'm afraid you'll have to."

"Your regular clientele? You'll see none of them here once it gets out that you're catering to the colored element."

"You make them sound like crayons."

"You're a businesswoman and you need to be practical." Triplet Number Three finally found her voice. "If you plan on selling to Negroes in this part of town, you might as well just close your doors right now."

"And that would be a shame," Number One said, tempering her voice. "You have a delightful store and your perfume is divine. It would be awfully shortsighted of you to go against the grain of popular opinion—"

"Honestly, ladies, I'm surprised at you!" Gwendolyn exclaimed. "You've got all the class and breeding and social advantages that money can buy." Hundreds of "women's pictures" had taught Gwendolyn that in order to clobber fools like these, a girl must flatter them first. "I know at least one of you went to Bryn Mawr."

"Sarah Lawrence," Big Boobs said. "I fail to see—"

"It frankly disappoints me that of all people, you three— " *flatter, guilt, shame* " —would come in here to my store—" *remind them who rules the roost* " —and stop dead in your tracks because you can't see past the color of someone's skin."

"Don't label us Jim Crow!"

"Yeah!" Number Two agreed. "This is California, not Kentucky."

"Ladies," Gwendolyn said, more placatingly now, "surely we can act like responsible, forward-thinking adults, and concern ourselves more with doing the *right* thing than the *done* thing."

Gwendolyn heard a noise behind her. Hattie and Dorothy stood a few feet away. "Thank you," Dorothy said, "but we'll be going."

"You stay right there," Number One told her, then faced Gwendolyn. "My husband is head of casting at Universal, and he personally saw to it that—" she aimed a lacquered nail at Dorothy— "this girl was cast in a picture with Una Munson. He raved about her audition and insisted she was cast."

"That picture was called *Drums of the Congo*," Dorothy said. "I played Princess Malimi."

"You see? My husband is progressive, and so am I."

Gwendolyn wasn't sure how casting a Negro actress in the role of a Congolese princess qualified as progressive.

"But that means we all agree!" Gwendolyn exclaimed. "Your husband casts colored actresses—at least he didn't put Maria Montez in blackface, right? Meanwhile, you shop where that same actress is looking at buying an outfit or two. It's all the same!"

Gwendolyn had meant to win the woman over, but Number One started shaking her head.

"You're being pigheaded!"

"Perhaps we all are," Gwendolyn countered.

"No!" Number Three insisted. "*We* are being realistic. Are you really prepared to sacrifice your living for—for—"

"For the sake of doing the right thing?" Gwendolyn prompted.

As though by some prearranged signal, the Tinseltown Triplets in their matching hair and twenty-inch waists that probably hadn't seen solid food since their high school proms spun around and stormed out of the store.

Gwendolyn kept her eyes on the window and tried to beat back her doubts. She felt a presence over her shoulder.

"They're right, you know," Hattie said. "You'll pay a price."

"I prefer to think this world is changing," Gwendolyn said.

"Perhaps, but if my experience is anything to go by, change comes mighty slow."

"Well," Gwendolyn exclaimed, spinning around, "fiddle-dee-dee!" Immediately, she wished she hadn't.

Hattie's face lit up, her round eyes bulging with recognition. "Lord have mercy! My screen test! With the fire, and the hoop skirt! I *knew* that I knew your face! Once they hauled you off to hose you down, they grabbed some poor script girl to stand in your place. Ten minutes later, I was back in front of them cameras. The next thing I know, our screen test is being bandied about town like you were some freak exhibit at the zoo. Every time I heard about it, I shook my head and thought to myself, 'That poor girl. The humiliation!'" Hattie raised a hand and cast around the store. "You've landed on your feet, though."

"Yeah," Dorothy said, "but for how long?"

CHAPTER 20

Marcus pulled into the parking lot of the Riviera Country Club in the Pacific Palisades. The place had an eighteen-hole golf course and a sprawling four-story clubhouse with five wings, which meant George Cukor could be anywhere.

The previous week, when Marcus received George's note to meet him there, he couldn't have been more delighted. The two of them had been close friends throughout the thirties and into the war years, but life had led them down separate paths. Marcus had always made a point of going to see a new Cukor picture, even the ones with tarnished reputations, like *Two-Faced Woman*, which Marcus didn't think deserved to kill Garbo's career. But now George was helming his third Tracy-and-Hepburn flick, so evidently life for him was on the upswing again.

But why had George summoned him? Did he have news? Had he waited until he was away from the studio to present him with an opportunity to lift him off the graylist? Did George even know of the graylist? He was a deliberate man, not given to whim or time wasting, and always had a carefully considered purpose for everything he did.

True to her word, Lucille Ball had set up full access for Marcus to shoot the writing, rehearsing, and filming of what had now become a runaway hit. Somehow, Mr. and Mrs. Arnaz had conceived a show that everybody in America wanted to watch.

Marcus admired Lucille's foresight and pondered the irony that television had brought her the astonishing fame that eluded her as she toiled away as a featured player and starred in B-list movies.

But it wasn't full-time work. It was enough to cover rent and gas, but barely, and Marcus couldn't live on it indefinitely.

From the parking lot, Marcus glimpsed a sparkle of the blue Pacific past the vast expanses of lush, green lawns. But nowhere could he spot the movie location trucks and vehicles that were the usual giveaway.

In his note, George said to meet him at the Riviera Country Club at noon on January 20. But where?

Inside the clubhouse's hushed marbled foyer, he asked the girl behind the desk if she could direct him to where MGM was shooting. Soon, a caddy appeared, escorted him to a golf buggy, and drove him to the farthest link tucked away in the foothills of the Palisades. An armada of identical cars was lined up with military precision along a grove of cypress pines, in front of which lay a boot camp of tents and equipment.

A young man in his twenties, sporting a bow tie and clipboard, came running. "You must be Mr. Adler?"

"I am."

"Mr. Cukor asked me to bring you to him."

He led Marcus to a large, square canopy of white canvas, under which George was seated at a café table with room for two chairs. A glass pitcher had already been set up. When George caught sight of Marcus, he brightened. "May the martinis begin!"

He rose to his feet and enclosed Marcus in a tight hug. "It's so very good to see you, dear boy!"

When he and George became friends, Marcus was already in his late twenties and felt he scarcely deserved the "dear boy" moniker, but figured if MGM's best director wanted to call him that, who was he to say no?

George started pouring the drinks. "I caught up with Garson the other day. He mentioned you were back from Europe."

Even now, all roads led to the Garden of Allah. Garson Kanin and his wife, Ruth Gordon, had been regular faces, either in residence or at parties. They wrote four of Cukor's last six movies.

"It was nice to hear from you," Marcus said.

"How long have you been back?"

In some ways, the past ten months had flown by; in other ways they'd crawled. In his more despondent indulgences, Marcus wished Oliver had taken the time to tell him face-to-face, but in perkier moments, he thought *Screw it.*

Marcus clinked George's glass. "Not quite a year."

The tiniest sip of martini took him back to Sunday brunches at George's house above the Strip where some of the brightest and smartest men in Hollywood gathered to dish the dirt and sample the gourmet fare that their host laid out in generous amounts. That life felt a million years ago, back when nobody had heard of Hitler, McCarthy, or the Black Dahlia.

"I had lunch with Mervyn the other day," George said. "He told me about the excellent job you did on *Quo Vadis.* You've become quite the photographer, it seems."

"I'm glad he was pleased."

"More than pleased!" He gestured to a lackey who was hovering outside the tent. "Evidently, you've got a cinematic eye, and you know how to tell a story with both a typewriter and a camera. He went on about it for quite some time." He waited until the lackey had served them a small Caesar salad and retreated to the shade of the cypress pines. "And what's this I hear about *I Love Lucy*?"

"I caught a lucky break."

George chewed his salad and nodded thoughtfully as Marcus described life inside the eye of the *I Love Lucy* storm. Not that it compared to directing *Gone with the Wind* or *Camille*, but still, the television show was now the talk of water coolers and coffee klatches all over the country.

George wiped his mouth. "You need to find steadier work than that."

"I know," Marcus said. "A guy can't live on beans and rice forever. But at least I'm working, thanks to Mayer."

"Mayer got you that job?"

"No, he got me off the blacklist and onto the gray one."

George nodded slowly. "So there is such a thing. Mervyn alluded to it, but he got uncharacteristically vague when I pressed him for details."

"It means I can work, but I won't get a decent job with decent pay until I'm off the list altogether. If you've got an idea or suggestion, I'm all ears."

"You need to align yourself with someone in power. The trouble is—" George gouged out a chunk of romaine lettuce from between his front teeth "—the power players are waning. Mayer's gone. *Pat and Mike* is Hepburn's farewell to MGM. My next movie is an adaption of a Ruth Gordon play, but after that, I think MGM and I will have reached the end of the road."

An afternoon breeze chilled by the Pacific swept through the tent. "An MGM without George Cukor is almost as unthinkable as an MGM without L.B. Mayer."

"Thank you, dear boy, but that's the reality we now live in. I fear we're on the far side of Hollywood's peak. At least, the Hollywood *we* know."

"Finding someone who can help me off the graylist is going to be tricky, isn't it?"

George sat up in alarm. "I was talking about stopping you from sliding back onto the *blacklist*."

The appearance of poached salmon and sliced tomatoes gave Marcus time to ponder an outcome he hadn't considered. The smell of the fish wafted up, nauseating him. He forced himself to pick up his fork and jab at the salmon as though he couldn't decide which part to eat first. *Back on the blacklist? Back in limbo? Back on the roll call of Hollywood's personae non gratae?*

George said, "Have you heard of this new evangelist?"

Marcus was unprepared for this abrupt change in conversation. "I'm sorry, what?"

"The one getting so much press lately. Sheldon Voss."

It was hard to avoid the onslaught of coverage Voss' proposed Sea to Shining Sea March had garnered. Newspaper editorials posited the theory that the rise of Billy Graham and Sheldon Voss heralded a swing toward a more conservative national outlook. The postwar economy was booming and nobody wanted to mess with it.

"Yes," Marcus said, "I've heard of him."

"Did you know that Voss and Joseph Breen are college pals?"

"That's a scary thought."

"They went to the same college in Philadelphia." George lowered his voice. "I've been following this Voss character, and it's become nauseatingly clear that both those bastards detest fairies. Don't kid yourself — they're coming for us."

This was the first time Marcus had heard someone else talk about this Lavender Scare. He gave up all pretense of eating and slid his fork beside the china plate. "Go on."

"I have a friend who lives in DC. He's well connected politically, and he said that Voss courted Hoover and McCarthy. Voss views homosexuals as perverted deviants, and thinks the ones who have married are subverting the American way. In his opinion, that's unforgivable, which is why he considers Los Angeles a cesspit of sin and debauchery."

"What's the bet he's never even been out here?"

"Listen to me, Marcus. I've read everything I can get my hands on about this Voss character, and I think he's got Kathryn in his sights."

"You think or you know?"

"It's more of an educated guess. Voss has gone out of his way to curry favor with Hoover, and Hoover is pals with Winchell, who is top of the ratings. But who's creeping up close enough to nip him in the butt?"

"Kathryn."

"And who did she marry at the end of the war?"

"Me."

"Which means yours was a lavender marriage, and Hoover knows that. So does Winchell. It would behoove you, therefore, to assume Voss does too. Cesspits of sin and debauchery are too abstract for regular Mr. and Mrs. Joe Public. They need a face to match all that self-righteousness."

"But Kathryn's practically Betty Crocker's sister these days."

"If I were Voss, I'd be looking to see how those HUAC vipers did it. They accused famous people. The more wholesome the face, the greater the shock, the bigger the headline."

A new lackey approached the tent. "Mr. Cukor? Miss Hepburn wants to know when we'll begin shooting."

"Tell her fifteen minutes."

Marcus waited until they were alone again. "So you think Voss is starting to connect the dots that will lead him to a big fish."

"That guy is plenty cunning. It won't take him long. You need to get off the graylist, pronto, before you find yourself on the blacklist. Or worse."

"There's worse than the blacklist?"

"There's always worse."

Cukor laid his linen napkin beside his plate and stood up. "You've barely touched your salmon," he noted. "There's no rush just because I've got to go. I ordered chocolate mousse for dessert. It's been lovely seeing you again. Sorry I've got to go, but this glorious sun won't shine forever. Take all the time you need."

The tang of the poached salmon drifted up to Marcus again. He pushed the plate away until he could no longer smell it.

CHAPTER 21

Kathryn sat in Joseph Breen's reception area and thought *Ugh, and double ugh!*
She had never imagined she'd be sitting outside the office of the Hollywood censor who enforced a code of behavior that went out with Queen Victoria, gas lighting, and chastity belts.

"You've got a job to do," Marcus had told her over banana splits at Wil Wright's. "Plus, it'll put you inside the enemy camp where you can sniff around like Rin Tin Tin."

Kathryn would have preferred a Nancy Drew comparison, but she took his point.

When he came home to the Garden to detail his lunch with Cukor, she felt as sick as Marcus had. Of all the people Sheldon Voss could target, he just *happened* to choose his niece? An unlikely coincidence, but as Marcus pointed out, "Thomas Danford didn't know he was your father and Francine hasn't spoken to her brother in forty years."

The irony was the sort of unexpected development around which a Hollywood movie would turn. And if this were just some Lubitsch farce or a bittersweet Wilder allegory, she knew she could distance herself enough to figure out her best move. But this was her own life poised to unravel and she only had her instincts to see her through.

Kathryn shifted in the uncomfortable chair. She pulled off her gloves and withdrew a notepad from her purse to look over a list of questions she and Marcus had dreamed up over port wine.

Liberal-minded Hollywood had always seen Breen as a disapproving meddler who reveled in hindering creative expression. Kathryn's transcontinental cake-baking trek had reminded her how easy it was to forget that people outside of Hollywood were more traditional in their outlook.

"What if," she'd speculated to Marcus, "I give him a chance to air *his* side? Ask him what *he* thinks and what *he* feels? After all, we've always seen him as the enemy."

"Which he is."

"I bet he doesn't see it that way."

Breen's secretary, a surprisingly relaxed woman of thirty, capable and efficient, announced that he would see her now.

The guy resembled L.B. Mayer closely enough that they could be brothers. They had the same small wire-framed glasses and harsh eyes peering back at her.

"Miss Massey."

It was neither a question nor a statement, but more of an expression of disbelief.

He stepped aside to usher her into his office. It was a decent size, and filled with the usual filing cabinets and stacks of paper. It could have been an insurance office on the outskirts of Omaha. She took a seat on one side of his desk as he took the other.

He said, "You mentioned some sort of interview?"

"That's right. You see, it occurred to me that you've spent nearly twenty years saying 'No!' to Hollywood, but nobody's thought to ask you how you feel about what you do. I want to hear *your* point of view."

His vacant expression didn't change. "My point of view about what?"

"Everything. The Hays Code and how you interpret it, how it's changed over the years, how you see your role in the film industry and by extension, modern culture at large."

It was this type of "big picture" article that Wilkerson wanted from Kathryn now that Mike Connolly was covering the bitchy gossip. When Kathryn begrudgingly admitted to Gwendolyn that Connolly had a clever, albeit irritatingly self-satisfied, way of writing about the who's-doing-what-to-who side of the business, Gwendolyn suggested that perhaps he was forcing her to up her game. It took Kathryn a couple of days to realize Gwennie was right, which is why she was sitting in Breen's unremarkable office.

Breen's thin lips soured at the corners. "Don't you people talk to each other?"

"Which people?"

"You and Mr. Connolly."

"Of course. Why?"

"He was here yesterday. Called for an interview, just like you did."

Kathryn folded up her notepad. "May I ask what he wanted?"

"He asked me what I thought about this march that Sheldon Voss will be mounting this summer."

What did that have to do with the adulterous movie stars Connolly was supposed to be writing about? "He did?"

"I'm Catholic. So is Mike."

The switch from "Connolly" to "Mike" wasn't lost on Kathryn.

Breen started threading a Chesterfield through his fingers without lighting it. "And Voss' style of firebrand fundamentalism appeals to us both. He and I have much in common." He made a show of consulting his watch. "I'm sorry, Miss Massey, but Mike Connolly has beaten you to the punch. As I'm sure you can appreciate, I am a very busy man."

He raised his hand toward the door.

* * *

The drive back to the office gave Kathryn a chance to think through what had happened.

She had to admit she didn't hate Connolly as much as she'd expected to when he joined the staff four months ago. He had trained his incisive wit to titillate, but knew when to retreat.

With a couple of Friday-night-after-work drinks inside him, he was funny as blazes. That is, until the third scotch.

It was almost chemical. Jekyll and Hyde in a crystal tumbler.

He'd drop his guard and ogle a handsome patron across the bar. And his droll humor disintegrated into bitter invective he aimed at anyone who wandered into his sight. By the fourth drink, he was merciless; by the fifth, he was a mess.

Kathryn turned into the parking lot. *And this guy is Catholic? As in "Holy Father" and "Thou shalt not" and "Bless me for I have sinned"?* Kathryn couldn't imagine Mike Connolly voluntarily walking into a confessional, unless maybe he had three slugs of Johnny Walker under his belt and the priest looked like Montgomery Clift.

When she walked into the clattering newsroom, she bee-lined for Connolly's desk.

"I've just come from seeing Breen," she told him.

He unwrapped a piece of Juicy Fruit and flicked it into his mouth. "Oh, yeah?"

She planted both hands on the side of his desk and bent forward. "I thought you were supposed to cover the gossip, and leave the big issues to me."

"That's right. Nothing's changed." His response was a little too breezy.

"And whose camp does the Sea to Shining Sea March fall into?"

"Voss' march isn't showbiz related, so I figured you wouldn't care."

"Then why do *you*?"

"Because I'm diehard Irish-Catholic. So's Breen, so I figured I'd get his take on it. Why the hell are you looking at me like I just ran over your cat?"

"I had an idea for an editorial, but you'd already beaten me to it, so I just ended up looking like a dumb cluck."

"You should support it, you know."

"Support what?"

"Voss and his Sea to Shining Sea."

"Why would I do that? You heard the guy — he thinks Hollywood's a cesspit of Commies and deviants. We know that's not true."

"Do we?"

"Why would I support that nutcase's attempts to exploit the people who work in the movie business?"

Connolly scoffed. "I've never met him, so who knows if he's a nutcase or the next Billy Graham. But he *is* rallying a groundswell. You know he's making twelve stops, right?"

"So?"

"Twelve, as in twelve stations of the cross. Of course, I'm not the one with a national radio show and ratings to think about. But if I were, I'd be cogitating on how I could use this. I don't know how you got Sinatra, but I heard the ratings went through the roof."

Kathryn had been jittery about having Sinatra on live, but he'd arrived sober and prepared. He was note-perfect, and his comedy skit with Betty Hutton broke the audience up so wildly that the listeners at home were treated to seventy-one continuous seconds of nonstop laughter. Kathryn heard later it was a record for the station and the suits were almost peeing themselves with glee.

But like the New York broadcast, the triumph was a one-off. Kathryn needed to bring in consistently high ratings. Her show was still in the top ten, but sat around the number seven or eight mark. She needed something only radio could provide, and Mike Connolly just handed it to her.

* * *

Later that night at Nickodell's, Kathryn hadn't realized how preoccupied she'd been until Leo tapped his spoon against her glass.

"You want to tell me what's on your mind, or am I supposed to play Madame Arcati and divine the answer telepathically?"

"I'm sorry." She dropped the steak knife she'd been using to score deep grooves in the white tablecloth. "I've been presented with an idea I don't particularly like, by someone I don't particularly care for."

"Are you ready to share it with me, or do you need some more time to chew it over?"

Kathryn loved that Leo seldom rushed or pushed, and gave her the space to make her own decisions.

She held off until the waiter cleared away their escargot. As she took him through her confrontation with Mike Connolly and his suggestion about covering the march over the summer, she could see the eagerness igniting in his eyes.

"That's a great idea!" he gushed. "I haven't told you this, but the Betty Crocker guys want to relaunch their chiffon cake mix with a new box and revamped advertising. This is going to dovetail perfectly!"

"How does a new box of cake mix dovetail with a Bible-thumping crusade?"

"The whole Sunbeam-Crocker market is middle America and its small-town happy homemakers. You can bet most of them are regular churchgoers. The overlap is massive. Oh my God, yes, this is *fantastic*!"

"Does it not concern you that Sheldon Voss is a crook and a charlatan, and that his march is just a big hoax to swindle money from unsuspecting little lambs?"

"You don't know that for sure."

Kathryn went to snap off a caustic retort, but forced it back. She hadn't told Leo that Voss was a blood relative.

After coming across that *Washington Post* article at the Bogie and Bacall party, Kathryn asked Marcus if they could meet with the private eye who'd tracked down Oliver after he'd disappeared.

She wasn't terribly impressed with Dudley Hartman at first. He struck her as altogether too genial, like the uncle about whom everyone says, "Doesn't he remind you of Burl Ives?" But Marcus insisted Hartman knew what he was doing, so she hired him to dig into Uncle Sheldon.

It took him several weeks to confirm that Francine's information was on the money: the petty theft and small-time cons that led Sheldon in and out of jails across more than a dozen states. Cunningly, Sheldon had built his reputation on being open about his dubious past, using it as proof of his redemption. On the walls of his revival tents, he hung "redemption boards" that listed the people and organizations he had grifted. Moreover, he had paid back every one with the donations he collected.

Hartman told her, "This is one slippery fish. When someone like this suddenly becomes Mister Honest Joe, it usually means he's hiding something. It's what magicians call misdirection. 'Hey! Look over there while I do this over here.' Whatever this guy is up to, you can bet your last bootstrap it's not what he says he's doing."

Kathryn stared across the table at Leo and debated whether or not this was the time to share Hartman's findings. Leo stared back, expecting her to answer him. She realized that as much as she loved him, his loyalties were divided.

"No," she said, "I don't know for sure that Voss is a crook. Let's call it a hunch."

"Your hunches are usually spot on."

"Voss is coming here to declare war on homosexuals."

Leo motioned the waiter for more wine. "I'm sorry, but that sounds far-fetched."

"He saw how far HUAC got with Commies, and he wants to do the same with homos. He's smart enough to dress it up like Billy Graham so nobody questions his motives."

"So now Billy Graham's a big faker, too?"

"I didn't say that."

A strained hush fell over the table. The waiter arrived to refresh their glasses, and they still weren't speaking when he returned to deliver Leo's New York steak and Kathryn's swordfish just as June Allyson and Dick Powell made a movie-star entrance. Normally, Kathryn would make a quick table hop after they settled and ordered drinks, but tonight she wasn't in the mood.

As she and Leo dug into their dinners, the silence stretched thinner. Kathryn was determined not to break it — not that she had anything she could say, aside from confessing what she knew about Voss, and she wasn't ready to do that.

In the end, it was Leo who broke the silence.

"Okay," he said, "here's what we know. Winchell is conservative, but he rarely covers religious stories. So he's not likely to cover the march. But *your* show covering it has merit and it'll let you pull ahead of Winchell. What if we hook up a line of local radio stars to take a mike into the biggest meeting at each stop? Have you noticed that Voss has scheduled them for Friday nights?"

"Right during my slot."

"We can do a live hookup. Winchell won't have that. And remember, there's another five hundred in it for you every week your show hits the top spot."

"Don't you need the approval of Mr. Sunbeam to put that sort of deal on the table?"

"You let me worry about that."

"The idea of my show hitting number one is all very well, but I seriously doubt — "

"You don't think this march will take America by storm?"

That's the whole problem; I fear that it will.

"If you're right," Leo said, "you get the satisfaction of telling me 'I told you so.' If I'm right, you get everything. Either way, you win, but wouldn't it be sweeter to finish with a huge bonus, beat Walter Winchell, and have the biggest radio show in America?"

Of course it would, Kathryn wanted to say. She scraped some swordfish meat with her fork. *I should be jumping for joy. Then why do I feel like a whore?*

CHAPTER 22

Hell broke loose in Hollywood on a Thursday. The sky was clear and crisp, giving no indication of the coming uproar.

For the first couple of weeks after that ugly scene with the Tinseltown Triplets, Gwendolyn opened her store each morning wondering if this was the day she'd regret choosing the right thing over the sensible thing.

She wasn't sure what to expect. Projectiles thrown from passing cars? Threatening telephone calls?

But day followed day with nary a moldy tomato slamming her window. Foot traffic continued unabated, appointments for fittings were made, and perfume sales remained consistent. As February flowed into March, her apprehension faded away.

That Thursday morning in March, Gwendolyn's head was filled with DeMille's latest effort, *The Greatest Show on Earth*, which she'd seen the previous night with Bertie and Arlene. It had broken box office records and was on track to be the highest grossing movie of the year, but Gwendolyn wasn't sure why. She thought it was a bit overblown and ponderous, and she was still brooding over what she might have missed as she unlocked the rear door to Chez Gwendolyn and heard the telephone ringing.

She picked up the extension on the back wall.

"Good morning, this is—"

"Thank God you're there." The caller sounded like she was gasping for air.

"Marilyn? Is that you?"

"Have you seen the papers?"

"Why? What's happened?"

"I didn't think it would be such a big deal. I really didn't. But I'm positively besieged! The press. They're all over the sidewalk in front of my hotel. I need to get out! Can I come over? They won't think of looking for me there. I can hide in your back room until I figure out what to do."

Marilyn had a reputation of moving two or three times a year. "Where are you?"

"At the Beverly Carlton on Olympic. But I can't walk out the front door. I'm trapped!"

"Surely they have a fire escape."

"I DON'T KNOW!"

Through the line, Gwendolyn could hear a dull roar in the background. "Service elevator, maybe?"

"Yes!" The tremble in Marilyn's voice faded. "There's a back alley. I think it leads to Beverly Drive."

"Take it and grab the first taxi you see."

"I'll knock four times, pause, then twice so you'll know it's me."

Gwendolyn didn't know why Marilyn felt a secret code was necessary until she raced to the Sunset Strip newsstand and bought copies of the *Times*, the *Examiner*, and the *Hollywood Citizen-News*. Slapped across all three papers was the news that Hollywood's biggest blonde bombshell since Lana Turner had posed nude for a calendar.

Marilyn was hardly the first actress to drop her drawers for girlie pics. But in the past, if any pics were so much as hinted at, her studio's fixer would pay off the photographer, or go out and buy up all the copies.

And yet here was Marilyn Monroe, Twentieth Century-Fox's big blonde hope, freely confirming to a United Press wire reporter that the naked tootsie roll stretched out on red velvet for a trucker calendar was her.

This was big. Shocking. Revolutionary.

It was no wonder the press had besieged her.

Gwendolyn heard four knocks, a pause, then two more. She raced to her back door and yanked it open.

Marilyn flew inside, pulling a black silk scarf off her head and huge sunglasses from her face.

With her bright blue eyes and skin that glowed from within, the girl was angelic. Her hair was quite short now, and not nearly so bleached. Marilyn ran her nails through it. "I must look a fright!"

"Let's take a deep breath and let it out slowly." Marilyn mimicked how Gwendolyn filled her lungs, held in the breath, and gradually released it through O-shaped lips. The *Citizen-News* was still open to the article. Gwendolyn lifted it up. "I have to ask: What were you thinking?!"

Marilyn shrugged. "Girls do it all the time. Everybody knows that."

"But you're about to film your first starring role, and your *Life* magazine cover will be coming out soon. Not to mention your date last week with Joe DiMaggio."

"Those bozos at Fox wanted to issue a denial, but I told them they were nuts."

"Gutsy move."

"It's obviously me; to deny it would make us all look like fools. I took those pictures four years ago when I was broke and did what I had to do. And anyway," she pulled at her bulky black sweater, "under our clothes, we're all naked, so what's the big deal?"

"I bet Zanuck thinks it's a big deal."

The first glimmer of a smile emerged on Marilyn's face. "You got any coffee going? I haven't had a thing since yesterday."

As Gwendolyn fussed with the percolator, Marilyn filled her in.

The producers of her next movie, *Clash by Night*, had learned about the calendar and leaked it to Aline Mosby from United Press International, who called Fox's PR people for confirmation, who in turn panicked. When Marilyn refused to play the "It Ain't Me" game, Zanuck set up an exclusive interview.

"But surely none of you thought that would be the end of it," Gwendolyn said, setting out the coffee cups.

"If there was a discussion about what to do once the article came out, nobody thought to include me."

"So they just left you to cope with the repercussions on your own? Sounds typical, but this is hardly likely to cool down any time soon."

Marilyn wandered over to Gwendolyn's worktable. She picked up a length of baby pink ribbon left over from one of Ella Fitzgerald's stage costumes and threaded it through her fingers. "I can't imagine it will."

"So you take control of it."

Marilyn narrowed her eyes. "How?"

"I'd call Kathryn Massey."

"From the *Hollywood Reporter*? You two are friends, right?"

"If you're in a jam, you want her in your corner. She could probably whip up some sort of rebuttal."

Gwendolyn eyed the pink ribbon. Ella said she'd be in for a fitting "real soon," but was vague on specifics. Most clients squeezed in dress fittings between luncheons and bridge parties. With all this commotion, any day but today would be good for a drop-in. She wondered if she could get hold of Ella, but tracking down a performer on tour would take Sherlock Holmes and a bloodhound.

"Honey?" Marilyn's voice brought Gwendolyn's attention back into the room. "Your coffee pot?"

Gwendolyn rescued it from boiling over and set it on the sink. "So shall I call Kathryn?"

"I already said yes."

* * *

Kathryn arrived less than fifteen minutes later and greeted Marilyn with a winded "OH, YOU POOR THING!" as though she'd run all the way from the *Reporter*'s offices. "Here's the line we should take. You were broke, the rent was due, and you did what you had to. Everybody can relate to that. No humiliation. No excuses. No embarrassment."

Marilyn let out a whimper of joy and hugged Kathryn. "Thank you! There's no shame in being nude. We're all naked at least once or twice a day."

The two women settled on the threadbare sofa, so Gwendolyn withdrew into her salon to prepare for the day.

When Marilyn wandered into the store a few years ago, she was unaffected by the buffeting that inevitably warps a pretty girl scaling the Hollywood ladder. Each time their paths crossed, Gwendolyn could see evidence of a slow transformation.

Marilyn's voice was lower now, and breathier, and she'd developed a habit of pulling her top lip over her teeth when she spoke. There was a new baby-doll quality to it, too. And the dreamy innocence that filled her eyes, like she was only half-listening and was happy to go along with whatever you were saying—that was new, too.

What struck Gwendolyn now was how all that had fallen away when Marilyn rushed into the back room this morning. That panting, little-girl voice and the doe-eyed gaze had disappeared. But just now, when Kathryn arrived, they were back.

The realization left Gwendolyn to ponder what it took for a woman to succeed in Hollywood. Did they have to invent a character to give audiences what they wanted, what the bigwigs expected? Were they supposed to switch it on in public and off when nobody was around? *What if you forget how to turn it off?*

Gwendolyn couldn't decide if Marilyn Monroe was the cleverest girl she'd ever met, or an emotional breakdown waiting to happen.

Kathryn and Marilyn burst out into a fit of giggles. "Oh, that's perfect!" Marilyn exclaimed. "Maybe this isn't the iceberg that sinks my career, after all."

In a heady rush, Gwendolyn realized that girl in her back room whose naked body everyone was scrambling to ogle was having the career that Gwendolyn came to Hollywood for.

Twenty years ago, *she* was the doe-eyed ingénue, desperate to be discovered. *She* was the one brimming with enough gumption to dance on a human billboard and present herself to David Selznick in hoops and crinolines. But if this was the price of stardom, Gwendolyn was glad she'd never had to pay up.

Kathryn and Marilyn had been in the back room nearly half an hour when Chez Gwendolyn's front door whooshed open. "Where the *fuck* is she?"

Darryl Zanuck stood in the doorway, all five foot six of him, a snarl etched into his face.

Gwendolyn walked around the counter and gave him a moment to recognize her. "It's nice to see you again, too, Mr. Zanuck."

"Oh, it's you." His fists slid from his hips. "I didn't realize—hello. Nice to see you." He took a breath to calm himself. "As you can imagine, I've had a shit of a morning."

Gwendolyn had dealt with this pint-sized power player enough not to be intimidated. It wasn't often that someone like her held the cards, and frankly, it was fun. "You think Marilyn is here?"

"You think there's anything I don't know about that girl?"

Kathryn slipped in front of the black velvet curtain that shielded the messy back room—and Marilyn—from sight. "You didn't know about the calendar."

Zanuck shook his head at Kathryn, almost smiling. "I swear to God. The way you people can sniff out a story makes a guy wonder if you've got ESP."

Kathryn crossed her arms. "I would've thought that you and those jumpy gazelles in publicity had more sense than to let Aline Mosby's story go out over the wires without a follow-up plan."

"Is she back there?" Zanuck pointed to the curtain. "She okay?"

"No thanks to you."

Zanuck closed his eyes as he nodded slowly. When he opened them again, he asked, "May I see her?"

Kathryn shot Gwendolyn a look. *If he's asking permission, it means he's screwed up and he knows it.*

Kathryn pulled open the curtain.

As Zanuck marched toward it, Gwendolyn told him, "Be kind."

Kathryn and Mr. Twentieth Century-Fox disappeared behind the black velvet as Gwendolyn went to close the front door, but she hadn't reached it when Ella Fitzgerald and Lena Horne appeared.

Gwendolyn used to see Lena at the Hollywood Canteen during the war. Bette Davis had been especially keen to recruit her to dance with the colored servicemen. Under Bette's orders, the Canteen had been desegregated, but allowing colored men to dance with white girls was too progressive—even for Bette.

Ella said, "Lena's got a gig in Chicago and needs a new outfit, so she tagged along."

Ella's dress was hanging on a rack in the workroom and Gwendolyn wasn't sure what damage she might wreak if she interrupted the drama playing out back there.

Ella laid a light hand on Gwendolyn's arm. "Miss Lena *always* knows what she wants."

Gwendolyn had only seen Lena in low lighting at the Canteen. She possessed the same glow as Marilyn did, as though lit from inside by a torch.

"I need something full length," Lena said. "Mermaid silhouette, sweetheart neckline, preferably strapless. Tight around the bust and hips. I want it in periwinkle. Iris in a pinch, but don't even think of showing me anything mauve."

Clients like these were a blessing and a curse. Women with specific tastes saved Gwendolyn hours of time wasted on screwy ideas that wouldn't suit. On the other hand, they would rarely compromise—even when their concept was impossible or unflattering.

Gwendolyn was about to tell Lena she had nothing like that in the store when the metal hoops of her velvet curtain slid across the rod. Darryl Zanuck stiffened when he spotted Ella and Lena in his path. He stared at them, stunned, as they stared back at him. He nodded briskly and stomped toward the sidewalk.

"A word, please," he told Gwendolyn. "Outside. Now."

Gone was the supplicating executive; the commander-in-chief was back. Gwendolyn followed Zanuck out onto Sunset.

"Kathryn's guaranteed me two thousand words by four o'clock," he said.

"So everything's okay?"

Zanuck jacked a thumb at the women inside the store. "What the hell are they doing here?"

"Ella Fitzgerald and Lena Horne are customers."

Though short in stature, Darryl Zanuck always managed to seem like he was looking down at someone, even if that someone towered over him by at least three inches. "What do you think you're doing?"

"I—"

"You can't have people like that in your store."

Gwendolyn half-expected this sort of blinkered attitude from the Tinseltown Triplets, but not from someone as sophisticated as this egotistical pipsqueak. "I can't?"

"One dumb bitch per day is my limit, so for chrissakes spare me that *W-w-w-what?* face. I'm grateful that you gave Marilyn a safe haven until we got this mess sorted out, so I'm doing you a favor." He tapped the window with a knuckle. "You cannot be catering to that clientele. Who they are is beside the point. As it happens, I admire those women, and have nothing against them personally."

A dark burgundy limousine pulled up at the curb beside them. Zanuck's uniformed chauffeur jumped out and opened the passenger door. "But you're downright stupid if you believe you can sell to them and think there won't be backlash."

Gwendolyn watched, speechless, as he climbed into the car and sped west, then she turned to observe Ella and Lena chatting with Kathryn and Marilyn. Feeling Gwendolyn's eyes on her, Ella turned to look at Gwendolyn and very slowly shook her head.

CHAPTER 23

Lucille grimaced. "You don't even know what crow's feet are."

"Sure I do," Desi replied. "They're just like pigeon toes."

The director held up his hand. "Technically, that's not the line."

Desi examined his script and read out loud, "Yes I do, they're like pigeon toes."

There were two sure things on the *I Love Lucy* set: Only Lucy could make fun of Ricky's Cuban accent, and Desi needed to read his script once to memorize his lines, and twice to memorize everybody else's.

Desi forgetting a line was a first, and Marcus wanted to capture the moment. He raised his camera and zoomed in on the guy's face. He half-pressed the shutter just as his stomach growled. A roiling gurgle followed.

He ignored it and captured a touching tableau of Desi marking up his script as Lucille watched her husband with unguarded tenderness. After filming thirty-three episodes, they only had two to go and the first season would be over. Marcus was sure Lucy would want that photo included in the official end-of-season album she had planned.

Marcus admired how well Lucille and Desi had coped with the enormity of their popularity. According to CBS, *I Love Lucy* was on track to become the first television show to reach ten million households. Thirty million viewers was staggering, but the most famous married couple in America simply came to work with a job to do, a script to finish, costumes to choose, and pratfalls to choreograph.

Marcus was deeply grateful that he'd managed to land in the eye of Hurricane Lucy, even though he was only scraping by financially. But he'd lived on very little before, and he could do it again.

Other blacklisted writers were doing the best they could. One he knew was a bartender at the Frolic Room on Hollywood Boulevard, another was editing the Diners Club magazine, and someone else drove a garbage truck. Meanwhile, Marcus was being paid to document a phenomenon that bloomed larger and brighter every week. Okay, so he wasn't being paid enough to live on, but he figured he was still in the game, if only on its periphery.

Back in February, the girls pooled their money and bought him a super-whiz-bang camera with an improved zoom lens and flashbulb. Lucille had been so thrilled with the results that she hinted at an end-of-season bonus. That was only two weeks away, after which there'd be nothing for a month.

The movie extra work that had been so easy to land a year ago had dried up just as he started thinking of it as a regular job. He understood now that it was just a lucky streak; suddenly he was "too old" or "too young" or "too honest" or "too hayseed." If it wasn't for *I Love Lucy*, he'd have moved out of the Garden by now and into some dingy boardinghouse.

His stomach rippled under his hand, sounding like a clogged drain opening up.

The director, Marc Daniels, stared at Marcus, then at the clock on the wall. "It's close enough to lunchtime, so let's break. See you all back in an hour."

Going without lunch the three days a week he was at the studio saved him nearly five bucks. Marcus lingered as the cast and crew wandered away, thinking he'd get some shots of the deserted set. He was loading a fresh roll of film when a voice from his past said,

"So the rumors are true."

Anson Purvis first came into Marcus' life not long after the war, back when Marcus ran MGM's writers' department. Later, it was Purvis who offered Marcus work on *The Lone Ranger*, which filmed at the same studios.

Purvis was conspicuously thinner and paler, and walking with a cane, which only served to highlight the contrast between the virile individual Marcus knew at MGM and the emaciated figure that faced him now.

Marcus shook Purvis' hand. "The last time I saw you, they were carting you away in a diabetic coma."

Purvis leaned against the Ricardos' kitchen counter. "And I woke up five days later."

"If I'd know you were back running *The Lone Ranger*, I'd have swung by to say hello."

It was a bromide, but Purvis acknowledged it with a nod. "I'm just a staff writer now."

"You should be writing for the movies," Marcus said, "not that cowboys-and-Indians tripe—no offense."

"You should be, too."

"Yeah, well, *Red Channels* had other plans. So, how are things with the Masked Man?"

"Fact is, I'm so bored that I want to stab myself in the eye with a hypodermic." Purvis scratched his scalp. "I miss the big ideas and big themes; lavish sets and casts of hundreds. And real stars with real star power. Come on, you must miss it, too."

Marcus hadn't permitted himself the indulgence of missing a job he might not ever be allowed to do again. Escaping the blacklist put him ahead of most of his exiled colleagues, but getting off the graylist was proving to be problematic. However, wallowing in a pit of yesterdays felt like a luxury he couldn't afford.

"I wish I could help," he said.

"Maybe you can. I was in the parking lot yesterday when I heard the writers from the *George Burns and Gracie Allen Show*. They were talking about Quentin Luckett over at Paramount. You're friends with him, right?"

"I am, yes."

"So I was thinking maybe you could . . ."

"Put in a good word?"

"I can try," he told Anson.

"I don't want to put you in an awkward position or anything."

"You once did me a favor when I needed it the most. The least I can do is make a phone call."

* * *

When Marcus called the next day, Quentin invited him onto the Paramount lot for "lunch or something." From what Marcus could gather, only people above a certain pay grade knew of the graylist. As head of writing at Paramount, did that include Quentin? Was the "or something" an escape clause?

Quentin stood in the doorway of his office, his arms outstretched and a genuinely warm smile on his face. "Such a sight for sore eyes! I can't tell you how happy I was to hear from you!"

Even in his forties, the guy had managed to retain his baby face, albeit slightly wrinkled around the edges, and his reddish-blond hair was now a whitish-gray. He pointed to the camera in Marcus' hands. "Is that the new model?"

Knowing that Quentin was a photography buff, Marcus had used his new camera as bait when he called. But now he almost felt guilty about employing such a ruse.

With enough room for a large table, Quentin's corner office was twice the size of Marcus' at MGM. Bright sunlight streamed in from two sides as the jaunty notes of a rehearsal pianist floated in through the open windows.

Marcus held up the camera for Quentin to see.

"I bet it zooms like a prince."

"More like a queen," Marcus replied, smirking.

His joke didn't quite land. Quentin's smile fell away. "Listen, I need to go over and crack some skulls on the *Road to Bali* set. You can loaf around here or meet me at the commissary."

"Or tag along maybe?"

After months at a second-string outfit like General Services Studios, Marcus longed to be on a "real" back lot, just like Anson Purvis did. He hated to admit it, but he envied the way Quentin marched past the soundstages and workshops, nodding at workers like the big man on campus.

"Do you ever hear from Trevor?" Quentin asked.

"Not since I left Italy. He was about to start filming a movie with Gina Lollobrigida."

"The one about the guillotine?"

"Trevor's playing Joseph Guillotin and she plays his wife."

"Ah, yes, *The Lady and Her Blade*. Horrible title."

Marcus could tell that he knew exactly what his ex was doing and where he was doing it. Trevor had been gone from LA more than two years; Marcus found comfort that he wasn't alone in finding it hard to let go of former boyfriends.

They entered a soundstage filled with formal gardens of what passed in Hollywood for a Balinese palace, with a painted dusk backdrop behind a forest of palm trees. In the center Bing Crosby and Bob Hope were incongruously dressed in matching gray-and-purple kilts. On a *Road To* picture, screen logic trumped real-life sense every time.

"Hopefully this won't take too long," Quentin said. "Just hang around here and I'll take you to the executive dining room later. My treat."

Marcus ran his hand along one of the palm trees. They were made of balsa wood and swayed at the slightest touch, but they were painted realistically. There must have been fifty of them planted carefully across the rear.

It reminded him of the day he wandered onto the set of *Honolulu*, an Eleanor Powell movie, and stumbled over a cable into a balsa palm tree, almost setting off a domino effect that would have toppled twenty trees if not for the producer's quick reflexes. Jack Cummings was Mayer's nephew and could have reported the incident to Uncle Louis, but he didn't. They got a *boy-that-was-a-close-one* laugh out of it and never mentioned it again.

Mayer often entered Marcus' thoughts these days. Lifting him off the blacklist was generous, especially as he hadn't asked for a favor in return.

"Excuse me." A young guy with a wispy moustache pointed to the camera in Marcus' hands. "Is that the new Leica?"

"It is. You want to take a look?"

"As a matter of fact, I was hoping I could borrow it." The guy grimaced like he'd just stepped on a nail. "I'm the production photographer and I just dropped my camera. This concrete floor busted it all apart and Mr. Hope's going to blow a gasket if I have to tell him."

"You don't have a backup?"

"Normally, yes, but it froze on me yesterday."

"You're not having a good week."

"No, sir, I am not. I was wondering if perhaps I could rent yours."

Marcus didn't really want to part with his precious baby, but his ears pricked up. "For how long?" He really meant, *For how much?*

"Today and tomorrow. How's about five bucks per day?"

Ten bucks bought Marcus a month of beans and rice. "Sounds good."

"Man, oh man, have you ever saved my bacon!"

Marcus fished out his card. "You can return it here any time over the weekend." Even though the guy accepted Marcus' camera like it was the crown jewels, Marcus panicked for a second and questioned the wisdom of handing over his sole source of income to a stranger. For all Marcus knew, he was just some nobody who'd snuck onto the Paramount lot. *Then again,* he told himself, *there was a time when* you *were a nobody who snuck onto the MGM lot.*

"And you are . . .?" Marcus prompted.

"Sam Dodds. I don't have a calling card, but I can be reached through the Hope Enterprises offices here on the lot."

"Hello, Sam." Quentin was back already. He clapped his hands together. "I'm famished and the commissary has a chicken pot pie you won't believe."

As they headed for the commissary, Marcus asked if he knew Sam, and more specifically, whether he could be trusted with his fancy new Leica.

"Yeah, Sam's a good guy. And pretty talented, too. He got this great shot of Hope and Jane Russell on *Son of Paleface*. Hope's staring at her chest like he was Ponce de León and she's the fountain of youth."

They passed a soundstage with *Come Back, Little Sheba* written in chalk on a blackboard out front. Quentin pointed inside. "The higher-ups thought we were going to lose that one to your old stomping ground. The script's terrific; I just hope it translates to the screen, but you never know."

Quentin babbled about movies and stars as they walked around the lot. He wasn't usually much of a prattler, so Marcus wondered what this stream of behind-the-scenes gossip and intrigue was masking.

"If you've got a busy day, we don't have to have lunch," Marcus suggested.

Quentin halted. "I know about the graylist."

Marcus jammed his hands into his pockets. "Yeah, I was wondering about that."

Quentin led Marcus into a deserted soundstage where a vaudeville theater still stood in case reshoots were needed on the new Dean Martin-Jerry Lewis picture. Quentin sat them down on a pair of seats at the end of the final row. "When you phoned me, I got the feeling that it wasn't purely a social call."

"It's not," Marcus admitted.

"Come on, then. Out with it."

Marcus told him about Anson Purvis, how he was stuck on *The Lone Ranger* and aching to do more.

"He wrote that war picture for you, didn't he?"

"*The Final Day* was his, and so was *Pacific Broadcast*."

"Would he work without screen credit?"

In the sunshiny days before the Hollywood blacklist, not getting screen credit was anathema to screenwriters. But now tons of writers were working for a fraction of their former salaries and giving the credit to other writers, some of whom didn't exist at all.

"He might," Marcus told Quentin.

"We've got this picture, *Jamaica Run*, an adventure yarn set in the Caribbean. The script's okay but it needs punching up. Done right, it could be pretty good."

"Shall I get him to call you?"

Quentin tilted his head away from Marcus. "I thought the favor would be for you."

Marcus laid out his predicament. Shooting on the set of *I Love Lucy* was great, but what he really needed was a way to get off the graylist. However, nobody could explain to him what the graylist was, and how it worked, let alone how to escape it.

"You need someone at the top of the food chain," Quentin said. "Now that Mayer's out of the game, Zanuck's your man. That's tricky, though. He works real long hours and his social life is largely marathon poker games with high rollers. But if you can get in front of him, you might stand a chance. You must know somebody who knows him."

George Cukor had said the same thing about Dory Schary, the new MGM honcho, but had offered no path to him. On the other hand, getting in front of Zanuck wasn't entirely out of the question.

When Kathryn tackled Marilyn's pinups on the air, she transformed a sensational headline into a sympathetic opinion piece of the industry's harsh treatment of vulnerable girls, and she'd heard through the grapevine that Zanuck felt indebted to her.

But was that enough to get Marcus within earshot of Zanuck to plead his case? Even if it was, would it be fair to ask Kathryn to call in a favor she might need for some future scandal?

"Hey, I promised you chicken pot pie." Marcus and Quentin strolled out into the noonday sun. "Did you know we're planning a movie about the *Titanic*? Maybe you can talk your way onto that one."

"Talk my way ONTO the *Titanic*? That's what I call fabulous irony."

CHAPTER 24

When Kathryn got out of the taxi with her mother, she could already hear the buzz spilling through the front door of Romanoff's and onto Rodeo Drive.

"Are you sure you're up for coming in?" Kathryn asked Francine. "I'll be working the room, so I'll have to desert you. You could just take this cab home."

It wasn't that Kathryn felt stymied by her mother's presence, but she had a lot to accomplish inside Romanoff's, and she could be more efficient if she didn't have to worry about her mother.

"Heavens, no!" Kathryn wasn't aware her mother's voice could even go that high. "I'm still trembling with excitement. I doubt I shall sleep tonight *at all!*"

"That was a heck of a concert, wasn't it?"

Francine bunched her gloved hands together. "When Judy broke out into 'The Trolley Song,' I broke out into goosebumps! All over my body!"

"You weren't the only one." Kathryn paid the taxi driver and guided her mother toward the front doors. "When she hit that note near the end — well, that did it for me."

As soon as Judy Garland walked into the spotlight earlier that evening, Kathryn knew it would be a night that divided people into two groups: those who'd be talking about it and those who'd wish they could.

During her one-woman show at New York's Palace Theatre the year before, Judy had put to rest any doubts that she was as washed-up as her critics would have it. Truthfully, she didn't just put those doubts to rest; she walloped them over their head, dragged them to the back alley, and bludgeoned them into bloody pools of mush. By the time she finished her nineteen-week run, she was ready for a triumphant return to California to prove there was a whole lot more life left in her.

Every song Judy sang and every joke she cracked at the Los Angeles Philharmonic Auditorium met with roars of approval. But Kathryn was most surprised — and touched — to see the man a lot of people blamed for Judy's crushing addictions and erratic behavior. L.B. Mayer was the one who'd insisted on force-feeding Judy uppers and downers to get her through her arduous schedule. And maybe he was to blame, but Kathryn knew he'd also footed most of Judy's medical bills. Or was that just another rumor?

Ever since Mayer's ousting from MGM, he and Lorena were rare birds on the social scene. Kathryn knew that the after party at Romanoff's would be a nut house, but it might be her only chance to corner Mayer and confirm these Judy stories.

She'd also heard talk of Mayer staging his own comeback with a new sort of movie house. With television slashing into movie attendance, the logical leap for the studios was toward even bigger screens. Was that what Mayer was up to? Kathryn felt sure he'd refuse to be sidelined, and she figured if she could find out what he was planning and convince him to return to her show to announce it, Winchell could kiss her sweet patootie.

There was also that little matter of why Mayer had so generously lifted Marcus off the blacklist. Her curiosity burned like a Roman candle.

She pulled open the heavy wooden door to Romanoff's; the chatter swelled. Mayer was nowhere to be seen, but Joan Crawford was circling Louella Parsons. Joan's fruitful contract at Warners was coming to an end, and Kathryn suspected it would be interesting to know her plans for her next move, because Joan Crawford always had a next move.

When Marcus approached Kathryn about getting in front of Zanuck, she'd put in several calls, but Zanuck was up to his armpits in *The Snows of Kilimanjaro*. His secretary told her that until the movie was in the can, he was scarcely returning any calls, so she shouldn't feel slighted. On top of everything else tonight, she was also on the lookout for Zanuck.

She spotted a cocktail waiter standing under a huge white double-R emblem on the back wall. The minimalist décor was unusual, but somehow the owner, Michael — who passed himself off as a European prince but who everybody knew was a pants presser from Brooklyn — made it work.

A pair of gimlets later, Kathryn had pointed Francine in the direction of Louella Parsons, who Francine knew through the Association of Hollywood Mothers. It left Kathryn free to strike up a one-sided conversation with Joan Crawford about the troubles she was having with her teenage daughter, Christina.

Joan was still bitching about Christina's ingratitude — "I should have left her where I found her!" — when a beaming Judy made her entrance to a thunderclap of applause. Judy's manager, Sid Luft, made a rehearsed but heartfelt speech about bringing Judy home.

Conversation was returning to its previous pitch when Kathryn spotted L.B. and Lorena. It was jarring to see the former king of Hollywood sitting alone with his wife, but it suited her purpose.

She opened with a bright exclamation about how marvelous it was to see Judy performing at the top of her game. Oh yes, they agreed, quite marvelous. She segued into the rumors she'd heard about L.B. developing a new cinematic format, but he clamped down like a prison door and murmured that he couldn't talk about that just yet.

It was a perfect opportunity to change subjects.

"My friend Marcus, you did him a huge favor. So many of MGM's writers got dumped on the blacklist. You could have helped any of them, but as far as I'm aware, Marcus was the only one."

"And you want to know why." Mayer rolled his cigar around his fingertips, mulling something over.

"Go on," Lorena prodded. "You might as well tell her."

"Okay," Mayer conceded, "but you can't tell him."

Kathryn shook her head. "We don't keep secrets from each other."

"I can respect that, so how about we drop it?" He jabbed his cigar toward a lone figure leaning against the deep rose suede that covered Romanoff's walls. "That character looks mighty suspicious. Do you know who he is?"

It was Winchell's rake. That's what Kathryn called the skinny moocher with the malleable loyalties she encountered the night of Lili St. Cyr's arrest. He held a steno pad in one hand while the other sped down the page like he was making a list. Kathryn bet it was names.

"Yes, I do." Kathryn hadn't given up on getting Mayer's reason for helping Marcus, but this was something she couldn't ignore. "Excuse me, please."

She headed straight for him. He didn't flinch when he saw her coming.

"You pop up in the darnedest places," she said.

"Don't I just?"

She flicked a finger at the pad in his hands. "Taking notes for Winchell?"

"Not tonight, Josephine."

"Awww, did he fire you?"

"He wasn't happy to learn that my allegiance was so easily bought. Nor was he surprised. He knows when you get right down to it, we're all whores. We just got different prices, is all."

"If you're not working for Winchell tonight, will it cost me another wad to find out who you *are* nosing around for?"

His smirk blurred with a flicker of warmth, possibly even genuine. "You're funny," he said. "You work a room like you don't care who's watching."

"Maybe I don't."

"Yeah, you care. But that's what I like about you."

"So show me your list."

"Who said it's a list?"

"I could tell by the way your hand moved down the page."

"Says the gal who doesn't care."

Laughter exploded from a large group at the center of the room. Judy hit a high C and held it, catching the rake unprepared long enough for Kathryn to snatch the notebook from his hand. He went to grab it back but she stepped away and scanned the page.

As she suspected, it was a list of people in the room. Not a full list, though, but an apparently random one. Husbands but not their wives, wives but not their husbands, agents but not their clients. There was no pattern that Kathryn could make out, so why did some of them have an asterisk?

"Who are these people?" she asked.

"Is there even *one* person in this room whose name you don't know?" He was getting smart-alecky now, and it was annoying.

"And why do some of them have an asterisk?" He stared at her, saying nothing. "Do I need to come up with some cash? Is that what that face is supposed to mean?" Still nothing.

"Fifty is yours if you tell me."

The twerp didn't react at first. Then, "I'm pulling double duty tonight. I'm what you might call an advance scout."

"Who for?"

"A New York publisher. He's planning to start a new magazine, probably another cheesy rag like his other efforts. I doubt you've heard of him."

"Try me."

"Robert Harrison. He's pals with Winchell, who recommended me for the job."

The name meant nothing to Kathryn. "What's your other duty?"

"Sheldon Voss." Kathryn felt a dull pain press against her chest. "He's hired me to scout LA for possible venues for his tent revival meeting. It's gonna be a doozie."

"You're going to suggest Romanoff's?"

"Hardly." He tried to suppress a smile. "He also wants me to recruit volunteers."

"The hell you are," she told him. *Your job is to provide my shady uncle with a list of people he can denounce during his big LA broadcast.*

"Kathryn? I'm getting awfully tired."

Francine's timing wasn't great. Her face was turning red — a clear sign that she was getting fatigued. Kathryn grabbed her mother's arm and guided her toward the exit. A taxi was already idling out front. Kathryn told the driver to take them to the Marmont, and fell against the back seat.

"That was certainly a night to remember," Francine declared.

"Sure was, Mom."

The driver made a swift U-turn and headed north. By the time he reached a deserted Wilshire, Kathryn's mind had drifted back to the asterisks on the rake's list. There was a pattern. She could feel it.

And what about Mayer? Had Marcus done Mayer a favor and this was payback? But surely Marcus would know if he had. Did something happen during the making of Quo Vadis? *Or did it have to do with Mayer's departure from MGM?*

As the taxi drove up Rodeo toward Sunset, she connected the dots between all those asterisks and let out a startled, "Oh!"

Francine grabbed her daughter's arm. "What's the matter?"

Kathryn faked a smile and wondered if Marcus was still awake.

CHAPTER 25

Gwendolyn was laying out the last of the punch cups on the patio table next to the diving board when Marcus called from inside the bar.

"What about now?"

She looked up at the trees. "Nope."

"Dammit!"

"Marcus, honey, forget about it."

"But they'll look so pretty if I can just figure this out."

Marcus had spent nearly two hours stringing up tiny lights among the trees surrounding the Garden of Allah's pool. But now that he'd hung twelve sets of them with yards and yards of wiring, the damned lights refused to glow. It felt cruel to keep his hopes up, but she knew why he persisted.

He didn't have the funds right now to contribute booze or food to the party, but he could string up the coils of lights he'd recently unearthed in the basement of the main building.

"I could at least add atmosphere." He'd tried to hide his embarrassment behind a chipper mask that probably would have fooled someone who hadn't known him for twenty years.

"And you could take photos," Gwendolyn suggested. "I'm sure Marilyn would love some pictures as a keepsake."

A few weeks ago, when Gwendolyn asked Marilyn if she had any plans for her twenty-sixth birthday, she was shocked that the answer was no.

Over the past year, the girl had become one of the most talked-about new stars in Hollywood.

Then she started dating Joe DiMaggio.

And *then* the news of her nude calendar broke. Suddenly the whole world was gaga for Marilyn and yet nobody was throwing her a party? Gwendolyn told her there would be a poolside potluck at the Garden and to invite anyone she wanted.

"What about now?" Marcus called again.

A warm summer breeze blew down from the Hollywood Hills and through the trees, stirring the top branches. But they remained lit solely by the setting sun.

"Nope," she told him. "I need you to hop over to Schwab's for the ice. They asked if you could go to the back door." No response. "Marcus? You haven't electrocuted yourself, have you?"

A thousand tiny bulbs suddenly bathed the oaks and maples around the piano-shaped pool in golden light. It was enchanting.

"I kept shorting a fuse." He stepped out onto the patio and rotated full circle. "Not too shabby, huh?"

Gwendolyn kissed his cheek. "James Wong Howe couldn't have done better. Now, scoot over to Schwab's."

He wasn't gone a minute before a squeal pierced the evening air. "You should have warned me!"

Marilyn walked through the bar's French doors wearing the purple gingham halter dress Gwendolyn made for her the previous week. Gwendolyn wasn't sure gingham was right for such a glamorous creature, but watching the girl totter onto the patio, it was clear that Marilyn could knock 'em dead wearing anything at all.

Gwendolyn swung her arms up. "You have Marcus to thank for the lights."

Billy and Dona Travilla emerged behind Marilyn armed with four bottles of champagne.

Marilyn carried two large platters. "I made cocktail knishes, chicken-salad cream puffs, and broiled mushroom caps."

"All that and she cooks, too!" Dona exclaimed.

Marilyn set them on the buffet. "Joe is Italian, and you know how they are about food. Admit you're serving store-bought and you might as well say you stole it."

Gwendolyn hoped Billy had made it onto Marilyn's guest list. She'd only just learned that, technically, Dona was colored. But she was so light-skinned that she passed for white, which meant far more roles were open to her. It also explained why she knew Ella Fitzgerald well enough to go backstage.

Gwendolyn hoped to find a moment to steer Dona into a quiet corner and ask why none of her Negro clientele had returned since the day Zanuck was in the store three months earlier—not Ella, nor Lena, Hattie, or Dorothy. Hadn't she made it clear how welcome they were? Had she offended them? Or had Zanuck scared them off?

Dishes of food, bottles of booze, and gifts for the birthday girl started arriving. The party kicked up a notch when Bertie arrived with her latest toy: a new-fangled Japanese transistor radio. Gwendolyn wasn't sure what transistors were, but it meant manufacturers could now shrink radios down to a portable size. Bertie switched it on and the smooth voice of Rosemary Clooney singing "Come On-a My House" floated among Marcus' twinkling lights.

Gwendolyn knew a few faces, but many were new. How refreshing to find they weren't the usual raft of hopefully-famous-one-day neophytes: self-consciously good-looking men and women unable to maintain eye contact in case they missed a once-over from a casting director or producer.

Instead, Marilyn's friends came across as people who actually read books. Gwendolyn was willing to bet that the cadaverously tall man in thick black glasses could read Dostoyevsky and Proust in the original. And behind him, two women in their early twenties dressed in identical tight black slacks and turtlenecks were discussing the black beret one of them wore.

She'd heard about these postwar teenagers who rejected marriage and motherhood in favor of avant-garde poetry and Sartre. Gwendolyn thought the somber garb and existential angst of these so-called beatniks was more suited to Greenwich Village than Griffith Park, but they were a welcome change from the usual polished baubles.

"Come with me," Marcus told Gwendolyn, coming up behind her. "You need to hear this."

He steered her toward a gray-haired man in the type of conventional suit usually found on a board member of a multinational corporation. "This is Charles Brackett."

Gwendolyn told him how pleased she was to meet the writer of *Sunset Boulevard*, which she'd loved so much she saw it twice. Brackett gallantly bowed his head, but not before Gwendolyn detected a discreet eye-roll.

Marcus explained, "Charles no longer writes with Billy Wilder. He's moved from Paramount to Fox." He placed subtle emphasis on the word "Fox," which Gwendolyn took to mean "Darryl Zanuck, who I'm desperate to meet."

Marcus continued, "He was just telling me that he wrote *Niagara*, which Marilyn starts filming tomorrow. And he's now working on *Titanic*."

"That must be interesting." Gwendolyn wondered why she needed to know any of this. She searched around for Dona.

Brackett nodded toward the beatnik girls. "As our friends over there might say, it's a gas."

"Gas is good, right?"

He nodded. "The sets really are a sight to behold. You might say they're titanic."

"But Charles," Marcus said, "tell Gwendolyn what you were saying about your recent trip back East."

Brackett pulled out a pipe and took his time lighting it. Off to the far right, Gwendolyn spotted Dona near the huge daisy bush next to Kathryn's villa, chatting with Bertie and Doris, Marcus' sister.

"I went to New York for a reunion of sorts. I once worked at the *New York Evening Graphic*. It was the most god-awful rag—the *PornoGraphic*, we used to call it—but a great bunch of fellows, nevertheless. For years now, we've caught up with each other on a regular basis. Over time, it's become just once a year, but the numbers swelled to include anyone who wrote for New York papers in the twenties and thirties, some of whom have gone on to national prominence, like Ed Sullivan—"

"And Walter Winchell," Marcus interjected. "Another regular is Robert Harrison."

The name rang a bell with Gwendolyn. "Remind me who he is."

"Magazine publisher," Marcus said.

"You're being too charitable," Charles said. "He's a low-level skunk who spits out prurient cheesecake rags called *Eyeful* and *Beauty Pageant*. Evidently, he's launching a new one, and plans to fling mud using the lowest common denominators."

"I dread to ask what they are."

"Commies, Pinkos, celebrities with criminal backgrounds, homos, mixed-race couples. But it's the homos he's really got it in for. You should have heard his rant. I started thinking perhaps the lady doth protest too much. I don't think he's that-way inclined, but he does know how to write a headline. People love to be appalled. And he kept on bringing up Sheldon Voss."

Marcus shot Gwendolyn an eyeful of *This is news to me* and brought two fingers to his lips. He emitted two short blasts, one higher than the other, followed by a third.

It brought Kathryn into the group, with Leo trailing.

"What's going on?"

Marcus gave Kathryn and Leo a recap of what Charles had related so far. Kathryn let out a grunt when she heard Voss' name.

"Harrison and Voss, they're cut from the same cloth," Charles continued. "They just love to provoke controversy. I guess they figure queers are an easy target because they've got so much to lose, and the stigma attached to them is like the stink of being accused a Commie—it doesn't wash off easily. Mark my words: If Voss gets his march on the road, Harrison is going to be riding it for all it's worth."

"That's what George Cukor told you, isn't it?" Kathryn said.

Marcus nodded. "It sounded a bit alarmist at the time, but now . . ."

Leo stood off to Kathryn's right and behind her far enough for Kathryn to miss the look on his face. Gwendolyn could see the gears churning as they calculated the probability that Sheldon Voss would take his blasted march as far as Los Angeles, and if he did, would he really start a campaign-by-insinuation? Or would it be a full-frontal attack with Kathryn in the bull's-eye?

"Tell Gwendolyn what you told me about Zanuck," Marcus said.

"Harrison knew about the day Zanuck came to your store."

"What exactly did he know?"

"He knew some coloreds were shopping there."

"Ella Fitzgerald and Lena Horne are hardly 'some coloreds.'"

"Any time blacks and whites mix in a nonsubservient context is going to cause trouble. Harrison boasted about how that's exactly the sort of story he intends to cover in *Confidential*. An intentionally ironic title I assume, considering once Harrison gets going, nothing in Hollywood will be confidential for long."

The sharp sound of a spoon hitting the side of an empty champagne bottle cut through the hubbub. "Ladies and gentlemen?"

Billy Travilla stood on the diving board with Marilyn standing next to it, fidgeting with her gold necklace.

"We are gathered here today — oh my goodness, that sounds like a funeral! Let me start over. This is a celebration, but not just of our friend's birthday. She's just shared with me some wonderful news." He nudged her arm with his knee. "Little Miss Keep-It-Quiet here was informed this afternoon that she's been cast as Lorelei Lee in *Gentlemen Prefer Blondes*. Isn't that wonderful?"

He led everyone into a trio of hip-hip-hoorays.

Charles said, "That movie's got a huge budget. If *Niagara* does as well as we hope, and she follows it up with *Gentlemen Prefer Blondes*, she could be the biggest thing since Harlow."

Gwendolyn leaned her chin onto Kathryn's shoulder and whispered, "Best you elbow your way over to Marilyn — Sidney Skolsky just walked in."

Short, dark, and chatty Skolsky wrote for the *New York Post* and had a monthly column in *Photoplay* called "From a Stool at Schwab's," which helped make Schwab's famous, and him along with it. He had been an early and vocal champion of Marilyn's.

As Kathryn approached her, Gwendolyn circled the perimeter of the group, keeping tabs on Skolsky. He, too, was heading for the birthday girl, but Jack Paar rerouted him into a conversation with the beatniks.

Gwendolyn caught Dona standing alone. "Isn't it wonderful news for Marilyn?"

"There'll be no stopping her now."

"I have a question I'd like to ask you."

Dona ran her hands down her front. "It's a Schiaparelli knockoff, but don't tell anyone."

"Have you spoken to Ella Fitzgerald lately?"

"I saw her the other night when she played at Jazzland. Why?"

"It's just that I haven't seen her at my store lately. Nor any of the others."

"What others?"

"Lena Horne, Hattie McDaniel, Dorothy Dandridge. I was wondering if they're staying away on purpose."

"Of course they are."

"Was it something I said? Or did?"

"Miss Ella and Miss Lena, they think you're lovely, and they adore your clothes." Dona gently shook her head. "But they're not blind or stupid."

"I never said they were."

"But weren't they at your store the day that whole ruckus erupted about Marilyn's calendar? They saw the way Zanuck pulled you out into the street and gave you a talking-to. Ella said it was plain as day."

"But I don't have a problem with any of those ladies."

"They know that, but they don't want to be the cause of any trouble for you."

Gwendolyn wanted to tell Dona to let Ella and Lena and everyone else know that her invitation still stood, but the news of this Robert Harrison guy ate at her resolve.

Dona pointed to her husband. "Billy's just tugged at his right ear — that's his signal. Sorry, but I must rescue him."

She hurried away leaving Gwendolyn alone until Marcus appeared at her side.

"All those New York guys seem to be in cahoots."

Somewhere at the store, Gwendolyn had the number of Ella Fitzgerald's West Coast manager. *Should I ask him to pass on a message?* "New York guys?"

"East Coast, anyway. Winchell, Hoover, McCarthy, Breen. And now this Robert Harrison. The way I see it, they're a right-wing cabal linking up to squash the liberal agenda. And it looks like Sheldon Voss has wormed his way into their good graces."

Or maybe the smart move would be to call the day Zanuck came in a close shave and just leave things be.

"What's a cabal?" she asked.

"It's a secret ring of conspirators, like in some film noir about Nazi spies, only this gang is even more dangerous because they're out in the open."

"How do you fight someone like that?"

"Beats me."

"Sounds like they're coming after Kathryn."

Marcus slung his arm around Gwendolyn's shoulder. "And maybe you, too, my sweet."

CHAPTER 26

By the summer of 1952, the bloom was off the rose in Hollywood.

Gleeful reports of double-digit growth in aviation, automobiles, manufacturing, and oil signaled an economic spree the country hadn't seen since the twenties, but as Kathryn reported in her column, cinema admissions had dipped below sixty million — down from the hundred-million postwar high of 1947 — causing three thousand movie houses to switch off their neon lights. Even more depressing was her follow-up report that Americans were spending more money on fishing tackle and ten-pin bowling than movies.

From the sidelines, Marcus could see he'd chosen a dicey time to shove his foot back in the door. So he was surprised and a little mystified when Sam Dodds, the photographer Marcus met at Fox came knocking at the Garden of Allah one morning, catching Marcus swimming his regular fifty laps.

"Is this a social call?" he asked Dodds as he toweled himself dry.

"Did you see *Daily Variety* this morning?"

"I'm more of a *Hollywood Reporter* guy."

"Fox has announced pay cuts of twenty-five to fifty percent."

Fox was the box office champ, so if it was hurting, surely the other studios would follow its lead.

"Sounds like the Depression all over again."

"For some, maybe." Dodds broke out into a leering grin that gave Marcus pause. "I saw this coming when the studios let their still photographers go. Not the glamour portrait guys, but the on-set shutterbugs. Poof! Gone." He squatted down on the diving board. "I've got more work than I know what to do with."

Dodds' skin stretched taut across his face, giving him an almost translucent quality that reminded Marcus of Cary Grant in *Topper*. An ability to remain unobtrusive was quite possibly the prime skill necessary for a production photographer trying to capture authentic, candid shots.

"I want to know if you could take some of it off my hands."

"Sure," Marcus said. "What've you got?"

Dodds pulled three index cards out of his jacket pocket. "*The Jazz Singer* remake at Warner Brothers. Danny Thomas is starring, with Michael Curtiz directing."

Curtiz had one of the shortest tempers in the business and an almost impenetrable Hungarian accent. "What else?"

"*The Bad and the Beautiful*. Lana Turner, Kirk Douglas, Walter Pidgeon, and Dick Powell, with Minnelli directing." He held up the card. "It's a class production."

Marcus had worked closely with Vincente Minnelli on *Till the Clouds Roll By* and *The Pirate* and had found him an unflappable and erudite gentleman, but it meant returning to MGM. He nodded toward Dodds' third card. "And that one?"

"You don't want it."

"Try me."

"*The Star*. It's about a washed-up actress who's intent on making a comeback and is offered the role of a has-been who can't face the fact that it's all over."

"Who's the lead?"

"And the Oscar does *not* go to . . ." Dodds drummed his hands on the diving board, "Miss Bette Davis. Yeesh! Talk about art imitating life."

"Who's doing it?"

"Twentieth Century-F—"

"I'll take it."

"I'm offering you the *Jazz Singer* remake or the new Minnelli, but you're choosing the one where Bette Davis will be grumpier than a constipated camel because she's taking a role that's a sad reflection of her own life? Why would you do that?"

"Do *you* want it?" Marcus bluffed.

"Hell, no!"

"I've met Bette a few times. She's a good friend of a good friend." He plucked the index card out of Dodds' hand. "When do I start?"

* * *

The set was cheerlessly mundane. Beige walls bare of decoration. A battered Franklin stove sat against the right-hand wall next to a cabinet filled with second-rate kitchenware. The only piece of furniture was a scruffy rocking chair. In the middle of the floor sat a bucket filled with sudsy water and a scrubbing brush.

Marcus took some shots. *God almighty, Bette, you're as far from* The Private Lives of Elizabeth and Essex *as I am from Zanuck.*

If Marcus had taken the time to properly read Dodds' index card, he'd have seen that *The Star* was only being distributed by Fox. Like so many movies these days, Bette's new project was an independent production filmed at a studio for hire called the Motion Picture Center on Cahuenga Boulevard, a million miles from Zanuck's studio. Marcus' disappointment cut deep, but a job was a job.

He hadn't seen Bette before she left to film *Another Man's Poison* in Britain with her husband, Gary Merrill. Despite being helmed by her *Now, Voyager* director, Irving Rapper, the picture had been a monumental disaster and, Marcus imagined, a sobering come-down from *All About Eve*.

And now this.

Dodds' comment about Bette being grumpier than a constipated camel replayed in Marcus' mind as he wandered around the dreary set.

It was now eleven o'clock, but still no sign of the leading actress. There were only so many interesting photos he could take of unremarkable kitchens without Bette's luminescence to brighten things up. He asked one of the key grips, "Have you seen Miss Davis yet?"

"None of us have. I hear she's in her dressing room." He took in Marcus' camera. "If you're thinking of heading over there, you better proceed with extreme caution." He let out a long, low whistle.

Undaunted, Marcus knocked on Bette's dressing room door.

"Who is it?" came Bette's unmistakable rasp.

"A friendly face."

Bette jerked open the door; her scowl melted with palpable relief. "Thank Christ! Get in here!"

Her dressing room was freshly painted in light green with white trim. The smell still hung in the air, lending the place a surprising crispness. Photos of her mother and sister, and a cute one of Merrill and their daughter, B.D. lined the edges of her makeup mirror. But otherwise the room was as sparse as the set.

Two years ago in *All About Eve,* Bette played a handsome woman two years past the dreaded forty but still more than capable of holding her own—especially with the full powers of a top studio's makeup, hair, lighting, and cinematography departments behind her.

But seeing her now, it seemed like ten years had passed. Gone were the reliable technicians to create her mask. Gone, too, was the huge salary, most of the trappings of movie stardom, the custom-designed clothes, and the legions of fans who couldn't get enough.

What was left?

A tough, middle-aged broad who still had fight left in her, whose family completely relied on her, and who didn't regret a single cigarette or single-malt whiskey or inappropriate affair.

Bette pushed Marcus into the chair next to her mirror and tapped the top of his camera with an unvarnished nail. "You're our photographer? How wonderful! I wish I'd known. Now I won't have to endure this cinematic masterpiece all by myself."

"I saw the set."

Bette shrugged as though to say, *It's work, isn't it?* "I decided the best way to tackle this job was to ignore the obvious parallels and try to enjoy myself."

"And are you?"

"My goodness, yes! I'm basing my characterization on Joan."

"Crawford?"

A wicked smile slithered free. "I've even convinced the hair stylist to copy Joan's 'do from *Harriet Craig*."

"Would you be offended if I called you a bitch?"

"As a matter of fact, the hairdo rather suits me, which is as frightening as it is hilarious." She tugged at the sleeves of her housecoat and fiddled with the limp collar drooping around her neck. "But I think I shall scream if I have to talk about this picture any more. Tell me about yourself. Is it really true that you're taking pictures on *I Love Lucy*? And how was Italy? I was always too busy making pictures to travel as much as I'd have liked. You must tell me *everything*."

Marcus launched into an abbreviated version of how he came to be documenting the biggest television show in America. He stopped when someone knocked on the door and told Bette they'd be ready for her in two minutes.

"We can pick this up after you're done," Marcus said.

"Did you see that bucket out there?" Bette lit a cigarette. "If they want me down on my hands and knees scrubbing floors, they can damn well wait for the privilege. So, what were you saying about Zanuck?"

"I'm trying to meet him. Kathryn thought she could pull it off, but he's not great at returning calls. Do you know him? I thought maybe for this picture . . .?"

She pulled a very Margo-Channing pout and jabbed the cigarette butt like it was a tiny dagger. "We had negotiations during *All About Eve.*"

"What was he like?"

"Tough as tacks, but fair. You can't ask for much more than that."

Another, louder knock on the door.

"I'LL BE THERE WHEN I'M READY!" She cleared her throat and turned back to Marcus. "Why are you so keen to meet him?"

"I was blacklisted, but Mayer arranged to have me taken off it."

"Why, that's marvelous news! Congrat—"

"And put onto the graylist."

"There's a *gray* one?" She faced herself in the mirror, picking at her hair, disheveling it lock by lock. "This world is insane."

"I'm stuck in No Man's Land and I don't see how I can break free without help."

"I can tell you that he won't agree to see you just because you ask. Even *I* had a devil of a time getting in to see him." She stood to tie a shabby apron around her waist and examined herself in the mirror. "God, this is awful. Tell you what, though. Some of the people Fox have let go, they're bound to pop up in independent places like these."

Bette made a good point. More and more lately, independent producers packaging scripts with freelance stars and directors were the ones putting movies together. The old studio system of signing everyone to long-term contracts was showing signs of stress.

"But I'll only be around until December," Bette added. "Gary and I are getting the hell out of this insidious hellhole. We're moving to Cape Elizabeth, halfway up the coast of Maine."

"Maine?!" Marcus couldn't have been more shocked if she'd said Mars.

"I'm sticking around until the premiere, then getting the hell out of Dodge. I can't wait."

Marcus held open the door for her, and Bette stomped toward her bucket of soapsuds. He pulled the cover off his lens and peered through the viewfinder, framing a great shot that took in the huge camera, the glaring lights, and the patient crew on the periphery of a set that reeked of desperation and despair.

CHAPTER 27

The day of Ava Gardner's ceremony outside Grauman's Chinese started with a typical October chill, so Kathryn dressed in a snug cream suit. But by midmorning, the sun had crept into the theater's forecourt raising the temperature into the eighties. Kathryn felt sweat collecting under her bra and knew Ava must have been feeling worse, dressed in a heat-soaking dark blue woolen ensemble.

As the workmen lowered the carpeted platform into place, Kathryn studied the fans clustered along Hollywood Boulevard for a fan club president, some press, or a past costar who needed fresh publicity. She could usually unearth somebody whose story could give her article some oomph, and readers liked oomph. They always let her know after her radio show or when they saw her in public at Perino's or Mocambo.

But the face she was surprised to see belonged to Walter Winchell. She studied it, wondering why she was so startled, considering his infuriating knack for popping up in unexpected places.

Winchell usually announced in his column when he was going to LA, which was often for a specific reason, like the Oscars. But the only noteworthy event he'd mentioned was — *Oh, wait. Bingo.*

Earlier in the year, when Hedda Hopper declared that she was writing her autobiography, she'd been met with jaded indifference. Divulging the real secrets in her files would leave her open to libel. That left watered-down versions tattled through rose-colored glasses. *Yawn.*

Kathryn forgot about Hedda's book until the week it became a national bestseller. Knowing that she couldn't *not* read *From Under My Hat*, Kathryn bought a copy and found with some satisfaction that she knew enough of Hedda's stories to know that most of it was sheer invention. The book virtually qualified as fiction and was clearly intended for a public that'd been trained to swallow whatever the studios' publicity departments were churning out that week.

Still, a bestseller was a bestseller, which was no mean feat, so Kathryn sent a congratulatory notecard to Hedda, and received an invitation to a party at Lucey's Restaurant opposite Paramount. The prospect of watching Hedda crow about her success held all the appeal of a pelvic exam, so she declined.

None of Kathryn's tipsters forewarned her of Winchell's arrival, which meant he'd slipped into town on the Q.T.

When Winchell spotted her, he gave his hat a token tug. With anyone else she would have returned the gesture, but that smile of his, so smug, so acidic . . . it was enough to give a girl trench mouth.

She guessed he was feeling superior about his recent stunt: He'd become the first person to broadcast his radio show simultaneously on television. To ensure maximum exposure, he'd secured Betty Grable and Arlene Dahl as his guests, but it probably hadn't been necessary. The whole setup garnered him inches of press.

Ava laughed when Grauman's manager almost lost his grip as a second chap guided her foot. The manager, a genial lookalike of David Selznick, would have been horrified if a star ended up face first in wet concrete.

But that sort of mishap made a lively story and Kathryn almost wished the guy's reflexes had been a little slower. Ava would have been the first person to shriek with laughter at such a calamity.

But Ava dutifully squished her feet and hands into the cement and inscribed the date without tumbling ass over dumplings.

Meanwhile, Kathryn edged her way to Ava's elbow and offered her a handkerchief to dab away the sweat collecting on her face and neck. In return, she got a great quote about getting fresh cement out of cracks where the sun don't shine.

Kathryn spotted a woman who, despite looking twenty years older, resembled Ava in that confident, boobs-out posture, despite her threadbare five-and-dime outfit. She was the sort of person Kathryn knew would have a story to tell concerning the star du jour.

Winchell stepped into her path.

"Hello," she said flatly. That pompous smile still filled his face, but whatever he was dangling, she wasn't buying. "If you'll excuse me, I have someone I want to talk to—"

"I'm surprised you weren't at Hedda's bash. She told me she invited you."

"I'd already RSVP'd to a charity dinner at the Ambassa—"

"It was quite the swell affair. You've read her book, I presume? What did you think?"

Kathryn watched the woman with the interesting face dissolve into the tide of humanity emptying the sidewalk. Winchell had an agenda, and it probably involved her.

"I think people like you and me are fortunate to be able to read between the lines."

"That's exactly what I told Felix Miller last night."

"Is that one of your tipsters?"

"He is, but surely you know that."

"I do?"

"You've met him at least twice."

She searched her memory for a Felix Miller, but drew a blank.

Winchell asked, "Are you in the habit of handing over wads of cash to strangers whose names you don't even know?" He brought a lit cigarette to his mouth. "Really, Kathryn, I'm surprised. You've always struck me as such an inquisitive girl." Somehow, he managed to make it sound like being inquisitive was outlawed in nineteen states.

"If we're playing Twenty Questions, what number am I up to?"

"Felix Miller is the guy you encountered at Ciro's, and again at Romanoff's."

The creep with the notebook and those goddamned asterisks.

In retrospect, Kathryn wondered why it took so long to recognize what the names in that notebook had in common: they were all homosexuals, or rumored to be, or had married one to deflect suspicion. Hollywood queers and dykes had been marrying each other so long it had become a way of life that nobody questioned. Nobody in Hollywood, anyway.

He crushed his cigarette butt out on Shirley Temple's hands. "He mentioned meeting your mother."

That night at Romanoff's was six months ago. "Is that right?"

"Specifically, how closely she resembles Sheldon Voss."

SHIT! "Have you met my mother?"

"I don't believe I've had the pleasure, no."

"If you had, you'd understand why people are always telling her that she looks like someone, or reminds them of someone. It's happened her whole life."

"I suppose I should tell Hoover not to bother looking into it."

Kathryn faked a laugh. It almost sounded real. Maybe he bought it. "So you get the head of the FBI to spend tax dollars on looking into the resemblance between a bag of hot air and a switchboard operator based on the say-so of some jerk whose loyalty is open to the highest bidder?"

Winchell didn't miss a beat. "Quite the coincidence, isn't it?"

"You have a far more elastic interpretation of the word 'coincidence' than I do."

"So it's just a coincidence that the sponsor of your radio show has also signed on as one of the sponsors of Voss' Sea to Shining Sea March?"

That explained the smile, even if it was baloney. "If either Sunbeam or Betty Crocker is sponsoring that march, I'd know about it."

"So my information is inaccurate?"

It'd damn well better be. "It is."

"In that case, I should call New York to change my column. I'd hate to say anything that I knew wasn't true."

He tugged his hat again and headed for the curb to hail a taxi. By the time it whisked him away, Mike Connolly was approaching her.

Kathryn no longer feared that Connolly was any sort of threat to her status as the paper's key columnist. He seemed content to splash around in the shallows, filling his column with celebrity pairings and unpairings, movie-star casting announcements, and far more blind items than Kathryn would ever dream of.

Still, she couldn't help thinking that she was one thoughtless stumble away from him pole-vaulting over her.

"What did *he* want?" Connolly asked, casual as a schoolboy.

Kathryn didn't even want to consider the possibility that Winchell could be right about this new Sunbeam sponsorship; to have Connolly rub it in her face was almost as bad.

"The usual insertion of knives between ribs."

"My money was on this rumor I've heard that Sunbeam is sponsoring the Voss march. I was hoping to get your reaction but you've been out of the office all morning."

How could Leo make such a decision without consulting me?

"What *is* your reaction?" Connolly pushed.

The fans were now thinning out.

"What do you think my reaction is?"

"Hard to say," Mike replied, "but 'mixed emotions' would be my guess." He suddenly yanked his hands out of his pockets and hung them from his hips. "Tell you what, though, I'm royally pissed about it."

"What have you got to be pissed at?"

"I've mentioned Voss and his march at least twice a week since his announcement. And I'm Catholic, for chrissakes. You've barely mentioned him at all, but it's *your* sponsor that's pledged to help fund the march. Then again, your sponsor is also your boyfriend."

Kathryn itched to point out that Connolly was only a lip-service Catholic, and everybody knew that he was a lush and a homo, and that he had no radio show to sponsor, so what the hell was he getting so hot under the collar for? But they were in public and she could see a quartet of frumpy housewives marshaling the courage to approach her for an autograph. And anyway, she realized, Mike Connolly was not the villain here.

The villain was in a sleek office on Wilshire Boulevard. If she hurried, she could catch him before he went to lunch.

* * *

Driving south on La Brea Avenue, Kathryn spotted a payphone and pulled over. She called the *Reporter*'s offices and asked Cassandra on reception if there had been a press release announcing Sunbeam's sponsorship of the Voss march.

Yes, there was.

Yes, they had.

No, there were no messages from Leo.

It took effort, but by the time she'd parked outside the Sunbeam building, Kathryn had recouped her poise. Leo's secretary wasn't at her desk, but his office door was open, so she strode straight in. He looked up from the papers in front of him. "I've been trying to get a hold of you."

"I was at Grauman's for Ava Gardner."

"You haven't been into the office yet?"

She stood quite still as she watched the pen tremble between his fingers.

Eventually, he pulled out one of his visitor chairs. "In that case, I've got news."

Instead of taking a seat, Kathryn kicked Leo's office door shut and dropped her handbag onto his desk. "You know where I learned about your lousy sponsorship deal? In the middle of Grauman's forecourt. From Winchell. Do you need a moment to picture the sanctimonious look on his face? It was the exact same look I got from Mike Connolly when he confirmed it."

She started tugging at the fingers of her gloves. She didn't like wearing them but in moments like these, they were useful for underscoring her points.

"You might have picked up the phone and said, 'Hello, my darling, just thought you'd like to know . . .'" She slapped her gloves against the palm of her hand. "Jesus, Leo, there are plenty of events you can sponsor. If you're so hot for marches, what about the March of Dimes? But Voss'? Really? You know who he is. You know how I feel. And yet you go right ahead and sponsor a dishonest, manipulative phony who's only motive is to — to . . ."

He took advantage of the break in her salvo.

"Shut up! Shut up! Just shut UP!"

Open-mouthed, she dropped into a chair.

"Sorry," he said, looking at his clasped hands.

"You think I don't have a point?" she asked.

"Of course you do. But hear me out."

"This had better be good."

"None of this was run past me. It all happened with my boss and my boss' boss."

"You're Mister Public Relations, Advertising, and Marketing. How could they not include you?"

"Don't think that wasn't the first question out of my mouth. I told them that I had good reason to suspect Voss was doing this march for unscrupulous motives, and that Kathryn Massey will most definitely *not* be okay with this."

"So they just ignored you?"

"It was already done. Voss himself went directly to the head of the company. At any rate, there was nothing I could do. We just have to accept the deal."

"What is the deal?"

"We're now one of three sponsors for the Sea to Shining Sea March, and you're required to mention it on each of your weekly radio shows."

"Required?"

Outside Leo's office window stretched a picture-postcard vista of Hollywood from Culver City in the west across to the downtown skyline. It was hard to see the buildings through the smog.

"It's been a long while since I've read my contract," she said, "but there must be some loophole or other."

Leo pointed to the papers on his desk. "I was looking for exactly that, but darling, I'm afraid there isn't."

She got to her feet and gathered up her handbag and gloves. "I feel betrayed. Maybe not by you specifically, but certainly by the company you represent."

This was the first time she wasn't confident that Leo's loyalties lay wholly with her. She needed time to sort that out and decide what she could do.

"So for now," she said, standing, "I think it's best that we separate our personal lives from our professional ones."

He pulled her back into the chair and took the one next to her, their knees brushing together. "Business Theory 101: Turn a negative into an opportunity."

A voice in Kathryn's head that sounded suspiciously like Gwennie's told her that he deserved a chance to speak. "Go on."

"Your show is no longer in the top ten. Two weeks ago it came in at number eighteen, and once it crashes out of the top twenty-five, Sunbeam-Betty Crocker can cancel our sponsorship with no advance warning."

"I would rather lose my show than endorse that shyster — oh! You're telling me that all I need to do is put out a bunch of rotten shows, and let *Window on Hollywood* fall out of the top twenty-five. Problem solved. I love Business Theory 101!"

Leo shook his head. "Voss' march is a hot potato. It's gathering momentum week by week. If you include the latest updates and exclusives — which is part of the contract with them — it's guaranteed to lift you back up in the ratings."

"It's bad enough that we're going to have local broadcasters yammering about him on my show each week. I don't like it, but I get it. We're dovetailing, as you put it, with an event that everyone's talking about. And as long as I don't have to actually talk to Voss, I guess I can live with it. But *sponsoring* this circus? It's too much. I'm horrified, Leo. HORRIFIED."

"And that's exactly the word I used when I addressed the executive committee. I told them how horrified you'd be, and that they'd better sweeten the pie if they wanted your cooperation."

"Did they tell me to go take a long walk off a short plank?"

"Not at all. They like you and are keen to keep you happy. So now for the good news." Leo cleared his throat. "If *Window on Hollywood* is still on the air once the march is over, they're willing to look at sponsoring your own television show."

Kathryn stared at Leo, not quite sure how to respond.

Winchell thought he was the king of the castle with his single, solitary broadcast. When he hears I've got a regular TV show, he'll spit up his last five Long Island Ducklings.

Leo leaned forward and took Kathryn's hands in his.

"Business Theory 102: Think big, and think long-term. Your ratings aren't dying because people don't like your show. It's because *radio* is dying. Everything is moving to television. That's where the money is because that's where the public is.

"We figure radio's got a couple more fruitful years. After that? Deadsville. Both Sunbeam and Betty Crocker have benefited extraordinarily well out of our association with your radio show. So we want to ride it for as long as it's worthwhile and then jump ship when it starts to splutter. Voss' march will run over the summer, ending in LA sometime in August. By then, we'll have wrung all we can from radio. And if you thought radio money was good, wait till you get a load of what television pays."

CHAPTER 28

Gwendolyn paced the sidewalk outside the United Artists Theatre on Colorado Boulevard. Doris was cutting it awfully fine.

Was she not coming? Did she get a flat tire? Did she have an accident? *When did I become such a worrywart?*

The answer came to Gwendolyn instantly: *Since the night of Marilyn's birthday party.*

All that talk of Marcus and the East Coast cabal: Winchell, Hoover, McCarthy, Breen, and now this Harrison creep. Were they really going to expose all the homosexuals in Hollywood? As far as Gwendolyn knew, there weren't that many Commies in Hollywood, and yet HUAC got huge mileage out of pursuing them. But the queers were a different story.

"Gwendolyn! Is that you?"

It wasn't the voice she was hoping to hear.

Eleanor Oboler was one of Gwendolyn's regular customers. In fact, she was the ideal customer: a svelte figure who wore every style well, high-class taste, oodles of money, and time to shop.

Her husband had written, directed, and produced a movie called *Bwana Devil*, which Eleanor described as "a Moby Dick tale set in British Equatorial Africa — wherever that is — but with lions. My husband dreams big, so I hope for his sake that it's not quite so schlocky as it sounds. I'm recruiting people to a sneak preview. Would you consider coming and give some honest feedback?"

Killer lions in Africa weren't Gwendolyn's idea of a fun night at the movies, until Eleanor added as an afterthought, "It will have the distinction of being the first feature released in 3-D." Gwendolyn figured Marcus might enjoy the novelty but he got caught late at a taping of an *I Love Lucy* episode that wasn't going well, and suggested she might ask his sister.

Doris had jumped at the chance and said she'd meet her in Pasadena. But where was she?

"I'm so glad you could make it," Eleanor said. "It's about to start. Shall we go in?"

"I'm waiting on my friend. I told her quarter of, and she's usually so reliable. Why don't you go in? I'll give her another minute or two."

"Don't forget—we'll be passing out feedback cards afterwards."

As Eleanor swanned into the theater, Doris came rushing up. Her hair was windswept, her coat hung off one shoulder, and in her hand was a huge tote bag. She wore a startled look.

"I've got it!"

"They're about to start—"

Doris pulled a folded magazine from her tote and held it up for Gwendolyn to see.

Confidential magazine was every bit the tacky rag Gwendolyn had imagined. Across the top was a black-and-white banner: *Exposed: Love in the U.N.!* The rest of the cover was taken up with four tawdry photos of people Gwendolyn didn't recognize. Beneath each one blazed a caption:

> *O'Dwyer: Saint or Sinner?*
> *Showgirl Sells Shares in Self*
> *Athletes Are Lousy Lovers!*
> *Hoodlums Paradise.*

Gwendolyn took the magazine from Doris. "It's out already?"

"Not for another week. This is an advance copy."

"Where did you get it?"

"A guy I work with at Columbia, his brother works for Fred Otash."

"That slimy private eye is connected with this?" Gwendolyn handed the magazine back.

The two of them took cardboard glasses from the usher at the door and dashed inside. They grabbed the first pair of empty seats, put on their specs and settled in.

The movie was as good as something called *Bwana Devil* could hope to be. The 3-D effects kinda-sorta worked, which made it kinda-sorta interesting, but not enough to redeem the wooden acting and woeful plot. Gwendolyn's attention started to wander. She saw now that the assassin in Doris' tote, with its stink of desperation and attempt to rake muck where there was none, seemed inconsequential.

And yet . . . and yet . . .

Fred Otash.

Otash was a former policeman turned private eye who'd been lurking around long enough to earn a reputation for having a conveniently pliable respect for privacy.

You want dirt on your cheating spouse so you won't have to pay alimony? Go see Otash. You suspect your accountant is embezzling your dough and gambling it away at Santa Anita? Otash is your man. Some bastard is trying to blackmail you because you ran over someone while driving home drunk from Robert Mitchum's? Otash will fix it for you.

He wasn't just any Hollywood private eye; he was *the* Hollywood private eye because he wasn't afraid to skirt the blurry edges of the law to deliver results. If *Confidential* was using Otash to exhume deeply buried humiliations, it wasn't above publishing anything about anyone.

The lights came up and the audience took off their cardboard glasses. As they walked into the foyer, the same usher handed them comment cards. Gwendolyn spotted Eleanor hovering near the front door, a look of hopeful expectation filling her face. Gwendolyn grabbed Doris and steered her into the ladies' room.

The bathroom was tiled in seafoam green with lavender trim. A colored attendant in a starched black uniform had just finished cleaning the six mirrors. Gwendolyn and Doris took the last two seats.

"The wife of the producer is a customer of mine," Gwendolyn told Doris. "She's the loyal-wife type so I don't want to be too harsh, but my mind wandered in and out. What did you think?"

"Put it this way," Doris said. "We've got a new Johnny Weissmuller-Jungle Jim picture coming out next week called *Voodoo Tiger*."

"Which one's better?"

"Believe it or not, the hour and a half of hooey we just sat through. At least the 3-D effect worked—to a degree."

"So I'll say, 'It's better than *Voodoo Tiger*.'"

"Oh, Gwendolyn!" Doris laughed. "We can't write that!"

An approaching figure caught Gwendolyn's eye in the mirror.

"Ma'am?" The attendant was very dark-skinned with bright pink fingernails and a hesitant smile. Her nametag read *Suzannah*.

"Yes?"

"S'kuze me for asking, but I was wondering if you were the lady who runs that boutique up on the Sunset Strip?"

"Why, yes, I do have a boutique on the Strip."

"It's just that I know the owners of the Dunbar. We go to the same church. They give me extra work from time to time, and the other week, Lena Horne performed there. She needed a dresser and whatnot, and they asked if I would step in. Of course I said yes.

"And when I helped her into her dress—it was the prettiest thing I ever saw. Blue like juniper berries, but with sparkles. When I helped her into it, I saw a label what said 'Chez Gwendolyn.'"

Lena had ordered that dress the day Zanuck told Gwendolyn she couldn't cater to "people like that."

After Zanuck roared away in his limo, the mood inside the store chilled, but Gwendolyn ignored it and continued with Lena's instructions about the blue dress. After Gwendolyn took her measurements, Lena paid in full and wrote out a delivery address, insisting that returning to the store for a fitting wouldn't be necessary as long as she stuck to the exact measurements, and she hustled Ella out before Gwendolyn had a chance to thank her.

Gwendolyn pushed her comment card aside. "But how did you know it was me?" she asked Suzannah.

"That night, Ella Fitzgerald came backstage to say hello, and Dorothy Dandridge was with her. They all got to chatting and Miss Lena's dress came up, and so they were talking about you, too. Admiring your work and the way you welcomed colored folk in your store. So when I heard your friend here say your name, I just wondered, on account of I figure there can't be many Gwendolyns around. Leastways, I never heard of none. And now that you're here in my powder room, I wanted to say thank you."

"Whatever for?"

"For doing right by Miss Ella and Miss Lena and the others. It took guts for them to venture up to the Strip. Miss Ella talked about how she came to the back door of your store but you insisted she use the front." She cocked her head to one side. "Did that really happen?"

"Sure it did."

"That right there says to me and everyone else that you is the sort of white folk we don't often come across."

"Has Miss Ella told many people about the back door-front door thing?" Doris asked.

"Oh, yes, ma'am! She done told pert-near everybody, so far as I can tell."

A gaggle of women burst into the ladies' room, one of whom was Eleanor Oboler. Suzannah withdrew to attend to them, leaving Gwendolyn and Doris to scribble honest but encouraging comments. They pressed the cards into Eleanor's hands and fled for the front doors, right into the path of Herman Dewberry.

"My goodness!" Gwendolyn exclaimed. "What are you doing here?"

"My friend Russell did the special effects on this turkey."

Gwendolyn spotted a discarded feedback card on the floor. "I'm glad I've bumped into you. I wanted to get a sense of how my perfume is doing."

"Are you not getting your checks?"

Not only had royalty checks been coming in regular as a Swiss clock, but they had been gradually increasing.

"I just wondered what sort of responses you're getting. People still like it, right?"

"Oh, yes!" Herman said. "Why would you think otherwise?"

"What would you say to extending the line?" she asked. Herman tried to keep a poker face but his eyes crinkled up at the corners. "Specifically, eau de toilette, cold cream, face powder, and eye shadow. And perhaps lipsticks?"

When Gwendolyn first produced her perfume, it was a seat-of-the-pants operation. If it hadn't worked, Chez Gwendolyn might have gone under. But its success had provided a comfortable cushion to help her through slow months. Now that the couture side of her business was on shaky ground, it occurred to her that, handled right, an expanded line could give her the financial freedom to run Chez Gwendolyn exactly how she wished.

"That's a capital idea!" Herman gushed. "I have a cosmetics manufacturer in Pomona we can use."

"So what's the next step? What do I need to do?"

"If you're serious about this, I can work on a formal agreement next week."

Over Herman's shoulder, Gwendolyn spotted Suzannah emerging from the ladies room in a fraying cloth coat.

"Excuse me a moment, will you, Herman?"

Gwendolyn stepped to one side and stopped Suzannah. "The next time you see Lena, will you tell her that I just got in a bolt of exquisite apricot chiffon that will look great on her? And I've got a design that will suit her every bit as spectacularly as the juniper dress."

Suzannah thanked her and said that she didn't know when she'd next see Miss Lena, but if she did, she'd surely pass on the message.

Gwendolyn turned back to Herman, but he was a different man. Gone was the gracious little Mr. Dewberry, grateful that she'd never blabbed about his preference for floral prints.

"I—I—must be—going," he stammered, backing away from her.

"Is something wrong?"

"No—I—it's just that it's gotten so—so very late, and—" He whipped around and disappeared through the doors.

"I'm glad you're still here." It was Eleanor Oboler. "I just realized I'm going to need a new outfit for next month. We've got tickets to that industry preview of *This is Cinerama*. You've heard of it, I'm sure."

This is Cinerama was the great white hope of the film industry: A super-widescreen format developed to counter the inroads made by that pint-sized upstart in everybody's living room. It required three projectors, which meant extensive theater remodeling, and that cost money. But money was in short supply because the moviegoing public was staying home. If the movies were going to lure people back into theaters, the vicious cycle needed to be broken. The novelty of 3-D wasn't going to do it—not if they only used it on crummy pictures like *Bwana Devil*.

Gwendolyn watched Herman's silhouette dissolve into the dark of night. "Yes, I have heard of it," she told Eleanor.

"I suspect the preview will be one of those I-was-there-when nights. I've got a Native Daughters of the Golden West meeting not far from your store next Friday. Shall we say around three-ish?"

"I'll be there." Gwendolyn bid her good night, but didn't follow Eleanor out of the theater.

"Are you all right?" Doris asked.

"I didn't like the look on Herman's face."

"It was a bit odd."

"Maybe I should have kept my mouth shut."

CHAPTER 29

Marcus tapped Gwendolyn's shoulder with his *This is Cinerama* program. "Bwana Devil Lady was right. All the big cheeses showed up."

He pointed across the foyer of the Warner Hollywood Theatre, where Stanley Donen and Gene Kelly were huddled at the foot of the stairs with John Ford. Not far from him, Louis B. Mayer was tête-à-tête-ing with Cary Grant, Cecil B. DeMille, and Vincente Minnelli.

"If the Big One hit right now, it'd take out half of Hollywood."

Gwendolyn slapped him back. "Don't even say it!"

Kathryn appeared with Leo. "What are we talking about?"

"Earthquakes."

"Pretty much the only thing they didn't throw at us," Leo said. "That sure was one heck of an experience. I liked the Cypress Gardens sequences well enough, but that rollercoaster was something else."

When Marcus first heard Mayer's ambitious plan for a triple-projector screen format, he thought it smacked of desperation. His experience on *I Love Lucy* had shown him the best defense against television was to embrace it, especially now that Lucille Ball was pregnant. The hullabaloo over whether or not anyone could say the word "pregnant" on the air had cannonballed the show to saturation-point popularity. They'd already shot the episode where Lucy goes to the hospital, and the network hoped to air it the day Lucille gave birth.

Better to join it, he thought.

But then Bette Davis sent him two tickets that she couldn't use to the special industry preview of *This is Cinerama*. Kathryn and Leo already had tickets, so he brought Gwendolyn. As he watched the film unspool, a pyrotechnic montage of possibilities pinwheeled through his imagination: pirate battles in the Caribbean; the explosion of Krakatoa; the London Blitz; wildebeest stampedes in Africa; gladiator tournaments in the Colosseum. And that was just off the top of his head.

"The whole movie was a rollercoaster," Marcus said. "But they'll need more than travelogues."

He craned his neck to see past Joseph Cotton and watched Mayer's hands blur as he and Zanuck tried to persuade DeMille, whose arms were crossed over his chest and mouth was pressed in a hard line. Finally, Zanuck threw his hands into the air and broke away.

Marcus stepped forward to flag him down but Zanuck took an abrupt right turn toward the men's room—hardly the place to buttonhole a heavy-hitter about the Lavender Scare.

As he waited for Zanuck to emerge, it occurred to Marcus that in a lobby full of A-listers, at least one or two others would want to bend Zanuck's ear. He shouldered the swinging door just as Zanuck was zipping up and heading toward the line of basins.

"Mr. Zanuck." The mogul didn't even look up. "My name is Marcus Adler, and I've recently heard some information that I think you need to know."

Zanuck held his hand out for the restroom attendant to place a towel in his grasp. He arched an eyebrow. "So you're the photographer my PR guy's been raving about."

"He has?"

"I've seen the photos you took on *The Star*, and let me tell you, they were exactly the sort of production shots I've always wanted. There was one where Bette's sitting on that sofa, with those Venetian blinds behind her."

"And the Oscar?"

"Yeah! You positioned it over her shoulder, like her best work is behind her, and she's got that wild-eyed look only Bette Davis can get. Now, *that* was a thousand-word photo." He pulled a fat cigar from his jacket and threaded it through his fingers, but didn't light it. "Can you come to the studio tomorrow?"

"Sure."

"We've got a real big picture in production."

"*Titanic?*"

"That's the one. The production photographer has done a god-awful job. I'll leave your name with security at the main gate."

He walked out, leaving Marcus to stare at the attendant. *What just happened?*

* * *

The next morning, Marcus drove to the gates of Twentieth Century-Fox and gave his name.

The security guard handed him a brown paper bag containing twenty rolls of film. There was also a letter from Zanuck's office informing Marcus that he'd been granted full access to all seven *Titanic* soundstages. If there were any problems, he was to contact Zanuck's office directly.

He parked next to the soundstage alongside a dozen golf carts. Inside, the *Titanic's* majestic dining room filled most of the stage. The cast, in full costume, dotted it like fragile dolls, blocking a complicated scene where the boat starts to tilt and the characters realize they're in deep doo-doo.

Marcus loaded up his camera and started clicking.

The set was on top of a hydraulic mechanism robust enough to raise it at one end, sending movie stars, dress extras, furniture, and china sprawling into a cinematic heap.

Three rolls later, Marcus felt a tap on his shoulder. Half-expecting a stern reprimand, he found instead Regina's friend, Linda Sunshine, fitted out in the most glorious pink coat of patterned brocade with a white fur collar and a tea-length hem.

"Howdy, kid!"

"Look at you!" Marcus raised his camera to his eye. "Let me get a shot."

Linda leaned against the ship's railing and struck a series of early-Pickford poses, her hands pressed in horror against her over-rouged cheeks.

"You've seen the iceberg!" Marcus said. "It's huge! We're heading straight for it! We're gonna — we're gonna — oh my God, no, we're gonna *crash*!" He snapped off a bunch of frames. "I bet they don't give you costumes like that on *Kit Carson*."

"You better believe it. This coat's got 'Lillian Gish' stitched into the collar. I get to be a snooty duchess and quaff pretend champagne. What a step up, huh? But tell me, what are you doing here?"

Marcus lifted his camera. "This is what I do now."

It was the first time he'd said those words out loud. They didn't feel as foreign in his mouth as he expected. It's like what Zanuck had said: he still told stories, just with pictures instead.

A loud bell rang out. "There's my cue to haul my carcass onto that monstrosity. When we all fall through the set, be sure to get my good side!"

The director strode into the center. Jean Negulesco was a dapper Eastern European in his fifties with a string of high-profile pictures to his name. He had the aura of someone who was the calm eye of a frenzied storm — an especially handy skill when re-sinking the *Titanic*.

Marcus took a few photos of Negulesco pointing to a lighting guy up in the rafters. The director frowned at him and beckoned him over.

"I hope you're better than the last guy." Negulesco swept his hand across the *Titanic*'s dining room. "We've gone to a great deal of trouble and expense. I want you to capture that. Also: drama, humor, detail, opulence, scale, and contrast."

"I'll do my very best."

Negulesco turned so his mouth was closer to Marcus' ear. "Zanuck and I believe Barbara Stanwyck and Robert Wagner are screwing. Or are about to. Try to catch them looking at each other the way that people do when they're hot for each other."

No pressure. "Okay."

"And don't waste film on the extras."

Oops. "Yes, sir."

The crew started bombarding Negulesco with questions just as Stanwyck and Wagner appeared from their trailers, and Marcus melted into the shadowy periphery. It was obvious they were trying not to look at each other. This meant one of three things: they were either fighting, or fucking, or both.

As they rehearsed their lines, Marcus took two rolls of film hoping to catch the flirty knowing smiles they exchanged with nearly every line.

It was four o'clock when he finished the twentieth roll and figured maybe if he showed up at Zanuck's office, an opportunity might arise.

The executive floor was lavishly appointed with thick, dark carpeting and walls paneled in mahogany and modern art: Matisse, Kandinsky, Klimt.

Zanuck's outer office was like a small hotel lobby. On the left stood a pair of desks awash with paperwork. On the right was a woman at a typewriter. She stopped bashing the keys long enough to look up at him.

"My name is Marcus Adler, and I've been shooting production stills on *Titanic*. I was hoping to see Mr. Zanuck. I just need a couple of minutes."

She pointed to the closed doors behind her. "Yes, Mr. Adler. You can go right on in."

"I don't have an appointment or anything—"

"If he's not there, he won't be long, so just take a seat."

This was altogether too easy.

The office beyond the redwood doors was twice as large. A Jackson Pollock hung behind a remarkably neat desk, and to the right, picture windows overlooked the studio water tower beyond a conference table for twelve. Zanuck was nowhere in sight.

Marcus took the middle chair in front of the desk and waited. Two or three minutes ticked by, then four, five, six . . .

A hidden door in the mahogany paneling squeaked open to reveal a moderately attractive blonde with a 36-inch chest stuffed into a 34-inch sweater.

She let out a high-pitched "Oh!" and tried to retreat, but Zanuck shoved her ahead of him into his office. "What the hell—?"

Marcus hopped to his feet. "Your secretary told me it was okay—"

"Oh, she did, did she?" Zanuck nudged the blonde toward the fire escape on the other side of the picture window. "She thinks she can shame me. You're just her patsy."

He patted the girl on her behind. "Thanks, doll." The girl tried to preserve as much decorum as her tight skirt would allow as she climbed onto the fire escape and down the metal staircase. By the time she was out of sight, Zanuck was in his chair, piercing Marcus with a suffocating stare.

"Did Negulesco tell you what we wanted?"

"Vis-à-vis Stanwyk and Wagner?"

"I hope you got some shots I can use."

"I believe so."

"That's what I want to hear. Can you come back tomorrow?"

"I can."

"We're also shooting *Call Me Madam*."

"Please don't tell me Ethel Merman is laying Donald O'Connor."

Zanuck let fly a whoop of a laugh that sounded like Francis the Talking Mule with bronchitis. "That's funny!" The braying subsided as the glare returned. "Last night. In the men's room. You said there's something I ought to know. I can give you ten minutes, but five would be better."

"The Red Scare that had us running around like Chicken Little? You might want to know there's a new one looming." Marcus paused a moment to let the implication sift through Zanuck's brain. "Senator McCarthy's got an agenda."

"You're going to have to do better than that."

"He's going to put the spotlight on the homos in government first, because they're open to blackmail. But he's also seen the attention HUAC got by storming Hollywood, so he's on his way here. The difference is, there were only ever a few Commies in Hollywood."

The mogul kept up his piercing glare. Kathryn warned him that Zanuck was no fan of fairies, but was realistic enough to know that he couldn't produce great movies without them. "How do you know this?"

"McCarthy's in bed with Hoover—so to speak—who is close chums with Winchell. And Winchell is all pally with Robert Harrison, the cretin behind *Confidential*. Have you read it?"

"Flipped through it once or twice."

"Harrison is circumventing the usual paths between magazines and publicity departments. He's engaged Fred Otash."

The mention of Otash sparked Zanuck's eyes. "I didn't know that."

Marcus pressed harder. "Harrison went to college with Joseph Breen, who would love to see every last homo and dyke fitted with concrete loafers and dropped into the Pacific. We're talking hair, makeup, costume, set design, scripts. Not to mention one or two of your marquee names." That hit the bull's-eye. "Haven't you already lost enough people to the blacklist and the Red Scare?"

The two men stared at each other for what felt like several ages of man until Zanuck said, "You're real smart." Marcus wasn't sure it was a compliment, so he kept his trap shut until the studio boss asked, "Got any other arrows in that quiver of yours?"

Marcus had walked in with every intention of telling Zanuck to embrace television like Harry Cohn had. But now that he was sitting here like a supplicant before a maharaja, he could see that Zanuck was a movie man through and through.

"I do."

"Give me a for instance."

"*The Robe.*"

"What of it?"

"You should get the screen rights."

"Why?"

"*The Greatest Show on Earth* has made nearly twelve million, and it wasn't even all that good."

"You got that right."

"According to Kathryn Massey, DeMille wants to remake *The Ten Commandments.*" Marcus waited until he got a guarded nod. "If you grab the rights for *The Robe* and immediately put it into production, you could out-do DeMille."

"You think so, huh?"

"Turn it into a widescreen production. You saw *This is Cinerama*; didn't your mind pop with possibilities? If you do it right, you could present the Roman Empire like never before. Not just an empty travelogue, but a spectacular movie event about the crucifixion of Christ, using one of the biggest books of the past ten years. And you'd be the first to pull it off."

"I don't even know who's got the rights to *The Robe.*"

"RKO."

A few weeks ago, Marcus and Quentin went out for a night on the town that took in four bars, two nightclubs, and some circus-themed dive down the grubby end of Santa Monica Boulevard where Mexican pimps hung out. Somewhere between the third bar and the first club, Quentin spilled how Howard Hughes was ramming RKO into the ground and might end up selling to Paramount—and if they did, Quentin would love to get his hands on *The Robe*.

"Someone's done his homework." Zanuck was snide but impressed. He leaned on the desk. "Any other big ideas?"

"I do, but I want quid pro quo."

"Of course you do."

"I want your help getting off the graylist."

"Why would a photographer be on the graylist?"

"Because once upon a time I was the head screenwriter at MGM and fell afoul of HUAC."

"You're *that* guy? The one who told the committee to shove their inquisition up their ass?" Marcus nodded. Zanuck chuckled. "No wonder you've got an eye for drama."

"Mayer got me off the blacklist, but I can't get back to work until I'm off the gray one."

Zanuck started threading his cigar through his fingers like he had the previous night. "Personally, I think you're better off sticking with photography, but if you really want to go back to screenwriting, I'll see what I can do."

"That'd be swell."

"It might take a while, though. Got anything else?"

"You hold the rights to a play called *The Greeks Had a Word for It*."

"Jesus fucking Christ!" Zanuck hurled his cigar at the window, which the stacked blonde had left open. "A homo play? What the hell—"

"You've already filmed it twice. Once in the late thirties as *Three Blind Mice*, and later as *Moon Over Miami*. You could put your waning blonde, Betty Grable, together with your rising one, Marilyn Monroe. If you relocate the movie to New York, imagine all the panoramas of the city you'll be able to get shooting it in widescreen."

Zanuck's face took on a distant look as his fingers groped for the gold cigarette lighter that was just out of reach.

CHAPTER 30

Kathryn set a pineapple upside-down cake on the coffee table and announced to the gang collected in front of her television, "In case you're wondering, I didn't bake this. It's store-bought. So if it's inedible, blame Greenblatt's."

It wasn't like anybody expected a homemade cake from Kathryn, even though her name was becoming synonymous with Betty Crocker. But her conscience was eating at her like rust.

The night of Monday, January 19, 1953, was noteworthy. Not because Eisenhower, the first Republican president in twenty years, would be inaugurated tomorrow. Tonight, America belonged to a zany, squawking redhead whose nine-month condition everybody knew but couldn't be specified on the air.

Lucy Ricardo was finally—and no doubt hilariously— going to give birth. The other three networks, ABC, NBC, and DuMont, might as well have sent everybody home. Nobody was going to be watching them after nine o'clock.

Everybody in Kathryn's living room froze. Marcus shot her a frown. "Duly noted," he said gingerly.

"I would have baked a cake," Kathryn said, "but I ran out of time. I worked late at the office and—never mind. Coffee will be ready soon." She withdrew to the kitchen. There was nothing to do but wait for the coffee to boil, so she wiped down her already-clean counter.

"You want to talk about it?" Marcus stood in the doorway. Behind him in the living room, Gwennie, Doris, and Bertie were pretending not to listen.

"No," she lied. This was a big night for him, and she didn't want to spoil it.

His production photographs were in high demand. Every week brought new requests from all the popular magazines: *Women's Wear Daily, Colliers, Reader's Digest.* Even one that hadn't started yet — *TV Guide* — had come calling. Lucille Ball had generously split the royalties with him, so at last he had some decent money coming in. But the photos he took during the rehearsal and filming of "Lucy Goes to the Hospital" really commanded big bucks, especially now that Lucille had delivered a healthy baby boy. Kathryn couldn't remember the last time art paralleled life quite so perfectly.

"Bullshit," he said.

"It's just that — not tonight. Maybe — "

"Lucy's water won't break for another twenty minutes. You going to tell me why you've been so antsy lately? Quite frankly, I'd rather not endure another night of you and Leo snapping at each other."

Marcus was referring to the cocktail party in Chasen's back room following the premiere of Bette Davis' movie, *The Star.* Kathryn and Leo had a tiff on the drive to Grauman's over the silliest thing: his new hair tonic. By the time the cocktail party was in full swing, they were at it worse than *The Bickersons.* Even Bette, no stranger to discord, kept her distance.

Truth be told, it wasn't just that fight. Since *The Star's* premiere on Christmas Day, they'd had several squabbles.

"Has it anything to do with why Leo isn't here tonight?" Marcus ventured. Kathryn nodded. "Come on. Out with it."

"It's this deal that Sunbeam negotiated with Voss."

"You hate it, don't you?"

"Of course I hate it."

"Do you hate Leo because of it?"

"I'm trying not to."

"Do you need to try harder?"

She pitched the dishrag into the sink. "I got my lawyer to comb through my contracts with NBC and Sunbeam to see if he could spot a loophole, but he couldn't find anything to use as leverage."

"Even though you're likely to get your own television show out of it?"

She felt like the worst kind of money-grubbing gold-digger. The prospect of the money she could get with her own TV show hypnotized her into ignoring how she'd first have to swallow her conscience like a cup of cod liver oil. Now that she'd had time to think it over (and over and over), she didn't know if she could go through with it.

"I keep telling myself the ends justify the means, but now I have to promote a charlatan who fancies himself the second coming of Moses swooping in to purge Sodom and Gomorrah of all its debauchery."

"And who knew you'd turn out to be Moses' niece?"

"Don't you just love irony?" Kathryn cast around for her cigarettes but she'd left them in the living room. The coffee finished percolating. She started pulling cups and saucers from her cupboard. "So instead, like the mature woman I am, I've started to take all this out on Leo."

"Why keep provoking the poor guy?"

She shot Marcus a naughty eye. "The harder we fight, the better the sex."

"I think they call that 'make-up sex.'"

"I call it 'almost worth it.'"

"But you know it's not sustainable, right?" Marcus said. "And it's not what normal couples do."

"Do you *know* any normal couples in Hollywood?"

"You planning on breaking things off with him?"

"No." The response shot out of her so fast, it caught her off guard. "I'm such a dummy."

"No, you're not." Marcus picked up a pair of coffee cups. "Well, maybe just a little." He put them down again. "What if you got someone to step in for you?"

"Step in for what?"

"Be the voice of *Window on Hollywood* that reports on the Sea to Shining Sea March so that you don't have to."

"You mean like a special correspondent?"

"I guess I do, yes." He picked up the cups again. "Now, for God's sake, buck up. Nobody wants to sit next to Little Miss Down-In-The-Mouth while watching television history in the making."

* * *

Hollywood was still talking about "Lucy Goes to the Hospital" at Marilyn's premiere a few nights later.

When CBS announced that the episode captured an unheard-of seventy-one percent of American television sets, columnists whipped themselves into a frenzy of predictions about the beginning of the end of the motion-picture experience.

But then Kathryn watched *Niagara* unfold on the Carthay Circle screen and realized that steamy, sordid tales of murder, sex, and suicide could never be told on TV's tiny screen. There was room for both forms of entertainment.

As a sultry Marilyn plotted murder in glorious Technicolor, Twentieth Century-Fox's publicity department set up a cocktail party in the theater's foyer. After the movie, the audience gravitated to the bar and Kathryn roamed the lobby for Mike Connolly. He hadn't been in the office for the past few days.

Severe laryngitis was the official excuse, but Kathryn suspected "severe boozing-itis" was a more likely cause. She hadn't seen him enter the auditorium, but she would have bet her last dollar that Connolly wouldn't miss this night.

A glimpse of white flashed among the tuxedo forest. *Of course he's wearing white linen to a formal premiere. God forbid anybody should miss him.*

She was maneuvering toward Connolly when Leo stepped in front of her. "Can I get you a drink?"

She told him she'd love a sidecar. "You'll need to give me a minute, though. Mike Connolly and I have business to discuss."

Leo knitted his brows. "Isn't that what offices are for?"

She told him Hollywood was a twenty-four-hour town and zigzagged until she could position herself in Connolly's line of sight. She summoned him toward her.

"You look . . . intense," he said.

She smelled brandy on his breath. "I have a problem!"

"And you're coming to me? Why, Miss Massey, I'm flattered."

No, you're not. But you're curious as hell. "It's this march. I'm in over my head."

"I find that hard to believe."

"You know how Sunbeam and Betty Crocker are sponsors? Well, they want me to report each week on their progress across the country."

The guy's smile curdled. "We talked about that."

"The trouble is, I don't know Jesus from Jerusalem. I'm scared to death that I'm going to either offend people or come across like an ignoramus."

"Or both."

Yes, you brandy-soaked turd, or both. "Exactly!"

"So what do you want from me? Bible classes?"

"I was thinking along the lines of a crash course."

"Aren't there plenty of priests you could ask?"

"I can't imagine there are many priests who are as savvy with the media as you are." *Bait and hook.* "To be honest, I wish you could take the whole thing off my hands."

"What whole thing?"

"Reporting on the march each week on my show."

And reel him in.

"Why don't I?"

"Why don't you what?"

"Handle the march."

"But how would something like that work? Unless you mean—like a special segment?"

Connolly deposited his drink on the shelf next to them. It clanged on the marble. "I could be your special correspondent!"

Kathryn shook her head. "You heard Wilkerson when you came on board. I handle the broad issues; you stick to the juicy gossip. It's worked well so far—"

"Lookit, I'm the perfect choice. I'm very publicly pro-religion and pro-Catholic." *You left out pro-personal publicity.* "You just convince your Mister Sunbeam boyfriend, and leave Wilkerson to me. I'll talk him around."

That wouldn't be hard. Yesterday afternoon, in the middle of a discussion about how to tactfully report on Rita Hayworth's upcoming divorce from Prince Aly Khan, Kathryn dropped in a couple of comments about how well she and Connolly were working together.

"Honestly," she told Gwennie and Doris later, "men can be so gullible, it's almost no fun at all."

"Do you think you can?" Kathryn asked. "In my experience, Wilkerson prefers to come up with his own ideas."

"Or thinks he does."

She nudged his shoulder. "Oh, you *are* a sly one."

"Much can be accomplished with a good old-fashioned man-to-man chat."

Marilyn entered the foyer, dazzling in a chic concoction of purple lace supported by ten black petticoats. She spotted Kathryn and waved.

"We should congratulate her," Kathryn said, just as a thicket of admirers besieged the girl of the moment and Kathryn saw she wouldn't get close.

Across the room, a hand held a bright orange cocktail in a martini glass above the heads. It was Leo—she recognized the wristwatch.

"Say, wait a minute. What's your angle?" Cagey mistrust now etched Connolly's face. "You've always been the face and voice of the *Hollywood Reporter* and now you're being selfless. I don't get it."

"I'm being the opposite of selfless, if you want to know the truth." A trio of reporters elbowed past Kathryn and Connolly en route to Marilyn. She waited until they were past. "When it comes to all that religious stuff, I'm a fish out of water. I do not relish the prospect of flopping around on the deck gasping for my last breath while I'm live on the air with twenty million people listening. The whole Jesus thing is more up your alley than mine. I'm happy for you to do the Voss stuff and save me any possible humiliation." Kathryn counted slowly to five. "Of course, if you've changed your mind . . ."

She watched panic replace the suspicion in his eyes. "I didn't say that."

"Do you need time to think about whether or not you're up for the job?"

"No," he shot back. "I'd love to."

Leo was still holding Kathryn's sidecar above the heads of the crowd. One of the reporters bumped him, moving the cocktail into the light cast by a fixture over the bar. It looked like a beacon now. *Come to me . . . come to me . . .*

CHAPTER 31

Lauren Bacall burst into Chez Gwendolyn amid a flurry of apologies for being so late. "Leslie's just started teething. Bogie and I were up all night with her, so none of us got much sleep. I finally conked out around five this morning."

"Don't worry, you're here now." Gwendolyn led her into the workroom. "I just read Kathryn's column. Congrats on the new contract."

This morning, Kathryn broke the news that Lauren signed a contract with Twentieth Century-Fox that required only one picture a year. Despite her rough night, the woman burned with the vitality of a star at the top of her game.

When Lauren asked for a dress for the Academy Awards, Gwendolyn was very flattered. Although neither Lauren nor Bogie nor any movie they were in had been nominated, it was the first time the ceremony would be televised, and everybody would be on show. A number of industry stalwarts sniffed that it was like allowing the lunatics to run the asylum for a day, but Gwendolyn agreed with Marcus—television was the way of the future. Why pretend otherwise?

At a wholesaler in downtown LA, Gwendolyn had recently come across a bolt of silk the same shade of Lauren's eyes and snapped it up. "I hear your first movie will be *How to Marry a Millionaire*."

Zanuck lost no time following through with Marcus' suggestion to film *The Greeks Had a Word for It* for a third time, and in a matter of only days word at the studio got around that Nunnally Johnson was already at work on the screenplay.

"We start filming next week." Lauren ran her hands down the material and hummed her approval. "And with Marilyn Monroe, no less. She's a client of yours, isn't she?"

Gwendolyn pulled out her sketch. Cut low across the chest, tight around the bodice, and made of interlocking triangles. "She is, yes, but how do you know that?"

"For the same reason I wondered if you thought I wouldn't show up."

Lauren Bacall was one of the most punctual people Gwendolyn knew. "Why would I think that?"

"The new issue of *Confidential*."

Gwendolyn held the silk up to Lauren's face. Now that she could compare the material to her eyes, she saw the shade didn't quite match. It was darker, but it suited her complexion. "I saw the first one, but it was so tacky. Honestly, I'm surprised you bother with trash like that."

"You really haven't seen it?" Lauren's tone had turned serious.

"Are you saying I should?"

Lauren retrieved a copy of *Confidential* from her bag and flipped to a sycophantic article about Walter Winchell. It trumpeted the bravery he displayed on a weekly basis by reporting on mobster mayhem, police bungling, celebrity marital shenanigans, and dubious political maneuverings. It ended with a florid declaration that the publishers of *Confidential* looked forward to working alongside such a proud and bold patriot.

"A bit over the top," Gwendolyn commented.

"No, no, the other page." Lauren pointed to an article halfway down.

> *Here's a cautionary tale of sartorial suspicion if ever we've heard one. It concerns a Sunset Strip boutique with the oo-la-la Frenchy sobriquet —*

"What's a sobriquet?" Even as Gwendolyn asked the question, she already knew she didn't want to hear the answer.

"Just a fancy word for nickname," Lauren said, "but this magazine likes to think it's up there with Steinbeck and Hemingway."

> *— which caters to the Noir trade. La Madame-in-charge used to sell under the cover of darkness — pun most assuredly intended — but now conducts business openly as though the whole world approves. And it doesn't stop with the selling of frocks. Evidently, La Madame holds mixed-race cocktail parties in the spacious back room where guests have been known to swap cocktails as readily as they swap clothes.*

"WHAT?!" If this had been her own copy, Gwendolyn would have hurled it into the alley. "Mixed parties where people swap clothes? How in the name of Jesus, Mary, and Joseph can they be allowed to print such tripe?"

"Nobody appears to be stopping them. Keep reading."

> *But don't assume they confine themselves to sticking with their gender when it comes to petticoats and garters, neckties and tuxedos. All you need to know is the password. It's "Licketysplitter" — but don't even ask what that refers to!*

Gwendolyn slammed the magazine onto her workbench. She was too shocked to even whip up a cuss word.

"Have you sold merchandise to colored women?" Lauren asked.

"Ella Fitzgerald, Lena Horne, Hattie McDaniel, Dorothy Dandridge."

"What about the cocktail parties?"

"That is a complete fabrication!"

Lauren pointed to the last sentence. "What do they mean by Licketysplitter?"

Not long after the war, Gwendolyn discovered her boss at Bullocks Wilshire was a cross-dresser. Gwendolyn sewed him a flattering gown that made him the belle of the ball at a cross-dresser bar called The Midnight Frolics. The regulars referred to it as "The Licks," and called themselves "Licketysplitters." Soon, Gwendolyn was making dresses for most the patrons, who hailed her Queen of the Licketysplitters.

All this led to Gwendolyn opening her store, which was ironic because soon after, the Licketysplitters defected to a dressmaker who worked for half the price.

"Licketysplitter is just an old private joke."

"Not so private, apparently. Let's forget about this." Lauren slung the magazine back into her bag. "If the Academy Awards are going to be televised, we'll need to come up with something that looks good from all angles."

* * *

As Gwendolyn cut wedge-shaped panels of moss green silk, Herman Dewberry's face popped into her mind. Or more specifically, that odd look on his face that night of the *Bwana Devil* preview.

She got busy with the Christmas and New Year rush and didn't worry too much that she didn't hear back from him about extending the Sunset Boulevard line. January came and went. By the time February rolled around, she figured maybe his boss had put the kibosh on the whole idea.

But that was before *Confidential.*

Noir trade.

Madame-in-charge.

Cover of darkness.

Mixed-race cocktail parties.

The more she thought about it, the madder she got. Questions that wouldn't have plagued her now popped up like groundhogs. Had *Confidential* suckered Herman into being a source? But what sense did that make? Why would he tell them about the Licketysplitters?

It took significant willpower to stop herself from jumping on the phone, but touchy matters like these were better handled once the initial blast of fury had subsided. She waited forty-eight hours, but when she called his office, he wasn't available and she had to leave a message.

When he failed to return her call, disappointment became annoyance, which mutated into suspicion. She resented how a no-good pile of hogwash could force her to doubt a gentleman like Herman Dewberry. But after a week of unreturned calls, Gwendolyn decided there was nothing left but to confront the man face-to-face.

Fortunately, he was a creature of habit. He took his lunch at the same time each day, at the same table in the Bullocks Wilshire Tea Room.

As an employee, Gwendolyn never ate at the store's restaurant, but she liked its calming spearmint green and earthy terra cotta Southwest color scheme. A few freshly coiffed ladies of leisure sat at scattered tables, but none were within eavesdropping distance of Herman.

He didn't look up from his fruit cup until she was close enough to clobber him. His face paled. She sat down without an invitation.

"I've left five messages for you over the past week. Did you not receive them?"

He wiped a linen napkin across his mouth with exaggerated care. "I've received them."

"That night of the *Bwana Devil* preview, you said you were going to set to work about extending the Sunset Boulevard line. That was months ago, Herman. If you've changed your mind, all you had to do was say so. There was no need to leave me dangling."

"First of all, I want you to know that I did exactly as I promised. I worked up a presentation to my boss. As per usual, he took his sweet time getting back to me, but when he finally did, he wanted a comparison of rival products."

"Is that unusual?"

"Not at all. I expected it. But it's a lot of work—facts, figures, graphs, pages of statistics. Everything pointed to exactly what I hoped, so I sent the report upstairs to be rubber-stamped."

"So why didn't you make the offer?"

"Because nothing happened. After a couple of weeks, I cornered him and asked him what gives? That's when I learned my boss goes to the same church as Joseph Breen, and it's a big supporter of this Sea to Shining Sea March. You know how that is—it's all one big boys' club."

Gwendolyn thought of Marcus' comment the night of Marilyn's birthday. "It's a cabal," she said, "but what does any of this have to do with extending my line?"

Herman gave a theatrical sigh. "I would have clued you in if I'd known what was going on, but they've kept me in the dark."

"What *do* you know?"

"Nothing for sure. But from what I've been able to piece together, Voss is chummy with Winchell, who is chummy with Breen, who is chummy with my boss, who is now very proud of the fact he's become chummy with Winchell." Herman ran his hand over his thinning hair and started chewing his lips. "Have you read the latest *Confidential*?"

"Why do you think I'm here?"

"According to the girl who runs the executive typing pool, Winchell sent my boss an advance copy of that article."

"I can guess the rest," she said. "Just be straight with me. Is it too late? Is the deal off? Because if the answer's yes—"

"It's not officially off, so that's good. I think it can be saved, but only if you swear that nothing in that blind item is true."

"The guff about the back-room after-hours parties is *completely* made up."

"How do you explain" —he lowered his voice to a whisper— "the Licketysplitter reference?"

"Truthfully? I wondered if it came from you."

"ME?" He drew back like a dowager in an Oscar Wilde comedy.

"I couldn't think of any other way. But *Confidential* has Fred Otash on the payroll, so with that lowlife snooping around, anything's possible."

"But what about this business of catering to the Negro trade? That's what it comes down to."

His face remained neutral as she took him through the same list she'd told Bacall.

"Chez Gwendolyn is your business," he said, "so you get to run it however you see fit. But if you continue with the Negro trade, you can forget about Bullocks extending your line of cosmetics. Furthermore, if you fail to convince the higher-ups that the whole article is a sham I wouldn't be surprised if they dropped your perfume altogether."

It wasn't like Gwendolyn had come to depend on her perfume. Chez Gwendolyn was doing okay without the Bullocks royalties. But larger profits meant she could expand her business. She wanted to advertise more, and to work her connections with people like Lauren and Marilyn and Travilla. That would lead to employing dressmakers and leave her free to work toward opening up a chain of stores. Anyone who thought her plans began and ended with just one boutique gravely underestimated her.

"My dear," he said, "it's time to make a decision."

He was right. Sooner or later, she was going to have to choose. She realized that she didn't resent Herman, or his boss, or Winchell, or the publishers of *Confidential* nearly as much as she resented being made to choose between being an ambitious businesswoman or a modern woman of the world who only saw skin tones in terms of which hues of silk and chiffon they matched best.

Why can't I be both?

CHAPTER 32

Marcus wondered how he was going to fit the entire penthouse into a single shot. The production team on *How to Marry a Millionaire* had obeyed Zanuck's decree — "We're going wide, boys. As wide as we can!" — and built a set that filled the longest soundstage on the Fox lot. And now that it was jammed with dress extras playing guests at the wedding of Lauren Bacall's character, it was Marcus' job to capture the vast pandemonium of it all.

The twinkling New York skyline wasn't going to fool anyone in the theaters, but it was still a spectacular feature. They only had a few more takes to do before everybody would be let go for the day, so time — as it always did on a movie set — was speeding by.

What he needed was a ladder.

The gaffer would know where to find one, but Marcus couldn't see him. He asked a couple of crew members, but they didn't know. The key grip was up on the camera crane and beyond shouting distance.

He'd have to improvise.

The *Millionaire* set had been harmonious, but Marcus had shot enough production stills by now to know that not all sets were created equal.

Sam Dodds procured him a week's work at Warner Bros., documenting their first 3-D movie, *House of Wax*. The director, André de Toth, only had one eye and was therefore unable to see the third dimension, which made him the least logical choice to direct a 3-D movie. The frustration and tension were palpable.

Marcus was glad to return to *I Love Lucy*, now even more popular since the well-orchestrated birth of the most famous baby in television. In early April, the first edition of *TV Guide* featured a cover photo of "Lucy's $50,000,000 Baby." The photo wasn't Marcus', but some of the shots included in the story were, for which he received an unexpected windfall.

Despite all this, when he walked onto the set of *How to Marry a Millionaire*, he was surprised to be referred to as "the *Lucy* photographer." While this morsel of recognition helped his self-confidence recover from months and months of near-starvation, it also had a downside.

Until now, he'd been able to sneak around sets as he caught stars, directors, and crewmembers in unguarded moments. It was the actors he really had to watch out for. They spent their lives developing a sense of how they came across on camera, which side was their most flattering, and what lighting conditions favored them best.

But now that he was "the *Lucy* photographer," everybody knew his face. Whenever he raised his camera, they straightened up, smiled wider, and held their pose.

Gwendolyn suggested he go undercover. He wasn't sure if it was the brown duds, his new rimless specs and surprisingly thick salt-and-pepper beard, or maybe people just got used to him, but as the shoot progressed, Marcus found it easier to slip around the cameras and lights to get the shots he wanted.

Whenever he ran his hand over his beard, he wondered what Oliver would think of it. It was now two years since they'd seen each other. Did Oliver think of him as often as he thought of Oliver? Was he happy in the seminary? Did he ever stop to question his choice? Maybe Kathryn was right when she said he'd reverted to form.

Jean Negulesco strode onto the penthouse set with the poise of a symphony conductor. He raised his hands for silence and waited for the hubbub to drop off.

"We're having trouble with these new widescreen cameras. They must be synchronized perfectly, but that isn't happening. Hopefully we'll get underway soon."

As the scattered conversations resumed, Marcus spotted an unusually large shipping crate and was searching around for a stepladder when he heard a familiar voice behind him.

"Marcus, is that you?"

He hadn't seen Regina since he started work on *Lucy*.

She patted his beard. "I hardly recognized you!"

Marcus stepped back to take in the resplendent sight of Regina in a gown of cranberry taffeta. "And get a load of *you*."

"A Travilla original, doncha know! There's a tag on the back that says 'Nora Prentiss,' so I like to think Ann Sheridan wore it." She twirled to show off the full skirt. "Ain't it something?"

He suspected she'd had her hair and makeup done at the studio. Seeing her so well put-together, he could glimpse the captivating flapper she'd once been. It was also the first time he'd been close to her and hadn't smelled the lingering tinge of marijuana.

"You're a sight to behold," he told her.

"Oh my goodness, 1953 is shaping up to be my busiest year ever! I'm up for a part on the *Dragnet* TV show as Officer Frank Smith's mother. They want to flesh out their characters and give them some depth and background story. It's not a big part, of course, but it'd be regular. Or semi, at least."

"I think that's called a recurring role." Marcus hunted around for a stool or stepladder to help him up onto the shipping crate.

"That's probably why they asked for a head shot."

"Did you send it in yet?"

"I don't have any taken this side of the war."

"Why don't I do it?"

"Really?"

Marcus ignored Negulesco's admonishment on *Titanic* to not waste film on extras. He was now friendly with the guys in the photograph lab and they sure didn't care.

"You look like a million bucks. The bedroom set's got lovely pale gray and cream floral wallpaper. I need to shoot this set now that it's filled with extras, so give me ten minutes and meet me there."

Regina scuttled away as Marcus scrambled on top of the crate and got the shots he needed. Ten minutes later, Regina was waiting for him with her hair re-fluffed and her lipstick refreshed.

He pressed the camera to his eye; Regina broke out a winning smile. "I know someone who works on *Dragnet*," Marcus said. Snap! Snap! "More of a friend of a friend." Snap! Snap! "He works in wardrobe, so perhaps he could put you in something memorable." Snap! Snap! Snap!

"Oh my goodness, Marcus, that would be wonderful. What's his name?"

"Horton Tattler."

"You mean Tattler's Tuxedos?"

"Yep. Lift your chin." Snap! Snap!

"I couldn't ask for anything more—oh! Hello, Mr. Negulesco."

Shit! Shit! Shit! Marcus lowered his camera. "I just asked this lovely lady if she could assist me with a couple of test shots. The lighting here—"

"Please excuse us."

Regina disappeared.

"I'm sorry we haven't had a chance to say hello again," Negulesco said.

"You've been awful busy."

"The publicity department sent me a stack of the stills you've been taking."

His distant manner made him hard to read. Marcus said, "Your set is so long that I'd have loved to climb up top but there are union rules about that."

"And we cannot upset the union. Listen, I wanted to tell you how impressed I was with what you did on *Titanic*. Fine, fine work."

Marcus never did hear if the photos he'd taken of Stanwyck and Wagner had caught the intimacy Zanuck was looking for. He searched in vain for signs. "Thank you. I'm glad you liked it, Mr. Negulesco."

"You're very good at catching the drama."

"You're very good at directing it." Marcus' compliment resulted in a slight curling of the man's lips.

He pointed to Marcus' film bag. "Once you've handed in your work, I'd like to choose my favorite photos and have them bound into a book like Mervyn LeRoy did on *Quo Vadis*."

"I'm sure everybody would appreciate the gesture."

"I want you to have a copy," Negulesco continued, "but I need to double-check that I've got your name right."

Asking Marcus to spell his name was the usual way people tried to establish if they were talking to the guy who'd blown up in front of HUAC.

"A.D.L.E.R. And yes, I'm *that* Marcus Adler."

At this point in the conversation, most people either pretended they had no idea they were talking to *that* Marcus Adler or feigned indifference. The more impassioned ones would launch into their own brush with anti-Communism, or HUAC, or the *Red Channels* booklet, often in the context of a neighbor or family member, invented or otherwise.

But Negulesco didn't flinch. Nor did he give any indication that Marcus had been the subject of discussion between him and Zanuck.

One of the second assistant directors appeared in the doorway of the bedroom set. "Excuse me, but Bruce sent me to tell you that they've nutted out the problem and need about thirty minutes."

"Tell him we'll go into overtime so make it twenty."

The kid bolted and Negulesco turned back to Marcus. "As soon as I wrap on this picture, I'm to start immediate work on my next project."

Kathryn had already made the announcement in her column. *"There's No Place Like Rome,"* Marcus said.

"That's right."

"It's a terrible title, if you don't mind my saying."

For the first time since Marcus walked onto the *Millionaire* set, Negulesco's stoicism broke and he smiled. "I told Zanuck that it sounds like *The Wizard of Oz* set in Tuscany."

"I'm surprised Zanuck's in favor of it."

"He's not. It's one of two titles the screenwriters came up with." Negulesco deadpanned a Buster Keaton mug. *"We Believe in Love."*

"Even worse. Isn't it based on a book?"

"Three Coins in the Fountain."

"That's your title right there. Everybody wants to go to Rome and throw a coin in the Trevi fountain."

The smile faded from the director's face as capriciously as it had appeared. "Production will first be here at the studios. After that, we move to Italy: Rome, Venice, and Merano. Zanuck gave me a rundown of your history, including your time on *Quo Vadis.*"

"I had four or five months there. Rome's getting back on its feet again. For such an ancient city, it's very youthful, very fresh—"

"I feel that you could be a useful addition to my team."

"As your still photographer?"

"Of course, but perhaps also tour guide, location scout, etc. I find that when shooting on location in a country with a foreign language, all manner of misunderstandings and complications can crop up."

"My Italian's pretty rusty," Marcus warned.

"It's a damn sight better than mine, which is nil. Between now and then perhaps you could brush up. I've been led to believe you're very skilled with language. In particular, *written* language."

Marcus' mouth went dry. "Mr. Negulesco, there's something you need to know."

"If you're referring to the graylist, Zanuck and I have already had that conversation. It might be possible to get you off it if we can show that you've been working in a creative and contributive capacity."

It hadn't escaped Marcus' notice that Negulesco had couched this conversation in vague and noncommittal terms.

"When does production leave for Rome?" Marcus asked.

"This might be your only chance to get off the graylist. Does it matter what date we leave?"

Lately, Kathryn's misgivings about the sponsorship deal and her consumption of scotch had snowballed. Almost every night now she would drop into Marcus' room, bottle in hand, but he hardly felt justified in stopping her. After all, he'd committed alcoholic hara-kiri in the past, and she'd never tried to take away his Four Roses. But as he watched her refill her glass night after night like it was iced tea, he felt he should at least try.

In the end, he promised that no matter how many plagues heralded the Four Horsemen of the Apocalypse, he would be with her when she walked out in front of all those people at the Los Angeles tent revival to introduce Uncle Flim-Flam.

"No," Marcus told Negulesco. "I just need to plan ahead."

"We fly out the first week of August."

"Good. Great."

"So that's a yes?"

"Absolutely. And thank you!"

Marcus was still nodding when the director told him his production coordinator would be in touch with the arrangements and left to rejoin the cast and crew on the penthouse set.

Marcus tried to do some mental math. Voss' march kicked off next week, which meant around May 20. If it was a twelve-week trek, that would put him into Los Angeles—

"Gee, Marcus, I hope I didn't get you into no trouble." Regina leaned against the doorjamb, worry creasing her face.

"Not at all." He walked her back into the wedding scene just as Negulesco was calling the actors to take their places.

"You looked awful serious back there," Regina whispered.

"You ought to scoot. You don't want your director to call you out in front of the whole cast and crew."

He stood on the sidelines, watching the stars replace their stand-ins. Even in her cat-eye spectacles and demure suit with a fur-lined collar sitting high on her neck, Marilyn still managed to draw every eye in the room. She tapped her glasses with a gloved finger and mouthed, "I like your new specs!"

He mouthed back his thanks and snapped off a few more frames.

So, May 20th plus twelve weeks comes out at . . .

Marcus' heart seized up when he realized that the *Fountain* crew would already be in Rome when Voss and his caravan of crazies hit LA.

CHAPTER 33

The first thing Kathryn did when she got to her dressing room was break the unbreakable rule. She gently kicked the door closed behind her and pulled out a chrome hip flask to swig a nip of scotch.

She knew she'd been hitting the Johnnie Walker a little too much lately, and she was thankful that Marcus hadn't said anything, even though she could see the disapproval in his eyes whenever she landed on his doorstep. But she'd never indulged before a broadcast. Not once. Not ever. But tonight was different.

She closed her eyes and waited for the warmth to unfurl across her chest. *Ah!* She took another nip and let her head flop back onto her shoulders as she leaned against the wall. The muffled sounds in the corridor outside her dressing room receded. What a madhouse it was out there.

Today was the big day: Sheldon Voss was kicking off his march with a revival on the steps of the Lincoln Memorial in Washington DC.

In every broadcast and interview, Voss trumpeted the same message: America's traditional values were being trampled to death amid the unprecedented postwar boom bewitching the country.

In principle, Kathryn didn't disagree with Voss' message of sticking to one's values, but she lost patience the night she read a transcript in the *L.A. Times* of his speech at a fundraising rally in Madison Square Garden when he declared,

"Everybody has their place in society. Men go out to win the bread, and women stay home to tend the young. An organized society is an orderly society is a successful society. Read your Bible, folks. It's all laid out right there!"

Kathryn had never read the Bible, but she knew a load of horse hockey when she heard it. Conformity, fitting in, and staying in your place was fine if you were white and male and married and Protestant and rich.

"What about us women who *enjoy* working?" Kathryn screeched later to Marcus and Gwendolyn. "Or for whom getting married isn't the be all and end all? Or who have no interest in what the Bible says? Or who are Jewish? Or colored? Or who have six kids and can't afford to live off one salary?"

There was a lot Kathryn wanted to say over the spring of '53, but her sponsors were over the moon about Voss' traditionalist stance. Their target market was Mrs. Happy Homemaker Mom, and they were moving merchandise like never before. It was hard to pitch a fit when your radio ratings were surging.

Kathryn told herself, "He's only giving them what they want to hear," but found little comfort in it. She was glad she'd asked Mike Connolly to be her special correspondent—the less she had to do with Voss, the better.

But then Voss announced that he'd received a lengthy excerpt from Alfred Kinsey's forthcoming *Sexual Behavior in the Human Female,* and declared his dismay over Kinsey's claims that more than half of American women were not virgins when they got married, and that a quarter of married women had extramarital affairs. He saved his most blistering outrage over Kinsey's most shocking revelation of all: Women enjoyed sex.

Overnight, he raised the timbre of his vitriol. He held Kinsey up as the perfect example of American society going wrong. Who was he to stick his nose into America's bedroom? How dare he propagate the idea that it wasn't unusual for American women to have premarital sex or indulge in affairs?

None of Kinsey's findings surprised Kathryn, and as far as she was concerned, the more Voss talked, the more out of touch he sounded.

But then he crossed the line and Kathryn couldn't stay silent.

In Nashville, Tennessee, Voss not only denounced Alfred Kinsey as the male representation of everything wrong in America, but held up Marilyn Monroe as his female equivalent.

Twentieth Century-Fox had started to release publicity stills from Marilyn's upcoming movie, *Gentlemen Prefer Blondes*. Most of them featured her in a pink strapless gown surrounded by a dozen chorus boys as she grabbed at the jewels they offered her in a number called "Diamonds Are a Girl's Best Friend."

"Marilyn Monroe is a hussy!" Voss thundered from the cover of *Time*. "An amoral gold-digger who thumbs her nose at the principles that have kept Americans on the path of righteousness. We only have to look at that shameful calendar to know the sort of Jezebel she is. By our actions shall we be known. By Miss Monroe's actions we know her as the personification of lust and greed against which we must fight if we want entrance to the kingdom of heaven."

Kathryn feverishly banged out an article refuting Voss' outrageous statement. All her pent-up frustrations of the past year gushed onto her typewriter. When she was done, she sent copies to Wilkerson, Connolly, Leo, and Leo's counterpart at Betty Crocker. Within hours, Wilkerson had called a summit in his office.

Leo tried not to be angry, but Kathryn could tell he wanted to throttle her. The Betty Crocker guy, however, had no such reservations. He charged her with treachery and demanded she be replaced with the public face of Betty Crocker, Adelaide Hawley.

Ironically, the coolest head in the room belonged to Mike Connolly.

He suggested that the *Hollywood Reporter* carry a full-page spread: *THE PROS AND CONS OF SHELDON VOSS.* "He called Hollywood 'the Sodom and Gomorrah of the West which must be purged of its debauchery,'" Connolly reminded them, "so our readers do have some skin in this game. Why not carry Kathryn's piece alongside one by me taking the opposite view, and let readers make up their own minds?"

The resulting article set many Hollywood tongues to wagging, but only until the execution date of convicted spies Julius and Ethel Rosenberg was set for June. Soon after that, Senator McCarthy accused former President Truman of supporting Communism. Americans had other matters to infuriate them, and the article was forgotten.

But not by Kathryn Massey. She was still mad. And still skeptical that she could get through this broadcast without losing her composure.

She reminded her reflection in the NBC dressing-room mirror that there was a grand prize in play for her after this summer of righteousness was over. She took another nip and was slipping the flask into her purse when someone knocked on her door.

"Ya decent?"

Kathryn had originally wanted Marilyn on this auspicious show, but Voss' attack put the kibosh on that. Instead, Zanuck offered up Jane Russell. She was Marilyn's costar in *Gentlemen Prefer Blondes,* so the movie still got a huge plug, and she could sing her main song from the movie, "Ain't There Anyone Here for Love?" It also helped that Jane was openly, devoutly, and unapologetically Christian.

Jane looked breathtaking in a black cocktail dress loaded with sequins. "I'm not Marilyn, but will I do?"

"You'll more than do."

Jane checked in Kathryn's mirror for lipstick on her teeth. "Is it true you've got Kate Smith on tonight?"

That was another compromise Kathryn had made to get her tirade into print. Given that the live broadcast from Washington was the pole holding up tonight's circus, Kathryn agreed to Leo's suggestion that the Songbird of the South could be tonight's musical guest.

"Yes," Kathryn said. "She's singing 'The Rosary.'"

Satisfied with what she saw in the mirror, Jane asked, "Does that mean I won't have to sing?"

NBC had given *Window on Hollywood* an extra half hour of *Dragnet*'s time. Despite the successful TV version, the radio incarnation was still a winner, but the NBC execs wanted to maximize ratings for the big night. Perhaps even take her show to the very top?

An extra half hour was a lot of airtime to fill, so Kathryn enlisted a comedy writer who'd spent three years on *The Jack Benny Show* to write a skit for Kathryn and Adelaide Hawley. He wrote a riot of a script about baking a cake during an earthquake that everybody loved. It had been a herculean task to fill every moment of the broadcast; Kathryn didn't want to answer Jane's question.

"If you don't sing, we'll have a hole in the—"

"Don't worry about that. I have a great story about filming that number. I was surrounded by all these weight-lifting hunks, miming my ever-loving tushie off, and one of them kicks me into the pool!"

"On purpose?"

"Nah, but Howard Hawks got such a laugh out of it that he restaged everything. Now it ends with me getting lifted out of the water wringing wet, but still singing!" She read Kathryn's doubt. "Don't worry, it'll be hilarious. Between Sheldon Voss and Kate Smith, you might need some levity."

Kathryn was surprised at that, given Jane's faith, but she was grateful. On the other hand, she wondered whether a story in which the actress with the world's most famous bosom talks about being plunged into a pool of bodybuilders was appropriate for a program featuring Kate Smith singing "The Rosary" before a tent revival meeting.

"Trust me, hon," Jane said. "I know the difference between show biz and God biz."

Leo appeared in the doorway. "Miss Russell, I wanted to introduce myself and wish you the best of luck out there."

"You mean break a leg, don't you?"

"Jane was wondering if it's necessary for her to sing tonight," Kathryn said.

"I can get by in a recording studio, but in front of a band and a live audience?" Jane let out a low whistle.

Leo nodded. "I've asked Kate to sing a second number. She suggested 'It Could Happen To You,' which the band's bound to know."

"Great!" Jane exclaimed. "What a relief!"

Although it was an easy fix to a last-minute hiccup, Kathryn felt as though her show was being hijacked.

When she started dating her sponsor, she knew it could lead to a thorny tangle of ethical dilemmas. In the intervening three years, she and Leo had negotiated their way through one briar patch after another. It hadn't been easy, but her anti-Voss speech had brought them closer to the brink of breaking up than ever before. Mike Connolly's proposal brought them back, but only just. The roses Leo sent on the twelfth of each month to commemorate their first date had faded away, as had their expensive dinners at Perino's. If she wasn't free to express herself, he was not the man for her.

The air in the dressing room suddenly felt dense. Luckily, Jane was nobody's fool and told Kathryn she'd see her in the wings. Leo closed the door behind her.

"You're okay with that change, aren't you?" Leo asked.

Kathryn shrugged off her sour mood. She had a big show to prepare for and she needed to be free of distractions. "Sure."

He closed the space between them to a more intimate couple of inches, near enough for her to smell the musky aftershave balm she'd given him for Christmas. "Tonight's show could push you ahead of *Lux Radio Theatre*, *Amos 'n' Andy*, and even Winchell."

She smiled up at him. "Wouldn't that be great?"

"You're going to do a wonderful job tonight."

It sounded like the instructions of a boss until he ran his hand along her arm, across her shoulder, and up her neck until it looped around her mouth and ended at her chin. He tilted it upward and placed a tender kiss on her lips. "I'm so proud of you."

She thought of her father. Did the inmates at Sing Sing even have access to the outside world? It was possible the place was on lockdown. The Rosenbergs had just been executed for conspiracy—surely emotions were running high over there.

Three raps on the door, then, "Ten minutes to air, Miss Massey."

Leo kissed the tips of her fingers. "Go get 'em."

When Kathryn arrived in the wings of Studio Two, Jane Russell and Adelaide were already standing in front of a television monitor that showed people filing into Studio One.

"We're under siege!" Adelaide declared, keeping her eyes on the screen. "NBC has put them into the *Dragnet* studio."

"There's more in the foyer," Jane added, "and they've even spilled out into the street. NBC is rigging up loudspeakers so the folks on the sidewalk can hear the broadcast."

On the other side of the stage, Mike Connolly stood alone, studying notes on a stack of index cards. He wore an ivory dinner jacket, black bow tie, black trousers, and patent leather shoes.

He looks like he's going to a gala at the White House.

Connolly waved; hesitation blurred his smile.

He's had a couple of nips himself.

Her producer, Wallace Reed tapped her shoulder and she strode onstage to thunderous applause. "Are you as excited as I am about tonight?"

On this night of all nights, Kathryn wished she could take comfort in seeing Marcus and Gwendolyn's faces. She scanned the audience, but couldn't find them anywhere. With all those crowds outside, she wasn't sure they were even in the building.

The stage manager counted her down to the short electronic beep, and a red light on the back wall of the studio glowed.

"Hello, America, this is Kathryn Massey."

She got through her opening monologue without a stumble. Her earthquake cake skit with Adelaide went over like Cracker Jack, and Jane managed to make her *Gentlemen Prefer Blondes* story sound like a swim meet with the local boy-scout troop.

Kate Smith was brave to follow Jane's clean-bawdy-funny story, but she sang her first song like it was the most natural thing in the world. She launched into her improvised number with such confidence that nobody could tell she and the band were flying without a net.

As Kate hit her final note, Kathryn caught sight of Mike Connolly taking a nip from a burnished copper flask. She smiled to herself at the thought that maybe they weren't quite so different, after all. But then he took a second nip. Then a third. Was he going to stagger out here half sauced?

Kathryn leaned into her microphone. "Gosh, but what a wonderful way Kate Smith has with a song. And now, folks, we come to the extra special part of tonight's broadcast. Joining me tonight, and for the next twelve weeks, is a *Hollywood Reporter* colleague of mine. Perhaps you've read his *Rambling Reporter* column. Please welcome Mr. Mike Connolly!"

He ambled on stage relaxed as Bing Crosby and gripped his microphone like it was a willing partner for the mambo.

"Ladies and gentlemen, boys and girls, this is Mike Connolly, your Sea to Shining Sea special correspondent. I'll be joining Kathryn Massey each week, and I do hope you'll tune in as Sheldon Voss journeys across these great United States."

His words flowed smoother than the Johnnie Walker in Kathryn's flask.

"Thank you, Mike," Kathryn said, "and welcome to *Window on Hollywood*. Do you know if—"

"Yes!" Cutting in like that was a major no-no. Kathryn flashed a frown at him, but he was playing to the studio audience. "Voss is about to commence his address standing at the top step of the Lincoln Memorial. Behind him is the nineteen-foot marble statue of Honest Abe himself, and collected around him are thousands of his followers at this auspicious beginning of what will no doubt be a memorable summer."

Oh, brother. Laying it on a bit thick, aren't you?

"Ladies and gentlemen," Connolly continued, "we're crossing now to the nation's capital."

"Hello, America. My name is Sheldon Voss, and I am speaking to you not just from the Lincoln Memorial, but also from my heart."

Kathryn had expected the voice of some local NBC reporter, not Voss himself.

"We had a tough time of it during the Great Depression, but we survived. We faced challenges of a different nature during the war, but we survived that, too. Since then, we have known unprecedented prosperity. The Great American Dream of owning your own home has become a reality for millions of people for whom it was only ever just that: a dream."

His voice! It was so warm, so kind, and so unexpectedly *human.*

"And not just a home," Voss continued, "but a car in the garage; a television in the living room; washing machine in the laundry; chickens in the deep freeze. All the conveniences of modern life are within reach of many Americans, if only on the installment plan. They're so close we can almost touch them, smell them, feel them in our grasp."

Who the hell is this? I've been expecting fire-and-brimstone. Not this . . . this . . . fireside chat.

"I hear you, friends. I do! I hear you ask, 'What's wrong with that?' To which I say there's nothing wrong as long as we do not allow ourselves to be seduced by our good fortune. If greed replaces obedience, if gluttony replaces compassion, and if our affluence blinds us to the teachings of the Lord, we shall soon find ourselves on a slippery slope, indeed."

Voss paused for a roar of enthusiasm. Kathryn went to pull out the handkerchief she tucked inside her sleeve before each show, but Jane and Leo had distracted her and she had nothing to wipe away the sweat coating her brow. She had no choice but to dab at it with the edge of her sleeve.

Sheldon Voss had always been more of a concept to Kathryn than a human being. A character in a movie. A grainy newspaper photograph. But not a *real* person. And certainly not this compassionate, thoughtful gentleman, troubled by what he saw around him.

I have an uncle and this is what he sounds like.

Kathryn hadn't forgotten her mother's warning: liar, cheat, thief, chiseler, fraud. But the sound of Voss' voice reduced her to that eight-year-old girl who had nothing for show-and-tell on "A Family Member Who Isn't Mommy or Daddy" day.

Through Voss' twenty-minute speech, Kathryn tried to reconcile the portrait her mother had painted with the beguiling voice flowing through the loudspeakers, cautioning her listeners to choose spirituality over shopping on the installment plan.

"Modern civilization might be the final civilization if we emphasize 'modern' over 'civil,' and the Cold War might be the final war if we choose to turn away from our souls," he concluded. "Folks, the good Lord tells me that Americans need to be reminded of what will shield us from the temptations that beckon us from the true path. Join me, won't you, as I march across this great land of ours. As Mark 3:25 tells us, 'If a house is divided against itself, that house will not be able to stand.' Thank you for listening, and may God bless America."

A tinny marching band started playing "The Stars and Stripes Forever" over the cheers of the throng. Kathryn gestured to Connolly to start talking, *because I don't know what to say. What if my mother got it wrong and my uncle isn't the grifter she thinks he is? What if he's genuinely seen the error of his ways?*

Kathryn wasn't sure what Connolly said. She caught his tone—upbeat, self-congratulatory, and enamored with Voss—and that was enough. She recited her usual closing thanks and signed off.

The red light extinguished and the whole studio ignited into an uproar, but Kathryn felt alone. She needed time, space, and silence to sort through what had just happened, and she wasn't going to get it in the middle of this post-show bedlam. She shouldered her way through the throng. If she'd just beaten Winchell in the ratings, it might all be worth it, but all she could think of was the sanctuary of her dressing room.

When she got there, Marcus and Gwendolyn were waiting. "Where were you two?"

"We fought our way to some seats in the *Dragnet* studio," Marcus said.

" . . . where we sat next to this fine chap."

Gwendolyn gestured to the snappy dresser in his early thirties standing next to her.

"I'm Army Archerd." He thrust his hand toward her. "Pleased to meet you."

"From the *Herald-Express*?"

Archerd widened his affable smile. "Used to be. I'm taking over for Sheilah Graham at *Daily Variety*."

Kathryn considered Sheilah's *Just for Variety* column direct competition to her *Window on Hollywood*. If the left-leaning Archerd was now writing it, their columns might become interchangeable. But was that bad? Kathryn's mind was too woolly to unravel that particular tangle.

Marcus wore a *brace-yourself* look. "Tell Kathryn what you told us."

"I have a tipster at *Confidential*," Archerd said. "Next month's cover article is a little something they're calling *The Lavender Skeletons in TV's Closet*."

A vein in Kathryn's temple started to throb. Wallace knocked on her doorjamb. "I have *Life* and *Harper's Bazaar* in the foyer, plus a *Look* photographer."

"Tell them I'll be out in a minute." She swung back to Archerd. "Did your insider tell you anything else?"

"He overheard one of the reporters talking to Fred Otash and the name 'Miller' came up."

"Felix Miller?"

"That's the weasel you encountered at Ciro's, isn't it?" Marcus said.

Kathryn nodded. "Talking about what?"

"Several times, he heard the name 'Floss.'"

"Floss or Voss?"

"He said Floss, but the smart money's on Voss," Archerd said. "Winchell and McCarthy came up, too."

It really is just a cabal for the boys. "So that baloney we just heard was a crock." *And I fell for it.* "My mother was right."

"Your mother knows Sheldon Voss?" Archerd asked.

Kathryn faced her mirror and started patting down her hair. "My mother has a theory about everybody."

Reed's face appeared in the doorway again. "Free now?"

"Do you think I can get away with seeing all three at once?"

Reed grinned. "After tonight, I'd say you can do anything."

Kathryn struggled to mount a convincing smile and longed for a shot of the scotch stashed in her pocketbook.

CHAPTER 34

Gwendolyn finished pinning Marilyn's hem and accepted a hand to pull herself to her feet.

"You really should get a little dais," Marilyn said. "Like the one you have at your store."

Gwendolyn dusted off her knees. "Perhaps I should now that *someone* is getting too famous to appear in public."

"It really isn't much fun . . . except when it is." Marilyn let out a giggle that dwindled into a sigh. "Joe hates it."

The more time Gwendolyn spent with Marilyn, the more she was glad her own misguided bid for stardom hadn't worked out. There was a lot to be said for blundering through mistakes and enjoying triumphs without reporters and autograph hunters trailing behind.

Marilyn had been into Chez Gwendolyn a handful of times over the past twelve months, and with each visit, a worldlier Marilyn appeared, more conscious of her effect on people and how to use it to her advantage. A guarded look shielded her eyes, along with a detachment that Gwendolyn described to Marcus as a cocoon of invisible cotton wool. "But then she steps into the back room, it's just the two of us and all that fades away."

However, since the release of *Niagara*, shopping at Chez Gwendolyn had become problematic. Between her *Photoplay* "Most Popular Actress" award, the buzz over *Gentlemen Prefer Blondes*, and her romance with DiMaggio, the press documented every date and spending spree. So Gwendolyn offered to meet Marilyn at the Garden of Allah, where she could slip through the side entrance unobserved.

"Joe's been famous since before the war," Gwendolyn pointed out. "Surely he gets how the game works."

"He knows what it's like, and what it can do to a marriage."

"Or maybe he's okay with fame, as long as he's the famous one." Gwendolyn adjusted a pin to straighten out the back hem. "Doesn't he come from a big Italian family? Guys like that are looking for a girl just like mama. Stay at home, cook, clean, and pop out a passel of babies."

Marilyn said nothing after that, not even a resigned sigh or begrudging grunt. Gwendolyn wondered if she'd gone a bit too far. After all, her love life was hardly an Edna Ferber novel. "How's the neckline now?"

Marilyn pulled at it. "Much more comfortable. Not that comfort has got anything to do with it."

When Marilyn and her *Gentlemen Prefer Blondes* costar learned they were to be favored with a Grauman's cement ceremony, Gwendolyn secretly wanted to create Marilyn's dress so her handiwork would be seen around the world. But Twentieth Century-Fox told Travilla to design matching outfits for the girls to wear.

But Marilyn called to say she'd need an outfit for the after party — she was sure she was going to get wet cement on Travilla's dress. When she came in for her fitting six days before the ceremony, Gwendolyn hoped she'd be happy — if she wasn't, they didn't have much time to start over.

Marilyn stood before Gwendolyn's full-length mirror and scrutinized her reflection. She rotated left and jutted out her derrière. "Perfect."

Marilyn pulled down the side zipper and stepped out of the dress. "Mind if I mooch around here for a while?"

It was a Sunday afternoon, so Marcus or Kathryn or Doris or Bertie were likely to come knocking with plans for cocktails in the bar, a cribbage game around the pool, or dinner at Ah Fong's.

"Don't you have plans with Joe?" Gwendolyn asked.

Marilyn started pulling her street clothes on.

"He's been back East and flew into LA this afternoon. Billy and Dona said they'd pick me up at seven. We're double-dating at Villa Nova."

"But don't the two of you want to be alone?"

"The last time Joe and I saw each other, it wasn't so great."

Gwendolyn wondered if Billy and Dona had been recruited unknowingly. "You're welcome to stay as long as you want. How about I put on some coffee?"

A knock on the door cut off Marilyn's reply. Her eyes flew open.

"Don't worry," Gwendolyn said, "it's probably just Kathryn. Or maybe Marcus. You remember him, don't you?"

"The photographer, right?"

"Yes, but not in his off hours."

She opened her front door to find neither Kathryn nor Marcus, but Ella Fitzgerald accompanied by a guy Gwendolyn suspected was her husband, the bass player for Dizzy Gillespie.

"This is a surprise!"

"Dammit!" Ella groaned. "I've got the wrong day, haven't I? You were right," she told her husband. "It was Monday."

"As a matter of fact, we agreed on Monday next week."

"I don't even have the right week?" Ella slapped her cheek. "Well, aren't I a dummy? Listen, I got a last-minute five-nighter at Club Flamingo in San Francisco. I was thinking-hoping-praying that seeing as how we're here . . .?"

Marilyn Monroe wasn't the only person Gwendolyn had to meet at the Garden instead of the store now.

She took inspiration from the middle road Kathryn found by using Mike Connolly as special correspondent. The *Hollywood Reporter*'s circulation was up; Connolly got onto the radio; sales of Mixmasters and cake mixes had increased; the march got nationwide coverage; *Window on Hollywood* shot to number one; and Kathryn received her promised bonus. Everybody won.

Gwendolyn called Herman and reassured him that she was no longer actively pursuing the colored trade, which resulted in Herman resubmitting the proposal to the higher-ups. Three weeks later, she received a letter spelling out their offer to add eau de toilette, cold cream, face powder, and eye shadow. If sales were encouraging, they would consider a line of lipsticks.

Meanwhile, Gwendolyn told Ella, Lena, Dorothy and their friends that pressure had been brought to bear, and proposed that if she went to *their* homes instead, nobody would be the wiser.

Ella told her that where she usually stayed in LA wouldn't be safe for a white woman, so Gwendolyn suggested she come to the Garden instead. It was the perfect solution.

Gwendolyn was still hesitating at her front door — she wasn't sure Marilyn would be comfortable with unexpected visitors — when she smelled a cloud of her own perfume behind her.

"Hello!" Marilyn cooed. "It sure is wonderful to see you again."

"Well, now, look who's here," Ella exclaimed. "We didn't have much of a chance to chat last time."

Gwendolyn shepherded everybody into her living room, where she presented Ella with swatches of material.

They were debating the last design when Marcus and Kathryn showed up with ingredients for champagne cocktails. Leo was with them, and so was the eccentric old lady friend of Marcus'. Gwendolyn had never met Regina, but she lived up to her reputation in a black lace dress that Gwendolyn would have killed for twenty-five years ago. When Gwendolyn asked what they were celebrating, Regina piped up, "I've just been cast in a recurring role on *Dragnet*, and I believe it's all thanks to your friend Mr. Tattler and the flattering dress he lent me."

Bringing up the rear was Quentin Luckett, who always appeared to be at a loose end now that his ex-boyfriend Trevor Bergin showed no sign of returning to the States.

Someone pulled out *Dinah Shore Sings the Blues* and suddenly the villa was filled with "Lover Come Back to Me." Arlene, Doris, and Bertie heard the commotion and appeared with more bubbly.

When Billy and Dona arrived early to pick up Marilyn and agreed to "a quick one or two for the road," everybody relocated to the pool area, where Marcus' lights were still rigged up in the trees. He switched them on, making the leaves glow like crème de menthe.

Dinah Shore became Dean Martin, and several bags of potato chips materialized. Gwendolyn could see that half of them might soon end up in the pool if she didn't fetch a bowl. She'd barely taken a few steps when she caught a silhouette lurking behind a hydrangea bush outside Villa Eight.

She heard the distinct click of a camera shutter.

"Did you catch that?" she hissed to Marcus and Ella's husband, Ray. She subtly jutted her jaw toward the hydrangea. "Someone's taking photos of us." Gwendolyn watched Marilyn giggling with Arlene and Bertie. Shots of her were worth major cabbage these days.

Marcus casually placed his highball glass on the diving board and lifted a foot to make out like he was tying his shoelace. "I don't like the look of this."

"I was a sprinter in college," Ray said.

Marcus muttered, "On the count of three, you go for his legs and I'll go for his neck."

"He doesn't have a clear shot to the street," Gwendolyn said, "but if he reaches Hayvenhurst there might be no catching him."

"Three. Two. One. GO!"

Ray shot forward as Marcus propelled himself over the diving board. The intruder darted across the gravel path and reached Bungalow Nine as Ray hurled himself at the guy's legs. He grabbed a handful of trouser and held on when the guy started kicking.

Marcus hooked his fingers in the guy's jacket pocket. It ripped away easily, but he managed to wrench the jacket off a shoulder, pushing the trespasser face down in the dirt. They hauled him back into the light around the pool.

Kathryn slammed her drink on the table. "YOU AGAIN!"

"You know this Peeping Tom?" Ray panted.

"This is Felix Miller. He's a professional snooper to the highest bidder." She faced Miller. "So whose business are you meddling in tonight? Or can we just go ahead and assume it's Marilyn? Because God knows the girl doesn't deserve five minutes of peace."

Miller's jacket and pants were ripped and stained like a hobo's. His hair was a mess, and gravel had grated the left side of his face. He made a halfhearted attempt to struggle out of Marcus and Ray's grips, and when that didn't work, he started laughing.

"I was sent to take photos of *you*," he told Kathryn.

"For Winchell, I presume? Trying to get dirt on me because I finally beat him in the ratings? Well, you can just tell him from me —"

"As much as my client hates fags, he hates coloreds mixing with whites more. Especially famous ones who —"

Ray slammed his fist into Miller's flank, causing him to double over.

Kathryn yanked the camera out of Marcus' hand, cleaved open the back, and pulled out the film. When she tossed it into the pool, Miller watched it sink as though he didn't give two hoots.

"I'm glad that wasn't *my* camera." He watched it hit the bottom of the pool. "I know where I'm not wanted." He turned to leave, but Ray blocked his path.

"What're you gonna do?" Miller demanded. "Hit me some more? I'll have you up on assault charges before the clock strikes midnight. And I got me a whole bunch of witnesses. Granted, they may not be my greatest fans, but none of them are gonna perjure themselves. And I can count on at least three of them who'd rather not be dragged into the papers."

The only sound in the whole Garden was Dean Martin warbling how when you're smiling, the whole world smiles with you.

Miller stepped around Gwendolyn and headed toward Hayvenhurst Drive, limping slightly.

Kathryn waited until he was out of sight. "I doubt that's the last we've heard of that son of a bitch."

"But who was he taking photos for?" Ella asked.

"Next month, *Confidential* is running a story called 'The Lavender Skeletons in TV's Closet.'"

"At least they won't have photos."

Marilyn pointed to a dark patch on the lawn behind Gwendolyn. "What's that? Is it a wallet?"

Gwendolyn scooped it up and brought it back to the center of the patio where the light was brightest. She pulled out Miller's driver's license.

"Where does that little weasel live?" The question was Kathryn's.

"Silver Lake."

"Good to know. What else is in there?"

There wasn't much cash, but it did contain a stack of business cards. She started flipping through them. "You're not going to like this," she told Kathryn. "There's Walter Winchell, Senator McCarthy's Washington office, and the New York office of Robert Harrison."

"The creep who publishes *Confidential*?" Ray asked.

"Yes, but who was he working for tonight?"

Kathryn polished off the last of her drink. "Quite possibly, all three."

At the bottom of the stack was a slip of paper. Someone with particularly neat handwriting had printed *Hotel Majestic, June 17 to 20, Room 314*, and a telephone number.

Arlene said, "There's a Hotel Majestic in St. Louis."

"There must be a Hotel Majestic in every city across the country."

"But you know who's currently visiting St. Louis, don't you?" Everybody drew a blank. "Sheldon Voss."

Gwendolyn flicked the paper back and forth across her fingernail. She spun on her heel and marched back to her apartment. "If Sheldon Voss thinks he can invade my home and my friends, he can think again."

Three chimes rang. When she asked for room 314, the operator asked her to hold.

A moment later, "Hello, this is Sheldon Voss."

He sounded just like he had on Kathryn's show—a kind uncle you hated to disappoint.

Gwendolyn grabbed Kathryn's hand for support. "Mr. Voss, I'm calling to see if the name Felix Miller means anything to you."

The silence at the other end of the line lasted an agonizing three seconds. "Who is this?"

"I'm calling from Los Angeles," Gwendolyn hedged. "I found his wallet."

"I see." The circumspection in his voice softened. "How considerate of you to report its loss."

"I'm calling to ask if you sent him to take photographs of people he has no business taking photographs of."

"You still haven't told me your name, my dear girl."

"I'm not your dear anything."

"Who, pray tell, are you?"

"My name is Gwendolyn Brick."

Another heavy silence.

"You haven't answered my question," she told him.

More silence.

"Felix Miller didn't just lose his wallet tonight, he also lost his camera. I'm calling to ask you if you sent him to the Garden of Allah Hotel on Sunset Boulevard to take clandestine pictures of the residents. You might want to tell him that I have his camera, and his film. However, I feel it only fair to warn you that if I find anything untoward on his negatives, I plan on suing for invasion of privacy. I cannot imagine that'll do your self-righteous cause any good."

"And what makes you think this underhanded monkey business is connected to me?"

"Because in his wallet was a slip of paper with your stay in St. Louis. I must say, Mr. Voss, you have very neat handwriting." That last part was a gamble. "If Mr. Miller would like his wallet back, tell him he can collect it at my store." Her tank now drained, Gwendolyn slammed down the phone. She raised her face to see a dozen people gaping at her. "Is there any champagne cocktail left? I think I need a double."

CHAPTER 35

It didn't occur to Marcus that he should be nervous until he saw the name *PREMINGER* on a brass plaque with an arrow pointing to the end of the corridor.

It wasn't like he'd had a terrible experience on *The Moon is Blue*, so why was he jumpy?

When Marcus was taking stills on *The Star*, Otto Preminger approached him to do the same for his next movie, which was about to start production at the same studios in the new year. He was shooting English and German versions simultaneously and he wanted Marcus to document the different approaches he'd be taking to accommodate American and European sensibilities.

The job was a mini reunion with David Niven, who'd been a neighbor at the Garden of Allah back in the thirties. He was playing one of two aging playboys vying for the affections of the same young woman, so he was perfectly cast.

Pretty soon, though, Marcus could tell this wasn't going to be a run-of-the-mill romantic comedy.

The dialogue shuttlecocked between Niven and Bill Holden included the Breen Office's three biggest Don'ts. The first time Niven said the word "virgin," Marcus nearly ruined a take. He was better prepared when another exchange included both "seduce" and "mistress."

It was times like these that Marcus longed to rush to a pay phone and call Oliver. "Get a load of what Preminger's doing!"

But the only sort of virgin Oliver concerned himself with these days was the Virgin Mary, and worrying about Joe Breen was no longer Marcus' job. So he stood back, took photos, and marveled at Preminger's chutzpah.

Marcus stared for a moment at the sign etched into the frosted glass—*OTTO PREMINGER FILMS*. He removed his fedora and let himself into the airy reception. Posters from earlier Preminger movies filled its walls: *Laura*, *The Fan*, *Daisy Kenyon*, *Forever Amber*. A fortyish secretary in plain brown tweed said, "It's noon, so you must be Mr. Adler." She knocked on the office door and announced, "Your twelve o'clock is here."

Hailing from prewar Austria, the balding Otto Preminger was Central Casting's idea of a German commandant. It was little wonder that Billy Wilder had cast him as a Nazi in *Stalag 17*. But in person, the man was on the convivial side of gruff. He was leaning over a table blanketed with photographs when Marcus entered his office.

"Ah!" Preminger beckoned Marcus to join him. "Thank you for coming in. Your timing is as striking as your work. I'm putting together the *Moon is Blue* press kit." He indicated a row of Marcus' production stills lined up along the edge. "I've narrowed it down to ten but only four are necessary. Help me choose."

Laying his hat on the end of the table, Marcus confessed, "I never expected that you'd get PCA approval."

"I didn't."

"So how did you get it past the Breen Office?"

"We are releasing the picture without their endorsement."

Marcus had ordered dinner at the Pig 'n Whistle with greater drama than the way this man dropped this bombshell. "But the PCA requires all films to be submitted."

"They rejected it, so screw them. We're releasing it anyway."

"That takes guts."

"Not really." He indicated a photo Marcus had taken of Niven on the Empire State Building observation deck. "I like this very much."

"What do you mean, 'not really'? When I was at MGM, I dealt with the Breen Office constantly. Don't you think you're asking for a whole mess of trouble —"

"It's time to take a stand against such ridiculously old-fashioned restrictions. Between the Hays Code and the blacklist, the right wing has taken over Hollywood filmmaking. It is time to take it back. Have you seen this moronic *Confidential* magazine? A new one came out this morning." He threw up his hands in despair. "What a piece of *Scheisse.*"

That night a few weeks ago when they discovered Felix Miller in the hibiscus bush, Marcus couldn't have been more proud of Gwennie's nerve calling Sheldon Voss like that. If they'd been sober, she might not have pulled it off, and everyone might not have cheered her on quite so loudly. Later, when their heads cleared, they saw what a dicey move it had been, but Miller never called for his wallet, and no photos had appeared in any of the second-rate magazines.

But still, lurking in the back of Marcus' mind was this rumor of an article about lavender skeletons, and every new issue of *Confidential* struck fear into the heart of every Hollywood denizen. He picked out the four stills he thought belonged in the press kit and explained why. Collecting his hat, he wished Preminger the best of luck and escaped into the street.

The Formosa Café was just around the corner on Santa Monica Boulevard, with a newsstand only half a block away.

* * *

The only person in the Formosa was the laconic bartender with skin as pale as those creatures shown in *National Geographic*'s article about the recently discovered Mariana Trench.

Marcus ordered a Moscow mule and installed himself on the furthermost bar stool. *Confidential*'s cover featured the usual snapshots of shocked celebrities and sports stars above headlines hinting at all-night sexcapades or drinking parties gone awry. The article Marcus had been dreading was on page six.

THE LAVENDER SKELETONS IN TV'S CLOSET

He scanned the introductory paragraph in which *Confidential* "bravely" aimed to "expose homosexuals in key positions as directors, producers and leading men," and went on to declare in its usual florid style how "vivid violets were giving the television industry a black eye."

Its first "case in point" was a popular comic who was the "shy sweetheart to one of Hollywood's tough guys." Example number two was a "rough and ready TV detective" so delicate in real life that writers were forbidden to include women's panties because he couldn't "control his compulsion to don the stuff." The third example was a hero of a "kiddie space drama" who loved to attend Greenwich Village parties "with taffeta skirts swishing at his ankles."

Marcus skimmed the rest of the article until a particular word caught his eye: "columnist."

"And don't think all the fruitcakes are on the screen," the article harped. "Somebody writes those tough-guy lines. And we have it from a *Confidential* confidante that too many of those scribblers have closets full of taffeta themselves. One of them is an ex-studio-but-not-ex-Commie powder puff who married a prominent Hollywood columnist to cover up his twisted inclinations. But fret not for the poor unsuspecting damsel—she was in on the charade. The gal in question can bake a mean cake so you can be sure she knows how to apply the right frosting to put people off the scent. All we need to say is: Point your sniffer down Sunset Boulevard."

This shitty little rag had managed to implicate Marcus, Kathryn, and Gwendolyn in one overwrought paragraph.

"Did you hear?" The bartender pointed to the radio behind him.

Marcus shook his head.

"That Joe McCarthy prick just held a press conference in DC yammering about high security risks within the government."

Marcus casually turned the page away from *Confidential*'s so-called exposé. "Risks from who?"

"The homos, on account of they're open to being blackmailed. He made it sound like all three branches of the government are teeming with them."

"Just like Hollywood's teeming with Commies?"

"Yeah, just like that." The bartender jutted his chin toward Marcus' empty tumbler. "Another mule?"

Marcus said yes and mindlessly turned the pages in front of him.

The timing was impeccable. For the first few stops on his Sea to Shining Sea March, Sheldon Voss had been careful to deliver his sermons in that just-us-folks voice he'd used the night of the kickoff.

But in Cincinnati, he introduced the words "vigilance" and "Lucifer" and expressions like "fire-roasted souls" and "the greed of Solomon." He uttered them with the same kindly-uncle tone, so if listeners weren't paying attention, they might not catch them.

His next stop was St. Louis, the night after Gwendolyn called him.

Gone were benevolent Uncle Sheldon and his gentle admonishments against getting caught up in wickedness. The St. Louis speech marked his return to Sodom and Gomorrah, the dangers of becoming Lot's wife, and the accusations that Marilyn Monroe was "the outrageous manifestation of Lucifer's lust."

The most recent broadcast was from Memphis; its theme was temptation.

"America has been called a modern-day Garden of Eden!" he thundered. "And with good reason. This is a land of plenty! Of riches! Of opportunity and choices! It is a garden of temptations such as Eve faced. Let us not fail to take heed."

Across the second-to-last pages of *Confidential*, a headline banner proclaimed:

A RAINBOW OF COLORS DANCING IN THE GARDEN OF EDEN

Beneath it lay a photo spread taken the night Marilyn was at the Garden with Ella Fitzgerald and Billy Travilla.

The center photograph showed Marilyn and Ella grappling each other by the elbows. Ella was bursting with laughter and Marilyn was bent at the waist, looking scandalized. Her bosom caught the light and looked enormous, casting Ella's face into half-shadow. It looked as though Ella was enticing Marilyn into a tryst amid the murkiness behind her.

Ten photos captured everybody either in full light or seductive silhouette as they "gamboled and guzzled, teased and tempted." Travilla, Dona, Kathryn, Marcus, and Gwendolyn were labeled by name and place of work. In the bottom corner was a shot of Gwendolyn pouring champagne directly into Marcus' mouth. It had been a silly dare by Bertie, who'd challenged Gwendolyn not to spill a drop. The photo presented the tawdriest idea of what middle America assumed Hollywood parties were like.

And worse: the caption referred to Gwendolyn's reputation as the premiere modiste to LA's crossdressers.

Half the photos included Hollywood's hottest blonde, and yet *Confidential* buried the spread in the second half of the magazine. It wasn't like them to be so coy.

Marcus swallowed the rest of his Moscow mule and rushed out into the June heat.

When he ran into the *Hollywood Reporter*'s raucous newsroom, he was dripping with sweat. Kathryn's mouth hung open, her copy of *Confidential* trembling in her grip.

"I see you've already . . ." He gestured at the magazine in her hand.

"I knew this Harrison guy was a skunk, but —" She rattled the magazine like it was stuck to her fingertips.

"Did you hear McCarthy's press conference?"

She stared at him.

He told her about being at the Formosa when the station made a live cross to Washington DC. "Does Wilkerson know about the *Confidential* piece yet?"

"I was just about to go in and face the lion's mouth. Come with me?" She tapped the Garden of Eden spread. "You were there, which means you can corroborate." She grabbed his sleeve and yanked him along with her. "The more outraged we are, the better. He responds to that."

Billy Wilkerson was from the litter of titans that nascent Hollywood spawned in one big, bloody mess. Like Mayer, Zanuck, Goldwyn, and Selznick, he was a big talker, big spender, and big gambler who lived life on an outsized scale. He was the one who instigated the blacklist that decimated the film industry, so he was hardly going to let a vicious little scrap of nothing like *Confidential* bring down the industry he loved.

Kathryn barged into her boss' office, announcing, "The new issue of *Confidential* hit the stands this morning."

"I've got enough toilet paper, thanks all the same."

"There's an article you need to see."

Kathryn opened the magazine to the Garden of Eden spread and laid it out in front of him. The lull lasted three seconds.

"JESUS GODDAMNED FUCKING CHRIST ON BASTARD BALLS OF FIRE! You need to find out who took these photos."

"A jackass named Felix Miller. We caught him in the act and broke his camera and ditched it into the pool."

The full flush of anger blotching Wilkerson's face abated. "Clearly, it wasn't the only roll he'd taken."

"Marilyn's in three of those shots, and they're not flattering," Marcus said. "You might want to warn Zanuck."

Wilkerson picked up the phone. "You two stay right where you are; he might want additional intel." He dialed Zanuck's number from memory and flipped the switch to speakerphone when a secretary answered the line.

"Monica, it's Billy Wilkerson here. I need Darryl, pronto."

"I'm sorry, Mr. Wilkerson, but he's in conference with Mr. Preminger right now. He left word not to be disturbed."

"You need to disturb him, Monica."

"It's a final production conference for the next Marilyn Monroe movie. Mr. Zanuck—"

"*River of No Return*? There's irony for you. I'll take full responsibility. Do it. NOW."

Silence, followed by several clicks. "What the hell, Bill? I'm in conference here."

"I've got you on speaker with Kathryn Massey and Marcus Adler. They've brought me the new issue of *Confidential*—"

"Who gives a cranberry-colored crap what—"

"There's a two-page photo spread of a party at the Garden of Allah. Marilyn's in three of the photos." Wilkerson ogled her bust. "You might call them compromising."

"How bad?"

"Drinking and dancing with coloreds, namely Ella Fitzgerald, and I think this other guy is Ella's husband."

Zanuck let out a long breathy groan. "Screw me drunk and shoot me up the ass. Okay, well, thanks for the warning."

"You also need to know about Senator McCarthy."

"What about him?"

"He held a press conference today. Adler's the only one who heard it, so I'm going to hand things over to him."

Marcus repeated what the bartender said, then added, "This is the shot across the bow that I warned you about last December."

The insistent tapping of Zanuck's pen against his desktop thudded through the speakerphone.

"That theory of mine about Robert Harrison being in league with Breen?" Marcus persisted. "Expand it to Sheldon Voss. Have you noticed how he's boosted the rhetoric?"

"Get to your point, Adler."

"It looks to me like McCarthy and Breen *and* Voss have put their heads together. They're no dummies; they can see what TV is doing. Looks to me like they plan to kick the picture business while it's down. Their weapons of choice are morality and abstinence, and they're using your biggest star to do it."

"Like I don't have enough problems with that blonde bitch."

"That blonde bitch is your most valuable asset," Kathryn put in.

"Don't remind me."

"McCarthy, Breen, and Voss are the unholy trinity." Marcus leaned closer to the speakerphone. "If you break one, you might be able to bring them all down."

"How do you figure on doing that?" Wilkerson asked.

"Mr. Preminger? Are you still there?"

"I am."

"Tell them your plans for *The Moon Is Blue*."

Preminger had barely finished explaining his plan to release the movie without approval when Zanuck burst out, "You gotta be shitting me!"

"If Mr. Preminger pulls it off, it means approval from the PCA will become irrelevant," Marcus pointed out. "Meanwhile, Voss is only halfway through his march. He's already talking hellfire and damnation, and he's still got six weeks to go."

"He needs to be stopped," Zanuck said.

"He has enormous momentum," Kathryn added, "but if you ask me, not everything's kosher with that march of his."

"You got something to back that up?"

"My gut tells me the financials are mighty fishy. Although how we prove that, I'm not sure."

"We should call Hoover," Zanuck said. "He's bound to have a file as thick as my d —" He cut himself off, but recovered quickly. " — as my dictionary. I'll call him once Otto and I are done. I'll get back to you if there's anything new. Oh, and Adler? Thanks for bringing this to us so fast. I owe you one."

"I'd like to cash that IOU in immediately."

Kathryn shot him a look of astonishment.

Zanuck snorted. "Go on."

"Push back the departure of the *Three Coins in the Fountain* company by a few days."

Longer pause. "I assume you've got your reasons."

Marcus ignored Kathryn's puzzled expression. "Uh-huh."

Even longer pause. "I'll see what I can do."

When Marcus and Kathryn got back to her desk, she scooped up her bag. "We should swing by Gwennie's store. That article isn't exactly great PR."

* * *

They pulled into the parking lot behind Chez Gwendolyn around four o'clock. The back door was unlocked and they let themselves in.

"Knock, knock!"

"We're out here."

Gwendolyn sounded like someone had just run over her grandma.

Marcus and Kathryn walked into the main salon where only a couple of lights were burning; the rest of the store was cloaked in gloom. Gwendolyn sat behind the counter, her elbow leaning on the glass and her face resting against her fist. Next to her, Doris and Bertie looked every bit as morose.

"So you've seen it?" Marcus asked.

"It's a little hard to miss," Bertie said.

"Oh, Gwennie," Kathryn said. "That photo of you with the champagne bottle!"

Gwendolyn lifted her head off her hand. "What?"

Marcus waved the magazine. He hopped from blank face to blank face. "Why are the lights out?"

"A little matter of . . ." Gwendolyn tilted her chin toward the Strip.

Someone had splashed paint across Chez Gwendolyn's front window. Marcus squinted. "What's that?"

Gwendolyn unlocked the front door and brought Marcus and Kathryn out onto the sidewalk. "You'll get a better view if you step back a little." She pulled them to the curb.

A large painted N with a bold slash through it took up virtually the entire front window.

"I don't get it," Marcus said.

"I've been vandalized!" Gwennie cried out.

"Yes, but what does it mean?"

"You dumb ass." Kathryn punched him in the shoulder, right where it hurt the most. "The N is for nigger."

"So the slash through it means—oh! No niggers."

CHAPTER 36

Kathryn stepped out of the heat baking Pershing Square and into the Biltmore Hotel's air-conditioned tranquility. The honking bustle outside melted away. "Do you see my mom?" she asked Leo.

He fanned himself with his white straw panama. "Nope. Maybe she's already in the tearoom." He took a step toward a baroque staircase carved with fruits and angels, but Kathryn pulled him back.

"Thanks for doing this," she said. "I know how busy your days can get."

He winked. "And yours don't?"

As she scrubbed the paint off Gwendolyn's front window, Kathryn realized she was featured in *Confidential's* two most explosive articles: lavender marriages and Garden of Eden parties. There would be fallout.

Although Louella Parsons had her faults, Kathryn suspected she didn't really care if Kathryn had married a homosexual for professional preservation, or that she threw a party where white people danced with Negroes.

By contrast, Hedda lost no time in slingshotting barbed accusations in Kathryn's direction.

One of the *Confidential* photos showed Kathryn attempting a Valentino-esque tango with Ella's husband. And there was hardly any point in denying her lavender marriage. Inside the walls of Hollywood, they were as common as divorces, and Hedda knew it. But Hedda's readers didn't, and her columns made it as clear as she could without putting Kathryn's name in print.

Consequently, twenty-two radio stations, all of them in Bible Belt states, dropped Kathryn's show. Hedda made a big deal of it in a follow-up column, but Kathryn had the last laugh when seventeen of them were back two weeks later after being deluged with listeners who wanted to follow Sheldon Voss' progress.

But what warmed Kathryn's heart was that Leo hadn't lost his faith in her. If the higher-ups at Sunbeam, Betty Crocker, or NBC were on his case to cut her loose, he never let on. The few times she asked, he told her, "The flak I'm getting is nothing to lose sleep over." She doubted the flak was inconsequential, but his willingness to shield her from it was deeply touching.

Between her schedule and his, they usually got together only two or three evenings a week, but now he'd upped it to four, sometimes five.

The night of Gwendolyn's window incident, he arrived with extra paint thinner, as well as takeout sandwiches and coffee from Schwab's. When Hedda started in with her no-names tirade, Leo reminded Kathryn, "Hedda's not the Supreme Court. You don't have to respond to anything she says. Take the high road and say nothing."

They mounted the Biltmore's ornate stairwell, passed the elevators, and stepped into the hotel's elaborately decorated passageway.

"Do we have time for a quick shoe shine?" Leo asked. He held out his foot to show her how scuffed his shoes were from crossing Pershing Square. The city had recently decided to build a parking lot beneath the square, which was a practical idea, but it meant pulling out all the shade trees. The square was now a wasteland of dirt and concrete. "I wouldn't want to show up looking like a lost Rat of Tubruk."

Kathryn spotted a bootblack sitting at his station at the end of the hall. "Let's make it quick."

They were only a few yards away when she realized it was the shoeshine from the Ambassador who had been one of her best tipsters.

"Delmar!"

"Miss Kathryn!" He tipped the patent leather brim of his cap.

"You work here now?"

"Have you been to the Ambassador lately?" His lopsided grin revealed a couple of freshly lost teeth.

"Not in a while."

He directed Leo to take a seat up on his stand, pulled out his brush, and set to work. "Traffic's gotten so poorly that I couldn't make no decent living. So when the bootblack here dropped dead of a bad ticker, I called 'em up and told them I could start straightaway. An' here I is."

"You make a better living here?" Kathryn asked.

"Oh, yes, ma'am. Traffic at the Biltmore don't know no end, especially with that march heading this way. The leader and his entourage are staying here when he comes to LA. Lord have mercy, but you'd think it was Jesus himself come riding into Jerusalem."

"Voss?" Leo said. "At the Biltmore?"

The Biltmore was one of the classiest hotels west of Chicago, so it struck Kathryn as an expensive choice for Voss' increasingly pious march. As he stormed through Dallas, Oklahoma City, Denver, and Albuquerque, his sanctimoniousness had become insufferable.

With each speech, Voss escalated his bombast, peppering his homilies with vitriolic attacks against a litany of "enemies of good, clean, God-fearing living."

In Albuquerque, he found time to denounce homosexuals, Communists, subversives, "loose-living entertainers who ignore the laws of the land, of nature, and of God," miscegenationists, unwed mothers, reefer-smoking beatniks, spineless alcoholics, shameless divorcees, and any non-Christian un-Americans. In other words, anyone who didn't fit into pretty-picture, white-bread, Eisenhower America.

During the Albuquerque broadcast, he referred to Hollywood as "the Sodom and Gomorrah of the West" four times. Listening to this hateful diatribe from NBC's Studio Two, Kathryn kept her sweet smile in place by reminding herself of the dressing-room advice Leo gave her: "You only have to put up with this hogwash for another couple of weeks and then we can start negotiating with NBC about a TV show."

The only person who enjoyed himself was Mike Connolly, which was ironic considering he fit into at least three of those categories. Whatever nerves he may have experienced on that first show were gone by the third week. The night of the Memphis broadcast, he walked into Kathryn's dressing room with such a glow that Kathryn was tempted to shove a light bulb in his mouth just to see if it would light up.

Voss seemed to be gearing up for a showdown in Los Angeles, but what gave Kathryn hope was his apparent failure to grasp how his labels described most people living there. If he was expecting his Los Angeles congregants to resemble those he'd encountered everywhere else, he was in for a letdown. Working under the Hays Code for the past twenty years had taught Angelenos to reconcile the reality that the conduct they put on the screen had nothing to do with their private lives.

"I'm surprised he's staying here," Kathryn said to Delmar.

"It's close to MacArthur Park. That's where he's pitching his tent."

"What about the Voss Vanguard?" Leo asked.

Whoever was handling Voss' public relations knew what they were doing. Angelenos couldn't pass a billboard, open a newspaper, or switch on a radio without hearing about the traveling circus. The latest proclamation revolved around the band of volunteers who set up base camp, raised the enormous tent, spread the word with handbills along the route. They were called the Voss Vanguard and their numbers grew at every stop.

"We've started to see them dribble in," Delmar said. "I thought I had one this morning. His shoes were real classy, like you'd buy at Silverwoods, but real muddy. So I says to him, you look like you been puddle jumping, only it ain't rained since April. Where the dickens did you find some mud around here?"

"What did he say?"

"He started right in with the big-noting. Telling me how he'd been scoping out MacArthur Park for Sheldon Voss. I asks him if he's with the Voss Vanguard, and he says, 'Hell, no, boy. I'm with NBC TV.'"

Leo gave a little start. "TV?"

"Yes, sir. NBC television is what he said plain as day."

Leo shot Kathryn a look. Why was this the first they were hearing about it?

Delmar curled a finger, leading them to a door camouflaged behind his stand. "Take a gander at this."

It was a storage room, fifteen by fifteen feet, filled to the edge with battered paint cans.

Kathryn felt vaguely let down. "What are these?"

"Why, them's the famous quarter cans."

At the end of each Sea to Shining Sea meeting, Voss sent his vanguard into the congregation to solicit donations. He asked for "only a quarter, and may the good Lord see fit to multiply them as he did the loaves and fishes." Typically, people donated more than one, so the dollars quickly added up. The cans became a symbol for donating to a good cause and a new expression entered the national lexicon: "I quarter-canned it!"

"So they really are just old paint cans," Kathryn said.

Delmar let out a high-pitched whistle. "He sure is going to clean up."

Leo paid Delmar and they headed for the tearoom. Halfway there, they passed a glass case where a display of Elizabeth Arden cosmetics was arranged against sapphire velvet. Beneath it, a sign proclaimed,

It was hard to know if it was the *Confidential* article or the "N" window, but Gwendolyn had received a curt letter from Herman Dewberry informing her that Bullocks had declined to proceed with her extended line.

Gwennie tried to make light of it. "I'll just concentrate on what I do best: sew stunning outfits!" They were brave, hopeful words, but business at the store had slowed to a trickle of what it had been a year before.

Voss sure had a lot to answer for. So did *Confidential*.

"KATH-RYN! MASS-EY!" Hedda Hopper's voice pierced the Biltmore's genteel hush. "You're even worse than I imagined." Red-faced and snorting like a bronco, Hedda charged at Kathryn, brandishing a rolled-up *Confidential* like a billy club. "I always knew you were one of those rag-tag leftists. You and all your Garden of Allah bohemians."

Oh, Hedda. I'm a forty-five-year-old woman who wears a girdle and subscribes to Reader's Digest. *I'm about as bohemian as Mamie Eisenhower.*

"Did you hear that?" Kathryn asked Leo. "I'm a bohemian."

"It wasn't a compliment." Hedda pressed her lipless mouth together and unfurled her *Confidential*. It fell open to the Garden of Eden spread. "Aren't you the least bit ashamed?"

After fretting over that article for a whole week, Kathryn had avoided looking at it again. As Hedda held it up, she saw it with fresh eyes. Instead of seeing whites and coloreds brazenly flouting convention by dancing together, she saw a bunch of people enjoying an uproariously good time amid a sea of champagne. In other words, it was no different from any of the countless dozens of Garden parties that preceded it.

"Hedda," Kathryn said, "do you have a point? I'm due to meet my mother in one min—"

"You should have heard Senator McCarthy when he called to thank me for mailing him a copy of this."

"I bet you sent it express."

"He and I have come to the inescapable conclusion that you are responsible—perhaps not in full, but certainly in a large part—for the recent breakdown of relations between Mr. Hoover and Mr. Voss."

Kathryn heard Leo's gasp in her left ear and hoped Hedda hadn't picked up on it.

After that day in Wilkerson's office, the plan to stop Voss in his tracks hadn't gone quite so well. Hoover had yet to take any of Wilkerson's calls. Zanuck had tried to put pressure on Breen, but Breen saw Voss as a white knight charging toward Sodom and Gomorrah. And if anybody needed a white knight, it was Joseph Breen. *The Moon is Blue* was in theaters despite its lack of PCA approval and its condemnation by the Catholic Legion of Decency, and it was a huge hit.

"Really, Hedda, you credit me with far too much power."

Hedda sneered back at Kathryn. "Do you think I've forgotten about that cozy little tête-à-tête you had with Hoover?"

"Which cozy little—?"

"The day of the *Spruce Goose* in Long Beach when you sat in his car and had a fine old natter. Oh, yes, I saw it. I recall it very well."

Howard Hughes' *Spruce Goose* flight was five years ago, maybe six. Kathryn wondered what sort of person hoarded information like that. But of course she knew: the sort who called MGM "Metro-Goldwyn-Moscow," who buried careers and personal lives without thinking twice, and who named names in front of HUAC without even being subpoenaed and then bleated about it in her column.

But what about Voss? Did Hedda think Kathryn had pull because of her radio show? She doubted this dried-up old cow huffing in front of her had rooted up the family connection.

"Whatever you think you saw that day down at Long Beach," Kathryn said, "it was anything but a 'fine old natter.'"

"What was it, then?"

Kathryn chose her words carefully. "There was a hatchet that needed burying. It was advantageous to bury it before it ended up in either of our backs."

"Regarding what?"

The hat on Hedda's head today was particularly ridiculous—even by Hedda's standards. It was a ring of puce silk roses inside a row of broad white ribbons dotted with black circles coiled into large loops. Kathryn wanted desperately to knock it off her head.

"Regarding *you*, if you must know," she told Hedda.

"You and Hoover were talking about *me*?"

"Not just you. But Louella, and Sheilah, as well as myself, Army Archerd and Mike Connolly, and all the other Hollywood columnists."

Hedda's eyes narrowed.

"He'd been after me to recruit us to help unseat Truman in the '48 election and put Dewey into the White House. He felt Democrats had been in power long enough and it was time Republicans had a go."

"Is that right?"

"I told him flat out that the Republicans will win the White House when the American public wants a change, and not because they'll listen to a bunch of Hollywood gossipmongers. I told him, 'If you want a sympathetic ear, go bend Hedda's.' And *then* I told him, 'I'm not her greatest fan, but she's sharp as a tack and has the courage of a lion.'"

Bull's-eye.

"We're late," Kathryn told Leo, "and you know how Mother is." She stalked away before the bitch with the world's worst taste in millinery could get in a final word.

The Biltmore Tea Room was a large rectangular space with a glass-smooth parquet floor, ornately carved ceiling, and enormous translucent skylight. The skylight was fake, but it lent the room a calming glow, which Kathryn needed—Hedda's ambush had drained her.

Francine greeted her with a cheek-press kiss and announced that she'd already ordered a pot of tea and petits fours.

"Thank you, Mother. That's very thoughtful."

"You're looking awfully pale."

Kathryn flicked her linen napkin onto her lap. "One of my tipsters showed us a broom closet filled with Sheldon Voss' quarter cans."

Francine rolled her eyes. "That old racket, huh? Some things never change."

Their waiter arrived holding a tray laden with a willow-patterned teapot and a four-tiered stand filled with bite-sized cakes. Kathryn told him that they were happy to pour the tea themselves.

"What old racket?"

Francine motioned for Leo to start pouring. "Back when we were kids, Cam—or should I say, Sheldon—used to steal pennies from Mom's purse. He figured she wouldn't miss them, and she never did. He'd save them until he had enough to go to the bank and change the pennies into a quarter. Then he'd take that quarter across town where he'd stand on a street corner and start to cry. He had such a baby face that it wouldn't be long before some poor sucker stopped to ask him what the matter was.

"He'd pull the quarter out of one pocket and turn the other inside out to show the hole he'd picked in it. He'd say he'd been saving his pocket money for six months to buy his mother a birthday present, but he'd only just discovered he had a hole in his pocket and he'd lost one of his two quarters. Every single time, they'd give him a quarter. He'd save those quarters and change them into a dollar bill."

"How long did that go on?"

"Years. He was still at it when he started hanging around with Joe Kennedy."

"The one who plundered RKO back in the day?"

"Mm-hmm." Francine bit into her petit four with the delicacy of a hummingbird. "They met at some Boston Catholic social club dance. Thick as thieves, they were—and you know what a straight arrow Kennedy is."

"I've met mobsters less threatening than that guy," Leo said.

Francine nodded sagely. "As soon as I heard about those damned quarter cans, I knew it was a scam."

"Money laundering?" Kathryn whispered.

"Nothing's impossible when it comes to Camden's feverish little mind. Coins aren't numbered like dollar bills, so nothing's traceable."

Kathryn stared at Leo, who stared back.

"How many quarters do you think would fit into one of those paint cans?" he asked. "Five hundred? A thousand?"

"Which means each can could hold around two hundred dollars," Kathryn said. "There must have been fifty cans in Delmar's closet."

Leo pulled a pen and a laundry receipt from his jacket pocket and made some quick calculations. "Ten thousand or thereabouts."

"And that's just LA."

"Multiply that by twelve stops," Kathryn said. "What if he gets a chance to appeal to America on television?"

CHAPTER 37

Gwendolyn slid the key into the alley door of her store but didn't turn it. She leaned against the bricks; at ten A.M., the August heat was already warming them. She strummed her fingernails against the weathered wood and considered going to the beach instead.

There seemed little point in opening up these days.

It had been disheartening to scrub away the "N" on her window. Leo's paint thinner helped; by midnight there was no trace. At least, not on the window.

It took effort to smile at people who offered platitudes. *Don't worry, things will pick up again . . . Nobody takes* Confidential *seriously . . . This'll blow over soon enough.*

At least Marcus and Kathryn hadn't tried to pretend. She'd asked herself countless times, "Why did I call Voss like that?"

Because champagne plus outrage equals folly.

And now she sat alone in her empty store feeling like she was the only person left in the world.

She shouldered the door ajar. The calendar in her workroom, opened to August 1953, reminded her that her bank statement should arrive today. She used to look forward to getting those, but now they were just a reminder of how long she could go on before she was forced to declare Chez Gwendolyn DOA.

She yanked the calendar off the nail and tore it in half, then tore those halves into quarters, and didn't stop tearing until shreds of cardboard were strewn across the floor.

She stowed her handbag in the bottom drawer of the filing cabinet and walked into the salon. Immediately past the velvet curtains, she smelled something. Car exhaust? No. Worse than that. Burned oil?

Everything looked exactly as she'd left it the previous night.

The sunlight creeping over the rooftops across Sunset caught on shards of glass on the carpet. Two steps closer, she felt a crunch under her heel.

A hole in the window the length of her arm let a warm breeze blow past her face.

Her foot brushed against a brick wrapped in newspaper held in place by a rubber band. She picked it up, pulled off the rubber band, and unfurled a page from the *L.A. Times*. It was the usual: a ceasefire in Korea, the new British queen's coronation, Mt. Everest had at last been conquered.

She turned the page over.

Under the *Hedda Hopper's Hollywood* logo, a headline screeched: *MARILYN MONROE – MODERN MOVIE STAR OR BRAZEN BOHEMIAN?*

Gwendolyn skimmed the article. *Immoral . . . blitzed . . . monkeyshines . . . unwed . . . Garden of Eden . . .*

It was a rehash of *Confidential's* story. Hedda cast Marilyn exactly as Voss had: a villainous expression of everything wrong with Western civilization.

Gwendolyn read the final paragraph.

> *Photographs in the most recent* Confidential *featured Chez Gwendolyn, a Sunset Strip boutique infamous for catering to Negroes. Miss Brick may ply her wares as she pleases, but I hear there's quite the rainbow in her back room. Mixing cocktails is one thing, but mixing races? Tsk, tsk, Miss Brick. Miscegenation helped bring the fall of Rome, and we know how that dark tale unraveled."*

Dropping the newssheet onto the glass scattered across her carpeting, Gwendolyn retreated to the counter and picked up the phone to call her landlord. The receiver felt as heavy in her hand as the brick had.

The landlord promised to send a glazier to measure the window and another guy to board it up. It would look ugly as hell, he said, but the store would be secure.

Secure from what, she wanted to ask. The hordes of customers charging into my den of iniquity?

She leaned a hip against her glove display while she smoked a cigarette and watched the lengthening morning light hit the fragments of glass, shooting tiny rainbows onto the cream walls.

Now there *is a rainbow for you, Hedda.*

She lit a second cigarette from the butt of the first and followed the light creeping from the floor to the walls. She told herself she'd set to work when it reached the ceiling.

It was only halfway there when the window guy showed up. He displayed genuine sympathy as he replaced the broken glass with corrugated metal. The whole procedure took forty minutes and he was gone.

Gwendolyn was still brushing shards into a dustpan when she heard the bell above the door jangle. *Nobody comes in for two weeks, and NOW they come shopping?*

Walter Winchell studied the metal window. "Is this a bad time?"

She wanted to hurl the dustpan at him, if only because he was the sole person around.

"What can I do for you?"

"I've come to negotiate a little business."

Gwendolyn led him to two chairs beside the trifold mirrors against her back wall. She let him sit first, then joined him. "And what might this concern?"

"I can fix this."

"You're a glazier, too?"

He indulged her with a smile. "I can fix your reputation and what I assume is your negligible trade. In one swoop."

It sounded like a deal with the devil. "How intriguing."

"In September, NBC is premiering an anthology series called *Letter to Loretta*. Personally, I think they should just call it *The Loretta Young Show*. At any rate, the idea is to have Loretta introduce the show each week. At the top of the episode, she'll make a dramatic entrance. It's a gimmick, but it'll work. And that's where you come in."

As long as I sell my soul.

"I have a very good relationship with the head of NBC TV and his wife. NBC is broadcasting live at Sheldon Voss' tent meeting in MacArthur Park, so they're in town. I've already told his wife about you. They're progressives, so this whole Negro situation isn't an obstacle. In fact, Mrs. NBC is keen to see what you've got. If you impress her, it won't take much to land you Loretta's gowns."

Gwendolyn kept her hands clasped in her lap as she ran through the reasons he was making this offer. What was in it for him? And what would she have to do in return?

"Mr. and Mrs. NBC," she said. "What's their name?"

"Crawley." Winchell leaned back and crossed his legs. "Patrick and Irene."

"Okay, so Irene is going to come in here and — what? I give her a dress?"

"How you impress her is up to you. She's rather nice in a Midwestern, liberal-arts-college, corporate-wife sort of way. But don't let that fool you. She's very smart, very savvy, and has her husband's ear like nobody else."

During this whole exchange, Winchell's gaze hadn't left Gwendolyn's face. He had parked his smile in neutral, but she could feel the heat of his scrutiny.

"Let's be honest," she said. "You're not exactly known for your philanthropy, so what's the catch?"

He snorted a quick laugh. "True enough."

"What do you want from me, Mr. Winchell?"

"When Irene comes in here, bring up Kathryn Massey's proposed television show. Tell her that despite what she may have seen on Golden Aerial Day, Kathryn Massey is quite unsuited for the role of weekly host and would be a national embarrassment to NBC if it goes ahead."

If that dustpan had still been in Gwendolyn's hand, she probably would have thrown its jagged contents at him. She got to her feet. "Kathryn is my best friend and you know it. Did you seriously think I'd say yes?"

He made no move to get up. "Mark my words, Miss Brick, *Letter to Loretta* will put Young back on the map. You'll be mentioned — glowingly — in my column. Fifty million people in over two thousand newspapers read me, and you'll have so much business that you won't know what to do." He rose from his chair. "You've seen what one article in *Confidential* can do. One mention in my column can *un*do all that. Now picture your life after a dozen flattering mentions."

His shoes crunched glass as he headed for the door. He paused to take in the metal plates, then told her he was at the Beverly Wilshire Hotel.

Gwendolyn counted to ten, then dialed Kathryn at her office.

"You'll die when you hear who just paid me a visit."

"I was on my way out the door." Kathryn sounded distracted. "Marcus is with me, we're going to the Town House."

"Can I meet you there?"

"In the middle of the day?"

"I can be there in half an hour."

* * *

The Zebra Room featured furniture upholstered in black and white stripes. On the walls hung murals of zebra wandering across a vista that struck Gwendolyn as more like Wyoming than Africa. She found Marcus and Kathryn in a corner booth.

"Somebody hurled a brick through my window," she blurted out. "Left a hole the size of a Mixmaster and broken glass all over the place."

"Were you looted?" Kathryn asked.

"No, just shaken."

"Have you seen Hedda's column?"

"Guess what was wrapped around the brick."

Gwendolyn recounted her morning and her conversation with Winchell, expecting Kathryn to explode, but Kathryn was unruffled.

"It's an incredible opportunity," Kathryn said. "You must take him up on it."

Gwendolyn blinked at her, wondering if Kathryn understood. "But what about you?"

Kathryn beckoned the waitress. They ordered club sandwiches and a pitcher of iced tea. Kathryn lit a cigarette and continued to shake her match long after it had gone out. She dropped it in the zebra-shaped ashtray.

"I can fight my own battles." She thrummed the pads of her fingertips against the table for a worryingly long time. "You know what I've come to realize about myself?" Her eyes took on a new sparkle. "Fact is, I rather enjoy a battle!"

The table fell silent as Gwendolyn and Marcus absorbed this startling admission.

"Think about it. I'm always in the trenches fighting someone about something. Whether it's Wilkerson over the blacklist or Hearst over *Citizen Kane*, not to mention my clashes with Louella and Hedda. And now my darling uncle comes along, trying to drag us back into the dark ages where women never leave the kitchen, men make all the decisions, and there's a moratorium on forward-thinking. I can*not* sit by and let that happen. I love jumping in the ring and putting up my dukes. Maybe I'll win, or maybe I'll go down for the count. In a funny sort of way, I don't really care."

"You can't really believe that," Marcus said quietly.

Kathryn stubbed her cigarette out on the zebra's face. "Don't get me wrong. I prefer to win, but it's the fight that I enjoy. Does that make me crazy?"

Gwendolyn started giggling. "In a good way, perhaps."

"At any rate, the point is, take Winchell up on his offer. This Loretta Young job could really open doors."

"But he's sure to know Gwendolyn's not going to betray you," Marcus said.

"All the more to bamboozle him. Do it, Gwennie. You'll regret it if you don't. And so will I."

"If you say so." Gwendolyn still wasn't sure. She needed to think it through. "Can I ask why we're at the Zebra Room, of all places?"

"Ah-ha!" Kathryn's eyes bulged. "Remember that bootblack at the Biltmore? Turns out his brother is also a bootblack, here at the Town House. Delmar called me this morning to tell me that his brother told him that a couple of nights ago all sorts of strange stuff was going on here."

"What kind of strange stuff?"

"Voss and his inner sanctum are staying at the Biltmore, but his herd is here. With MacArthur Park just a block or two away, it's easier for them to prepare. Delmar's brother, Fayard, goes on duty at one."

"So you're here to—?"

"Snoop around. See what we can see."

Lunch arrived and the conversation shifted to how Marilyn had hurt herself during a take on the Canadian set of *River of No Return*. Suddenly, it was one o'clock. Kathryn flagged down the waitress with a five-dollar bill and hustled them out to the foyer.

The Town House's shoeshine stand was tucked into a nook along a corridor between the reception desk and the parking lot out back. Fayard was a round-faced man with a shaved head and a full smile that belonged on a toothpaste tube.

"I can't just stand around chatting." He gestured to Marcus' shoes. They didn't need a shine but he hopped up onto the seat and rested his right foot against the angled platform.

"Delmar told me you think some strange things are going on around here."

"Those Voss people have been trooping in and out like they was planning D-Day all over again. I don't recognize half the stuff they've been carrying through here, 'cept of course those quarter cans."

"But aren't they at the Biltmore?" Kathryn asked. "Delmar showed them to me."

"Them's just the overflow. The real ones are out back." Fayard shook his head. "Too many to count. Sky high, they're stacked."

"Where are they?" Kathryn pressed.

"There's a little yard next to the parking lot beside the service lane."

"Can we see them?"

"They've got security out there, but he's a buddy of mine. Nate. Just tell him Fancy told you it was okay."

At the rear of the hotel, the parking lot lay to the right, a large loading zone to the left. Between them, a guy in a blue-and-gray security uniform stood around, his hands buried in his pockets.

It wasn't until they drew closer that Gwendolyn realized he was whistling a hymn she hadn't heard in over thirty years.

Back when she was a pigtailed kid, her mama would send her down to the liquor store on Sunday mornings to replace the gin she'd swigged the previous night. The quickest route to Polk Street Liquor was past the Baptist Church, which sang "Come Down, Angels" every other week during the years Gwendolyn's mama was sprawled on the sofa whining about her disappointments.

"You're Nate, aren't you?" Kathryn asked.

He eyed them up and down. "Nope. Nate called in sick today. Unless you're with the Voss party, I'm going to have to ask you to move along."

"We are with the Voss group," Kathryn said.

"Can I see your passes?"

"We just started," Marcus jumped in. "They said we'd get our passes by the time we were finished for the day."

"I'm sorry, but I got my orders."

In front of the brick fence behind him, three dark blue tarpaulins were draped over something huge. If these were the quarter cans, Gwendolyn figured there must be dozens and dozens of them.

"Tell me," she said sweetly, "but you weren't whistling 'Come Down, Angels' just now, were you?"

He pulled his head back as he took in the sight of a white girl quoting a Negro spiritual.

She started singing, "I love to shout, I love to sing, Let God's saints come in."

He joined her at the third line. "I love to pray my heav'nly King, Let God's saints come in." He uncrossed his arms. "How the heck does a girl like you know a song like that?"

She raised her hands heavenward like she'd seen the Baptists do, and with far more reverence than she felt right now. "Your God, my God, their God, our God," she said. "It's all the same God, isn't it?" She pointed to the tarpaulins. "They asked us to double-check all that stuff's in place. Won't take us too long."

The guy stepped aside and let them pass.

Marcus pulled away a tarpaulin corner and revealed stacks of old paint cans.

"There must be two hundred here," Kathryn said.

Marcus grabbed a couple of cans. "Get a load of this.'"

Someone had painted the bottom of each can with a small red 'X' or a small red 'Y.'

"Turn around and walk away," Marcus whispered.

"What?"

"Go into the corner and pretend to chat, but do it now. *Now!*"

They scuttled over to the far end of the pile, lifted up a corner of the tarpaulin and pretended to inspect the battered cans underneath.

"Can you see what he's doing?"

Gwendolyn snuck a glimpse past Kathryn's shoulder. "A couple of real volunteers have arrived with more cans."

They were a twin set of young girls, no more than eighteen years old, glowing with Salvation-Army purity.

"Marcus is showing them his camera."

"I asked him to bring it along. Is he photographing the cans?"

"He's getting them to pose in front of the cans and he's taking their photo. They're giggling. Now he's shaking their hands."

Marcus waved the volunteers goodbye and hurried over to Gwendolyn and Kathryn. "I think our guard is onto us. Come on." He nudged them toward the service lane.

As they hurtled west along Wilshire in Kathryn's car, he explained how he told the teenage vanguards that he was a photographer with the *Examiner* working on a story about preparations for the march into LA. All it took was a promise that their picture would be in the paper for Marcus to worm out of them the difference between the X cans and the Y cans.

"Their bank has told them that it'll be too much for one branch to handle. The cans marked X will go to a Bank of America at Wilshire and Normandie, and the Y's will go to 510 Spring Street in downtown."

The first bank branch, opposite the Ambassador Hotel, was the one Gwendolyn had used when she worked at the Cocoanut Grove. It was a tiny branch, and she wasn't surprised they didn't want the responsibility of counting up all those quarters.

When Kathryn pulled her Oldsmobile to the curb at the corner of Wilshire and Normandie, Gwendolyn asked Marcus what he was looking for. He scanned the Bank of America branch and confessed that he didn't know. "This whole X and Y business sounds shifty. I thought it was worth checking out, but there's nothing to see here."

By the time they reached downtown, the afternoon rush hour was thickening. They found a parking space on the 600 block of Spring Street and walked back.

Five hundred and ten Spring was nine stories of cream brick: pleasant enough to look at, but the least remarkable building on a block of richly ornamented banks and stockbroking houses built in the 1920s.

Standing out front, Kathryn said, "I've been here before."

They walked into the foyer and studied the list of tenants: the usual roll call of insurance offices, importers, and obscure organizations.

Gwendolyn pointed to the head of the list. "Nobody's registered for the eighth or ninth floors."

The guy at the reception desk shifted uneasily in his seat when Kathryn asked him who occupied the top two floors. He told them they were empty.

Out on the sidewalk, Kathryn said, "Two whole floors? Empty? I don't buy that for a minute."

The service lane behind the building was called Harlem Place. As they approached, the rear door swung open and a pair of colored women stepped onto the grimy cobblestones. They wore light worsted wool suits that were clean, pressed, and fitted them well. Gwendolyn guessed they were secretaries or supervisors of the typing pool.

"Excuse me," Kathryn said, "but I was wondering if you work in there."

"At 510?" the plumper of the two asked, her face filled with suspicion. She raised her handbag to her chest, preparing to brush past them, when her friend said, "Say, aren't you that white lady who makes dresses for Ella and Lena?"

Gwendolyn smiled tightly. "Yes, that's right."

"From that *Confidential* article, right?"

"Uh-huh."

"Oh, brother! Ella and Lena, they've been running to your defense every chance they got. I saw Miss Ella play the Dunbar some time back. Did you make that dress? The one-shoulder number in dusty pink?" When Gwendolyn nodded, she whistled. "Miss Ella never looked better."

Gwendolyn felt Kathryn nudge her in the back. "So, you ladies work in this building?"

"Yes, ma'am. We're with the National Council of Negro Women."

"We were in the foyer just now and saw there was no listing for the top two floors. I don't suppose you know who occupies them?"

"We're not sure who's there." The other one chose her words more carefully than her friend. "We've just heard, you know, rumors."

A puff of rotting garbage and exhaust smoke wafted past. "It'll go no further than this stinky back alley," Gwendolyn prodded.

The plump woman lowered her eyes as she leaned in ever-so-slightly. "We hear that those are the LA offices of the FBI."

Kathryn slapped an unprepared Marcus across his shoulder. "I knew I'd been here!" She turned back to the women. "Thank you, ladies. We appreciate your candor."

The women nodded unsmilingly and hurried away.

"Half of Uncle Sheldon's quarter cans aren't even going to a bank?" Marcus said. "There's a plot twist worthy of Hitchcock himself."

Kathryn started tapping her chin. "Wilkerson's been very put out that Hoover hasn't been returning his calls."

Gwendolyn angled her face upward until she could see the top floor. "Funny place for a laundry, huh?"

CHAPTER 38

Marcus zoomed in tight on the face of Clifton Webb.

"Why can't women play the game properly?" Webb declared. Marcus snapped off three frames. "Everyone knows only men can lie — look, I'm sorry, Jean." He looked up from his script. "But this photographer chap, is he necessary?"

Marcus lowered his camera.

"What's the problem?" Negulesco asked Webb.

"We're feeling our way through our first table read, and it doesn't help when you have Mister Shutterbug here distracting us."

"You didn't mind when we were shooting *Titanic*," Jean pointed out. "It's the same guy."

"That was different." Webb started fondling his silk cravat. "We already knew our characters, and that huge set camouflaged him. But here it's just the twelve of us sitting around a table."

Marcus had tried to be unobtrusive, letting his zoom lens do most of the work. They'd been reading lines for the best part of an hour without any sign that he was ticking off Webb.

"Clifton," Negulesco said, "I'm sure a performer of your stature, not to mention professionalism, is able to block out any distractions."

Webb cracked a sliver of a smile. "Flatterer."

"Jesus, Webby," Dorothy Maguire declared, "you survived the sinking of the *Titanic*; surely you can ignore one little photographer."

"I survived the *filming* of the sinking," Webb corrected her, "which was almost as uncomfortable."

Negulesco waved at Marcus to step back.

Marcus was keenly aware what promises meant in Hollywood — even earnest ones. Deals fell apart at the last minute; stars got better offers; screen rights were rescinded; scripts failed to come together. For four months, he'd waited for Negulesco to contact him about *Three Coins in the Fountain*.

As the sharp air of spring yielded to the balmy breezes of summer, Marcus became more and more antsy. Joining *Three Coins* in Europe was his best hope of getting off the graylist, but that was his priority, not theirs. When the final days of July approached and still nothing, Marcus decided it was time to give things a nudge.

But how?

The answer arrived the day he stood with Kathryn and Gwendolyn in that downtown back alley.

Marcus wasn't sure why he was so shocked to learn that the FBI had a hand in laundering Sheldon Voss' quarter cans. He was all too aware of how the Bureau dug its spindly fingers into every pie it deemed necessary, but this revelation rattled him to his core.

He suddenly needed some alone time to clear his head, so he escorted the girls to Kathryn's car, waved goodbye, then wandered down Spring Street. A block and a half later, he passed an art gallery with an oil painting in the window that glued him to the sidewalk.

It depicted a solitary figure in browns and reds with splatters of gold. It was a monk, or a priest, perhaps? Or maybe a friar? The man was on his knees with his face tilted toward a beam of light coming through a hole in the roof above his head. The stooped figure looked exactly like Oliver. The shape of his nose, the smudge of a dimple in his chin, the way his lower lip dropped when he was taken by surprise.

Marcus pressed his face against the glass and realized the eyes weren't the same. Oliver's were hazel flecked with green, but this disciple with the beatific smile had eyes so brown they were almost black. And his brows ran together in an unbroken line. But they were only superficial discrepancies—it was the expression that captured Marcus. It was just like Oliver's the day Marcus drove to Cloverleaf Sanatorium and asked him to come to Rome.

Anger shot out of Marcus like a swarm of hornets. *How could he leave me like that? After everything we went through, all I got was a crappy note?*

If Marcus was still in Rome, he would have marched up to that monastery and banged on its front doors until they let him see Oliver and demand an explanation. Vows of silence be damned.

But he wasn't in Rome. He was standing on a Los Angeles sidewalk with his eyes glued to an oil painting that reminded him of someone who'd rejected him for the Father, Son, and Holy Ghost. Someone he hadn't seen in over two years, and yet a random painting in a window could bring it all rushing back.

He couldn't stop himself trooping inside to ask about the portrait.

The owner gushed over an artist Marcus had never heard of in a tone that told him he should. The five-hundred-dollar price tag may as well have been five million.

Another piece caught his eye: a painting of Venice, with the dome of St. Mark's towering over a gondolier plying his trade on a sea of absinthe green. He had hoped to get to Venice while he was in Italy, but the opportunity never presented itself.

"And this one?"

"That's Jean Negulesco's work from the twenties."

"Negulesco? The movie director?"

"Yes, he was an artist in Bucharest and Paris before he moved to the States. All those are his." He pointed to a wall featuring a couple of nudes, a portrait of a haughty gentleman holding a pipe, the Venice landscape, a still life of an apartment spilling over with books, a blue chair, a white vase and a guitar, all rendered in bold colors.

The telephone at the back of the gallery rang. When the owner excused himself, Marcus snuck a bunch of photos of the paintings, thanked the guy and left. Only a few of them came out okay, but they were clear enough for Negulesco to recognize his own work. Marcus mailed them off to him at Fox, marking the envelope "Personal." A secretary called him a few days later with instructions about reporting to the set of *Three Coins in the Fountain*.

The director was too preoccupied corralling his cast to extend anything more than a hurried "You know what I'm looking for, yes?" The lunch break was nearly over when Marcus saw his chance to approach the director. Clifton Webb had hogged the man's time for most of the break, but finally left.

"You haven't had a chance to get some lunch," Marcus said. "I could run out and find you a sandwich."

"I have a Girl Friday for that," Negulesco said. "Oh, and sorry about Webb. It's his way of saying, 'I'm the most sensitive one whose needs must be met, so therefore all eyes on me.'"

"I spent enough time at MGM to know all the moves," Marcus reassured him. "I was wondering, though, did you get those photos I sent you? The ones of your paintings."

"Yes! Wherever did you find them?"

When Marcus told him about the downtown gallery, Negulesco asked if Marcus was free to take him there once they were finished for the day. This was the best of all possible outcomes. Negulesco would be his captive audience as they drove along Pico Boulevard.

But Negulesco dominated the conversation during the drive into downtown, reminiscing about the glories of his youth in Vienna, Bucharest, and Paris.

"Always with the ideas flowing from me like mother's milk. What a thrill to be reunited with some of them again. And so far from where I created them."

Eventually Marcus found a way to ask when *Three Coins* would leave LA, but got only vague commitments.

The gallery owner bubbled with declarations of how happy he was that the man himself had graced them with his presence.

He escorted them to Negulesco's paintings, and soon the two men were deep in technical art talk that exceeded Marcus' comprehension. He wandered to the front of the gallery and stared at the FBI building across the street until a young assistant in his twenties approached him.

Marcus had first heard the word *beatnik* in a *New York Times* magazine article called "This Is the Beat Generation." This guy wore drainpipe trousers and a black turtleneck sweater that couldn't have been comfortable in this August heat.

Marcus looked at the guy's pointed-toe winklepickers. "Do those pinch?"

"Surprisingly, no." He pulled back the cuff of his sweater to consult his watch. "It's nearly show time."

"What show is that?"

"For the last few days, there's been this procession of four white vans coming up Spring. The first day they screwed up the address. They wanted 510 Spring but came to us because we're 501. They were kinda nutty, especially the guy in charge who kept insisting they had the right address. I think they're part of that Sheldon Voss march. Eventually, I made them see they wanted 510 across the street."

"What do they do when they get there?"

"Turn around and drive back. I don't know what they're up to, but they come like clockwork. It's almost six now — they should be along any second."

The two men stepped outside the store and onto the sidewalk just as four white vans turned off Wilshire and headed toward them.

As they passed by, Marcus clipped off a bunch of shots. He peered back inside the gallery to find Negulesco still deep in conference with the gallery owner.

"If Mr. Negulesco asks for me, tell him I'll be back in a minute."

Marcus followed the procession into Harlem Place. He continued snapping as the Voss Vanguard pulled up along the lane and got out of the vans. One of them opened the back door and showed the others a paint can. The guy strained to lift it, letting out a groan that bounced off the surrounding buildings. He swung it back inside, then took it out again.

When Marcus returned to the art gallery, Negulesco and the owner were finishing up.

"You bought all five?" Marcus asked. "I hope he gave you a break, considering they're your own paintings."

"He tried to, but I told him that I would not accept anything less than the asking price. For me it is nostalgia, but for him it is business, and business must be respected, no?" He slipped his checkbook inside his jacket. "I cannot think of anything I'd rather buy than a piece of my youth."

"In that case, congratulations."

"Ah, but this would not have happened without you!" Negulesco exclaimed. "I'm glad you will be joining us in Italy. Your knowledge of Rome will be indispensable. You've brushed up on your Italian, I hope."

The day after Negulesco told him about joining *Three Coins*, Marcus bought a set of records: "Speak Like an Italian in 10 Easy Lessons." He was surprised to find that he'd retained more of Signora Scatena's jabbering than he supposed. "I've been working on it every day."

"Mayer told me you're conscientious that way."

"You know L.B.?"

"He'd been after me to direct a Cinerama picture for him. He wants to produce a narrative film set in the South Pacific, but it was too vague. Not long after that, Zanuck offered me *Titanic*."

"How did I come up in conversation?" Marcus asked.

"We bumped into each other at the first showing of *This Is Cinerama* in New York. He said you were a fine production photographer and an even better screenwriter, and with your experience on *Quo Vadis*, you could be invaluable. I hinted that I was surprised to hear him sing someone else's praises so highly. He said he'd been humbled by his ousting from MGM, and that he owed you a favor."

"Did he say why?"

"He did." Negulesco glanced away and pulled at his cuffs.

"You going to make me beg?"

A stiff pause, then, "It concerned someone who used to work for Joseph Breen." The knowing look on the director's face made it plain that he knew the whole story.

"What about him?"

"His name is Oliver, yes? Evidently, this Oliver person asked his old boss to recommend someone who could teach him Italian. I guess because Breen's so well connected in the Church? Anyway, Breen didn't know, so he asked Mayer, who recommended a school run by the Jesuits, which I thought was funny because Mayer is Jewish and—" The tension on Marcus' face cut him short. "Anyway, he feels responsible for leading your friend to the Church and leaving you out in the cold."

Marcus fell against the gallery's front window. It floored him to think that conservative Mayer gave two figs about a couple of queers splitting up.

"He didn't say it in so many words," Negulesco continued, "but I got the distinct feeling that he deeply regrets his cowardice with the blacklist, and that he didn't find the courage to stand up to HUAC like you did. If you ask me, getting you off the graylist is his way of apologizing."

Just when you think you've got someone pegged. "So, I am coming with you when you leave for Italy?"

"Of course!"

"And what day is that?" Marcus held his breath.

"We leave August tenth. I do hope that's okay with you."

Marcus started his engine. That was three days after Voss' tent revival. "I'll be there."

CHAPTER 39

The revival tent hulked across MacArthur Park like a dinosaur devouring bodies. Kathryn leaned against Marcus' dashboard and counted the peaks.

"God almighty! Six poles? You'd think it was the return of Caesar."

Marcus grunted. "It's not like we weren't warned."

For the past week, the *Los Angeles Examiner* had trumpeted Sheldon Voss' arrival.

Voss Vanguard reaches two hundred!

Sheldon Voss prepares to break radio records!

Revival to meet under largest tent constructed in California!

The photos showed Voss at a sunset prayer service in Surprise, Arizona; conducting a baptism in the Salton Sea; giving an impromptu sermon at the Mission Inn in Riverside captioned, "Bringing God's mission to the Mission." In every photo, his eyes were cast heavenward, so reverent it gave Kathryn the dry heaves.

Yesterday, when the march came within the LA city limits, she speculated that the reporters were out of superlatives and on their second go-round. Marcus reminded her that those same reporters were plugging her radio show in nearly every article.

Kathryn hated that her name was linked to this colossal charade, especially after Marcus showed her the photos he took downtown.

"But that's your deal with the devil," she told herself. "It's a means to an end."

Her association with Voss delivered astronomical ratings and welcome bonuses, and was paving the way to her own television show. But now that she could see the mammoth tent, her innards were churning like a turbine.

Just say your lines. First the sketch with Roz Russell, then a chat about faith with Loretta Young. Betty Hutton's going to pep up the crowd singing "His Rocking Horse Ran Away" and "Stuff Like That There." Then cross to Mike Connolly.

"HELLO!?!?"

Marcus' voice brought her back. "Sorry, what?"

Francine snapped her purse shut. "I said I've changed my mind about coming backstage."

"Are you sure?"

"The last time I saw my brother, I told him he was a no-account bum who wouldn't amount to a pile of cow dung. But to see him like this? No, thank you. I'll be plenty near enough in the audience, thank you very much."

They arrived at the western edge of MacArthur Park. Masses of the adoringly faithful and the agnostically curious filled the sidewalks and spilled over the curb.

Kathryn had never seen her uncle's followers in the flesh. They ranged from five years old to eighty, and wore everything from shabby hand-me-downs to elegant dresses.

"I wish Gwennie was here."

Marcus inched his car through the trooping flood of humanity toward a sign marked *PRESS PARKING ONLY*. "We should be helping her prepare for the inevitable."

They'd all shed tears that week when she announced that she was closing Chez Gwendolyn. Nobody was hiring her to design couture; nobody was buying her perfume; nobody wanted to shop where they might encounter colored people. *Confidential* had wrecked everything with a headline that would be forgotten by the next issue.

Marcus pulled his car into the slot indicated by a Voss Vanguard, and they got out. Kathryn's heels immediately sank into the grass.

* * *

Marcus took in the spectacle as they crossed the park to a red-and-white-striped circus tent with six soaring poles. Its sides billowed and shifted in the brisk August breeze, and it seemed even larger on the inside — perhaps because it still smelled of freshly mowed grass and eucalyptus, even with the heat, sweat and perfume of hundreds of people filling the vast enclosure.

After escorting Kathryn to the backstage door — really nothing more than an open flap — he and Francine crossed in front of the raised stage and stood at the front of the audience. They stared up the center aisle and watched the swarming masses slowly take their seats.

Louella and Hedda had secured front-row seats on opposite sides. Billy Wilkerson and his wife, Tichi, were not far behind Louella, and directly behind them sat Walter Winchell. Winchell and Wilkerson were shaking hands and talking. On the other side a couple of rows behind Hedda, Mr. and Mrs. Mayer were taking their seats at the far end of the row.

"Where are we sitting?" Marcus asked Francine.

She showed him their tickets: Row P. He was disappointed but not surprised; she probably thought Voss wouldn't spot her way back there. Marcus took her arm and led her up the aisle.

"Nervous, isn't she?" Francine said.

In the car, Kathryn's face had taken on the same ashen tinge it had the night she first heard Voss' voice. "She doesn't want to screw up in front of forty million listeners. Can't say that I blame her."

Marcus eyed Mayer. Ten years ago, the man would have been surrounded by hangers-on, but now he was chatting with his wife ignored by everyone around them.

Marcus saw Francine to their seats, then continued up the aisle, around the back of the tent, then down the side until he drew alongside the Mayers.

"Good evening."

Mayer peered warily up at Marcus. "I figured I might see you."

"It's a big night for Kathryn." Marcus crouched down on his haunches so that they were face-to-face. "I'm leaving for Rome soon."

"Congratulations."

Marcus dropped his voice to a loud whisper. "I wanted to thank you. You know, Oliver Trenton and everything that happened."

"Thanks are not necessary."

"I want you to know that I appreciate what you've done for me."

Mayer squirmed. "Really, there's no need — "

Lorena prodded him. "Would it kill you to simply say, 'You're welcome'?"

Mayer pulled himself up straight. "You're welcome, Adler."

"Are you going to tell him what we just heard?" Lorena pushed.

Mayer's smile pinched into a thin line. "Voss is going to launch that Lavender Scare today. He was watching McCarthy's witch hunt, and you know how much mileage that bastard got."

The papers had been screaming for weeks about the purge in DC: hundreds of men had been fired in disgrace. And now Voss was going to call attention to all the queers in Hollywood, and how they were intent on advancing the homosexual agenda. At the last two stops, Voss hadn't called Hollywood the Sodom and Gomorrah of the West, or Marilyn its Jezebel. Marcus assumed that someone had told him to quit it if he wanted to win over Angelenos.

"In front of *this* crowd?"

"In front of the forty million Americans who will be tuning in."

"Are you sure? How reliable is your source?"

"Last night, I met Winchell for drinks at the Beverly Wilshire. I wanted to quiz him about Howard Hughes off-loading RKO because I want him to sell it to me. Somehow the conversation deviated onto Voss."

He paused, drilling Marcus with his marble eyes.

"Kathryn should know what she's heading into."

Marcus nodded. "Thank you. I know she'll appreciate it."

"Marcus?"

Beside him, a wild look wrinkled Francine's face. Marcus stood up. "Is something wrong?"

"I went to say hello to Louella, but on my way over to her I overheard a couple of workers say that the line is broken."

"What line?"

"The radio and television lines are linked together somehow. They're not working and nobody's sure they'll be able to patch things together by air time. All those sound engineers are running around like headless chickens!"

No link to the outside world, Marcus thought, *means no one outside this tent would hear Voss' rant.*

"We should go tell Kathryn," Francine said.

"I'm sure she knows."

"I'm going backstage, Marcus."

He'd heard this tone before, usually from Kathryn. It wasn't hard to guess where she got it from.

"You might bump into someone you'd rather avoid."

"Are you coming with me or not?"

* * *

The evening breezes gusting along Wilshire shuddered the sides of the tent. Kathryn pressed her hand against the tarpaulin and felt the heat of the sun. Up close like this, the structure looked flimsy. Visions of a cross between *Titanic* and *The Greatest Show on Earth* crowded her feverish imagination.

Her dressing room was bigger than the one at NBC, but not as well lit. There was a makeup mirror with standard lamps set up on either side, but neither of them worked. Nobody had thought to lay down a floor, leaving her heels vulnerable in the exposed grass with every step.

The flap of striped canvas that worked as a door flew aside and Leo walked in. "Hello, darling! Ready for the big one?" The afternoon sun now hit the outside of the tent, striping the grass with bands of red and white. "I've had a request from Voss. He wants to meet you."

The enclosed space was starting to heat up. Kathryn fanned herself with a *Herald-Examiner* someone had left on her makeup counter. "I hope you told him no."

Leo indulged her with a less-than-genuine chuckle. "He feels your rapport will be greater if you meet beforehand."

"Isn't that what Connolly is for?"

Leo pressed his hands onto her shoulders. "This is not a negotiation."

"Pulling rank?"

"In a manner of speaking."

She brushed his hands away. "Fine. But I need to prepare, so let's get this over with."

Leo went to kiss her on the lips, but she didn't want to muss her lipstick, so she pointed to her forehead. He kissed it and said he'd be right back.

The twelve-piece NBC orchestra struck up a somber refrain that Kathryn didn't recognize. It was probably intended to introduce a level of solemnity, but it sounded like a funeral dirge.

Marcus burst in. "Have you heard about the link?"

"What are you doing here?"

"Both radio and television, they're kaput."

Why is he smiling? "But they're going to fix it, right?"

"Maybe. Or maybe you don't want them to."

Marcus had barely started relaying his conversation with Mayer when Kathryn had an overpowering urge to smoke. Normally, she abstained before a broadcast, but tonight she wasn't sure she could resist.

"So the worst-case scenario is they cut to *Toast of the Town* and America is spared his tirade," she said. "Have they alerted Ed Sullivan?"

"We bumped into your producer out there."

"We?"

"Your mom insisted we come backstage to tell you."

"Where is she?"

"Talking to him. I think she wants to see her brother up close. Our seats are halfway to Fresno. Let me go fetch her—"

"I want you here with me," she choked out. "Voss wants a face-to-face. I've never met a blood relative before."

Marcus offered her the gentlest smile she'd ever seen on him. "I'll be right here." He hooked her by the chin. "If the going gets tough, remember: You enjoy a battle."

She might have punched him, but Leo pulled back the flap with the flourish of a ringmaster. "Kathryn Massey," he announced, "meet Sheldon Voss!"

Kathryn's uncle was a slight man with a slender body, sloping shoulders, and soft, almost girlish hands. He moved with the grace of a ballroom dancer but exuded none of the charisma she'd expected from the *Examiner*'s staged photos.

THIS is who has been setting the country on fire? This dainty little pixie?

She hunted for signs of herself reflected back at her. His face was rounder, more like Marcus', and his eyes were green, like Gwennie's. His hair may have been her shade of brown, but sun-bleached streaks ran through it, making him look younger than sixty-seven.

"Miss Massey!" He grabbed her hand and shook it fervently. "Thank you so very much for your support throughout my march. It's all been so gratifying."

Kathryn slipped her hand from Voss' grip.

Talk about snake charm. You've even got a glisten in your eyes, as though you're moved to tears.

"Well, I'm sure you've got as much to prepare for as I do."

"I've been preparing all summer," Voss replied. "You could say I've been preparing my whole life."

"I'm sure." She lifted her hand toward the exit.

"Hasn't it been inspiring to see America respond to our message of traditional values?" Voss asked.

OUR message? Don't you lump me in with your bunch of backward-looking —

Kathryn realized that to him, she was no different from all those Mixmaster-blending, Betty Crocker-baking housewives whose apron strings he'd ridden across the country. She went to point out that it was close to air time when she heard Marcus whisper,

"Incoming at three o'clock."

"I was told Kathryn Massey was—"

Francine halted just inside the flap, her face frozen.

Voss was the first to speak. "Mary? Is that you?" He rushed toward Francine, who stepped backwards. "Is it really you? I don't believe my eyes! Sweet Jesus in heaven has brought my long-lost sister to me!"

"Knock it off, Camden, it's just us."

"Oh, how I've beseeched the good Lord that we might be reunited again. And here we are! On this night of all nights. Don't you see, Mary? He—"

She strode past him toward Kathryn. "My name is Francine. Francine Massey. This is my daughter—" She'd learned a thing or two about showmanship and paused for a moment. "—Kathryn Massey."

Kathryn watched the comprehension filter through his eyes. "That's right," she said, "I'm your niece."

"I'm your uncle!" He reached out for her, but she recoiled.

"No, my uncle is Camden Caldecott, who's got a warrant out in seven states. Passing bum checks in Providence; swindling a rich widow in Hartford; impersonating a member of the clergy in Poughkeepsie; embezzlement at the Vulcan Iron Works foundry in Wilkes-Barre." She leaned her head toward Marcus. "Aren't I forgetting one?"

"Toms River, New Jersey," Marcus said.

"Is that where you took money from the Presbyterians, Episcopalians, *and* the Catholics for two hundred gold-embossed Bibles and then skipped town?"

"I haven't hidden the mistakes of my past." Voss ditched his oily tone. "On the contrary, I've made it a central tenet of my teachings. It's the whole reason for my redemption boards. Up there for all the world to see."

Kathryn felt Marcus' hot breath in her ear. He whispered, "I'll be back in a jiffy," and dashed from the tent.

What happened to "I'll be right here"?

"The widow from Hartford isn't on your redemption boards, nor are the foundry workers from Wilkes-Barre. So not ALL your sins are there for all the world to see, are they?"

"I take it, then, that you haven't seen the boards here tonight?"

Oh, damnit.

"I have since repaid the Hartford widow, and the foundry workers. And as for the Toms River situation, two hundred and fourteen Bibles have now been gifted to the city."

Pilgrimages of forgiveness were the sorts of stories that the press leaped gleefully on like jackals, but there'd been no mention of the Toms River Bibles.

"But even if those warrants were still valid," Voss pressed, "and I was found guilty, my followers wouldn't desert me. My message is salvation through confession."

"Your message is a load of bunk!" Francine spat out. It was a rare tonic for Kathryn to see her mother so passionate.

Voss stiffened. "You couldn't be more wrong, Mary—"

"I haven't been Mary since I left Boston. I always thought my pregnancy caused something to tear inside you, and through that hole climbed a conniving little swindler. But I've been wrong all these years. It was more like pulling back a curtain. If the law landed your behind in jail, your followers would forget all about you soon enough."

Voss pointed at the wavering sheet of canvas that separated him from his devotees. "They'd stick with me, come what may."

* * *

Marcus navigated the obstacle course of cables, lighting rigs, and sound equipment and burst through the employee egress, almost colliding with a quartet of nuns decked out in white cornettes so stiffly starched they could take an eye out.

Skirting the Sisters of Charity, he ducked and darted across the rows of cars at the west end of MacArthur Park until he reached his own. He threw open the door and grabbed his briefcase. It was only there by chance. Ordinarily he wouldn't bring it to something like this, but he'd come straight from his favorite photography store on Fairfax. There wasn't time to sort through all the photographs, so he kicked the door shut and headed back to the tent.

As he neared the flap marked *NBC EMPLOYEES*, he saw Mike Connolly approaching from another direction. "Connolly!" he called. "Wait up!"

Connolly nodded mechanically, then recognized Marcus. "You're that friend of Kathryn's, aren't you?"

Marcus didn't appreciate the malicious tone, but there wasn't time to quibble. "There's something you ought to know." He held open the flap for Connolly, who passed through without acknowledgment.

"And what might that be?"

"Voss plans on starting up his anti-homo rant again tonight."

"Nonsense. He hasn't breathed a word about that whole lavender thing in weeks. And besides, he wouldn't try that on this crowd."

"He doesn't care about *this* crowd; he's going for the radio audience. He's got plans far beyond this march and we're not going to come out of it very well."

Connolly stared at Marcus, the color slowly draining from his face. "But I'm the one who convinced him to stop. After Oklahoma City, I called him. I made it very clear that nothing good would come of it, that Hollywood's too powerful and they'd beat him down, so he had to stop. He mentioned it in Denver, but it was more of a postscript. And after that, nothing."

"Yeah, well, he's changed his mind."

"But he promised me. Gave me his word."

Marcus eyed the flap into Kathryn's dressing room. He had to get in there now. "I have it on good authority that the guy's a low-down lying jackass."

Connolly wiped his brow. "What are we going to do? Can we stop him?"

"Do you know anything about broadcast cables?"

"Why?"

"The link is kaput. Both TV and radio. The NBC guys are trying to fix them. It will be helpful if we can prevent them from doing that."

"But how?"

"I haven't the foggiest." They were outside Kathryn's dressing room now. Marcus pushed it open. "Just give it your best shot."

* * *

Kathryn was relieved to see Marcus. Voss was still explaining why his followers would stick with him when she felt Marcus slip something between her fingers. They were the photos he took at the Town House and downtown.

She held aloft a close-up of one of the Town House quarter cans.

"Do your followers know about these?"

"They're as famous as my redemption boards."

She held up two more photographs showing the bottoms of two cans. "Do they know they're marked X and Y? And that the Xs go to the bank on Wilshire and the Ys go to the FBI downtown?" Voss' trembling chin told Kathryn all she needed to know. "Or is it the other way around?"

"You people!" he shouted. "You've been reading so much Raymond Chandler that you think everything's a byzantine plot."

As though on cue, the orchestra launched into the John Philip Sousa march, "The Crusader," that played every time Voss took the stage.

Tonight, the *Window on Hollywood* theme song would open the show, so NBC was playing "The Crusader" to signal everyone to take their places.

"Remember, uncle dear, I'm on first." Kathryn marched toward the flap. Francine and Leo stepped aside to allow her to sweep from the room.

Twice the number of people were now scrambling around equipment, checking lists on clipboards, staring into lighted consoles. She spotted NBC's head sound technician holding the thick black cord that usually connected to her microphone. Mike Connolly was peppering him with questions. It looked to Kathryn like he was making a nuisance of himself but was too stupid to realize it.

As she maneuvered around the equipment and over the snaking cables, she spotted the pasty-faced sneer of someone she hated as much as Uncle Holier-Than-Thou. Standing in the wings, he was accosting a middle-aged couple with a narcissistic monologue.

Kathryn zeroed in on him like a kamikaze. "YOU!"

Robert Harrison drew back, startled.

"Who the *hell* do you think you are?" she spat at him.

"Miss Massey." *Confidential*'s publisher possessed a well-honed poker face. "At last we meet."

"I've half a mind to punch you in the face." The woman beside him inhaled sharply. "You and your Rainbow of Colors Dancing in the Garden of Eden. So smart. So smug. Did you come up with that one yourself, you slimy little bastard?"

"I wrote both the headline *and* the article."

"The woman who owns that boutique on the Strip is a friend of mine. After your article came out, someone painted a big 'N' on her window. Then someone else lobbed a brick through it, and now she has to close her store. She's lost everything."

His casual shrug infuriated her more than his poker face. "The press cannot be held responsible for the consequences of the news."

"You're not the press!" she hissed. "A real journalist conveys actual news with objectivity, and doesn't manipulate the truth with whatever scandal he can scrounge up. Or worse, invent outrageous distortions and pass them off as fact. That's all you do, you bottom-feeder. I know you're aware of the damage your disgusting rag does, but your real crime is that you don't give a rat's ass. Chez Gwendolyn has to close down and I hold you entirely responsible, you disgusting sack of horse shit!"

Harrison waited to ensure Kathryn's harangue was over before formally turning to the couple beside him. "Kathryn Massey, may I present the head of NBC television, Patrick Crawley and his lovely wife, Irene."

Kathryn felt the heat of battle fade and her mind go blank.

"Chez Gwendolyn," Mrs. Crawley said. "I was planning on visiting there before we returned to New York. Walter Winchell talked it up like it was the best new show on Broadway."

The cymbal crashes of the Sousa climax trembled the air around them. Kathryn threw up her hands and headed for her producer, who was waiting in the wings with Roz Russell. They were deep in conversation and missed Kathryn's rant. She was halfway there when she heard Voss demand,

"Just you hold on a minute!"

Kathryn was tempted to keep walking, but it was better to have it out with him now before they faced forty million people.

He stuck a warning finger in her face. "You might go on first, but then it's my turn."

She shoved his finger aside. "Here's what is *not* going to happen. You're not going to mention anything about unwed mothers, the sin of miscegenation, all this so-called loose living in Hollywood, and you're *especially* going to lay off any denunciation of homosexuals."

"Fat chance. It's the centerpiece of my speech."

"Your speech? Or Joe McCarthy's? You couldn't be more wrong if you think those people out there are the same ones you've been duping all summer."

"Homosexuals in government are a grave risk to the security of this country, just as they are a risk to its moral fiber. They're out to insert the homosexual agenda into the movies. You should know! You married one. If anyone should be angry at the queers, it should be someone who was hoodwinked into living a lie."

Over Voss' shoulder, Wallace Reed waved his clipboard to attract Kathryn's attention. He pointed to his watch and held up six fingers. She ought to be standing with him and Roz and Loretta.

Behind him, Connolly was still arguing with the sound guy. Connolly was holding up a cable and the other guy was shaking his head. Then Marcus joined them.

Is he holding a hammer?

* * *

It was Regina Horne who provided Marcus with a mallet.

She barreled up to him as he was watching Kathryn give Robert Harrison hell. "Marcus! You do pop up in the most extraordinary places."

"I could say the same about you." He took in her simple black ensemble. "What are you doing backstage?"

"I'm a member of the Los Angeles Choral Society. Voss hired us to sing the Hallelujah Chorus from Handel's 'Messiah' as his exit music. I almost didn't come because I think he's full of crap, but then I figured, hey, it'll make for a good dinner story at Canter's. Did you hear that NBC is panicking like hell? Their equipment's out!"

Marcus saw the hammer in her hand. "Is that your plan to fix it?"

Regina hefted it up. "I just saw this on the grass and thought I ought to give it to them before someone trips over it."

Marcus told her he knew the head sound guy and took the hammer from her, wishing her luck with the performance.

As he approached the two men, he eyed the cable in Connolly's hand. Two thick prongs protruded from one end of it. He didn't know much, but it looked important. He mouthed the words "distract him" at Connolly.

Immediately, Connolly started lecturing the guy about electrical networks. It diverted the tech long enough for Marcus to grab the cable out of Connolly's hand and lay it against the trestle table. He raised Regina's hammer as high as he dared and slammed it down on the prongs.

* * *

Kathryn turned back to Voss. "We were in a tough situation."

"Marriage is a sacred institution, not a solution."

"I wouldn't mind so much if you truly believed what you're saying, but you're a fraud — and a thief. Half for your cause, and half for your pockets, right?"

Every seat in the audience was filled, along with hundreds of more congregants content to stand along the periphery. They all started to clap in a slow, rhythmic tempo.

Voss glared at her with cobra eyes. "If you keep mum about the quarter cans, I'll fix everything. Winchell and I, we're real good pals. I know he wants a chance at television, but I can talk him out of it. He'll listen to me. And I'm in tight with Hoover, too. I'll make sure he never learns about the cans."

Kathryn drew back from her weasely little uncle when she realized that Hoover didn't know anything about Voss' quarter cans. Trying to put one over on J. Edgar Hoover took balls, but he'd never get away with it. Hoover was too well-connected.

"You can shove your deal up your ass."

Voss grabbed Kathryn by the shoulders and dug his fingers in deep. "If you do anything to blacken my name, fair warning: I have the patience of Job." He pulled his lips back into a wild grin. "I waited years to exact my revenge on your father."

Kathryn ignored Wallace's frantic waves. "You had him *framed*? Is that what all this is about? Because he got Francine pregnant with me?"

"Thou shalt not covet! Thou shalt not bear false witness! Premarital fornication is a mortal sin! Your father's wanton desires—"

Kathryn leaned back and clocked him in the side of the head. He dropped to the ground like a bag of rocks.

Shaking her hand out, she marched toward Wallace. Roz Russell and Loretta Young smiled at her obliviously as she approached them, but Wallace's face was a mask of thinly veiled horror. "The show's about to begin."

"Boy, is it ever." Kathryn hugged Roz and Loretta and apologized that she wasn't there to greet them earlier. "It's crazy as a bug house back here!"

"There's a problem," the sound guy said. "We've been trying to fix the TV link but it's brought down the radio link. We need four or five minutes."

"We're due on the air in less than three!" Wallace said.

"I've alerted the studio, but it's the best we can do."

"What about the microphones?" Kathryn asked. "Are they hooked up? Will that lot out front be able to hear me?"

The technician assured her that they were, and that when they were broadcasting live, a red light at stage left would go on.

"That's all I need to know."

The collective energy of several thousand Angelenos swamped Kathryn as she stepped into the spotlight.

"HELLO, HOLLYWOOD!"

Her voice bounced from loudspeaker to loudspeaker strung up at regular intervals along both sides of the tent.

"Thank you for turning out tonight, and in such numbers! But guess what. The live radio and television feeds have gone AWOL." She slapped her sides with exaggerated irritation. "The busy bees backstage have assured me they're trying to get us on the air. They're sweating bullets, so let's give them a huge round of applause."

A boisterous ovation filled the tent. To the right, Wallace made the "keep talking" hand signal. To the left stood Voss and Connolly, who both looked like they were heading off heart failure. How odd, then, that they wore such different faces.

"Ladies and gentleman, may I be candid?" Ninety percent of the people in this tent worked in an industry dedicated to being heard. They roared their approval. "As Sheldon Voss brings his trek to a close tonight, his message of sticking to traditions may be more open to interpretation than perhaps he realizes. Our nation's capital is a very long way from — to quote Mr. Voss' words — the Sodom and Gomorrah of the West."

Someone up front jeered. Kathryn raised her hand to shield her eyes from the lights and identified Orson Welles. He wasn't the type to slip quietly into a room — even a room the size of a football field. Encouraged by Orson, a few people started booing.

"I wasn't sure how to take his accusation that Marilyn Monroe was the manifestation of Lucifer's lust."

The boos multiplied. Someone yelled, "Marilyn's wonderful!" and several people wolf-whistled their agreement. Scattered applause broke out.

Bolder now, Kathryn gripped the microphone stand with both hands. "Personally, I was a little concerned with his message that the proper place for women is in the home. As a working gal who loves her job, I have to question if it's as true as Mr. Voss would like."

More boos, louder this time. And applause. Somewhere in front, a woman yelled out, "You got that right!" It sounded like Judy Garland.

"I began to wonder if Mr. Voss understood that out here, we don't care where you come from or what your daddy does for a living. We stand on our own merits as we look to the future."

The booing flipped to cheers.

"But I'm here to tell you that I was wrong to worry that perhaps the Sea to Shining Sea March may have lost its moral compass."

A glint of color on the far left caught Kathryn's eye. The lamp tucked into the wing now glowed red. Marcus had tried his best, but now it was up to her.

"I wish the folks at home could see the enormous gathering tonight in MacArthur Park. Just a few minutes ago, Mr. Voss told me of an announcement he'd like me to make on his behalf. At the end of each sermon, the Voss Vanguard disburses with the famous quarter cans. I am thrilled to announce that the entire proceedings from tonight's collection will be donated to the National Council of Negro Women. After tonight's sermon, Sheldon Voss himself will lead a procession down Wilshire Boulevard to the council's offices at 510 Spring Street to present them with more quarters than they've probably ever seen in their lives. Isn't that wonderful?!"

The hair on Kathryn's arms stood up as the audience jumped to its feet. Not everybody was applauding for the same reason. From the expressions on their faces, she could see that some people supported desegregation; some supported Voss' capitulation to the values of the Sodom and Gomorrah of the West; some saw her announcement as jacking the middle finger to Robert Harrison and his grubby brand of muckraking. Kathryn didn't care why they were applauding. She knew she'd blown it with NBC and blown Gwendolyn's chance into the bargain, but at least someone was going to come out of this situation all right.

She leaned back into her mike. "And now, let's go on with the show!"

CHAPTER 40

Gwendolyn looked out across the women filling her store and tried not to be bitter. She had expected to spend the morning packing her remaining stock into crates before seeing Marcus off at Los Angeles International Airport, but at this point, she might not get out of there on time. Why was *this* the day everyone decided to show up?

A wide-hipped matron held up a Chanel-style suit and asked how much it was. She had no hope of fitting into it, and the sunny yellow did her pasty complexion no favors, but a sale was a sale.

"Fourteen ninety-five."

The woman wrinkled her nose. "It's a bit high."

Gwendolyn thought about the hours she'd put into the gold embroidery along the lapels. "Down from twenty-nine ninety-five."

"Will you take twelve?"

If you explain to me how the heck you plan on squeezing into it. "Sure. Tell Doris at the counter that we agreed on twelve."

Gwendolyn had only been open a couple of minutes when the first rush of customers charged through the door. Soon she was overrun and had to call on Doris and Bertie to lend a hand. Bertie helped out in the workroom that was currently a communal fitting room, and Doris was behind the cash register ringing up sale after sale.

Gwendolyn called Doris' name over the havoc, pointed to the suit, and held up ten fingers, then two. "Thank you for coming."

The customer missed the sarcasm in Gwendolyn's response, and instead took off for Doris, clearing a path for Lena Horne, who was standing behind her with an unusually feline woman in a skintight cashmere sweater.

"I'm sorry to hear you're closing," Lena said. "Ella wanted to be here but she couldn't so I brought my friend. Gwendolyn, I want you to meet Eartha Kitt."

"I'm a fan of your perfume." Eartha's voice almost sounded like a purr. "I'm here to buy as many bottles as I can afford."

"You're a singer, aren't you?" Gwendolyn asked.

"Singer, actress, dancer, fill-in-the-blank."

"Everybody's been talking about what's happened," Lena confided. "Not that it matters now, I suppose, but you've got a sterling reputation with us."

"Of course it matters." Gwendolyn started straightening a scarf display. "And thank you for telling me."

"You don't deserve this treatment."

"There are people out there who'd argue otherwise."

"So what are your plans now?"

"Get a job, I suppose. It'll be hard after being my own boss these past five years."

A pair of Beverly Hills matrons started arguing over a fragile ball gown. "I better go break that up."

Lena pulled her into a hug. "For what it's worth, we consider you a friend, and we won't forget the stand you took on our behalf."

"Thank you." Gwendolyn let Lena go and crossed the salon to reassure the two women that she had a number of similar gowns in the back.

Time flew by as the cash register sang like a nightingale. It was well past one o'clock now. Gwendolyn hated the thought of missing out on saying goodbye to Marcus.

"It's nice to see you so busy, despite the circumstances."

Gwendolyn hadn't seen Billy Travilla since the "Rainbow at the Garden of Eden" party. Not that she expected to. Nor did she blame him for going to ground when that horrible article came out.

She threw her arms open. "And it's nice to see you, even under these circumstances. If you're shopping for something, you better have at it while you can."

"I brought this lovely lady along." He half-turned to the woman behind him and nudged her by the elbow. She had the look of a woman of means who did her best with her God-given gifts while grudgingly surrendering to the inevitability of middle-age. "Gwendolyn, I want you to meet Irene Crawley."

Gwendolyn took the woman's offered hand. "Pleased to meet y—" She stiffened. "Did you say Irene Crawley?"

Billy's smile faltered. "I did."

Gwendolyn had been too busy preparing her store for closure to attend the final Sea to Shining Sea revival meeting, but she'd kicked herself for missing out on Kathryn's speech. Somewhere along the march to the National Council of Negro Women, Voss' promise to clean up the Sodom and Gomorrah of the West lost momentum. The NCNW hadn't finished counting all those quarters yet, but Kathryn estimated the windfall to be north of five grand.

He said, "Irene and I have known each other since our days at the Chouinard School of Art. I've been talking up your wares to her for ages, and when she heard you were closing down, she insisted that I bring her here."

Gwendolyn took in the woman's figure. "I have a floor-length gown in coffee-colored lace that would suit you, but only if you like off the shoulder."

"That's not why I came."

"The perfume, then?" Gwendolyn had two hundred bottles behind her sofa at the Garden of Allah. The more she could offload today, the better.

"I'm here about Kathryn Massey," Irene said. "Billy told me that you two are the best of friends, and I was rather staggered by her behavior backstage. Did she tell you about it?"

It was pretty much all Gwendolyn had heard about for the last two days. "She did mention it, yes."

"But then I had time to think it over, and I have to admit that I was rather impressed by it, too. I admire a woman who sticks to her guns."

"Did your husband have the same reaction?"

"Oh, goodness me, no!" Mrs. Crawley pressed her fingers over her mouth. "After the sermon, Patrick and I bumped into Billy and Dona. He told me that you were closing your doors and said I ought to look at what you can do and make up my own mind."

"Everything you see is half price," Gwendolyn said. "And I'd be more than happy to tailor anything."

Irene fluttered a hand. "I can see you've got what it takes. It's just that I didn't want to take Walter's word for it."

So Winchell kept his end of the bargain, after all. "I heard you two were friends."

Irene scrunched her face in disgust. "I wouldn't be caught dead talking to that reprobate unless it was essential to my husband's business interests. What a relief to find your work marvelous."

Billy pointed to a tea dress in pink tulle. "Can't you see Loretta in that?"

"Loretta?" Gwendolyn cut in. "Young?"

"That's right."

"Are you saying you'd still like to recommend me to do her costumes?"

"You are interested, I hope," Mrs. Crawley said.

"Of course!"

"Good. You just leave it to me. I know how to bend my husband's ear."

"Will you bend it for Kathryn, too? I understand there was a plan to transfer her radio show to television."

Irene shook her head. "Patrick can't abide women who don't act like ladies." She patted Gwendolyn's hand. "I'll see to it that someone from the show is in contact. Now, if you'll excuse me, I do see a few things I'd like to investigate before some of these women snap them up." She headed for the daywear.

"I have you to thank for this, don't I?" Gwendolyn asked Billy.

"I merely sang your praises."

"Thank you, Billy, so very much."

His aw-shucks grin fell away. "You're going to need a place to work on those gowns."

"I'm sure Loretta's production company will have some place."

"They haven't even rented offices yet. But regardless, wouldn't you like to have access to every fabric under the sun? And the services of some of the best seamstresses in the business? Not to mention how you're assuming this job will pay you enough to live on."

She realized he had a valid point. She'd only be required to build one dress per week. That wasn't a full-time job. "I get the feeling you're driving at something."

Billy stroked his cheek as though to coax the words out. "Marilyn's becoming a tad difficult to work with. I've seen it happen over and over. Insecurities come to the fore the bigger a performer gets. She trusts me, but that's about all. And even then . . ." He laced his fingers together and pressed his palms to his chest. "Did you see the article about her and DiMaggio in the new *Confidential*?"

It was hard to avoid seeing that rag these days. Every newsstand carried it front and center. The August issue screamed the headline:

WHY JOE DIMAGGIO IS STRIKING OUT WITH MARILYN MONROE!

"The cover was bad enough."

"I told her she shouldn't let it affect her so much, but . . ." He let out a heavy sigh. "I think it'll help if you can be there to assist with fittings and adjustments and such. Quite frankly, your just being there will make the process of costuming Marilyn so much easier."

Gwendolyn hadn't seen her since the night of the party at the Garden. She sent a card after *Confidential* came out, but had heard nothing back.

"The next project is dressing her for the *How to Marry a Millionaire* premiere on November fourth."

"That's three months away," Gwendolyn pointed out. "Surely it won't take that long—" Billy's deer-in-headlights expression cut her off. "Is it that bad?"

"She's a very strong girl who's overcome an appalling past. But fame has a way of magnifying flaws and insecurities so that they become the size of a zeppelin, and about as stable. The slightest disruptions have started to set her off."

"So what are you offering me?"

"A full-time job in the costuming department of Twentieth Century-Fox while creating gowns for Loretta's show. Are you in?"

* * *

When the taxi pulled up at the curb in front of the Pan Am terminal at LA International, Gwendolyn threw fistful of bills at the driver. "Thank you!" She raced inside and ran her eyes down the departures board.

Flight 706 – Lounge 9 – Boarding at 7:15

She darted up the stairs and into Pan Am's cluster of lounges. Number nine was at the other end—just far enough for her to wish she was wearing flats.

The tide of customers had retreated by five o'clock, when she was clean out of stock. Every last dress, gown, suit, jacket, glove, and scarf had been picked over by Beverly Hills vultures, leaving Chez Gwendolyn a bone-dry carcass.

She spotted Marcus and Kathryn in the corner next to the window looking out across the tarmac.

"I made it! I made it!"

"Gwennie!" There was a trill in Kathryn's voice. "What took you so long?"

"Things didn't quite pan out how I expected. But never mind, we're all here now." She took in Marcus' smooth face. "You shaved off your beard."

"It wasn't really me."

With its flecks of gray, Gwendolyn had thought it added five years and she was glad to see it gone.

She grabbed both Marcus and Kathryn by the hand. "Gosh, but this feels mighty familiar. Substitute Union Station for LA International and this could be a retake of three years ago."

"It's not the same at all," Marcus said. "Back then, I was skulking off into the sunset because I'd been banished from Hollywood. I had no idea what the future held and no definite plans to come back. This time, I know exactly how long I'm staying and when I return, I'll be off the graylist and ready to work again."

"Well, you better not disappear like some people." Gwendolyn pointed to a discarded copy of the *Examiner*. Its banner demanded: *WHERE IS SHELDON VOSS?*

It now was three days after the MacArthur Park revival, and the man who'd attracted the nation's attention all summer had dropped out of sight.

A voice over the loudspeaker announced that Pan Am Flight 706 for New York and Rome was now boarding.

Gwendolyn broke out into a nervous giggle. "All I know is that I'm suffering from déjà vu. Last time you didn't know if you were ever coming home and you were back in four months. This time you say you'll be back when *Three Coins* is finished, but what if you meet up with Oliver and find he's decided not to become a monk or a priest or whatever, and convinces you to stay over there for good? Or if—"

Marcus pressed his fingers to her lips. "You're babbling," he told her. "Shooting is scheduled to finish mid-September. Six weeks at the most."

"We're going to hold you to that. Just be sure you don't hammer any more cables."

Marcus threw up his hands in mock despair. "Hey! How was I to know it was just a backup? And anyway, things worked okay, didn't they? I'll be back at the Garden before you even realize I've gone."

"I doubt that very much." Kathryn slipped an arm around Gwendolyn's waist. "But I think we can manage six weeks, can't we, Gwennie?"

She nodded.

"I'll bring you back some of Signora Scatena's zucchini flowers," he said. "Or at least the recipe."

"Because we're such gourmet cooks?" Kathryn laughed. "People are starting to line up. You better go."

He embraced them both. "It's just six weeks." He gave them a final hug and picked up his cabin bag.

They leaned against the window and watched him shuffle to the front of the line until the stewardess waved him through. He smiled at them and raised his fedora before disappearing through the door.

They stared at the doorway, each lost in their own thoughts.

"I guess it does feel different this time," Gwendolyn said.

"He's not being railroaded out of town."

"He gets to start over."

"Speaking of, what are *your* plans for starting over?"

"Oh my goodness!" Gwendolyn exclaimed, "I didn't tell you what happened today."

Halfway through her story, Gwendolyn realized what was good news for her was a bitter pill for Kathryn.

"The National Council of Negro Women is a whole lot richer, and you got a terrific job offer," Kathryn said. "So two out of three ain't bad." A low thrum vibrated the large pane of glass to their backs. They turned around to see the propellers of Marcus' aircraft spin as the ground crew pulled away the stairs. "And how sweet to see all that momentum Uncle Ratface built over the summer sputter out completely."

"He is kind of rat-faced, isn't he?"

"And to think I'm related to him." Kathryn shivered. "Ugh."

"Let's not forget that speech you gave. You made a big impression on many important people. I wouldn't dismiss that, if I were you."

The plane pushed off from the terminal and started taxiing away. Gwendolyn and Kathryn stood in silence as it banked right before slowing to a halt.

"I wish I'd thought to tell Marcus about my job at Fox."

"It'll make a hell of a letter," Kathryn said. "If you post it tomorrow, he should have it in a week. He'll love that."

The Douglas DC-7 lurched along the runway just as the sun slipped out from behind a cloudbank. The wings gleamed like quicksilver as the aircraft picked up speed. Slowly, almost effortlessly, the nose tilted upwards. The wheels, now a blur, bounced along the tarmac once, twice, then lifted off the ground, picked up speed, and shot into the warm California dusk.

THE END

Did you enjoy this book? You can make a big difference.

As an independent author, I don't have the financial muscle of a New York publisher supporting me. But I do have something much more powerful and effective, and it's something those publishers would kill to get their hands on: a committed and loyal bunch of readers.

Honest reviews of my books help bring them to the notice of other readers. If you've enjoyed this book, I would be so grateful if you could spend just a couple of minutes leaving a review on the website where you bought it.

Thank you very much,
Martin Turnbull

ALSO BY MARTIN TURNBULL

Hollywood's Garden of Allah novels:

Book 1 – *The Garden on Sunset*
Book 2 – *The Trouble with Scarlett*
Book 3 – *Citizen Hollywood*
Book 4 – *Searchlights and Shadows*
Book 5 – *Reds in the Beds*
Book 6 – *Twisted Boulevard*
Book 7 – *Tinseltown Confidential*
Book 8 – *City of Myths*
Book 9 – *Closing Credits*

Chasing Salomé: a novel of 1920s Hollywood

The Heart of the Lion: a novel of Irving Thalberg's Hollywood

ACKNOWLEDGMENTS

Heartfelt thanks to the following, who helped shaped this book:

My editor: Meghan Pinson, for her invaluable guidance, expert eye, and unfailing nitpickery.

My cover designer: Dan Yeager at Nu-Image Design

My beta readers: Vince Hans, Nora Hernandez-Castillo, Bradley Brady, Matthew Kennedy, Beth Riches and especially to Royce Sciortino and Gene Strange for their invaluable time, insight, feedback and advice in shaping this novel.

My Proof Reader Extraordinaire: Bob Molinari

My thanks, also, to Susan Milner and Andie Paysinger for providing verisimilitude. I can only dream of these lives but Susan and Andie lived it.

CONNECT WITH MARTIN TURNBULL

www.MartinTurnbull.com

Facebook.com/gardenofallahnovels

Twitter @TurnbullMartin

Blog: martinturnbull.wordpress.com

Goodreads: bit.ly/martingoodreads

Sign up for Martin's no-spam-ever mailing list, be the first to hear the latest news, and receive *Subway People* - a 1930s short story exclusively available to subscribers.
Go to: **bit.ly/turnbullsignup**

Made in the USA
San Bernardino, CA
05 August 2020